Temptation

Also by Martina Devlin

Three Wise Men
Be Careful What You Wish For
Venus Reborn

Martina Devlin

Temptation

POOLBEG

This novel is entirely a work of fiction. The names, characters and incidents portrayed in it are the work of the author's imagination. Any resemblance to actual persons, living or dead, events or localities is entirely coincidental.

Published 2004
by Poolbeg Press Ltd.
123 Grange Hill, Baldoyle,
Dublin 13, Ireland
Email: poolbeg@poolbeg.com

13 5 7 9 10 8 6 4 2

A catalogue record for this book is available from the British Library.

ISBN 1-84223-182-0

Typeset by Patricia Hope in Goudy 10.75/14.25
Printed by
Litografia Rosés S.A., Spain

www.poolbeg.com

About the Author

Martina Devlin was born in Omagh, Co Tyrone and lives in
Dublin. She has worked as a journalist and started writing
fiction after winning a Hennessy Literary Award for her first
short story in 1996. This was followed by three novels, *Three
Wise Men*, *Be Careful What You Wish For* and *Venus Reborn*.
She has also contributed to a number of short story
collections. In addition to writing fiction, Martina is a
columnist for the *Sunday World* magazine. Her website is
www.martinadevlin.com

Acknowledgements

Thanks to Frank Coughlan for services above and beyond the call of duty in keeping me caffeinated.

Imelda Reynolds for her considered, caring advice – and always in such a salubrious setting. The Clarence should dedicate a corner of the Octagon Bar to her.

Lorraine Curran for the loan of her magazine rack story in chapter 8.

Sarah Webb for her generosity of spirit and awesome organisational skills.

The rest of the Irish Girls crew of writers – I won't name you all in case I leave anyone out, but life would be bland and sober without you.

Alison McDermott of the Carlisle Bookshop in Omagh, who never minds me popping in to clutter up her premises.

My agent Stephanie Cabot for her unflagging enthusiasm and positive attitude.

Gaye Shortland, a fabulous editor without whose help *Temptation* would be the poorer.

The highly motivated but also fun-orientated Poolbeg team, especially Paula Campbell, Sarah Conroy, Brona Loobey and Lynda Laffan.

And last (but not in my affections), the extended Devlin and English family for their loyalty in always buying my books – and sometimes even reading them.

For David Murphy,
at the front of the queue when credentials
were handed out to the good guys

Chapter 1

Being single is the ideal state, except when it palls. Which is how, on New Year's Day, Kitty Kennedy found herself lying in bed watching an old movie on televison and considering husbands. Not potential ones – her two discarded husbands.

"They had their uses," she conceded. "My first husband" – and didn't that phrase sound casually urbane and just a shade decadent, Kitty thought – "taught me the value of an orgasm. My second husband taught me the value of supermarket own-brands."

Tom Ewell wasn't paying the slightest attention to her. He was frantically dimming lights, activating mood music and camouflaging evidence of his status as husband and father, in preparation for a visit from his upstairs neighbour, Marilyn Monroe.

Kitty had faked most of her orgasms with number two, without any clear idea of why she'd bothered. Some misguided sense of politeness, probably. Or maybe it was so that he'd stop doing what he was doing to such little effect.

She resumed addressing Tom Ewell, who looked a little over-ripe to be intent on seducing Marilyn Monroe. Then again, all men in Fifties' films looked middle-aged, especially the really juvenile ones. "Ryan" – he was husband number one – "had no interest in shopping or supermarkets. If you'd explained to him that own-label Fruit&Fibre was cheaper than Kellogg's and tasted only slightly less appealing, he'd have called you pathetic or unstable or both."

Ryan had been an utterly focused person. His emotional telescope had been trained on Kitty for the two years of their marriage and the preceding six months of courtship – that magnificently quaint term which covered every activity from holding hands to the nightly creak of bed-springs. He hadn't been able to resist her, that's why he had been so irresistible. Ryan had made it his mission to give her pleasure, but she hadn't valued it. Pleasure, she'd assumed, would be more or less automatic in such circumstances.

Husband number two had cured her of that misconception. Kitty presumed she must have had her reasons for marrying Benjamin, but she was hard pressed to remember them now. At least with Ryan there had been the excitement of being swept off her feet in a tidal wave of post-adolescent passion. Plus she could always cite immaturity in her defence: "I was only twenty, Your Honour."

Ryan's response to her had been so compelling that how she felt about him had seemed irrelevant. At least initially. His intensity, however, had been why he started to chafe against her. So much attention had crowded Kitty, unable to lift a mug to drink her coffee but he'd offer her a refill. She knew some women would have felt cherished by such devotion, but she'd been unnerved, then sullen and finally cornered.

Kitty resumed her monologue. "You see, Tom, I thought all that spine-tingling pleasure and sitting pretty on a pedestal was normal, sap that I am. Nobody told me it was beginner's luck with Ryan." She jiggled the remote control to lower the sound; Marilyn's breathy whimsy was interrupting her. "Of course, with the benefit of hindsight, I dismissed Ryan too lightly – but hindsight is fool's wisdom, according to Noreen-dear."

Noreen-dear was Kitty's mother. Typical of the woman,

intruding on her harmless flirtation with Tom Ewell. She had no life of her own so she gatecrashed other people's, specifically her two daughters'. Kitty dropped the zapper, aware that she was in trouble: she hadn't yet phoned the woman who'd given birth to her to wish her a Happy New Year. The longer she left it, the more trouble she'd accumulate, for the woman who'd given birth to her had certain expectations. Kitty shifted uneasily, clasping her knees to her chest inside her nest of pillows and duvet: it wouldn't kill her to lift the phone – but her mother would cajole her into ordering a taxi and being driven to Number 16, Hunter Crescent, Bray. The seat of her jurisdiction. She was impregnable there. Kitty and her sister joked that Noreen-dear had a secret spring in the garden where she bathed to prolong her powers, like Ursula Andress in *She*.

Whatever chance there was of defying Noreen-dear at a distance, opposition was futile once you stepped into the kitchen in Hunter Crescent. Her mother was a singularly determined woman and Kitty lacked the energy for a close family encounter today. Family life was for parachuting into; isolated snatches of its borderline sanity were as much as anyone could manage. She couldn't face any of it today, however, for Kitty wanted to lie in bed mulling over what a banjax she'd made of her life.

It was how she always liked to start the New Year.

This voyage into self-examination invariably followed the same strangely comforting pattern: Kitty would dissolve in a welter of self-pity, tentatively wonder if she were the sinner or the sinned against, and rehash all the excruciating episodes that had dogged her year. Then a self-preservation instinct would intervene and she'd remember another year was dawning. She had a clean slate, she'd realise, with a heady sense of relief. New Year's Day was so liberating, it was the equivalent of an *ego te absolvo* from a bishop. Not that she went to confession any more – jettisoning that had been her eighteenth birthday present to herself.

She hadn't reached the liberation stage yet; she was still brooding over how astute she was in hindsight – and how dense the rest of the time when it actually mattered. She narrowed her blue-grey eyes at Tom Ewell, trying to lip-read his instructions to a woman with a notepad and the abnormally pointed breasts of all Fifties' secretaries. Men must have had some shock the first time they unhooked a bra. Tom was talking out of the side of his mouth, which meant he was lying – she remembered that from her dealings with Benjamin, husband number two. Benjamin never admitted to lies; he claimed people had shifting perceptions of the truth.

Kitty, who was training herself to think kindly of Benjamin because ill wishes had a habit of rebounding on the ill-wisher, hoped her second husband's face was jammed down a lavatory regurgitating his stomach lining. Ryan, she decided magnanimously, could enjoy a hangover-free New Year's Day – he could even have company in bed if he chose. Kitty rallied, encouraged by her vision of Benjamin cradling a toilet seat: she'd just remembered that hindsight did come wrapped around one valuable message.

"You may have to lose from time to time, but you don't have to lose the lesson," she lectured Tom. He looked as though he could use the reminder.

She groped beneath the pillow, hair knotting as she jammed her head against the headboard, and located her emergency packet of American Hard Gums. They'd gone soft, but she popped a white sweet into her mouth, where it clung to a couple of molars and gleefully set to work on dental decay. Kitty chewed as she reviewed her brace of husbands.

Ryan had shown her that love wasn't the answer and Benjamin had shown her it wasn't even the question. Benjamin and she had lasted four years – not because she had loved him twice as much as Ryan, but because she had been twice as reluctant to admit defeat by then. She'd managed to wangle an annulment from the Catholic Church so she could marry Benjamin, and for what? So she could turn around, choose wrong a second time and file for divorce all over again. Serve her right for pursuing an annulment for the sole convenience of Noreen-dear.

"One divorce is unfortunate, Tom, two divorces are a pattern." Even though the volume was now mute, Kitty pitched her voice an octave higher, competing for his attention. "Everyone's allowed a first mistake, but make a second and people start drawing unflattering conclusions. Conclusions you've been reaching yourself."

After four years with Benjamin, Kitty had recognised that she could not bear to stay married to him for a day longer, and so she had submitted to the repetition of failure. She had decided she deserved to feel like a love-bankrupt, if only because she had said yes to him. Fully aware of his problem with excess saliva. She shuddered at the memory of marriage to a man who had drooled – not even provocatively in a sexual sense – then she looked back at the television screen.

"I'll level with you, Tom. I told myself I could live with a little saliva, but it began to bother me. It used to congeal in the right-hand corner of his mouth, leaving dried-in tracks there. I'd wake in the morning and there it would be, clinging to the side of his mouth. Bubbles of solidified drool."

Tom was busy pushing back his eyes into their sockets, as Marilyn Monroe straddled a subway vent and the gust of air from a train sent her skirt billowing. Kitty could tell she herself was having no impact on him. Not even with her rueful story about marrying a man who needed less spit and considerably more polish.

She crawled from under the duvet's embrace and shuffled towards the kitchen, detouring to wince over her appearance in the bathroom mirror.

"Imagine winding up a sophisticated ruin without having managed to look sophisticated first," Kitty complained.

She left the unforgiving bathroom to its own devices and trailed downstairs, hands against the walls for balance because the staircase was steep. Time for a pot of Earl Grey tea – ordinary tea seemed too prosaic for New Year's Day. The phone rang while she was in the kitchen and she waited for the answerphone to screen her caller.

"Kitty, it's your mother, Noreen," announced the disembodied voice, carefully specific, as though Kitty had other mothers called Betty or Margaret. "Your father and I were hoping to hear from you. I'm cooking an extra large roast duck for dinner so there's plenty for everyone." A crackle of hesitation, then her mother continued in a more subdued tone. "I wouldn't mind some company, Kitty – your sister's still sleeping and your father has disappeared into the basement. I've seen neither hide nor hair of him since breakfast. Give me a ring, lovie."

Her mother was doing plaintive on her; Kitty had no resistance against that one. Domineering and interfering she could ignore, but melancholy left her defenceless. She slumped against a cupboard – a slight figure in her vividly patterned aubergine and gilt robe, a Christmas present from her younger sister Sunny who liked decoration better than Kitty did – waiting for the kettle to boil. Her mother could pantomime the forlorn old lady all she liked, but at least she shared her home with a husband and a daughter. Kitty didn't co-exist with so much as a goldfish.

She slid her hands inside the stiff, embroidered sleeves of the robe, brooding over why she was alone on New Year's Day. No wonder she was pouting. Here she was, a woman in her prime, a natural blonde, for the love of God, and you didn't get many of them to the pound outside Finland, and she had just spent New Year's Eve alone in bed. It was downright abnormal. She hadn't even been drunk when she'd reached her bedroom at an indecently early one a.m. Unaccompanied.

It was like picking at a scab, she knew that, fretting over her fundamentally unsatisfactory past, littered as it was with broken marriages. Well, two anyhow, but they felt like more. That was the January 1st ambush: it tricked you into looking backwards as well as forwards. Two-faced Janus had a lot to answer for.

With the blood thundering in her ears, Kitty Kennedy decided it was time to take the situation in hand. She added a tea bag to the tumescent belly of the teapot and rooted for a clean mug in the dishwasher, tutting as she was unable to find one. She should empty the dishwasher one of these days instead of using it as a cupboard for dirty dishes.

Now, she needed a New Year's resolution and what better day to make one than New Year's Day? The first New Year's Day since the age of seventeen when she wasn't lying in bed, nibbling toast and honey dusted with ground-up Paracetamol, moaning, "I couldn't, I wouldn't, I didn't" as the jigsaw flashbacks filtered through, inexorable in their mounting detail. Must be a sign of maturity, she thought smugly. Unless – she quailed – it was a by-product of old age. There was a certain virtue in being too incapacitated to think on New Year's Day.

Kitty trudged upstairs with a tray, where she collapsed on the bed, clicking the remote control to give back Tom Ewell his voice. It meant Marilyn Monroe was vocal too, but Kitty was determined to ignore her. Could be worse, she reminded herself, resolutely upbeat: Benjamin could be in bed beside her. She waited. That didn't perk her up as much as she'd anticipated.

Despite the name, Benjamin wasn't even Jewish, which would have lent him a certain cachet in her eyes because she was always attracted to men who made her feel they could tap into thousands of years' worth of persecution and endurance. Irish Catholics were adept at *feeling* persecuted, but they couldn't produce anything from their store of grievances to compare with the Holocaust. Kitty also favoured Jewish men because she knew they would sleep with an Irishwoman like herself, they would even be seen in public with her, but they would never, not ever, bring her home to meet their mothers. She found it reassuring, that innate assumption she was inappropriate, by reason of birth and religion, to be brood mare to their line. It meant their relationship had built-in impermanence, which suited her just fine and dandy.

Kitty heaved a sigh. "I tend to remember my marriages around New Year, Tom, because the end of one year and the onset of another always leaves me pensive, and sometimes maudlin – especially if I've been drinking champagne, which gets me drunk at jig-speed." She frowned, momentarily diverted by the unfairness of champagne's capacity to render her comatose, no matter how often she tried to acclimatise herself. "It generally strikes me that one marriage began in bed and the other ended in it. But I'd rather not talk about that last part just now, it's too painful."

Watching Tom Ewell's progress to a happily-ever-after that didn't convince, regardless of how often she replayed it, Kitty realised that she'd wrested something valuable from both marriages. What two husbands had taught her, and which she was laboriously coming to terms with, was that not all men and women were meant to live together. Indeed, some should not attempt it on any account, and Kitty included herself. She was better on her own, that much was obvious. She'd made a brace of attempts to subvert her nature, escaping relatively lightly with twin divorces. Strictly speaking she wasn't divorced from number two yet, but she had a formal separation – it was only a matter of time before the remainder of the paperwork followed.

Although she knew she was lucky, Kitty also felt unlucky. Specifically, she felt unfortunate at that precise moment because she'd come through a New Year's Eve with nobody clamouring to kiss her as midnight chimed. Whereas a husband would have been honour-bound to clamour, at least in front of their friends.

"Divorce hurts like the devil, even when you want the relationship to end, Tom," Kitty counselled him. "I never managed to reach the seven-year-itch stage – I only notched up six years of marriage between two husbands." Then she switched over to an episode of *The Waltons* on RTÉ. *The Waltons* were safer. The mood she was in, she'd start looking at her wedding photographs. Girls in long white dresses always made her cry, especially if she were that girl.

It sometimes struck Kitty – particularly when she was in a vestigial depressed state, which she was sinking into on this New Year's Day because she felt lonely, although not lonely enough to go home to her parents for dinner – that men and women were designed to meet at specified periods, mate, and then lead separate existences. Exactly like those tribes you read about it in magazines at the dental surgery. If people would only accept this, instead of perpetuating the "two hearts beating as one" fable, everyone would be less stressed trying to store water in a sieve and make monogamous, legally-enshrined partnerships work.

"I should use that for a column," she remarked, cheered by her observation.

Kitty's job required her to write wry reflections on life, the cosmos and the transitory nature of relationships for the *Sunday Trumpet* – a tabloid newspaper with broadsheet delusions – and she invariably found it reassuring when a pithy insight popped up of its own accord. Without even a deadline looming. None of it had to be original – heck, she didn't have an original idea in her brain. The knack to being a widely read columnist was to give those unoriginal reflections a judicious amount of spin. That, plus being merciless about quarrying your own life and those of your friends to entertain the *Trumpet's* audience.

She rallied enough to go downstairs again, this time to check that the central heating was firing on continuous instead of switching to the timer. The dial was just inside the door of the galley kitchen.

The house was in Blackrock, a village that had swelled to a suburb on the outskirts of Dublin city. It was close to the sea and to the Dart commuter-train network which whisked her into work in twelve minutes, plus it had a Café Java which served poached eggs on wheaten bread. What more could anyone ask?

There was a window above the kitchen sink and Kitty raised the blind, checking the weather. Dry but overcast. That was the trouble with Ireland; even when it wasn't raining it usually threatened. She reviewed the state of play in Bumpermac's carpark just beyond her backyard: no cars loitered there, one of the rare days in the year when the supermarket was closed. Kitty decided she preferred it with vehicles studding the concrete – a carpark looked so pointless otherwise. She withdrew upstairs.

It was then, on the third stair from the top, the one which always creaked, that Kitty was overtaken by a New Year's resolution. Her legs buckled and she plumped down on the step, a lilt of certainty eddying through her. It felt as though she had been scrutinising life through a haze, but now it had tilted into alignment and she could see everything with absolute clarity. For once, the impulses of her heart were endorsed by the logic of her head.

Or to put it another way, resisting temptation was about to become unnecessary.

Chapter 2

Back in bed, Kitty lifted a Christmas card from the unsent stack on her locker and scribbled on the back. Writing down the insight made it seem more real.

I've finally realised that my natural state is the mistress, not the wife, she wrote. Her fingers couldn't keep pace with her thoughts which were spooling out at such speed that she scrabbled to catch up. *I don't want a man so he'll be there for the wet Wednesdays – that's normally why people cling to marriages, the belief they'll have someone to keep their feet warm in bed when the chill sets in. Wet Wednesdays are covered by a woman's friends. What I want is a man who's there for the fun: someone who meets me for clandestine trysts, laden down with hotel-room keys and bottles of Bollinger, clumsy with anticipation because I'm his stolen treat. Laughing because he has me to look forward to and I'm the silver lining in the cloud of his daily grind.*

She read over what she'd written, apprehensive about the word 'stolen'. The lying and cheating ingredients in being a mistress didn't appeal; Kitty decided she'd have to gloss over that. Otherwise this idea she was formulating could come crashing down before it had a chance to take its first teetering steps.

The trouble was that other people's husbands were so much more fascinating than your own. Even other people's fiancés, at a push. Her number one, Ryan, had been engaged to someone else when they'd met and she'd been instantly riveted. Kitty twiddled the ends of her shoulder-length wheat-coloured hair, recalling the sense of exhilaration when Ryan had detonated that engagement to be with her. She had believed if she could inspire such worship that he'd abandon a student nurse, who emptied bedpans all day and only had his love to look forward to when her dreary shift ended, then it must be cataclysmic between them.

Of course she had reasoned in fairly hackneyed terms back then, she acknowledged that openly. But in her youthful idealism, a particularly callous state for anyone who might stray into its force-field – student nurses, for example – she had concentrated on how Ryan had been stirred by her and had ignored whether she had been affected by him. Kitty hadn't paused to consider whether she had loved him in return. Or had loved, simply, the idea of generating a grand passion. Granted, that had been irresponsible. But she wasn't a complete ninny, as she'd insisted to her sister, Sunny, during a show-and-tell session which had taken the wrong fork and had left Kitty stripped bare of all pretension. Too naked by far.

"I'd never marry a man just because he asked me. I must have had feelings for Ryan or I wouldn't have pranced up the aisle in an ivory dress with a train that everyone kept standing on. Remember the shoe-prints I found all over it when I took it off?" she'd whined to Sunny. Kitty always whined when she felt herself to be on shaky ground.

Sunny, although seven years younger than Kitty, was infinitely more worldly and forever searching for new parameters to strain against. She had sat there, a scathing smile twitching her lips as a response fermented. Something to let Kitty know how capricious she'd been. Kitty could never fathom how she'd managed it, but Sunny had inherited the older-sister gene. All the more galling since Sunny could teach master classes in being superficial, frivolous and downright irresponsible, but she still left Kitty feeling like an ingenue.

"I know how you think," Sunny had crowed. "You felt you owed Ryan a wedding day, on account of interfering with the one he'd already lined up with the nurse. That's why you married him. You were paying the debt. You should learn to be like me and live in the moment, instead of getting muddled up in expectations and obligations."

Sunny was so provoking, especially when she was spot-on.

Kitty accidentally sat on the remote control, switching off *The Waltons*, and savaged her lip, determined to succeed in this mistress stratagem. Her sister needn't imagine she was the only bohemian member of their family.

Marriage made absolutely no sense. It was predicated on property, heirs, giving your family a day out and getting caught up in the excitement of a wedding. Without rationalising that marriage was the inevitable corollary. Love wasn't necessary before embarking on it – and it certainly wasn't guaranteed within it. Obviously she should have reasoned this through before getting married, and if she hadn't done it the first time there was no excuse for neglecting it the second, but better late than never.

She felt sufficiently energised to throw off the duvet and step out of her purple and gold robe, which would look wonderful on Sunny, a full seven inches taller than Kitty at five feet nine inches. Her sister was always buying presents that would suit her better. Kitty hunted for sweatpants and a fleece, pulling them on without washing first because this was an officially designated slob day. Then against her better judgement, and before she adjourned to the sofa in the living-room with an escapist paperback received for Christmas, she rang her mother to wish her a Happy New Year.

"It's me, Mum. Did you stay up to welcome in the New Year?"

"No, Kitty, I did not, I was in my bed by eleven. Sure, one year's much like another when you reach my age and who knows if I'll live to see the end of it?" Kitty crossed her eyes. Her mother was sixty-four and forever predicting her own demise, although in contradictory robust health. "I suppose you were out until cock-crow?"

"Not at all, Mum, I only stayed at the party as long as decency allowed."

Her mother sniffed. "Your sister didn't come home until breakfast time – I heard her on the stairs at seven o'clock this morning. I shudder to think what she can have been doing until that hour of the morning."

Kitty could have managed a fair guess at what her sister might have been doing, but charitably decided not to speculate in front of Noreen-dear. If she hadn't worked it out by now, her mother was deliberately being obtuse. Sunny Kennedy had recently moved back in with their parents because her acting roles had evaporated. It was only a temporary blip, she'd assured Kitty, daring her to disagree. But it comforted Kitty all the same – her sister was in no position to condescend to her while she wasn't even living an independent life.

"So will I throw your name in the pot for dinner, Kitty? It would be nice if we could all sit down together as a family once in a while."

"We did that last week on Christmas Day." Kitty's protest was half-hearted; her mother had never lost the knack of making her feel guilty.

"Some families do it on a regular basis. It's called breaking bread together, an ancient tradition." Her mother's tone was conversational rather than accusatory, but there was a subterranean sting.

Kitty pursed her lips. She really didn't want to eat overcooked meat and listen to her sister rhapsodise about her acting career – by her account a heartbeat away from Oscar acclaim, although she'd never been in a film that hadn't zoomed straight to video.

"I had plans –" she began.

Her mother sliced across her. "I'm sure I'm not going to plead with my own daughter to come home on New Year's Day."

Kitty caved in, just as she'd known she would, even as she was dialling the number for the house in Bray.

So much for sloth. She ran a shower and hunted out her new velvet dress, the colour of fuchsia buds studding country hedgerows, because her father loved to see her in frocks and she was a daddy's girl at heart. Who had taught her to secrete sweets under the pillow? Not her mother. She should make an effort with her appearance because Sunny would look sensational, even if she'd been out all night. Not to compete – that was impossible – but to harmonise.

Kitty phoned for a cab to Bray, a town eight miles beyond the Dublin suburban sprawl – almost part of it now – then began applying her make-up. Her brain ticked away. She'd need some help locating the right man for her mistress scheme. It would require a certain amount of finesse: you couldn't just saunter up to a likely lad and offer your services, it might be misconstrued. Kitty had a discreet, honourable arrangement in mind. She didn't intend becoming some bored husband's one-night stand; she saw herself as a moral mistress, contradictory though she knew it sounded. She tried it out, rolling the phrase around her tongue: "A moral mistress." Yes, Kitty liked the ring of it.

"Here's the deal," she told the diminutive blonde reflected in the mirror. "He pays me attention, I reserve myself exclusively for him. We can have Thursday nights and Sunday afternoons together. It'll be just like a marriage, but without that feeling of mating in captivity. Best of all, we'll never have to look at paint charts together, or visit DIY superstores, or argue over whose turn it is to clean the bathroom. Life will be an intoxicating succession of candlelit meals, soothing back-rubs and bottles of carefully chosen wine sipped beside a blazing fire."

The doorbell rang while she rummaged among the presents under the Christmas tree, scattering pine-needles. Kitty believed wholeheartedly in the redistribution of gifts. Her mother could have either a box of Belgian chocolates or a set of miniature perfumes. The perfumes were handbag-sized and useful so she returned them to the pile, and dislodged the card on the chocolates which read: *Love from Auntie Sarah*. "I'll be right out," she called to the taxi-driver, setting her burglar-alarm and bundling herself into a claret-dark wool coat with contrast frogging. She was all but dancing as she deadlocked the front door of her terraced house with its jutting wooden eaves, facing Bumpermac's carpark and closer to a noisy dual carriageway than was strictly desirable. Being a mistress sounded so idyllic, Kitty could hardly wait to get cracking: never had a New Year's resolution glinted so beguiling.

* * *

Kitty asked the driver to pull over at the end of the street so she'd have a couple of breaths of icy air coursing through her lungs before braving the family. Not that there was anything terrible about the Kennedys – they weren't as dysfunctional or idiosyncratic as some families she'd encountered – but they had the capacity to wear her out. There were only three of them – her mother, father and sister Sunny. Imagine if she were one of six. She blanched.

The sunlight was apologetic, aware that its rays held no warmth, as she strolled along Hunter Crescent – a curve of 1930s semis, all of them pebbledashed in a self-conscious way. Most of the houses had fairy lights girdling the roof or strung about a tree in the garden, usually a palm-tree because the East Coast climate was so mild. The Mangans at Number 6 had lost the run of themselves entirely and had plonked a life-sized Santa in his sleigh, complete with Dasher, Dancer and all the crew, on their roof. This area of Bray counted as des res, because of its proximity to the seafront, but Kitty had barely tolerated it growing up. There had been no commuter-train network at the time to link Dublin with the towns abutting it and the capital had seemed a remote Xanadu.

She approached Number 16, with its holly wreath on the daffodil-yellow front door, and thought, "At least our front garden has a sundial instead of being paved over for an extra car-parking space." Two lines from Hilaire Belloc straggled across the sundial's face, and no matter how hurried, Kitty always paused to read them:

I am a sundial, and I make a botch

Of what is done far better by a watch.

Sunny repeatedly urged their parents to sell up and take advantage of the equity in Number 16, and every so often they'd go through the motions of considering options. Arklow, maybe, or Brittas Bay. Except, as Kitty reminded Sunny, their parents would never be able to buy anywhere else that suited them half as well. In any case, the sundial was soldered into place and their father would leave their mother behind before he'd abandon that.

Noreen Kennedy was pinioned to the ironing-board when Kitty walked into the kitchen, and waggled a couple of fingers at her daughter to indicate she needed to finish what she was doing. The older woman took pride in her expertise with the iron: nothing escaped its smoothing tyranny. She even pressed labels on clothes and nudged the tip of her Morphy Richards inside pockets.

"Ironing on New Year's Day, Mum?" Kitty slumped at the kitchen table, downcast at the prospect of being sixty-four one day and obsessive about household chores.

"Be with you in a minute, Kitty." Her mother didn't deign to answer the quip about ironing. What did bank holidays mean to her when her washing-basket contained laundry?

She was becoming a mistress to avoid precisely this class of behaviour, Kitty reminded herself. Comforted, Kitty approached and kissed Noreen's cheek, lips brushing one of the cheekbones that delayed the flight of her mother's beauty. Close up, she inhaled the clinical tang of ironing – a blend of heat, damp cloth and fresh air. Images of hospital beds and cans of Robin's Spray Starch jumbled in her mind as her mother continued whisking through a pile of embroidered tray-cloths.

"I ran them through a gentle cycle to freshen them up." She nodded towards the heap.

"You don't even use them any more – you're making work for yourself."

Kitty's protest was desultory, for ironing was more than housework to her mother, it provided a framework to her life. Or so

Sunny claimed. A full ironing-basket represented chaos, an empty one translated into order.

"I'm keeping them in proper condition to pass on to you and your sister." Her mother flicked back the ruthlessly hair-sprayed beige curl that flopped over her forehead and folded the cloth she'd been working on, aligning its scalloped edges.

"You know best, Noreen-dear." Kitty went back to the table and hunched over it.

It had been Sunny who'd initiated the campaign to have the family call her Noreen-dear, aping their father's absentminded endearment. Installed as a joke, it had coagulated into habit, and their mother no longer noticed when the girls called her Noreen-dear to her face. Sometimes she even thought of herself as Noreen-dear. She finished her final tray-cloth, unplugged the iron and checked the clock. "We just have time for a cup of tea before dinner, Kitty. You take the meat out to stand and I'll put on the kettle."

Kitty would have preferred a glass of wine, but knew better than to suggest it. Sometimes she wished hers could be the kind of mother who skulked around tipping Liebfraumilch into teacups, imagining nobody knew what she was up to, but Noreen was profoundly opposed to alcohol in anything. Even her sherry trifles were misnomers.

Kitty lifted out the roast duck, careful not to splatter juice on her velvet dress. "Where is everybody, Mum?"

Her mother's feet clacked across the tiled floor to the fridge in her Dr Scholls, worn winter and summer in the belief they would spare her from fallen arches. "Your father's in the basement and Sunny's in her room. You may as well call down to your father to see if he wants a cup of tea – he'll say no, but he can't pretend we never ask."

Tea-consumption had been a battlefield between her mother and father for as long as Kitty could remember. Her mother drank it every half-hour, sometimes more frequently, while her father could take it or leave it. However, Noreen Kennedy regarded it as her life's mission to convert him to something approaching her frequency. It seemed to have acquired the status of a personal struggle between the two, a war of wills, her mother forever chipping away at her father's resolve not to submit to more than three daily cups.

Kitty went into the hallway and opened the basement door, where a smell of damp earth assaulted her nostrils; she could never understand how her father tolerated it.

"Tell him," cried her mother, "Mr Donnelly from Number 28 says his cousin was found dead in his bed yesterday morning. They think dehydration may have been a factor."

A smile tickled Kitty's lips. "Dad, Noreen-dear wants to know if you fancy a cup of tea?" Her voice reverberated off the brick walls leading downstairs.

There was a scuffle and Denis Kennedy's sturdy frame appeared at the bottom. "No thanks, chicken. That mother of yours would have me swimming in the stuff if she had her way." His voice was slightly distorted from the sweet he was sucking.

Kitty's father was a tubby man two inches shorter than his wife. Although a moderate eater, his stomach protruded between the buttons of his trademark navy overalls. He seemed to have a sweet lodged permanently in his mouth – Sunny and Kitty had a theory that his Fox's Glacier Mints controlled his appetite but accounted for the pot belly.

"Dinner's in ten minutes," she called.

"Right-oh, tell Noreen-dear I'll be up in two shakes of a lamb's tail." He turned away, jaw still moving.

"Well?" asked her mother, when Kitty returned to the kitchen.
"No."

"No," her mother intoned, with more bitterness than seemed strictly necessary, given that her husband had been declining cups of tea for thirty-eight years. She carried the teapot to the kitchen table and poured two cups.

"Can I do anything to help with dinner, Mum?" Kitty was anxious to distract her from the palpable simmer of grievance.

"It's all keeping warm in the oven and the table's set in the dining-room." Noreen-dear shook her head, sorrow ricocheting from rigid curls. "Tea-drinking on your own is a solitary business, Kitty. It wouldn't hurt that man to accept the odd cup, whether he wants it or not, to keep me company. Then there's Sunny, who only takes perc-u-lated coffee, even first thing in the morning. I keep telling her it's too harsh for her stomach before it's had a chance to wake up, but sure when did your sister ever listen to me?" She sipped her sugary tea and rallied. "Have you made any New Year's resolutions?"

Kitty's glance skittered off her mother's face: this was one resolution she had no intention of sharing with Noreen-dear. "I might try and walk into work the odd day."

Noreen nodded. "Walking is great exercise altogether. The car culture's throttling the art of walking."

Was there an art to walking, Kitty wondered? Just then Sunny padded barefoot into the kitchen.

"I'm starving, I could eat the hand of God." She stretched, massaging the back of her neck. "Hello, Kitty-cat, how was your New Year's Eve?"

"Dull," admitted Kitty. "I hear yours was the business."

"Just the usual sex, drugs, rock 'n' roll, and passing around our knickers for a guessing game to see who wears what." Sunny yawned, clicking her jawbone.

"You didn't," protested Noreen-dear.

"All right then, we didn't." Sunny winked at Kitty and wandered over to the duck, picking at slivers of meat. "You really ought to make more of an effort, Kitty – if you can't rustle up a decent party on New Year's Eve, it's a poor show."

Kitty bristled. "If I lived at home and relied on Mum to cook, clean and do my laundry for me, I might have more free time to organise a social diary."

"It's probably just as well you didn't meet anyone interesting at your damp squib of a hooley – you'd probably be engaged to him by now," Sunny sniped.

"No bickering, girls," murmured their mother automatically.

Kitty simmered. Was she never to be allowed to forget that she'd managed to marry and discard two husbands by the time most of her peers were still working up to the first set of wedding invitations? Some people were able to develop a forgiving amnesia regarding their mistakes. Not her.

Meanwhile, Sunny knitted her eyebrows. Kitty knew exactly where to slide in the knife. Sunny wasn't thrilled about living at home, but efforts to move out inevitably culminated in disaster. Once she signed a tenancy agreement there was no guessing what might happen. Acting jobs that appeared to promise months of security suddenly petered out – shows closed prematurely, backers filed for bankruptcy, someone else was chosen for the role all her friends agreed nobody could play except her.

"I'll call Dad for dinner." Sunny flounced out of the kitchen, her toe-ring twinkling against the spray-on tan on her feet.

Kitty was immediately penitent: she shouldn't have needled her sister. She could use Sunny's contacts in the theatrical world to line up a lover – maybe a director or a playwright. She fancied someone arty. Not an actor, though – they were too narcissistic.

After dinner she suggested a walk to her sister as a way of mentioning her New Year's resolution without their mother eavesdropping.

"Are you mad? It's dark out there and the wind would cut you like a knife," her sister responded. "Besides, I was thinking of meeting some of the crew for a drink in town in the Princeville."

Close to the Abbey Theatre in the city centre, the Princeville was an eccentric hybrid of thespian rallying-point and old codgers' local. Cramped, unventilated and one of the few unrenovated pubs in Dublin, it flouted the Government's smoking ban in public places. This meant it was a favourite haunt of Sunny's, who could secondary-inhale there to her heart's content if funds didn't stretch to a packet of cigarettes.

"It's too early to go there yet," wheedled Kitty.

"It's never too early or too late for the Princeville." Sunny scratched her stomach.

"I'll buy you an Irish coffee in Barracuda afterwards," bartered Kitty, naming a popular restaurant-bar on the seafront with views across the bay. "Come on, it'll be invigorating, and to be honest I want to canvass your advice."

Sunny studied her with suspicion: Kitty never asked for advice. Her sister was more mature and infinitely more organised. Seven years older and seven inches shorter, the coincidence used to amuse them. Well, it entertained Sunny more than Kitty, who felt aggrieved that her legs were stumpy compared with the willowy Sunny's. But Kitty had achieved so much more than she had, thought Sunny, overlooking the additional years. Not only was she a columnist on a Sunday newspaper, she'd managed to buy her own house. Sometimes Sunny suspected she was doomed to live permanently with her parents. Still, Kitty was hopeless at relationships, for all her high-achieving life – or possibly there was a connection, but Sunny hadn't the spare brain-cell capacity to mull it over now. She'd assassinated too many of them at the New Year's Eve party and the survivors needed time to regroup.

She narrowed blue eyes still outlined by last night's mascara and considered Kitty. Although she'd married and cast off two husbands by the time she was thirty-three, she was remarkably gauche when it came to dealing with men. Maybe she wanted to quiz her about boyfriends – obviously there was a famine on that front. Sunny prided herself that she might not have a home of her own, she might not have much of an acting career – she hadn't even been offered a part in pantomime this year – but at least she always had a man on the go. Sometimes several. "A walk it is, Kitty-cat," she complied. "Wait until I find some shoes."

They ambled along by the seafront railings, orange and turquoise paintwork peeling, surprised by how many others were pacing the promenade. Fairy lights bounced off the silvered surface of the sea, while parked cars with their headlights switched on lined the route. Passers-by stamped briskly, but many let their glances linger on the sinuous length of the white-blonde Sunny, with her prominent bone structure inherited from Noreen. Kitty's was the more winsome face, but few noticed her beside her captivating sister who, sensing admiration, tossed her head so that her neck-length hair fluttered in the breeze.

"So last night was a damp squib?" Sunny challenged Kitty.

At least it felt to Kitty as though she was being challenged; in fact, Sunny was offering her an introduction.

Kitty shrugged. "I've had better nights."

"You should be fighting them off on New Year's Eve – it was a barbarian's stronghold at my party."

"I could have had company if I'd chosen, Sunny. There were at least two men willing to go home with me, if it weren't for the inconvenience of wives at their elbows. There are never any single people at parties any more – not at the parties I'm invited to, anyway. You start to suspect they're swapping invitations and hissing '*Don't tell Kitty Kennedy*'." She pressed a knuckle into the corner of each eye. "I was queuing for the bathroom behind two girls so drunk that one was trying to explain to her friend that sherbet was something you ate and Herbert was a man's name, when the countdown to midnight started. The girls bolted for the sitting-room where everyone was holding hands, but I perched on the banister and thought, 'There's nobody here I even want to kiss'. How defeatist is that?"

Sunny slid her arm through Kitty's. "We'll have to find a lovely chubby man for you to settle down with, Kitty-cat. Someone you can stay home with on New Year's Eve." She hugged Kitty's arm, for her disposition was as cheerful as her name. She'd been christened Sunniva – their parents had been going through their Celtic-princess phase. Kitty had always counted it fortunate that when she'd been born, it had been a name-the-baby-after-Granny stage.

They were at the end of the promenade now, Bray Head rearing before them, with the distinctive spiked peak of the Sugar Loaf mountain over the rooftops to its right. Some hardy souls were tramping the path twirling down from Bray Head, having made it along the cliff-top to Greystones and back before the night settled in with an assured finality. Kitty and Sunny were unanimous in feeling they'd exercised quite enough, however, and retraced their steps.

A thought struck Kitty. "What *were* you doing until seven a.m., Sunny?"

"Having sex, naturally. Deliciously repetitive, gloriously life-enhancing, casual sex with a stranger. You should try it some time instead of always getting married."

"As a matter of fact, that's what I wanted to talk to you about."

"Casual sex with a stranger?" Sunny was amused, for Kitty wasn't the type. Then again, you never knew if you were the type until you tried it.

"Not exactly." A squat white dog on the end of a leash sniffed at her boots and Kitty quickened her pace, throwing a reproachful look at the owner.

"Casual sex with someone who's not a stranger?" prompted Sunny, intrigued.

"No casual sex and no strangers." Kitty was definite. She'd had six lovers in her life and none of them had been one-night stands. She wasn't about to set foot on that particular slippery slope. One-night stands were only glorious and life-enhancing and all those other bracing adjectives if you had the capacity for them. Kitty knew she didn't. She'd tried it once and ended up marrying him – that was Benjamin. No, Kitty planned to be a moral mistress.

Sunny lost interest. "Did you bring your mobile? Mine's out of credit. I need to check if there's any action tonight."

"I'm going to become somebody's mistress – I'd make an ideal one," gabbled Kitty. "I wouldn't want a man to leave his wife for me, or marry me, or set me up in a penthouse, because I like my terraced cottage. I'd appreciate the odd present – not much point to being a mistress without gifts. Bouquets of exotic flowers, say, or maybe the odd weekend away in a smart hotel. Even a piece of jewellery now and again, nothing too extravagant because I'd feel guilty about depriving his children of their school fees, and I suppose his wife is entitled to her little luxuries, to compensate for a cheating husband."

Sunny was astounded. Kitty wanted to be a mistress? Granted, it sounded glamorous the way she described it, but she wasn't convinced it was her sister's calling in life. Just because she had no desire to marry again didn't rule out being a girlfriend. Sunny unbuttoned her waist-length shearling jacket, suddenly over-heated.

"That's wrong, isn't it?" resumed Kitty, noticing Sunny's silence. "I'm not supposed to care about the wife's feelings, let alone whether my trifling with her husband affects the household budget. I need to toughen up if I'm to make a success of being a mistress."

"Don't be ridiculous," exploded Sunny. "You're not mistress material, Kitty. I've never heard such nonsense in all my life. Mistresses cause pain, you prize idiot, and they're usually on the receiving end of quite a lot of it too."

Her tone was so venomous that Kitty was cagey, studying her sister's reddened complexion. Then the familiar rivalry snaked between them. "I suppose you think I'm not sophisticated enough. I expect you believe if anyone in the family has a shot at being a mistress it should be you."

Sunny quickened her pace, a nerve fluttering in her left temple, leaving Kitty's shorter legs to pump as she raced to catch up.

"The truth hurts, doesn't it, Sunny?" she jeered.

Sunny stopped walking and spun on her heels towards her sister, voice subdued, so that Kitty strained to hear. "I was a mistress, Kitty, and believe me, I wouldn't wish it on my worst enemy."

Chapter 3

This was news to Kitty. Then again Sunny had always been selective about confidences. They trudged along mutely, engrossed by the chuckle of the waves as they nuzzled the pebbled shore. Approaching Barracuda, where lights flaunted an invitation, Kitty suggested, tentative, "How about that drink I promised you? Something hot with a dash of alcohol through it sounds promising from where I'm standing."

"Me too," Sunny agreed, eyes bleak as the rocks guarding the shoreline directly ahead.

Barracuda was under new management and had opened on New Year's Day to win customers. Upstairs tables with a view of the coast were reserved for clientele ordering food, so the sisters sat elbow-to-elbow at the bar on the ground floor. Both women preferred it that way; it meant they didn't have to meet one another's gaze.

There was a dislocation between them, not just at that moment, but in general, for they had little in common. Yet they were conscious of their bond as sisters and valued it.

"Sorry about the outburst," Sunny apologised eventually.

"No problem." Kitty dabbled a teaspoon in the cream floating on her Irish Coffee, wondering if she should risk a question. She and Sunny had been so close once; as a girl Sunny had been her shadow, trailing after her, forever begging to be allowed to sleep in Kitty's bed. They used to lie facing one another, Sunny's little finger twined around hers on the pillow. A wishbone embrace. How had that worshipful small girl grown into a brittle stranger?

"I don't suppose I'm naturally virtuous. But I've learned that if you put your hand in the fire it burns," began Sunny, "and if you become involved with a married man you end up scorched. My red-hot coal was called Nick Shooter. He was an actor, from Swansea originally, but when I knew him he was part of the London set." Her eyes acquired an introverted glaze. "I should have known better than to get involved, but I couldn't resist him. He had the chiselled, almost painfully perfect features of a matinée idol. Wavy black hair, eyes the colour of green marbles, cleft jaw. No wonder he was an actor. He had a wife considerably older than him, at least that's what he said, a home and two children in the Mumbles, and he assured me the marriage was dead. What can I say without making myself look feeble-minded? I believed him."

Kitty was afraid to react in case it interrupted the flood of recollection. Naturally she'd heard of Nick Shooter; he was one of the best Shakespearean actors of his generation, but handsome enough to attract the schoolgirl audience with his face alone. She scowled at a party of six men and women who erupted into the restaurant, laughing inside an eddy of cold air, and was relieved to see them escorted upstairs.

Sunny wasn't aware of the intruders. She dragged fingers through her hair, leaving tramlines in their wake. "I lived with him while he appeared in *Antony and Cleopatra* at The Gate – he played Mark Antony, naturally. We were together for three glorious months of folly. That's when you all thought I was sharing a flat with my friend Quentin in Arbour Hill. But I was spending every day at the theatre listening to Nick captivate audience after audience, and every night at his penthouse in Temple Bar being a

27

spellbound audience of one. Sometimes Nick would tell me he had to make private calls and I'd leave the apartment and sit in the Norseman nursing a bottle of lager, or walk up and down the boardwalk on the Liffey if funds were low. I didn't mind, no matter how cold or wet it was – I thought those phone calls were about making arrangements to divorce his superannuated wife and marry me." Sunny reached for a cigarette, realised she wasn't allowed to smoke in Barracuda, and mangled her unlit cigarette in a glass ashtray. "I met her, you know. She wasn't an antique after all. When the play ended he told me he had to fly to Los Angeles for a few days to see an American agent who might be useful. He suggested I go home to Bray so I wouldn't be lonely in the penthouse. 'We'll have all the time in the world together soon enough,' he promised, and he kissed the tip of my nose. He liked my nose." Sunny touched it, awed. Then she positioned her lips into a smile which lent no warmth in her face. "What happened next was a cliché. I moved home, but I had to meet someone in town on the Sunday afternoon, and who should I see parting the Red Sea of the crowds on Grafton Street but Nick Shooter. He had a little wavy-haired girl riding on his shoulders and another clutching his hand, and his arm was draped around a tall, auburn woman. They were laughing, Kitty, they were a family." She paused, tongue flicking her upper lip, tasting the shock again. "I suppose he hadn't taken on board what a village Dublin is – he imagined it was as anonymous as London or New York. I was so angry that I marched right up to them. 'Nick,' I said, 'imagine seeing you here!' He didn't flinch. He's a damned good actor, I'll grant him that. He pretended we were nothing more than members of the same cast – that was a joke, I had two lines as Cleopatra's handmaiden. If he hadn't been sleeping with me he'd never have noticed me. Nick introduced me to his wife, who might have been all of a year older than him at a push; she took my hand and looked into my eyes and her gaze was pitying. That was the truly humiliating part. She knew. She felt sorry for me." Sunny squinted through a spasm of pain.

"Still, I wanted to believe there was an explanation. He didn't bother meeting me to palm me off with one. He sent a text message to my mobile phone saying he'd decided to give his marriage another try – that he owed it to his daughters. A text message! He didn't even have the decency to speak to me. Nick's in Tuscany now, filming with Francis Ford Coppola. See how I keep abreast of his movements? I heard his wife went with him and I can't say I blame her. If he couldn't be trusted in Dublin for three months, he definitely couldn't be turned loose in Italy for six. Will we head home?" She started to get up.

Kitty touched Sunny's elbow, guiding her back into her seat. "I had no idea," she whispered.

"It wasn't something I wanted to shout from the rooftops." A suggestion of desolation clung to Sunny, face drained of colour. "He lied to me and I believed him, I was a victim. But I wouldn't have been fooled so easily if I'd spared a thought for his wife and children. I didn't care about them, you see, all I cared about was hooking Nick. That's why I was punished."

Was that why she had random sexual encounters with strangers, Kitty wondered? Less complication – less chance of a broken heart. It was unusual to see her sister so sombre, for Sunny was always rushing around, crying: "Life's not a dress rehearsal!"

Kitty didn't prefer this blank-eyed sister to the frenetic one, but each version made sense of the other. She curled her little finger into Sunny's, their wishbone embrace, and was rewarded with a fleeting smile.

* * *

Sunny stayed on in Barracuda after her sister struck out for home, although Kitty had been reluctant to leave her.

"I'm going to have another drink, then I'll head for the Princeville. The crew will be congregating shortly," predicted Sunny.

Kitty's expression was doubtful as she studied her sister,

unconsciously puckering her forehead in a carbon-copy of their mother. "I'll keep you company until you're ready to go, Sunny."

"I'll be fine – shoo! I just fancy a quiet coffee while I collect my thoughts."

Still Kitty hesitated, her voice snagging on the words. "You're not going to . . . you're not going to do something wildly spontaneous, like ring Nick Shooter and beg him to see you again?"

Sunny shook her head, impatient. "Kitty, I may be a flibbertigibbet, I may be that all too common phenomenon, a resting actor, I may be twenty-nine and living at home still. But I do retain some shreds of self-respect – and contacting Nick Shooter to offer him the opportunity to spurn me all over again is not on the agenda, I promise you. Besides, he's probably busy working his wiles on another impressionable girl. So many sacrificial lambs, so little time to plunge in the knife." Sunny noticed how Kitty relaxed visibly – she'd really worried her sister by confiding in her about Nick. She began to feel goaded by the fluttering way Kitty was watching her. "Listen, Noreen-dear will be hounding poor Dad. If it's not the lack of blank tapes to film her soaps, she'll be obsessing about taking a toothbrush and some bleach to the bathroom grouting. Go home and rescue the man for an hour – it's the least you can do on New Year's Day."

As Kitty gathered her bag and coat, Sunny stood too. "I'll step outside and have a quick cigarette between coffees."

"You smoke too much, you'll end up with cancer." Kitty had her back to Sunny and was walking towards the door.

"You worry too much, you'll end up with cancer," retorted Sunny. Then she regretted her acerbity. "Happy New Year, Kitty-cat. Make another resolution, there's still time."

Sunny couldn't hear her reply, juggled by the wind. She huddled in a sheltered area near the doorway and lit one cigarette from the stub of another, smoking until her throat ached and her eyes stung against the plumes – forgetting to flick off her ash so that it dangled, precarious, over her clothes. She only stopped when she realised her cigarette packet was empty. Indoors again, she ordered a coffee and asked the shaven-headed barman if he sold cigarettes.

"You have to use the machine on the wall, I'm afraid." His smile was unusually apologetic, for there was something about Sunny that persuaded the eye to dawdle on her. It wasn't her sculpted cheekbones, or her downy bleached hair, or her long, slender limbs, but the combined package. The sum of her total added up to considerably more than any individual part. "Do you need coins?" he volunteered, although it wasn't encouraged by the management, fearful of a change shortage.

"No, I'm all right." Sunny checked her pocket and turned away, not so much impervious to his admiration as so accustomed to generating it that it scarcely registered.

He was still watching her when she returned to the stool. "Is there anything else you'd like?"

His English was perfect, there were even traces of a Dublin accent, but she guessed he was East European. Polish, maybe. He had hands the size of shovels; she could easily imagine him on a farm. She wondered idly why he wore his hair cropped close, so that his skull resembled a giant egg.

"An espresso, please." Sunny jingled some coins and met his gaze.

"One espresso coming up." He smiled, gum glistening.

"And a brandy chaser to go with it," added Sunny. Why not? It was New Year's Day. She shouldn't really mix her spirits, especially after the previous night's bacchanal, but revisiting the emotions surrounding her relationship with Nick Shooter had left her churned up and scrabbling to regain her equilibrium. It wasn't that alcohol would restore her balance – she'd learned that much – but it was a palliative. At least for a time.

"A large one?" asked the barman.

"May as well." Sunny rewarded him with her Oscar acceptance smile. *All right, Mr de Mille, I'm ready for my close-up.*

He stretched towards the optics, debating his chances of

persuading Sunny to accompany him to Captain Atomic's nightclub.

Towards the end of her brandy and espresso Sunny wearied of flirting with Karl the barman, and grew introspective. A flash of self-loathing gripped her as she realised she was drinking to feel better – but she was still a failure. No matter how many brandies she ordered, she'd remain a failure. Here she was, on the cusp of yet another year, a year in which she'd go to auditions and be chosen for some parts, rejected for more, and what were the chances of seeing her name in lights? Remote to zero. Being beautiful wasn't enough, being talented wasn't enough. You needed luck.

Except luck, ruminated Sunny, draining her glass, wasn't that easy to chance by. She could book facials and sun-bed sessions to maintain her looks, she could use a drama coach or reach inside herself to emote, but there was no-one she could approach for an extra nugget of luck. A talisman of promise to keep by her: *in case of emergency break glass*. She was tired of her friend Quentin telling her the universe was benign and she should tap into that benevolence. If it was true it was a passive kindness – she wanted something to intercede actively on her behalf. Some force that would look at Sunny Kennedy, struggling actor, reluctant telephone salesperson, and say: "It's her turn, let's give her a chance."

She stood, scraping her stool against the floor. Moping was counter-productive – she'd catch up with the crew at the Princeville. Someone was bound to know of a new play or film, or even a commercial that was being cast. Karl saw her prepare to leave and raced across. "It's the tradition in my country that the barman always buys the third drink." He lifted her balloon glass and placed it under the up-ended bottle of Hennessy.

"That must prove an expensive custom for the barman." Sunny continued to shrug on her jacket.

"We only do it once every evening and we choose the most exquisite lady on the premises to receive our tribute."

Sunny winced at the mawkish overture. Still, the brandy was

poured, the barman was smiling through even teeth and she could hear the wind howling outside. Sunny sat down again. Perhaps, while she was drinking this, she could make a New Year's resolution of her own. She sipped the gilded fire in her glass, smiling vaguely at Karl, who was plotting to tell the owner he had a toothache and needed to leave early.

Sunny, unaware of the role she was playing in Karl's subterfuge, decided she'd give herself a year to make it as an actor. If she were still drifting this time next year, she'd re-enrol in college and study for her drama teacher's qualifications. "But you were born to burn bright, you're radiant with star quality, you've known it all your life. This is your destiny," chimed the inner certainty which had always allayed her doubts in the past. Sunny concentrated on it, feathered blonde head inclined to one side. How could she know if her inner certainty was an ally . . . or an agent provocateur? Maybe it wasn't self-belief but self-delusion.

"I can't keep on trying to sell myself to casting agents. I'm a person, I'm Sunny Kennedy, not a slab of meat who might fit this role or that," she whispered. There was no response from the inner certainty. Sunny listened, holding her body taut with the effort, giving her inner certainty a chance to dissuade her. Nothing. Just silence, replaced, then, by a faint drumbeat of fear. This was it: the die was cast and her New Year's resolution made. In a year's time she'd know whether her life would be played out in the spotlight. Or behind it.

The realisation sobered her. She hooked her toe under her handbag strap to lift it without bending, looking for Karl to say goodbye, but there was no sign of him. Sunny stepped into the wind. A shaven-skulled figure in a battered flying jacket materialised on the promenade beside her. "I have the rest of the night off – would you like to go somewhere and celebrate the New Year?"

Sunny thought she should probably say no. She knew nothing about Karl, not even from which East European country he originated. "All right then," she acquiesced.

Chapter 4

Kitty reviewed her mistress machinations as she set the alarm-clock, for she was back at work at the *Sunday Trumpet* in the morning. She tried to reassure herself they were still water-tight, despite Sunny's unfortunate experience. The day she took advice from her underdressed, overwrought sister was the same one she'd start relying on the psychic hotline for guidance with crunch decisions. Besides, the cases weren't comparable. Sunny had intended to lure her man away from his wife and children, whereas she was keen for hers to stay with his family. She didn't want all of him, just a couple of hours twice a week, spiced up with the odd weekend away. Sharing could work under those circumstances. Yes, it could, she contradicted the dissenting voice in her brain. However, she wouldn't be able to rely on Sunny to supply possible candidates; she'd be obliged to track them down herself. Such a prospect was profoundly unsatisfactory – you had to visit nightclubs and meet strangers, an unnerving prospect. They were crammed with stunning teenagers, all flawless skin and skimpy tops that showed off the belly-bars piercing their navels. Kitty cudgelled her brains for an alternative and remembered Rose McBride from the

picture desk at work. Maybe she should confide in her and see if
Rose could suggest a man in need of a mistress.

You'd never imagine, Kitty thought bitterly, punching a pillow,
it was going to prove so difficult to have an affair.

While Sunny was seeking oblivion in the arms of Karl, whose
bed-sit close to the Bray Wanderers football club grounds was
furnished with a variety of flavoured vodkas conducive to oblivion,
Kitty thrashed inside a nightmare. In it, both Ryan and Benjamin
appeared to her, and when she recalled this in the morning she
found it unsettling. They'd never been in one another's company
and she didn't appreciate their united front in her dreams. "You
have a commitment phobia, Kitty Kennedy," they intoned in
unison.

The words stayed with her as she gulped coffee and tried to find
footwear that matched the silver-grey suit she was wearing. Kitty
had a collection of neat Doris Day work suits, all with knee-length
hems and slits that would never raise office temperatures. She
abandoned the search for her court shoes with silver heels and slid
her feet into all-purpose black-patent ankle boots, trying to
remember if Sunny had borrowed the missing footwear. If so, she
might never see them again. The last shoes of hers that Sunny had
purloined, she'd lent to a stranger so he could drink pink
champagne from them.

"I couldn't ask for them back, Kitty-cat – he passed out stroking
them."

As Kitty's ankle-boots rapped a castanets' rhythm along the
deserted street leading to Blackrock Dart station, the dream
gnawed at her. Maybe she did have a commitment phobia. But
there was only so much critical self-analysis one woman could cope
with. Besides, it was galling that both exes appeared to be
conspiring against her in her dreams. Unless. She paused, rotated
the possibility in her mind and decided it made sense. Unless it was
her subconscious ordering her to learn from her mistakes.

Kitty bought a three-day pass from a surly youth who grunted when she wished him a Happy New Year. "In the US," she told him, "all businesses, by law, must post up a sign in the employees' rest room saying: *If you come within twelve feet of a customer, smile.*"

He pushed the change towards her, impassive.

"I don't believe it either." She moved away before the two women behind her, bent on January sales shopping, mutinied.

Imagine having to go back to work on January 2nd – she felt wronged by life as the commuter train rounded the corner and juddered to a halt at the platform. At this time of year, she always wished she could be a schoolgirl again and on holiday until after the feast of the Epiphany, eating the remnants of selection boxes and watching daytime television. Nothing like it for learning the latest American slang. She was still trying to figure out how to use 'she's such a cheerleader' in a column. Then she fell to pondering how to kick-start her mistress scheme, a dilemma which continued to occupy her as she arrived at the *Sunday Trumpet* offices near Grand Canal Dock station, on the fifth floor of a purpose-built block constructed with breathtaking brutality.

The receptionist, Irene, reached Kitty a pickle-green balloon with a Danish pastry attached to the ribbon as she walked in.

"It's from a new public relations firm – they've sent Danishes to everyone in Editorial," said Irene.

"One question: why?" Kitty was already eating the cake and had discarded the press release.

"It's in the press release." Irene looked reproachful, for she found journalists too flippant and not at all appreciative of their freebies. "They say they can do everything except make your coffee in the morning – even supply breakfast," she clarified.

"Nice try," Kitty mumbled, cramming the remains of the Danish into her mouth and retreating to the Ladies' to repair her lipstick. She had learned in journalism college that a perfect shorthand note and a lavishly lipsticked mouth carried you through all emergencies. Provided you were a female journalist. Men had to make their own arrangements.

Kitty strolled the subdued length of the newsroom, past four wall-mounted television sets tuned to Sky News, nodding to a couple of reporters. She saw the latest recruit, fresh out of college, huddled alongside the news editor. It was a conversation where you knew from the body language that one of the parties was being lied to – and since the news editor made Pinocchio look like George Washington, she assumed he was telling it like it wasn't to the new kid on the block.

When she reached her desk, the post was stacked and waiting for her to open.

Kitty's haul contained:

– a free set of stick-on nails

– an invitation to a new lap-dancing club (she was invited to one every week, since writing a diatribe denouncing them – they thrived on the publicity)

– a press release for a conference on rape which she pushed to one side for the newsdesk

– a book on flirting with lots of quizzes to tick, showing how adept you were at sending out and receiving signals

– a reader's letter complaining that she hadn't received her free CD in the last edition of the paper and could Kitty sort it out personally because she had a kind face. People were always using that line on her – a cheap trick, but it worked every time.

She switched on her computer and checked her email. There were three messages from her stalker. He still thought her columns were rubbish, that she was a man-hater, but only because she hadn't met the right one, and he'd booked dinner for eight o'clock tonight at Thornton's and expected to see her there. Hmm, change of year, change of venue. Last year he'd ordered her on a weekly basis to meet him at Shanahan's on the Green. Kitty deleted the messages and wandered off to the kitchen to make a mug of instant coffee.

What had her last column been about anyway, to spark that flurry of communication from her email stalker? Oh yes, high heels. She'd described how stilettos had survived feminism and post-feminism, concluding that some objects of desire exerted too powerful a pull to be discarded – whether you burned your bra or preferred to flash it. Her friend, an assistant picture editor at the *Sunday Trumpet* called Rose McBride, claimed she'd nominate for canonisation whoever invented the elegant flat shoe. "But I'm not holding my breath," Rose had added. "By the way, left and right shoes were only devised in the early 1800s, until then both were identical. Sorry about that, my brain stores trivia." Rose was always foisting her opinions on Kitty's column onto Kitty herself, and since they were generally reasonably supportive – or at least not too negative – she and Kitty were friends.

Rose was in the staff kitchen, also brewing up coffee. Rose and Kitty both knew they probably wouldn't gel particularly well under normal circumstances, except they had decided early on that they were the only rational people at the *Sunday Trumpet* and ought to form a united front, in the interests of preserving their sanity.

Sometimes Kitty thought she wouldn't be able to carry on working there if it weren't for Rose. Everyone else was too peculiar – not interesting and eccentric peculiar, introspective and egotistical peculiar. The pair didn't often go out together socially because Rose retreated to Slane every weekend for at least one night. Slane was known for its annual summer rock concerts in the grounds of the castle, which lent it a nonconformist reputation. But to hear Rose describe the small town north of Dublin, just too far away to commute from although that didn't deter some people, it was a desert of tedium. Which is probably why, when Rose did hit the town, she was the life and soul of the party. At the newsroom Christmas bash she'd announced deadpan to Peter Webster, the special investigations reporter: "*I find that alcohol, taken in sufficient quantities, can produce all the effects of drunkenness.*" It had taken him until the scramble for taxis more than an hour later to decipher it. He still imagined Rose had been the one to coin the phrase.

Rose McBride wasn't much above average-looking, but people forgot that five minutes into conversation with her because she could make a weather bulletin sound fascinating. Kitty puzzled over the secret of her friend's allure and could only conclude that she had charisma. Rose was spaghetti-thin, although fond of food, with pearl-pale skin that was virtually unlined, lending her a youthful appearance. Her eyes were her most unusual feature – blue on the outer ring, hazel on the inner one – and people tended to pause and check them at first sight. Unsure whether they were strangely attractive or just strange.

Rose was more indifferent about her appearance than Kitty, who was continually making self-destructive comparisons to Sunny and buying eyeliners and face creams which would bridge the perceived gulf. Rose wasn't prepared to expend the effort, which is why she had been dyeing her hair with a home-kit for years. She was the first to buy coffees or donate to charity collections, but she couldn't be bothered with a professional job on her hair. Kitty had deep reserves of affection for Rose, but she wished she'd spend money on her appearance.

"Happy New Year, Kitty. This week it's your turn to fancy Peter Webster and mine to have Des Redmond from features," said Rose, debating low fat or full-cream milk in the staff kitchen.

"Same to you. Now give me a break – anyone but Peter. It's not worth working up to a drool over him," objected Kitty.

"The umpire's decision is final." Rose was implacable.

"All right then, but I'm only fancying him from afar – this is strictly hands-off and fantasy-based." Kitty tossed her blonde hair.

It was a game they played regularly, although both agreed the raw material left much to be desired.

"Met a man at the weekend." Rose was conspiratorial now, checking the door in case any colleagues were in the vicinity.

Kitty wheeled around. "How?" She was astonished and didn't trouble to mask it.

"What do you mean how? The usual way – at a social event."

"But you insisted you weren't going anywhere for New Year's Eve, Rose, you said you'd be seeing the old year out in the kitchen of your parents' house with a glass of Asti Spumanti."

Both Rose's mother and father were elderly and she felt obliged to spend as much of her free time as possible with them. She was forever complaining about her lack of foresight in being born an only child to middle-aged parents who didn't even live somewhere convenient such as the city centre. However, Kitty realised that Rose's weekends with her parents were evidence of her kind heart – and not a cash-saving exercise like Sunny's. Nevertheless it needled that both Rose, who went home for at least part of nearly every weekend, and Sunny, still living at home, had rampant sex lives. Yet here was Kitty with her own place in Blackrock and she couldn't rustle up a date for New Year's Eve.

Rose leaned against the worktop. "Our next-door-neighbours were having a silver-wedding anniversary dinner and they hired caterers and set up a marquee in the back garden. In the middle of winter, can you believe it? They must imagine they live in Tenerife. The parents insisted I had to go to represent the family. They invited half the county, the place was heaving." A mournful look flitted across Rose's pointed features. "You see what I'm reduced to? Meeting men at silver-wedding anniversary parties. I'll be giving widowers the glad eye at funerals next."

All their conversations featured men sooner or later and sometimes Kitty and Rose despaired of themselves. But mostly they accepted that it helped to pass the time.

Kitty studied Rose's face for signs of being in love, lust or friendship. "What's he like?"

"All right, I suppose," Rose sniffed. "Too young for my taste, but passable enough. Not wet behind the ears, for all his baby down."

"So what happened?" Kitty prodded.

"Well, it was all exceedingly affected at the party – they had a seating plan." Rose pulled her mouth sideways. "I was trapped beside this fellow with halitosis who was boring me rigid, talking about how much his house was worth and how successful his business was. I hardly bothered replying, but that didn't discourage him. On and on he droned. I wanted to ask him if he'd ever had a homosexual experience or dressed up in his wife's underwear, just to establish if his life was really as dull as it sounded."

"Did you?" Kitty wouldn't put it past her friend.

"No, I was rescued before I disgraced myself. It was quite exciting, really. A fellow I never laid eyes on before yanked me over to his table. He said I looked as though I couldn't stand another second of your man twittering in my ear, which was absolutely true, and" – her voice dwindled to a whisper – "I was so grateful that I slept with him." Rose propped her chin in her hand. "I promised myself I wasn't going to start doing that, just to get even with Father Damien."

At least you never married someone out of a sense of obligation, thought Kitty, stifling a sense of envy that Rose's life was so much more intriguing than hers. She even managed to have an adventure in the next-door-neighbours' house. "You made me promise not to let you talk about Father Damien," Kitty reminded her. "Besides, you know he's not Father Damien yet, he's only done a year in the seminary."

"Right, thanks." Rose mangled her lower lip. "No more mentioning Father Damien. It's just that if I keep calling him Father Damien, I'm hoping it will remind me he's off-limits. I saw him over Christmas and he's actually started looking like a priest – he had this clerical aura about him. He even stands differently, with one hand folded over the other and his head bent forward to listen to the faithful. How do you suppose they teach them that at priests' school?"

"Maynooth's a mystery to me." Kitty's manner was brisk. "So, about your man from the party, the masterful lad who saved you from being bored catatonic – you didn't sleep with him then and there in the marquee, did you?" Kitty wasn't entirely ruling out the possibility, although she thought it unlikely, for Rose had escapades but she wasn't another Sunny.

"No, we had a couple of drinks and a dance. He had absolutely no sense of rhythm, let me tell you. Then he offered to see me home. I pointed out that since I could be home by jumping over the garden wall if someone gave me a leg-up, it was a redundant gesture."

Kitty pushed aside her coffee – this was so much more fulfilling than caffeine. She made an impatient circular gesture with her forefinger to indicate that Rose should cut to the chase.

"Since he couldn't walk me home, I walked him home – or at least to the house he was staying in for New Year. It turns out he's a cousin of the Garritys a few doors up. They were still at the party so I went in for peppermint tea and –"

"Wait," Kitty interjected. "You really went in for peppermint tea?"

Rose radiated indignation. "Certainly I did, Kitty, you know I never turn down a mug of peppermint tea. When he offered it, I took it as a sign."

"That you should sleep with him?"

Rose's look was reproving. "That I should go indoors and drink tea with him."

"Then what?"

"We kissed, had sex and afterwards he gave me his email address – this seems to be what people do now." She wrinkled her nose, doubtful. "His name is Feargal Whelan. I always think of Feargal as a verb. It makes me imagine a man in a flat cap and tweeds, whistling up the greyhounds and telling his wife he's off out for an afternoon's feargalling."

"Feargal's a fine name," Kitty consoled.

"He looked like a greyhound too – you'd find more meat on Good Friday." Rose still seemed dubious about the wisdom of her fling.

"You and my sister are a matched pair – she says casual sexual encounters are therapeutic." Kitty checked her watch. "I have to get a move on, I'm due into conference with the Exalted One."

In addition to a weekly column, Kitty also wrote features, interviewing whichever celebrity the paper decided to garrotte. It was becoming tedious because, as she complained to Rose, Ireland didn't have an excess of celebrities. There was just U2 and some boy bands. Kitty had to brief the editor – better known as the Exalted One – about who was lined up, because he was protective about his newspaper and choosy about who to feature in it. He had this bizarre notion that subjects needed to earn their place in the *Sunday Trumpet*, which was all very well in a country where stars were limitless, but they weren't exactly thick on the ground in Ireland. Especially as the Irish were such a nation of begrudgers they refused to countenance other Irish people's celebrity status. Sometimes she thought it might be preferable to abandon the hatchet-jobs – sorry, the in-depth profiles – and become an accessory to the crime rather than an assassin, as features editor. Des Redmond, the current title-holder, was forever grousing about interference from the Exalted One and threatening to resign. But he had never actually put pen to paper. Rose maintained he'd developed Stockholm Syndrome and was addicted to the abuse routinely heaped on him by the editor.

Kitty was always booking interviews with subjects and being obliged to backtrack and cancel. Generally without using the real reason given by the editor, which tended to run along the purely subjective lines of she's too ugly/he wears a moustache/they're has-beens. Just before Christmas he'd given Kitty his mission statement, accompanied by a gratuitous amount of hair-pulling (his own, fortunately), to indicate he was surrounded by imbeciles: "I keep telling you, I want more top women in my paper." But they had to be beautiful top women, or at least pretty and willing to have a stylist turned loose on them. Plain ones didn't count.

"Never mind the editor." Rose was reluctant to allow Kitty to scurry off to conference. "What about the sad excuse for a human being that is me? I didn't have sex for therapeutic reasons. I did it to get even with Father Damien, who never wants to sleep with anybody again and doesn't care whether I do or not." She rinsed her mug under the tap. "Furthermore I did it with a fellow who could pass for a twelve-year-old."

Kitty knew better than to allow her to talk about her ex-boyfriend Damien Crowe – that always led to a wallow. They'd courted for eight years, but immediately after setting the date he'd developed cold feet and had entered a seminary instead. The ignominy of it flailed at Rose. She said she could have handled it if he'd run off with another woman, or even another man at a push, but to be thrown over for God was too humiliating by far.

"I could see it if he wanted to have sex with someone else instead of me, but to choose to have sex with no-one else instead of me . . ." she'd wailed at Kitty during the office Christmas party.

An inebriated nineteen-year-old had lurched up to them, slopping an opened bottle of wine over his shirt front. He didn't even work for the *Sunday Trumpet*. "I can get you into the VIP section," the gatecrasher had ingratiated himself.

"We're already in the VIP section," Kitty had slapped him down. Then she'd dragged Rose to her feet, as Hot Chocolate's *You Sexy Thing* blasted from the sound system. Boyfriends decamping to the priesthood were not something you could rationally discuss at a Christmas party. "Dance him out of your system," she'd urged Rose. "Get those hips moving. Shake it, girl!"

There was no syncopated rhythm to distract Rose in the office kitchen now – and from the look on her face Kitty was afraid her friend might start weeping. Which wasn't a sensible idea in a newspaper office: you ended up labelled a neurotic. Kitty harried her brain-cells for a subject to divert Rose from Damien. "Are you going to email Feargal?" she asked.

"No."

Was that a snuffle? Kitty's speech pattern accelerated. "Where's the harm? Do it while I'm being pilloried by the Exalted One for losing that interview with Madonna. It'll be quiet on the editorial floor; everyone who's not in the meeting will be straining for shrieking sounds from the editor's office. Then we can judge Feargal's suitability based on his answer. I'll meet you for a sandwich across the road at one."

Rose didn't say yes, but she didn't say no either, so Kitty assumed her plan appealed. More importantly, the tear-ducts seemed to have closed for business. Kitty really couldn't divine how being pursued by a younger man counted as a dilemma; it was hardly in the same sphere as trying to isolate likely candidates to commit adultery with.

On the subject of which, Kitty had just thought of a contender.

Chapter 5

All through the conference Kitty speculated on the editor: perhaps she could become his mistress. Linus Bell was a testy, fretful-haired man, not tall but sturdy, with pale eyes barely contained by their sockets. Aside from the inconvenient fact that Kitty was repulsed by Linus because he was hectoring, arrogant and utterly devoid of charm, it might be a shrewd career move. Besides, disliking someone didn't preclude chemistry.

She toyed with the possibility while Linus crowed over his exposé of a newly appointed RTÉ newsreader's former career as a sparsely dressed hostess in a Tokyo bar – he'd even managed to buy a grainy photograph. "Nobody can criticise us because this is in the public interest," he chortled, making a gratuitous remark about the paucity of the newsreader's cleavage. The men guffawed dutifully, while the women kept their expressions immobile and mentally updated their CVs. Kitty twiddled an earring and concluded that she couldn't seduce him. It was depressing enough to suffer Linus Bell during working hours without volunteering to spend free time with him. A mistress was supposed to be charming to her lover, share scented baths with him – she'd itch to hold Linus's head under the water.

A quiver convulsed Kitty and the editor's roving glance landed on her.

"Kitty, when's the Madonna interview happening? Is she still convinced she has Irish roots?" His wintry eyes were inexorable.

She took a deep breath; Linus despised failure. "No, apparently she's changed her mind about having an Irish heritage so there's not much point in interviewing her."

Linus's nostrils flared. "Are you seriously telling me there's not much point in interviewing Madonna for my newspaper?"

"You're always saying we shouldn't waste our time on celebrities with no Irish connections." Kitty sensed she was skating on thin ice, even though the Exalted One was forever complaining about being palmed off with non-Irish celebrities.

"There's always room in my newspaper for a star of Madonna's stature." Linus's voice was dangerously low and his eyes had started to bulge.

No help for it, she'd have to tell the truth. "I was still willing to do the interview," Kitty confessed, "but her people rang to say she's feeling over-exposed. I can have Puffin O'Mara instead." Puffin was last year's Miss Ireland. "Puffin's been taking lessons and is now a fully-qualified breathing instructor – it's a new twist to her roller-coaster life." Kitty forced herself to meet the editor's gaze. She always wanted to shuffle and keep her eyes on the floor when dealing with Linus Bell.

"The nancy-boy game-show-host's daughter!" There followed a string of profanities which made it clear how little he valued her substitute interview, and how he'd prefer his newspaper to be filled with free advertisements for the Scientologists – a sect he particularly abhorred – than give Puffin O'Mara an inch of space. "Who does she think she is, teaching us how to breathe?" he roared, moving seamlessly on to fume about a TV3 weather-girl who bore a passing resemblance to Puffin and who had excited his wrath by accidentally snubbing him at a party.

Kitty caved in to instinct and fastened her eyes on the stone-coloured carpet in his office – all the other journalists in the room had their eyes lowered too.

Finally, when he'd wound down like a clockwork toy, although still tugging at fistfuls of hair – she was permanently amazed he had any left on his head – Kitty risked speech. "So do you want me to say yes or no to Puffin?"

"Well, yes, of course, Kitty, or we'll have no celebrity interview this week." His scorn was withering, but she'd learnt to ignore it.

She began to relax as Linus moved on to interrogate the social diarist about his movements for the week, with the air of a man convinced vital information was deliberately being withheld from him. His relentless eye grazed the showbusiness editor and Linus remembered he was incensed about a rival paper's scoop. "I don't care if the *Sunday Globe* paid that boy band for the interview, they should be coming to the *Trumpet* pleading with us to run their stories." He was petulant. "We tell our readers what to think, and if we tell them not to buy their records, that band of untalented no-brainers are history. It's your job to put that message across to their manager, *capisce?*"

The showbusiness editor resigned himself to a tongue-lashing, thinking about the holiday home on the Costa Blanca he was buying thanks to this turbo-paid, turbo-stressed job. He hoped he didn't die of a tumour before he had a chance to enjoy it.

Kitty returned to daydreaming about becoming a mistress. Although not Linus Bell's – you'd be worn out from conversation with him never mind any further pandering he might expect. Maybe she could become the proprietor's – that would keep Linus Bell on his toes. Except since she'd only glimpsed the proprietor in the distance once as he'd sailed through on a goodwill visit, becoming his mistress might prove a shade difficult. Still, fantasies weren't meant to be foiled by an inconvenient bagatelle such as reality.

"We've been offered serialisation rights to a new book on Eamon de Valera." Des Redmond, the features editor, intruded on Kitty's reverie.

"De Valera . . . remind me, who did he shag?" quizzed Linus.

"His wife," faltered Des Redmond, aghast. "He was our greatest statesman, our founding father, architect of the Irish state. I don't think –"

"That's your trouble, you don't think," snorted Linus. "It's no feckin' good if he didn't sleep with anyone he shouldn't have. I'm not spending the newspaper's money for revelations about a man who spent nights tucked up in bed with his missus. Our readers want revelation and they want it glitzy, *capisce?*"

Linus always said *"capisce"*, pronouncing it *"capeesh"*, like a cinematic Mafia don. Or as much like a Mafia don as a sandy-haired man from Dundalk could sound. Glitzy was his mantra, the newspaper's zeitgeist – all the executives parroted it, as if simply sprinkling the word in conversation could keep the sales-chart buoyant.

Des was on his feet, which left him at a disadvantage because he either had to slouch and look slovenly or stand to attention as though being court-martialled. This was a ploy on Linus's part to discomfort his staff: he deliberately ensured there'd be one chair too few in his office so the last suit through the door had to stand. Being last was a social solecism of treacherous proportions in Linus Bell's rulebook because it showed lack of commitment. His capital-punishment crime.

Kitty had to attend editorial meetings at the beginning of every week, but Linus was also prone to calling short-notice brain-storming sessions with the senior executives (fortunately that ruled her out) to debate direction i.e. how to squeeze more skin into the newspaper while still assuming a middlebrow mantle. "The *Sunday Trumpet*'s not a tabloid, we're a compact newspaper," he'd insist, sandy hair erect. Compact or tabloid, there had to be room for Andrea Corr, on whom he had a fixation. He always wanted articles on her – complimentary or savage, he had no preference. Just so long as he could run her photograph. It had to do with both of them coming from Dundalk, according to the old lags in the office. She was his equivalent of the girl next door, except he hadn't known her when he'd lived there, which provoked him intensely.

Linus eventually dismissed the staff and they stampeded towards the door.

"Wish I was still at the *Daily Digest*," moaned Des Redmond, as they funnelled through to the editorial floor.

"Did you leave on sour terms? Couldn't you go back?" asked Kitty.

"No." He bristled. "The *Strumpet* has me used to twice the money I was on at the *Digest*. I'm trapped, cunning bastards."

Kitty put in a lightning call to Puffin O'Mara to confirm the interview, which she'd already accepted as a fallback position two days before Christmas Eve, and then it was time for lunch. There was no sign of Rose at her desk in the photographic department with its view of Boland's Mill – staff took pleasure in pointing it out as a nerve centre of the 1916 Rising to English visitors from their sister paper in London – so Kitty assumed she'd gone ahead. She followed, encountering Linus as he emerged from the Gents' opposite the lifts. His private lavatory was out of order. Linus scowled because people taking lunch breaks vexed him; he was born in the wrong century. Bank holidays made him truculent too.

"I want that nutty bird's interview on my desk by six p.m. today," he blustered.

"I'm not meeting Puffin until later in the week," Kitty protested.

He squeezed his eyebrows together until furrows popped up all over his forehead, but couldn't think of a more caustic reply than, "Make sure you get revelatory quotes. Remember, I need some commitment around here."

As though she'd go to the trouble of interviewing Puffin O'mara and not bother trying to do a proper job . . . The man behaved as if he was convinced he had a shower of wastrels working for him. Kitty fumed as she stood beside him in the lift. She noticed how he didn't even have the manners to allow her out first. A slap on the back of his legs when he was growing up would have worked wonders for him. Then a chilling thought intervened: Linus Bell had a mistress as well as a wife. Was he the class of oaf her grand scheme condemned her to couple with?

"I have to escape this place," Kitty told Rose, who was saving her a seat in Café Society.

"Linus Bell?" Her tone was sympathetic, but not overly so, because never a week went by without one of them moaning something similar.

"The one and only."

"What was your man's expletives-tally at this week's meeting?"

"Twenty-two fucks and fifteen bastards. String of fecks as well, but I didn't bother counting them."

"About average," concluded Rose. "I thought he'd be in worse form after all that time at home with Mrs Exalted One over Christmas."

Kitty rallied. "Never mind Linus Bell, tell me all about Feargal. Has he replied to your email yet?"

"No, because I haven't sent him one." Rose spooned the froth from her cappuccino. "His kisses were clumsy. If that's not a warning from the universe I don't know what is. Leave well alone, that's my instinct. You're always advising me to listen to my instincts."

"Now is no time to break the habit of a lifetime and start acting on my advice." Kitty was stern. "All kisses can't glide along perfectly, especially at the start – some have to fumble a little and feel their way. I wouldn't write off someone on the basis of an inept kiss – that's just plain profligate, Rose McBride."

Rose looked humble, defiant and doubtful, all in the space of a few seconds. Then she adjusted the diamanté clips in her black hair which streamed below her shoulder-blades.

"You're only sending him an email, not offering to have his babies," Kitty encouraged her. "Now, have you made a New Year's resolution?" This was her opening gambit to confide her own, in the hopes that Rose might know a married man scouting for a mistress. Kitty had already overcome her wobble in the lift, convincing herself she'd never be so desperate as to wind up with a Linus Bell.

"Absolutely not." Rose ejected a crescent of onion from her ham-salad sandwich. "New Year's resolutions are a tiresome habit. You can never make the ones you'd really like, such as arranging only to be seen by candlelight, and the resolutions you are in a position to make are too depressing. They're all about self-improvement. I don't hold with them."

Kitty waited for her to ask if she'd made one, but Rose continued scrutinising her sandwich for onion. "Aren't you going to ask if I've made a resolution?" Kitty nudged her.

Rose shrugged. "Naturally you have, don't you do it every year? Last year's was to visit the gym twice a week, I seem to recall."

"Never mind that. This year I'm going to become a mistress, that's my resolution." She sat back, arms folded, exhilarated by her determination.

Rose studied Kitty, jaws working. "That's an old-fashioned concept, surely?" she suggested, swallowing some semi-chewed food.

"That's where you're wrong, Rose – it's a post-modern solution to a post-modern problem." Kitty gulped black coffee. "You know how marriage and myself aren't compatible, right?"

"*Marriage has many pains but celibacy has no pleasures,*" quoted Rose, wondering where on earth the conversation was headed.

"Father Damien's the man to tell that to, not me." Kitty was impatient at the interruption or she'd never have mentioned Father Damien. References to him turned Rose morose.

"You think I haven't reminded him?" Rose retorted. "Anyway, what did you want to polemicise about? I hope you're not practising a column on me."

"No theory, this is for real." Kitty inhaled and began. "You see, Rose, there's a batch of women nowadays who don't want men for the traditional reasons: to put a roof over their heads and father their children. They've supplied their own homes and don't intend to have babies. So where does that leave men? I don't need one to repair my leaking bath, I pay a plumber to do that. I don't need one to put up shelves, I have a drill I can manage myself." She beamed, enraptured by her logic. "But I could use a man for entertainment – and what's a mistress but someone to divert yourself with? It's a win-win situation for both of us."

"Isn't the mistress the one supposed to do the entertaining?" Rose cavilled.

Kitty shook her head. "Only if she's a kept woman and has to sing for her supper. You're confusing it with concubines and geishas and the like. What I'm suggesting is a contemporary solution to a contemporary problem: the man shortage."

Rose scrabbled in her bag for spectacles, worn when she was attempting to convey gravitas, and swiped her black fringe out of her eyes. "You must realise there's a thumping great ethical flaw in your argument, Kitty."

"Ethics are subjective." Kitty parroted Benjamin, husband number two. She didn't believe that, but it sounded convincing. Rose disagreed, judging by her snort. Kitty abandoned that position as untenable. "I'd be a moral mistress," she explained. "There's no question of marriage-wrecking. I'd be copper-fastening his marriage, if anything. It would be quite a wholesome arrangement. You see, myself and marriage aren't compatible, so this is the best possible compromise."

Rose pushed her slipping rimless spectacles back along the bridge of her nose. "Maybe not the best possible compromise for his wife."

Kitty gnawed at a rag-nail. Why was everyone so set against her scintillating idea? "It is if it keeps him in the marriage with her – I'd be no threat to a relationship, in fact I'd be a safeguard against it breaking up. Imagine the ructions if he took up with a twenty-five-year-old who was determined to have him all to herself, come what may."

"I can't decide," Rose pulled a side-plate with its slice of chocolate cake towards her, "whether you're being deliberately impenetrable or if it's an act." Kitty was wounded and her expression showed it. "You see, Kitty, you haven't mentioned love in any of this. What if you fall in love with whichever nominee you have in mind for your hare-brained scheme?" Rose doodled a cake-laden fork through the air. "That's when reasonable plans tend to evaporate. People turn maudlin and want to spend every minute of the day with one another – they don't allow minutiae such as previous intentions about arrangements of mutual convenience to deter them. They have a disconcerting tendency to pack their bags and turn up on your doorstep chirruping, 'Let's be together always, darling, there's room in your house for both of us. By the way, I know you won't mind if we spend every weekend taking my children to the zoo or McDonald's.' So much for your champagne lifestyle then, Kitty Kennedy."

That halted Kitty in her tracks. She'd assumed the man would be grateful at the offer of a relatively uncomplicated relationship; now Rose was painting him as a clingy squatter. No, she reassured herself, before her perfect scheme developed cracks and was subverted by Rose's uncompromising version of reality – he'd have too much to lose. He'd be sacrificing his marriage, his family and his home. Of course he wouldn't want to abandon them for her. And if he did she wouldn't permit it.

"Incidentally, whose mistress have you decided to become?" asked Rose.

"Don't know yet." Kitty was downcast at the prospect of accidentally becoming involved with a man determined to divorce his wife and marry her, after all.

"This is all so Parisian," reproved Rose. "You'll be demanding jewels as an insurance policy for your old age next, like the *grandes horizontales* of past centuries. I read about one courtesan who used to have her maid parade behind her with all her gems piled high on a velvet cushion, to prove how adept she was at pleasing men."

"I'm doing this to please me, not some man."

"You won't be doing it at all if you don't please the man."

"Anyway," continued Kitty, "this isn't a cash transaction. It's actually a form of independence: I'd be having a relationship on my own terms."

"Doesn't sound like much of a relationship. Takes two to have one of those."

Kitty pretended she hadn't heard. "I'm liberating myself from archaic ideas about being a wife or a chattel."

A dense silence settled between them. Rose felt an unwelcome sense of prissiness, but she had an instinctive opposition to the idea. A moral mistress, indeed. Who was Kitty trying to fool? They were mutually exclusive concepts. As for Kitty, she felt unfairly judged.

"If you're really determined to go through with this – and I don't recommend it – how about the Exalted One?" Rose suggested. "I know Linus Bell is vile, but at least he might treat us both a little better if you were his bit on the side. His reserve bit on the side, I mean, since he has a mistress already."

"Call me impossibly romantic but I have my heart set on at least liking my lover," Kitty quibbled. "Anyway, your moral scruples vanished fairly sharpish at the thought of some benefit to yourself."

"They did," Rose acknowledged. "You don't think you could bring yourself to like him, even just a little? He's gifted at what he does."

"You're right, Rose, he's a gifted bully." Kitty couldn't admit that she'd dallied with the idea of seducing Linus Bell only a couple of hours earlier. "Linus prefers his women to look like Andrea Corr but with Rubenesque breasts. I'm not having silicone implants for anybody."

"Push-up bra? Only joking, I'm not trying to pimp for you. Listen, I have to get back to work, we'll talk about this again."

"Don't forget to email Hot Lips," Kitty commanded.

"No way, he's thirteen years younger than me. I was panicked into going home with him – it was the New Year's Eve factor."

Kitty paused, a vacuum-sealed moment during which her mind grappled with the figures. Thirteen years younger than Rose who'd turned forty recently? That made him twenty-seven, even younger than the wilfully immature Sunny. Thirteen years was definitely an age gap, whichever prism you viewed it through. She could try reassuring Rose that forty was the new thirty. But everyone knew that was just a line dreamed up by some magazine editor or style guru to mask the fact they'd turned the corner on the decade themselves. "That's what I call an inter-generational relationship. How do you do it, Rose? I'm not saying for one minute you look your age –"

"I know, I don't look a day over thirty-nine," interrupted Rose, removing her spectacles.

"– but what is it about you and younger men at the minute?"

"Don't ask me," Rose was glum, "and don't go using me in your column as an example of some trend or other. It's not as if I'm proud of attracting little fellows. I keep telling them I'm way too ancient for them, but they seem to think it's a joke or a challenge or some kind of tease. I'd much prefer an old boy with a few grooves gouged into his face and a bit of slack at his jaw, but since when did what I want count for anything? Old fellows think I'm Methuselah's mother and young guys think I'm mysterious. Meanwhile the only man I ever wanted is devoting himself to God." She heaved a quivering sigh that whisked chocolate crumbs off her plate. "Even when I slept with the little lad on New Year's Eve, I half-expected him to stop in mid-session and say: 'Yuck, your body is saggy, I can't go through with this!' And did he? No." Her face radiated accusation. "He tried to foist his email address on me. He'd be text-messaging me by now if I hadn't lied about having a mobile phone."

Kitty tapped a thumbnail against her coffee-cup handle. There was something inherently unfair in her own assets being frozen while Rose's were in sizzling demand. But this New Year was going to ring in some changes, she was resolved on that. "What's so terrible about Feargal?"

"He's twenty-seven."

"He won't be twenty-seven forever."

"You think twenty-eight is much better?" Rose sounded outraged. "Besides, he looked twelve – I felt like his, em, big sister."

Kitty stood her ground. "Where's the harm in kicking up your heels, Rose?"

Rose had no objection to fun, but not with a baby like Feargal Whelan. He was still playing with Action Man when she was out there grappling with men who thought they were his personification. Only with more class and sex appeal. But it was too difficult to explain to Kitty, who saw nothing wrong with toy boys – or borrowing other women's husbands and pretending it would preserve a marriage, not jeopardise it.

Rose looked at Kitty, sitting there so wholesome and fresh-faced, and felt an unfamiliar jag of dislike for her.

Chapter 6

Rose hunched over her desk pretending to adjust the light and shade on a photograph of Liam Neeson, but in reality dwelling on why she'd gone home with Feargal Whelan on New Year's Eve. Was it to punish Father Damien Crowe, the man she wasn't supposed to think about any more? Rose leaned across to filch a stick of chewing-gum from the picture editor, reassuring herself she was over Father Damien. She could even say the name aloud and it would have absolutely no effect on her. "Father Damien," she announced.

"Looks more like Liam Neeson to me," said Gerry Harty, the bearded picture editor.

"Looks can be deceptive," she mumbled, soured by her memories. Wait a minute, why was she obsessing pointlessly about Father Damien Crowe when she could be obsessing profitably about Feargal Whelan? Father Damien persistently cluttered up her life, there was no budging him. Rose didn't believe in New Year's resolutions, and she was a day late with hers, but she suspected she needed to make one this year after all. This would be the year she'd get over Father Damien, using whatever ammunition came to hand.

Feargal Whelan, if necessary.

It puzzled Rose why she'd decamped with Feargal on New Year's

Eve, for it was uncharacteristic of her. It wasn't because she'd been drunk, although she hadn't stinted on wine; it wasn't because Christmas had been dull, although it had been far from exciting, stranded in Slane with a set of elderly parents. She loved them, of course she did, but she was their only child and sometimes the responsibility weighed on her. So why had she strolled off into the night, arm in arm with a juvenile stranger? It had been irresponsible in the extreme; serial killers could have winning smiles as well as a knife collection. Just because he was a cousin of the Garritys didn't make him safe – serial killers had relatives too.

Rose's sensory memory disengaged from her nagging consciousness and lingered on the encounter with Feargal Whelan.

In the beginning came a kiss.

The wrong kind of kiss.

If ever a woman received a cosmic warning, it arrived gift-wrapped in that kiss. But Rose ignored it.

"I like you," he murmured, then kissed her.

Rose supposed she'd started out as an onlooker rather than a participant. So she had watched with detached curiosity when he'd leaned forward and removed her mug of peppermint tea, cradling her face between his hands, brushing his thumbs against her jaw-line. He'd touched his lips to hers and, with infinite tenderness, stabbed his nose into the corner of her eye. Leaving it there. As though there was nothing unusual, or even uncomfortable, about a nose jammed in your eye.

She should have recoiled. Any woman with an ounce of romance – and no, romance didn't come in kilograms, Rose didn't care what the eurocrats claimed – would have cut her losses after that substance over style introduction. Where was the point in building up a database over years of experience about when to resist temptation if she didn't log on to it when it mattered? But she hadn't. That was mistake number one. Or number two if you counted letting him reach her mouth in the first place.

Instead of leaping up and leaving, reproof for his unrefined technique, she had moved her head to one side and had dislodged his nose. Simple as that. After which the kiss had flowed smoothly. Indeed, it had generated a level of response to catch her unawares. She had stopped watching and had become a party to the proceedings, distracted by the tingling of all those nerve-endings crammed into the lips.

Except.

Except Rose had a theory about first kisses.

They should be perfect. Or at least, if they weren't flawless, they should not be so inept that one partner in the venture was distracted by the need to jolt the other partner's nose out of their cornea. Which was never designed as a resting-place for anyone's nose.

Except.

Except Rose had wanted him to kiss her.

She knew she was being inconsistent, but she had. After all, why had she gone home with him, if not for kisses? So that's why he had kissed her – a man could always sense when a woman wanted his mouth against hers. Some men, according to Kitty, in her last but one column, had an additional instinct for never entering a relationship with the least hope of lasting the pace. They were programmed for failure and they liked it that way. Maybe Feargal was one of those no-hopers, attracted to Rose because there was no question of a relationship. Anyway, she thought, clicking her computer software to remove the shadow from Liam Neeson's neck that gave him a double chin, Kitty shouldn't be there. This was her first kiss with Feargal and there was only room for two of them in it.

Except.

Except she couldn't kiss anyone without Father Damien muscling in.

Metaphorically, of course. Not that Father Damien would recognise a metaphor if it bought him dinner and asked for his telephone number afterwards. She didn't ever plan to be civil or mature about Father Damien Crowe. He was her villain – even if he did want to be a missionary and minister to devout African Catholics with smiles that could power electricity generators. But Father Damien shouldn't be in the kiss either; this was about Feargal, whom she was never going to see again. Probably.

Looking back, it was unfathomable why she had sat on a sofa in his cousin's house on New Year's Eve, going through the motions with Feargal, who couldn't kiss a girl without blinding her. If she hadn't closed her eyes a millisecond before he'd planted it on her, there could have been lasting damage.

Except.

Except after she'd moved his nose out of her eye, where it had no business intruding, but before she'd remembered that this must stop because he was too young and she still loved Father Damien, there had been quite an agreeable part.

All right, there had been fireworks. A liquid interlude in the kissing episode where Rose had enjoyed it and had overlooked how unsuitable Feargal was, even simply for the purposes of showing Father Damien that she was a desirable woman. During those kisses she had forgotten Father Damien and how he'd warped her, with his unflattering preference for celibacy. She had been too preoccupied to wonder, yet again, if he'd been thinking about God while they had made love, in the latter months. Or if he'd felt guilty about being with her; if he'd gone to confession and beaten his breast over her. *Mea maxima culpa.*

All Rose had been aware of was how delectable kissing could be – it was the most self-absorbed activity you could engage in with another human being. But then the cogs in her brain had clunked into gear to interfere with the pleasure and she'd recollected that she shouldn't be doing this. A kiss would move along the dynamics between Feargal and herself to a stage she was unready to enter.

For all her spirited talk with Kitty, Rose hadn't gone to bed with Feargal. She'd only pretended she had to seem interesting to her friend, who led an infinitely more glamorous life. Who didn't need to dye her naturally blonde hair. Who still had almost four years to go before colliding with forty. Rose suspected Kitty felt sorry for her, sequestered in the wilds of Meath weekend after weekend with her parents, miles from the action. Sometimes forty seemed impossibly old to her. Her birth certificate told her it was her age, so did her passport and her driver's licence, but Rose's brain refused to register it. How could she have reached forty without noticing? It was all Father Damien's fault; he'd appropriated the prime years of her life and then had the cheek to tell her he'd pray for her. "I'll dedicate my first Mass to you, Rose," he'd promised. Oh, he was crafty, she'd grant him that, but she was still livid with him.

Meanwhile here was Kitty, who had everything in life, including two ex-husbands – infinitely more stylish than an ex-fiancé who'd answered the call to God. As if she hadn't been blessed to excess already, Kitty even had a stalker. Well, an email stalker, a reader who contacted her every week to discuss her column, psycho-analyse her and attempt to make a date. Kitty had decided he was harmless and couldn't be bothered changing her email address.

Rose abandoned Kitty's stalker to his emails and thought about Feargal Whelan. She'd discovered something during that New Year's Eve encounter – remembered it, really – mouths had a tendency to forget about circumstances when they were exploring other mouths. Mouths were conscienceless when they fitted one another. And lacking in prudence. The fit was all that mattered. That was why mouths were so dangerous; bewitching, too, of course.

Rose had another theory about kissing. It atrophied the brain, attacking logic and common sense. Hers had been in free-fall until Father Damien had intervened, a little later than usual but in time, nevertheless, to remind her of her obligation to separate her lips from Feargal's while she had the willpower left to do it. She had learned a lesson from her time with Damien Crowe, before he had set off to Maynooth to become Father Damien Crowe: distrust physical attraction. So she had eased herself from Feargal's arms and suggested he walk her home.

He had stood up straight away. With unflattering alacrity, in fact – she wouldn't have objected to a little coaxing first. "How about another peppermint tea and then I'll do it?" That class of approach. Feargal had shown a gentleman's instincts – laudable in principle but, frankly, he should listen to them more sparingly in particular scenarios.

He'd escorted her home, skimming her cheek chastely at the door. She'd been stupefied and insulted in equal measure. Then he'd given her his email address and said: "I won't pester you, it's up to you if you use it." Who else was it up to, in the name of God? The confidence of the younger generation was beyond belief. Obviously, Rose told herself, staring sightlessly at her computer screen, she couldn't email him and allow him to ignore her, and naturally he would. What would a man of twenty-seven want with a woman of forty? Feargal was sweet – her favourite dismissive word – but unsuitable. She should never have allowed him to kiss her, it had eroded her certainties. Even crooked kisses that somehow straightened out and bloomed into . . .

"Get a grip, woman," she muttered aloud, attracting a sidelong glance from Gerry Harty, the picture editor.

He could see she wasn't concentrating on the job, but said nothing. Gerry was keen on Rose in that self-deluding "if I weren't a happily married man with three children" way.

Rose hadn't wanted to sleep with Feargal, but she had experienced a crackle of something. Desire, she supposed, wistful at the realisation she could feel it for a man other than Father Damien. She'd have to consider carefully whether or not to contact Feargal. Kisses weren't safe, Rose knew that much.

Although if she were serious about this New Year's resolution to forget Father Damien, she'd need help from any quarter she could find it.

* * *

While Rose was thinking a great deal about Feargal Whelan –

although telling herself he meant nothing to her and anyway he was the lesser of two evils – Kitty was ripping open a package delivered by courier. Inside the padded envelope was a book sent in the hopes she'd review it, *Mistresses Without Masters*. A statuesque woman, her clothing in a state of artful disarray, was draped across the cover and her eyes were lanced with a significant gleam. Now this definitely fitted Kitty's interpretation of divine intervention.

She flicked to the last page and saw the phrase "influence leading to empowerment" which reassured her sufficiently to turn to page one. It began with a definition of mistress, explaining it was derived from the feminine form of *magister*, Latin for "master": "female of Mister, now written Mrs, a woman well-skilled, employer of servants, a woman loved and courted, a concubine." That covered a multitude of possibilities. She liked the sound of "a woman courted".

Just then the phone rang, a junior from a public relations firm asking if she'd be attending a launch for National Jogging Day. She transferred the call to the newsdesk – slyly doing it via the switchboard because the news editor was forever remonstrating with Kitty about palming off her reject calls on him – and surveyed the office. Nobody to fancy, not even at a distance.

Kitty watched one of the sub-editors use the photocopier near her desk and willed him to make eye contact with her. Nothing, not so much as a passing glance. There was nobody in the building worth having an affair with, they were all too pedestrian. If she should become somebody's mistress, it must be an individual with panache. She wondered where Ryan was and what he was doing; it never failed to strike her as odd that she didn't have a current address for someone whom she had once promised to love, honour and cherish all the days of her life. Husbands. They just seemed to slip through her fingers. Kitty hoped that when she became a mistress, she didn't spend as much time thinking about her ex-husbands as she was currently doing. Fortunately her phone rang again, distracting her.

"It's Rose." She only sat a few desks away, but took the sensible precaution of ringing. If she'd ambled up for a chat Linus Bell would have slammed open his office door and stalked through the newsroom, and when he saw people gossiping – he could always detect the difference between work-related and private conversations – he'd pile more assignments onto them. "I've thought of someone who'd like a mistress – he's ideal for you," whispered Rose.

"Who is it?" Kitty was thrilled.

"I'll tell you in the pub after work."

* * *

They sat on cracked leather armchairs in the Treasury with abstemious glasses of fizzy water, since Christmas and New Year had taken their toll on both livers. The pub was called Sheridan's, but the reporters had renamed it because all their money seemed to gravitate there. It was a bit of a dive, yet there was never any question that it would be the officially designated office local – journalists always used the closest watering hole, it was their only criterion.

"So who is it?" Kitty asked.

"He's a bit on the old side," warned Rose.

"Old as in mature or old as in hoary?"

"Better an old man's darling than a young man's fool." Rose looked prim.

"So he's antiquated." Kitty pouted. "Rose, I'm not doing this for money or as an act of charity, I need to like the fellow. I'm meant to be getting something out of the arrangement, you know."

"You would be getting something out of it, Kitty. He's a name – a famous artist."

Kitty reflected. The notion of being muse to a painter appealed – it had a bohemian ring. Rose knew all sorts of unconventional folk; she'd handled the public relations for an arts centre in Temple Bar before switching to picture editing. "Who is he? Not" – a bolt of horror tingled through her – "that old goat with the glass eye who wanted to paint me nude, but only my torso, not my face? You foisted him on me at the launch party for the Dublin Fringe Festival. I couldn't fancy him, no matter how gifted an artist he might be. It's fundamentally insulting to be told your face isn't suitable for a painting, only your body parts."

"No," Rose reassured, "he's between wives at the moment – I understood you wanted a married one. I was thinking of Hubert de Paor, the fellow who paints the beautiful people and turns them all into shifty bookies."

Kitty chewed a strand of hair. The name rang a bell, but she couldn't supply a face. "Would I like him?"

"You might." Rose drank some water, then rubbed at the damp halo around her lips, ink-stains on her fingers. There was always something slightly messy about her appearance, whereas Kitty was invariably groomed. "He's well-preserved, pickled really, and has a wife he's in awe of called Flora. There are a couple of sons away at university in England. Hubert has a studio in Howth while Flora runs the family farm in Kildare, so they're apart a good deal. Opportunities, if you follow my drift. They've been married for aeons. I met Hubert at a gallery opening a few months ago and I remember him telling me that he and Flora were childhood sweethearts, then rather woefully adding that she'd been fabulous at sixteen. With the subtext that she wasn't fabulous any longer. Not that he's an oil painting himself, but men never seem to consider that." Rose pilfered a handful of Kitty's peanuts. "He's devoted to Flora, there's no question of a divorce, but if ever I saw an affair waiting to erupt, it's stamped with the name Hubert de Paor."

This sounded promising. "Describe him," Kitty commanded.

"Medium height, medium build, brownish-grey hair, slightly overhanging belly, sings when he's drunk, convinced he's God's gift to women, could talk the hind leg off a donkey."

She'd just described half the male population of Ireland. Still, if he was devoted to his wife he might learn to worship Kitty too. She chewed a knuckle. Artists were practically obliged to have mistresses, it went with the territory, so if it wasn't her luring him astray it would only be someone else. He didn't sound particularly attractive, but she was willing to sacrifice looks for talent, someone whose career she could help nurture – everyone knew artists suffered from blockages periodically and needed encouragement. She mentally replaced the jewellery her intended lover would woo her with for canvases of his most inspired work. The fantasy reached the stage where she was refurbishing the lean-to shed in Blackrock as a makeshift studio and tripping out to Hubert with thermos flasks of coffee, when reality intervened in the shape of Rose.

"I'd say he's mid-fifties," she estimated. "He won't be able to believe his luck with you."

Kitty hadn't banked on quite such a pronounced age-gap. Still, he might be well- preserved; she shouldn't be narrow-minded about it. Genius was ageless. "When can I meet him, Rose?"

Rose flicked back her long black hair and beamed. "This Sunday evening, no time like the present. He's showing an exhibition of his paintings at the studio in Howth – I've been sent an invitation. The wine will taste like urine lovingly blended with paint-stripper, but it's an ideal opportunity to give him a covert once-over and see if you could be tempted by him."

"Or if he could be tempted by me. What if I'm not his type?" worried Kitty.

Rose barked out a single-note laugh. Kitty was slim and blonde; she was everyone's type.

Marianne O'Leary walked past, winter-white fake fur draped over her shoulders and a pair of designer sunglasses perched on top of her head.

"Why on earth is she wearing sunglasses in January?" hissed Kitty.

"She'd wear sunglasses in the bath if someone told her John Rocha recommended it."

Rose and Kitty disliked the fashion editor: she was one of those women who suddenly adopt a baby-girl voice and say, "Me not put any money in parking meter – who will feed nasty machine for Marianne?" She never suggested these errands to women, only to men, because they responded so much more willingly. Men always humoured her because Marianne had the golden skin of her Mauritian grandmother, as well as silken light brown hair, parted in the middle and falling in two burnished sweeps to her shoulders. She always wore white and it always looked clean. The sheer unfairness of the latter rankled with Kitty and Rose. Still, she was a work colleague and appeared to be on her own in the Treasury, so Kitty and Rose nodded at Marianne, who blanked them.

"Everyone thayth I have the perfect Paul Coth-telloe body," Rose lisped, and they sniggered.

Marianne had revealed this once, in an uncharacteristically forthcoming moment with people who weren't men, supplying the duo with more ammunition against her than they'd ever need in their lifetimes.

Linus Bell loomed in the doorway of the Treasury – for a man of average height, he had an above-average knack for looming – and his appearance precipitated a rash of dropped glances. Nobody wanted to make eye contact and have to talk to him – they'd be labelled a toady.

"Linus," called Marianne, "over here!"

Kitty and Rose exchanged glances. Had the editor actually arranged to meet Marianne O'Leary in the Treasury? Surely he'd realise half the office would spot them and add two and two together, ending up with multiplication. Or copulation at the very least.

"This kip is even more distasteful than I remember," snarled Linus. "Let's go to Patrick Guilbaud's straight away – it's got a bit of glitz about the place. My driver's outside."

Marianne delayed for Linus to hold open the door, but he bowled out ahead. A buzz of conversation was generated by their departure.

"Why do you suppose the Exalted One is taking Marianne O'Leary to Patrick Guilbaud's for dinner?" wondered Kitty.

It was one of Dublin's most select restaurants. Linus Bell had brought her there once, before she'd joined the *Sunday Trumpet*, and wouldn't order any wine because he disapproved of lunchtime drinking. Also of freedom of choice. Still, the food had been mouth-watering and she'd seen two politicians, a shock-jock and a model-agency owner rumoured to have undergone so much plastic surgery she couldn't sit near an open fire for fear of meltdown.

"It's too obvious to assume Linus and Marianne are having an affair." Rose's eyes were slits as she considered the possibilities.

"Besides, he's busy having an affair already, with a Filipino midwife." Kitty rustled her packet of peanuts but found them empty.

"Do you really believe the Exalted One is having an affair with a Filipino midwife, or is it just a rumour he started to make himself seem more touchy-feely?" Rose also jiggled Kitty's packet of peanuts, locating a nut missed by Kitty. "You don't expect newspaper editors to have young ones on the side who do worthwhile jobs. You imagine if they're going to behave like a cliché they'll have the model who's trying to break into films. Mind you, the one consistent point about the editor is his inconsistency."

Kitty reflected. "The book of evidence seems to suggest there's definitely a relationship in place with a midwife – and since he doesn't do either paternal or fraternal, it has to be lecherous."

"So is Marianne O'Leary lining herself up as the midwife's replacement?" Rose's hazel-to-blue eyes were speculative.

"He'd be insane to take her on." Kitty spoke with more conviction than she felt, because everyone knew Linus was certifiable and Marianne was incontrovertibly stunning.

"I bet it's a red herring. My money's on Marianne being a friend of the Filipino girl's and Linus using her as cover. He can't have liked that dig in *Phoenix* magazine about a certain well-known editor from Dundalk, which narrowed the field to just him – unless you count the editor of the *Dundalk Democrat* – and his trips on the Orient Express. His wife probably savaged him over it – she thinks she should be totty enough for him."

They finished their drinks, agreeably picturing Linus Bell's wife giving him hell at home.

"Since when did you start using sexist expressions like totty?" challenged Kitty.

"Since I joined the *Strumpet*," admitted Rose.

Their mouths drooped in unison.

"Anyway," concluded Rose, "let's not waste our off-duty time on the Exalted One or the rag he edits, even if we contribute to its raggedness. Are you still on for assessing Hubert de Paor's mistress-keeping potential?"

Linus Bell's activities had stripped the lustre from Kitty's stratagem but, even by her slacker standards, abandoning a New Year's resolution on January 2nd smacked of the quitter. "Suppose so," she muttered.

"We don't have to go if you're having second thoughts," offered Rose.

"I'll do it if you email the twelve-year-old," Kitty negotiated.

Rose prevaricated. "He couldn't tie his shoelaces when I started dating. I was at college before he knew how to read or write. I was earning a salary when he was still doing a paper round for pocket money. Even" – she savoured her *pièce de résistance* – "my record collection is older than him."

"It's just a bit of fun – nobody says you have to kidnap him and abscond to Gretna Green."

"You strike a hard bargain. But it's a deal."

They shook hands on it, then Rose rushed off because she hadn't phoned home yet to speak to her parents and they never went to bed until she'd checked in with them.

This left Kitty on her own. Peter Webster, the pock-marked special investigations reporter, broke off his conversation with the sports editor about whether or not Lotto winners were morally obliged to share their jackpots with siblings. He signalled to Kitty to join him. She declined – he had more hands than one of those Indian mudras statues. Plus he was single, so she wasn't about to waste her time on him. There was absolutely no point in being a bachelor's mistress; it lacked that smack of the illicit.

"Aren't you going to buy me a drink, Kitty?" Peter called, seeing her reach for her briefcase.

Typical of the single Irish male, his idea of a chat-up line was to ask you to buy him alcohol. She was bemused how they'd ever managed to earn a reputation for charm. "I'm saving myself for Hubert," she announced.

Peter turned to the sports editor. "Who's Hubert?"

"I knew a boxer called Hubert once, lost a packet on him when he threw a fight."

They watched Kitty sashay out of the pub, eyes lingering on the twin hemispheres of her bottom.

"That Hubert's a lucky man. Same again?"

Chapter 7

It was noon on Saturday and Sunny lay on the bed rehearsing her Oscar acceptance speech. "Ladies and gentlemen, some of the most significant words in the English language are the shortest . . . words such as love, baby, yes. I have another important word for you all here tonight: thanks." Cut to camera panning slowly over ecstatic audience – including Noreen-dear and her father beaming with parental pride and Kitty, overcome at being related to Sunny – then returning to her own face irradiated by a modest smile, hand cradling the statuette. Hand. Sunny sat up, banging her head on the headboard. She ought to have a manicure before the reception, no point in half-measures.

She sank back, strategising. This could prove to be the most crucial evening of her life. A Hollywood casting agent was in town and her agent, Malachy Curran, had wangled her an invitation to his drinks party. Mr Hollywood had better watch out, Sunny Kennedy was coming to get him. Downstairs she could hear her mother moving about the kitchen, and the odd muffled crash from the basement which meant her father was fiddling with some DIY project or other. She checked her watch, adjourned to the bathroom where she washed off her mud mask, then phoned her hairdresser and cajoled until she agreed to slot her in without an appointment that afternoon. Next she tossed a selection of dresses onto the bed, thinking longingly of the Jenny Packham oyster-beaded cocktail frock she visited occasionally at the Powerscourt Centre. It was too expensive for Sunny to contemplate buying, but she liked to check it was still there on its hanger, so she'd know God was in his heaven and all was right with the world.

Then Sunny phoned Kitty. "I have an important date, Kitty, I need The Bag. I also need you to deliver it because I won't have a chance to collect it." Sunny was shameless and accustomed to being indulged.

"Monster." Kitty was resigned to being the spoiler rather than the spoilee.

Beaded and bewitching, the communal evening bag had cost so much that when she had acceded to its siren lure, Kitty had promised herself it would become the Kennedy family evening purse. Thereby reducing the price-tag via her personal brand of mental gymnastics. Her mother and sister would borrow it, so it was really only costing a third of the price.

"I'll have the loan of your star-spangled wrap as well," added Sunny.

"You make it sound like the American flag," Kitty complained, nevertheless trying to remember where the filmy length of material might be housed. "I'll drop by with the bag and wrap later this afternoon." She rubbed her sleep-deprived eyes until they stung, for the baby in the house next-door was teething. "I promised Noreen-dear I'd call in today anyway, so I may as well run your errands for you."

"Thanks, babe," burbled Sunny, refusing to be shamed. "I'll remember your sacrifices in my Oscar acceptance speech."

Sunny would have liked to dawdle a little longer on the bed fantasising about this performance, which she continually refined, but there was no rest for the wicked. A Hollywood casting agent was in town that evening and her horoscope had told her Venus was in the ascendant, always a promising sign. With her inner certainty back in place following that unnerving New Year's Day wobble, Sunny was convinced her bound towards stardom was imminent. It had taken a little longer than usual to retrieve her inner certainty this time, a state of affairs which had left her feeling indistinct, as though an eraser had been pointed at her outline and her definition smudged. This didn't suit Sunny's self-portrait at all. When she thought of her smile, she saw it stretching to fill a cinema screen. When she imagined a tear sliding down her cheek, she wanted it to touch the emotions of millions. The prospect of existing on a life-sized scale appalled her.

She prepared a bath before the inner certainty had time to develop another fault-line, reviewing her career as she submerged her body. Her meatiest role to date had been as a detective in a gritty cop drama which hadn't made the transition from pilot to series. The production company had gone belly-up, although public reaction to the pilot had been positive. One newspaper review had described her as "sassy". Sunny still mourned the loss of *Beat It*. She had even been given a catch-phrase never afforded the chance to win the hearts of the nation: "Looks like rain, Sarge." To be delivered with the twitch of an eyebrow, or a wry smile, or a wink, or sometimes pokerfaced, depending on the episode.

Sunny had earned her Equity card from a pantomime season in *Sleeping Beauty* at The Gaiety – playing a singing squirrel and a serving wench who managed to interest the prince until the unfair competition of the leading lady had intervened. Apart from a Synge revival at the Peacock last year and a bottled-water advertisement, repeated on television so often it was keeping her in funds, she was doing virtually no acting currently.

Kitty was forever teasing her about the way she moaned her curriculum vitae must have constant additions to keep it fresh. But it was an insatiable monster. Kitty didn't understand how many prettier, younger girls were out there – talent barely signified. "My CV needs that part in *Fair City*. My CV needs this documentary voice-over. My CV needs fresh blood and the internal organs of a Transylvanian virgin," Kitty would joke. It was all right for her, she didn't have to compete on her looks every day of her life. She didn't have to bank down panic if she woke up and discovered a line on her face that hadn't been there the night before. Sunny knew she should have moved to Los Angeles, or at the very least London where there was more work, but to date she remained in the lilac bedroom with the sloping eaves which had been Kitty's before her. Fear, she supposed, was the root cause; she was measuring out her life in J Alfred Prufrock's coffee-spoons, although she had sworn that was exactly what she would never do.

Between acting stints she earned money from a succession of temporary jobs – right now it was telephone surveys. To entertain herself, she acquired a different accent for each call she made. Sometimes she was a Russian émigrée, at other times a Southern belle. Once she pretended to be Meryl Streep for an entire afternoon, but nobody recognised the impersonation. Which was disheartening, because voices were supposed to be her strong suit.

"A twenty-nine-year-old has no business living under the same roof as her parents," Sunny told the taps. At least Kitty had shown enough sense to move out, before the prospect of self-sufficiency became too frightening. She felt a coil of uncertainty ripple within her – what if she never made it? What if she were fated to live in the lilac bedroom forever? "Looks like rain, Sarge." Sunny tried to strike a defiant note, but only managed a tentative one. She pulled the plug on the bath water: time for action if she intended to be a player.

* * *

Kitty trailed down the passage to the bedroom to collect her evening bag and shawl for Sunny, wondering where she was bound. Her sister yearned for the femme-fatale days of celluloid glamour and recreated what she could in Bray. Even on a relatively dowdy day she'd slash on twin crescents of vivid lipstick, the colour of something that could only have started life in a jam-jar. "It's an anti-depressant, it needs to be bright," she'd lecture Kitty, who was more inclined towards pearlised pinks. Kitty liked nothing better than to see the curve of colour transferred from her mouth to wineglasses and coffee cups – it bolstered the illusion of being grown-up. Looking the part was half the battle – Kitty had learned that much from a sister who was an actor.

She tended to feel a little faded by comparison with Sunny. Sunny said Kitty was a sepia version of her glorious technicolour; she was given to extravagant statements, but Kitty had to admit it was accurate in this case. Sunny meant it in a complimentary way, insisting sepia had its charm. Kitty's hair was golden fair to Sunny's artificially refined coconut-milk white, while her eyes were neither blue nor grey but a mingling of the two shades. Sunny's were cobalt and always sparkled, charged from deep within her. Kitty's eyebrows were almost natural, apart from a little judicious plucking at the camber, whereas Sunny's were tortured to an arch that lent her a permanently surprised expression. Both had inherited their mother's cheekbones, a sweep from temple to chin that wasn't beauty, exactly, but which marked them out from the herd. However Sunny had an ancillary gift, one which Kitty envied – a zest for life that she lacked, an anticipation of skies as clear as her eyes.

The jet evening bag was where she expected to find it, in the top drawer of her cherrywood bureau. The gauzy wrap proved more elusive, but she located it finally, hidden under a raw silk bolero on a coat-hanger, the spangle of stars in the dim interior of the wardrobe betraying it. As Kitty reached in, a sliver of paper peeking from the bolero's breast pocket caught her eye.

She recognised it before she read it. The knowledge seeped through her. It was an admission ticket for a one-man show at the Gate: Simon Callow as Charles Dickens. That had been the night when she and Benjamin had savaged one another during the interval, carelessly public in their mutual disdain. The taste of the quinine in the gin and tonic Kitty had been drinking rushed back into her mouth, forming sediment, and she swallowed, queasy. She had stalked from the theatre without returning to the auditorium for the second half, while Benjamin had stayed out until dawn.

He had stumbled, drunk, into bed as light streaked the night sky. The hot, acrid gush from his bladder had woken Kitty thinking, in her dream state, that she was standing under the shower. Benjamin had urinated in bed, a prolonged discharge that had reached across the sheet to soak her. After her shrieks of enraged horror and his sluggish apology, she had thrown the nightdress she'd been wearing into the bin, adding the sheet and duvet-cover for good measure. They had never shared a bed again. There. That's what she'd meant about one marriage beginning in bed and the other one ending in it. A tilt from the sublime to the ridiculous – someone had taken the script of her life trajectory and transposed the pages.

Negativity as nebulous as a vapour ambushed her when she pulled the ticket-stub from the jacket. She held it at arm's length between the tips of two fingers. Theirs had not been an easy relationship to walk away from, despite the flamboyance of their arguments. Her not-quite-ex-husband's swarthy face with its twin moles, one on top of the other above his left eyebrow, swam before her eyes. Life had certainly backed her into a cul-de-sac with Benjamin. Fortunately it hadn't been an irreversible manoeuvre.

Kitty crumpled the ticket, dispelling the chill. Mistresses should be light-hearted, their capacity for frivolity was integral to their charm. Ex-husbands weren't going to deter her.

Chapter 8

Kitty folded her arms and leaned against the wall at the bottom of the basement stairs because Denis Kennedy didn't like his den to be invaded. "What are you working on, Dad?" she called through the open door.

"Just having another crack at Sunny's magazine rack, chicken. Can't make head or tail of those end pieces." He rearranged the sweet in his cheek and scratched his head. "I don't know why everything has to come in kit form these days."

Although currently without a regular boyfriend, Sunny was compiling her bottom drawer. So far she had bought a magazine rack which defied attempts to assemble it, a rocking chair, giraffe-headed salad servers and some guest towels with crocuses embroidered on a panel. "That's the tray-cloth genes coming out in you," Kitty had noted, to Sunny's dismay. You never knew when those latent genes would pounce. There were more than 30,000 of the little beasts in each of them, waiting in the long grass to spring their biological surprises.

The magazine rack had been the first and least successful purchase. It had reached the stage where Sunny insisted she'd marry the first man who could assemble her rack. It was her glass-slipper test. All the Kennedys knew she was only joking . . . then again, Sunny was capable of it. She had bought it from Ikea in Wembley a year before, during a long weekend in London – intended to deliver her a part in a controversial Almeida Theatre production. Instead she'd come home with the magazine rack, minus the instructions, and had never managed to turn the strips of wood and metal into anything resembling a useful item of furniture. But she harassed any men who strayed into her force-field to have a crack at it. It troubled Denis Kennedy, who couldn't enjoy the jigsaw puzzles he usually spent his days working on, knowing it was lying there beside his drill. Unassembled.

"Do you want a hand with the magazine rack?" offered Kitty.

"Ah no, chicken, you go and keep your mother company over a cup of tea. It'll distract her from the ironing and save her having backache tonight. The teapot never cools when that happens."

Kitty returned to the kitchen, where her mother was arranging cups and saucers on the table. She even had sugar lumps in a bowl, although neither of them took sugar, and a crochet cover for the milk jug with beaded weights holding it down.

"That looks lovely, Mum, are you expecting company?"

"If I can't do things properly for my own daughter who can I do them for?" Noreen Kennedy's blue-grey eyes that matched Kitty's surveyed her china and glimmered their approval. "Sunny never notices when I set out my best ware."

Kitty sat down, elbows leaning on the scrubbed pine table. "Sure she couldn't manage without you, Mum. She'd know all about it if she went back to one of those dives she used to rent. You have her ruined here, with your fetching and carrying."

It was exactly the right approach. While thrilled to have something as unconventional as an actor in the family, her mother's patience was sometimes tested by Sunny. Particularly when she wasn't acting and her plummeting self-esteem led to multiple random sexual encounters. Not that her mother knew about them, but she did find Sunny's erratic hours a trial. She split a scone with an onyx-handled knife, also earmarked for her daughters' heirlooms collection whether they liked it or not, and was soon gossiping about Sunny's auditions. Noreen-dear could never mask her delight in her younger daughter's theatrical lifestyle, despite complaints about her eating breakfast at two in the afternoon or the way she flung her clothes on the bedroom floor instead of hanging them up, the way she'd been taught.

Kitty only needed to spare a fraction of her attention for Noreen-dear. She was thinking about Rose's promise to introduce her to Hubert de Paor the following day and wondering whether she had it in her to inspire a series of paintings. Kitty Kennedy as Queen Maeve, proto-feminist in the Celtic era; Kitty Kennedy as Maud Gonne, patriotic aristocrat who renounced her class; Kitty Kennedy as Grace O'Malley, pirate queen and another of those independent vixens. Maybe she was self-aggrandising: just because she fancied an affair with an established artist didn't mean he fancied an affair with her. Still, the possibilities were intriguing and she'd always preferred to travel hopefully than to arrive.

"There's a furtive smile licking at the corners of your mouth." Her mother eyed her closely. "You seem very pleased with yourself, Kitty."

She hadn't meant to say anything, but her tongue made a unilateral decision. "I have a sort of a date tomorrow, Mum." Where had that sprung from? Kitty wasn't expecting it, let alone her mother. Anyway, it wasn't what you'd call a date with Hubert de Paor, more a prelude to a date. Affecting nonchalance, Kitty peeled off the price ticket from a sauce bottle left on the table since Sunny's midnight raid on the fridge.

"A date – that's wonderful, Kitty – buy yourself something fetching to wear." Her tone was encouraging.

"I have a wardrobe full of clothes, I don't need anything."

"Or you could borrow something of Sunny's." Noreen steamed ahead. "Every brass farthing she earns goes on her back – I'm sure she'd have an outfit to suit you, although you might have to do something about the length. You wouldn't wear anything of mine, I suppose?" She adjusted her cardigan cuff, hoping Kitty would beg to borrow one of her Peter Pan blouses. Noreen-dear had an infinite collection of them in ice-cream shades, all identical to the naked eye but for the colours. When Kitty didn't respond, she compressed her lips. "Too old-fashioned for you, I dare say. But remember, Kitty, no man will ever mistake you for anything other than a lady in a smart blouse with a brooch at the collar or a string of pearls."

"Considering the men I meet, that would be casting pearls before swine." Kitty might be a conservative dresser by Sunny's standards, but she drew the line at Peter Pan blouses. "Thanks, Mum, but I don't need anything."

"It's not about need, it's about confidence, lovie."

"Anyway, I'm thinking of cancelling."

"Why? A date will do you the power of good. The hours you work are too long. A dose of admiration is healthy." Her mother was appeasing.

"He's miles too old for me, Mum."

"How old is he?"

"Mid-fifties, twenty years older than me."

Her mother wrinkled the patch of skin on her forehead which she used to express emotion. "You can't be in your thirties, Kitty."

"I'm thirty-six, Mum. Since November the eighteenth. The four of us went out to dinner and when we left the restaurant Dad realised he'd locked his car keys in the Nissan. We were just about to call a locksmith when you remembered you had a spare set in the pouch of your handbag."

"A handful of years off forty," intoned Noreen. "It doesn't seem possible."

"Yes, well –"

"Forty," she repeated. "The years just fly by and nothing to show for them."

Rancour whooshed through Kitty, staining her neck brick-red. This was shaping up to be a repeat of her mother's conversation that November night, when comments on the meal, Denis's forgetfulness and Sunny's stellar performance in her bottled-water commercial had been interjected by regular recitations of "a few years off forty, it doesn't seem possible, the years just fly by and nothing to show for them". Thirty-six was light years away from forty, everyone knew that. Kitty contained her pique. "Mum, I'm thirty-six," she said firmly. "You may not like it but trust me, that's my age."

"If you say so, lovie."

"So it doesn't make any sense for me to go out with a fiftysomething," she continued, hopeful of contradiction. "In this case, it isn't so much a generation gap as a pothole. What do you think?"

Her mother stalled.

The pause shrieked and Kitty pounced on it. "You think I should be grateful for anyone I can get, with my track record," she howled, reading censure in her mother's silence. "Two divorces make me flaky."

"I see what you mean," murmured her mother. However, it was a holding statement as opposed to agreement. For although Kitty didn't realise it, her mother's silence was one of reflection rather than rebuke. She was aware how the failure of both her marriages had maimed her daughter, who sometimes tried to pretend it was liberating to be a double divorcée. But whose bravado didn't fool anyone who loved her.

Kitty's parents had never been able to grasp why she'd separated from Benjamin. They had managed a glimmer of understanding about Ryan because Kitty and he had both been so young, still at college, but when Kitty had left Benjamin they'd been mystified. "We grew apart," had been the nearest to an explanation she'd managed. This hadn't seemed appropriate grounds for divorce to either Noreen or Denis Kennedy, who'd grown apart with a consistency bordering on determination within several years of marriage. There were other, more pressing reasons why Benjamin and Kitty couldn't stay married, but they weren't readily explicable. Kitty's vocabulary couldn't rise to the challenge.

All right, she'd thought once, stirred by their bewilderment, she'd try. "He stifled me – I felt consumed by him. I needed vacant possession of my life."

Her parents had bandied identical accusatory glances: she gets this from your side of the family.

"I see what you mean," murmured her mother now, adjusting the beaded cover on the milk jug. Then she struck a haltingly encouraging note. "You know, Kitty, it mightn't do you any harm to go out. You're still a bit of a catch, with your own house and a job with a pension, despite all that other business."

This was a considerable advance on her mother's usual stance, which was that Kitty had wasted all her chances by marrying twice. She never mentioned divorce, no matter how often Sunny tried to trip her up, tenacious in referring to it as "that other business". She'd implied for months after the second separation that Kitty should stay at home in the evening and retire from gallivanting. The chador had all but been proffered to her during one particularly fraught exchange. Now here she was calling her daughter a catch. To reward her, Kitty poured them both more tea and remarked, "Have I ever told you grateful I am that my name is Kitty Kennedy? It's perfect in print, you couldn't invent a better one. Alliteration always works well for newspaper columnists, it rolls off the tongue."

"Really, lovie?" Her mother looked gratified. "We thought long and hard about your name, your father wanted to call you Philomena, but I insisted on Kathryn with a K, Kitty for short. 'Denis,' I told him, 'any time you'd care to go through an eleven-hour labour you're free to choose the name.' That settled it."

Kitty contemplated life as a newspaper columnist called Philomena Kennedy, sending her opinions floating out into the world to incense, tickle and entrance readers. Or not. For all she knew, they could turn the page without bothering to read her musings on why women thought they could have it all when they couldn't even kill spiders. Apart from the stalker, of course, she could always rely on him to read her column, if only to deconstruct her arguments. She couldn't imagine herself doing it if she were called Philomena Kennedy.

"Do you like being a columnist?" asked her mother.

Kitty reflected. The best part about the job was being allowed to inflict opinions on a wider audience than the dinner-table. The worst part was that other people had opinions about you. It was outrageous and there was nothing to be done about it. She'd been labelled left-wing and right-wing, a feminist and a traitor to the legacy of the suffragettes, a pseudo-intellectual and a bimbo, downmarket and élitist. Then there were the readers who always thought a good hard shag was all she needed. Preferably from them, and would she ever print her home address at the bottom of next week's column so they could drop by and sort her out.

Kitty felt the photograph the *Sunday Trumpet* used of her was slightly more flattering than the reality, which always made her feel dishonest. It wasn't unbelievably glamorous, but it was her best possible angle on her best possible day, with her head precisely positioned to enhance the cheekbones and her hair arranged to curve around her face. No wonder the weirdo element responded to it. Safer by far to have a cross photograph at the top of her column, but the editor insisted on a smiling one.

Kitty opened her mouth to explain some of this to her mother when Sunny burst in. She was fizzing with energy in a newly acquired halo of curls and a pair of seamed fishnet tights. The exuberance of her walk always reflected her frame of mind – which in turn was influenced by the progress of her career. That afternoon she was upbeat because of the film industry mogul's reception. She twirled for her mother and sister before joining them at the kitchen table. "Mr Hollywood has no chance against me tonight," she hugged herself.

"Who is Mr Hollywood, lovie?" asked Noreen-dear.

"My walking, talking, cigar-smoking, beautiful big break. At least I assume he smokes a cigar."

"Not if he's based in California, he doesn't," Kitty pointed out. "California's the state that put the health into health-conscious."

Sunny intercepted her mother's stare at her hosiery. "The end justifies the seams, Noreen-dear."

"When I was young, stockings like those spelled ruin for a girl's reputation," said her mother. "Mind you, I have to say they look very fetching on you, Sunniva. Are they draughty on the leg?"

"Warm as toast. But the seams are a nightmare to keep straight, I've a crick in my neck from checking them." Sunny lifted Kitty's knife and buttered a scone. "I shouldn't eat this because I'm going out tonight in a dress that leaves too little room for my stomach and too much room for my chest. Although its inadequacies aren't the frock's fault, they're Mother Nature's." She bit in. "Did you remember the spangles, Kitty-cat?"

"Of course. I'm glad to see my accessories have an outing. Where are you taking them?"

"We'll be the centre of attention at the Four Seasons."

Sunny had a breathless way of speaking, as though she had too many words to force out and a finite amount of time to do it in – it always reminded Kitty of Dad's gabbled Noreen-dear. Sunny launched into one of her galloping explanations.

"It's being hosted by an American casting director who thinks he's Irish because his great-grandfather was born here – and had the sense to clear off as soon as he could scrape together the passage. I'm determined to catch Mr Hollywood's eye. There's only so much double-glazing I can sell down a phone-line before I run screaming for sedatives." She tossed her head to set the platinum curls dancing. "How do you like my new image? I thought about having some henna added in case he's angling for the colleen look, but then I decided on Shirley Temple meets Jean Harlow. Cover all the virgin-to-vamp options."

Kitty smiled. It seemed only yesterday since her sister used to climb into her bed and curl fingers into their wishbone embrace. Now here she was tweaking her options for a Hollywood casting director.

"How come you look so alluring and I don't?" Kitty asked, affection swelling.

"Allure wouldn't be so alluring if everyone had it," Sunny explained. "But relax, all the Kennedy girls have allure, and that includes Noreen-dear."

"Sure isn't it me you inherited it from?" Their mother was complacent as she picked crumbs off Sunny's lap.

"Word is," Sunny carried on, "he's casting for a remake of *The Quiet Man*. Pearl Roberge" – she mentioned a double-Oscar winner who monopolised all the plum female roles – "is lined up for the Maureen O'Hara part. I see myself as one of the barefoot village girls, captivating and natural. "

"Natural takes too much work," Kitty teased.

Sunny was immune to baiting. "Tell me about it. Anyway, mustn't sit about gabbing all day, I have to transform myself into star material by six thirty. Clarke T Maloney won't know what's hit him." She stood, brushing down crumbs.

"Kitty has a date tomorrow, Sunny," said their mother.

"I wouldn't exactly call it a date."

"You hedge more than a country lane," laughed Sunny, delighted that her sister seemed to have forgotten all that nonsense about becoming a mistress. "A date for you is hardly a big deal – it's not as if your future career depends on it, the way mine does. You're not going to be sized up by some casting director who has the power of stardom or obscurity over you. Lighten up, get out there and enjoy it. These could be the best days of your life and you're frittering them away. The race isn't always to the swift, you know."

"But it's the way to bet," Kitty mumbled.

Sunny rested her arms on her hips. Kitty could tell from the set of her that she was about to recreate her feisty young widow role, as performed at the Tivoli the year before last.

"Kitty Kennedy, you're turning into a spinster – and don't tell me you're a divorcée because spinsterhood is a state of mind. I know spinsters who've been married for thirty years and produced half a dozen children." Now she was wagging a finger. "Take yourself home and paint yourself up for a date. There's nothing like it to set the adrenaline pulsing. It doesn't matter if the date is a damp squib, it's the fact you could be bothered to go on one that counts. Otherwise you might as well shrivel up and die."

"There's more to life than dating." Kitty felt badgered, especially as what she had lined up for the next day couldn't be counted as anything as flattering as a date, precisely.

"Of course there is," agreed Sunny, "but it's time you rinsed the nutter formerly known as Benjamin out of your hair. With a man who's available," she added emphatically. "Just because you had a roller-coaster ride with Benjamin shouldn't put you off – it's a glittering fairground out there. Check out the attractions, pick something you fancy and hand over your money for another go."

Now it sounded like one of Sunny's film scripts.

"Life's not a carnival," Kitty protested.

"Life's not a carnival? I'll let you in on a secret, Kitty, it can be."

"She has a point, lovie," said their mother. "Perhaps it's time you found yourself a boyfriend."

"See, even Noreen-dear agrees with me." Sunny sucked butter off her thumb.

"You're ganging up on me. I'm a mature woman of the world, far too old to be intimidated by these tactics. But fair enough, I'll go." Kitty felt a tickle of pleasure. Little did they know what she had in mind for Hubert de Paor. "You'd think it was a crime to have a night in on your own," she added.

"You'll have plenty of nights in on your own when you're at my stage of life." Their mother returned to the iron, lifting it with the determination of a woman tackling an international humanitarian crisis.

"But Dad's always with you," Kitty objected.

"Exactly. This shirt is very creased, I should have seen to it while it was damp." Noreen licked her index finger, testing it against the metal.

"Dad never takes her anywhere," Sunny translated. "The only time they have a night out is when they go to someone's wake to pay their respects to the dead."

"Leave Dad alone," Kitty warned.

"It's unnatural," Sunny protested. "Human beings are social animals. Noreen-dear needs to get out more."

"Denis likes to be in bed by eleven." Noreen exuded martyred forbearance.

"So do something about it yourself, Sunny – take her to your drinks party at the Four Seasons."

Kitty flung out to the hallway. She hated it when Sunny and her mother joined ranks against her father. He was contented in the bowels of the house, doing nobody the least bit of harm – he'd eat his meals on a tray down there if it were allowed. Kitty opened the door to the basement. "I'm off, Dad."

He appeared at the foot of the stairs. "Fair enough, chicken. See you soon."

She closed the door, then re-opened it. "Dad?"

"Yes, chicken?"

"Do you think I'm a spinster?"

"Of course not. Didn't you make a gorgeous bride?"

She had made a transcendent bride, everyone was agreed on it. Both times. It was only as a wife that she left something to be desired. Kitty had a flashback to her second wedding day. Even Sunny hadn't been able to overshadow her in that strapless emerald gown she'd sidled off and bought, before Kitty could remind her they'd agreed on an antique gold colour scheme. Imagine having a flawless wedding day and a blemished marriage. Where were the harbingers of doom when you needed them?

"Who's been calling you a spinster?" Indignation flooded her father's already sanguine face.

"Sunny."

"That's rich coming from someone who's never even been engaged."

Kitty nodded, mollified. Not that there was any sin in being a spinster – the single life could be an affirmation as opposed to a rejection. She decided against sharing this with her father. Imagine if it left him wondering whether he'd made the right choice himself, for he was a man inherently attuned to the bachelor lifestyle. Kitty decided to be magnanimous. "I don't think Sunny meant it unkindly, it's just how she is. She has a robust way with her."

"Never you mind, chicken, you won't stay a spinster. You'll find someone else, someone who deserves you and treats you properly."

"Thanks, Dad." She blew him a kiss.

He reached out his knobbly hand and caught it.

Kitty closed the basement door. She could hear Sunny pounding about upstairs in the bedroom that had once been hers – she'd annexed it the day Kitty had moved out, claiming she needed more space to practise her samba routines. Restless, Kitty returned to the kitchen.

"That one makes enough racket to wake the dead." Their mother was ironing Sunny's frock for impressing the important casting agent.

No wonder Sunny humoured her, telling her their father didn't appreciate her. Kitty noticed how her mother had turned inside out the flimsy net circus costume masquerading as a gown, so the material wouldn't become shiny. She pegged her clothes lining-side out on the line too; laundry had life and death importance in Noreen Kennedy's value system. Kitty's mother inhaled sharply at a stain on the bodice and set down the iron to search a drawer for brown paper to draw out the grease.

"I'll head on, Mum," said Kitty.

Noreen rummaged with her back to her daughter. "Enjoy yourself tomorrow with that fellow. Oh, and Kitty," Noreen faced her, a used brown envelope in her hand, "there's no need to tell him your real age."

"He's the one who's decades older than me," bleated Kitty.

"I know, but you're thirty-six with all that other business behind you – it's verging on shop-soiled." ·

Kitty opened her mouth and closed it, inarticulate. She tried again, but the necessary syllables of indignation wouldn't form.

"I'd call myself twenty-nine if I were you, love – borrow Sunny's birthday," added her mother. "Sure what's a year or seven? I know women who never let on their true ages to their husbands even after they've been man and wife for decades on end. Your father's mother lied about her age on her marriage lines. She thought it was none of the priest's business."

"It feels dishonest."

"Honesty between men and women will never catch on, trust me on this, lovie." With that her mother returned to the ironing-board, positioning the envelope over the stain.

Kitty ruminated on the issue of honesty as she walked across the railway tracks to Bray Dart station, listening to the seagulls squabble. Was deliberately setting out to become a mistress dishonest? Or was it so searingly candid it had no chance of success? Her mother obviously believed that "honesty is the best policy" was one of those truisms that had sneaked into the lexicon when nobody was paying attention. Ambiguity about her plan jangled within Kitty. Then she shook herself. She mustn't give up so soon, it showed weakness of character. It wasn't as if she was inventing the wheel here: the ancient Greeks had taken mistresses – Aesop, who wrote the fables, and the sculptor Praxiteles, whose lover was a high priestess.

"I'm only trying to work out a modus vivendi that's best for me," she told one of the seagulls, defensive beneath its gimlet eye. "It's not as if I'm setting up a new sect that specialises in training women to become courtesans. I'm not recommending it for other people, just for me. Besides, it's an experiment, it might fail."

That was too negative; she had no chance of becoming a mistress with such a pessimistic attitude. Successful people expected success. Look at Sunny, preparing to dazzle her Mr Hollywood: she was behaving like a diva, thus improving her chances of becoming one. It all hinged on positive thinking. Focus, Kitty reminded herself, don't let anxieties about dishonesty trip you up. "I'm about to become a mistress because being a willing mistress is less dishonest than being a reluctant wife," she told the seagull, which flapped its wings and was airborne. "That's my definition of morality," she called after it.

Chapter 9

Rose re-read the email. *Great to hear from you. Could we meet? You choose when and where. I'm embarrassingly available and never learned how to play hard to get. Love, Feargal.*

Love, Feargal? That was hyper-keen. On impulse, and to test just how eager he was, she keyed in one word and hit send. *Tonight?* It was Saturday afternoon and Rose was still at work, but she'd be finished by six and was having an entire weekend in Dublin for a change. Instead of going home to collect her decrepit Honda Civic and nose it into the early evening traffic, navigating towards the small town of Slane thirty miles north of Dublin, she could stay on in her apartment in Ranelagh. Her parents had decamped to her aunt's house in Carlingford for the weekend. A nephew had even been despatched to fetch them, on the basis that he had a new company Mercedes and it deserved to be admired.

This meant a slice of time from six p.m. on Saturday evening until ten a.m. on Tuesday morning was hers to do with exactly as she pleased, a rare treat. Tonight she had planned to go to the Treasury for a few drinks with her colleagues, afterwards collecting an Indian takeaway and a video on her way home. Not the most exciting option but self-indulgent enough to appeal. Then Feargal replied to her spur-of-the-moment email and she decided to submit to temptation. She'd meet him again.

Back whizzed the response. *Brilliant. How about coming with me to hear a torch singer I can recommend? She's doing a cabaret act upstairs in Faye's pub on Georges Street – I'll leave a ticket at the door for you. Show starts at 8.30 p.m. See you inside about fifteen minutes before that so we can have a drink.*

Hoist by her own petard, whatever a petard might be. How many times had she learned that you should only call someone's bluff when you were one hundred per cent convinced they were bluffing? Rose considered the permutations and decided there was no help for it but to meet Feargal. At least he'd made an effort to suggest something different. She and Father Damien had developed the habit of cinema visits every Saturday night; no need to talk that way. Disengage brain, chew popcorn, enjoy the comfort of a familiar shoulder against yours.

The trouble with Feargal was there was nothing familiar about him. It was a leap into the unknown. She was too old for these feelings of anxiety, for the dating bear-pit, for starting over with someone new. Yet not starting over was more depressing still, for it was capitulating on life. Deep breath: she could do it.

* * *

Rose couldn't help but notice how Feargal's face illuminated when she walked into the bar. He didn't have that effect on her, of course, but the fact she had it on someone else was (a) flattering, (b) still flattering and (c) left her feeling chastened for having spent the past nine hours wanting to parachute out of the arrangement. He had one of those faces that looked plain and somewhat severe until he smiled – when its contours altered and people felt a tickle of recognition, even if they didn't know him.

Feargal was so thin he made the skinny Rose feel plumply rounded, with dark hair that flopped forward however often he pushed it back from his face, and a narrow face that defied the Irish climate to remained lightly-tanned, winter and summer. He was wearing a navy T-shirt with the name of a band she'd never heard of emblazoned across it, but he'd swapped his usual jeans for a pair of Dockers.

He was positioned near the door so he could watch out for Rose – because, as Feargal explained later, a former girlfriend had told him how those anxious first moments of scanning were the most uncomfortable for a woman on a date. He had this courtly view that he never wanted any female to feel uneasy on his account. Honestly. Rose did a double-take when he admitted it, checking whether she was being baited.

"You look fantastic," Feargal smiled. His smile started in the crinkles around his eyes and meandered down to identical lines rimming either side of his mouth. He had an English accent – she'd almost forgotten that, between his Irish name and because they'd been communicating by email. She smiled back. "You should have seen me an hour ago: I had wet hair, a slice of cucumber on each eye and I was wrapped in a mangy old robe."

"I bet you still looked fantastic."

"Well, if you're determined to be partisan."

There was a whisper of heat between them as he placed his hand on her elbow and guided her to a seat. His touch was transitory, but her instantaneous reaction panicked her. The last man she'd responded to in this way had been Damien, before he'd started on a fast track to becoming Father Damien. Proof that she couldn't trust her instincts.

"What would you like to drink?" Feargal remained on his feet, looking down at her.

"Let me get them in." Rose stood too; it made her feel more in control of the situation. She was startled to find herself on eye level with him, for although slight, he gave an impression of size. Perhaps it was due to his relaxed confidence.

"You can buy the next round." His dark grey eyes were luminous with amusement. They had the capacity to glow so that his eyelids seemed inadequate shutters for them.

"I can't stay long so I'll buy them," Rose insisted, feeling her control recede by the second.

The amusement ebbed from his eyes and she saw the veins in his lids as they lowered to half-mast. "Why not?"

"I'm forty," she blurted out.

Feargal didn't flinch. "Well then, I should think you're old enough to stay out as late as you like. Have you decided what you'd like to drink? No? I'll just order you a glass of white wine to be going on with, I know you like that."

She sat in a tangle, forgetting to smooth her tunic over its matching trousers and crushing it to a rag. Feargal hadn't reacted. Not even some quip about being well-preserved for her age. Obviously he was deliberately playing it cool, but she'd expected some response. Surprise, at least. She might just as well have told him she was Capricorn or her favourite colour was turquoise.

Feargal slid into the seat beside her, carrying her glass by the stem so the temperature of his hand wouldn't heat the wine. The same former girlfriend had advised him about that, too. Rose would buy her a drink if she had the chance. The work women did, preparing boyfriends for the next female after them, was largely unsung. Rose batted a sidelong look at him. If it weren't for that aquiline nose his face would almost strike a feminine note. The nose that had wedged in her eye and almost dissuaded her from seeing him again.

He lifted his beer, oblivious to her assessment. "The singer has a voice that conjures up midnight in a deserted bar and last orders being called. She's my landlord's sister. Ian is probably somewhere around here too – he's her roadie."

This was ridiculous, thought Rose – he was taking the cool game to polar extremes. She was entitled to some reaction. "I just told you I was forty," she prodded.

"You did."

"On New Year's Eve you were under the impression I was in my mid-thirties."

"This is true."

"So doesn't the correction interest you?" She scrutinised Feargal's face, puzzled by his serenity.

"Not much. Age is just a number as far as I'm concerned. My sister – you'll have to meet her, you'd like each other – believes people should never say their age in numbers: 'I'm thirty' or 'I'm fifty.' That categorises you in your own mind and other people's. Patricia claims we should say 'I was born in 1978' or 'I was born in 1966' and then it minimises the baggage." He swallowed a mouthful of lager and angled his body so they faced one another.

"I'm not in the market for a relationship," Rose announced. Why had she said that? It implied she didn't expect to see him after that evening, but she was on for a bit of jiggery-pokery in the meantime. She was having a particularly obtuse night, but Rose was panicked by Feargal – by his equilibrium. He had no right to be so self-possessed at twenty-seven going on twelve, it was unnatural.

"I understand."

"Excellent." She felt deflated.

"Here's where I stand on it," said Feargal. "I'm ruling nothing and nobody out and I'm ruling nothing and nobody in. Certainly not on age grounds, which seem far too arbitrary. I believe in keeping an open mind."

Rose's fingers betrayed her jittery state of mind. First they worried at one of the buttons on the front of her tunic, then they drummed on the table, finally they twined themselves around her glass of wine and brought it to her mouth. How come she wound up as the immature one and he had all the choice lines? It was pointless being forty if it didn't give her an edge dealing with twenty-seven-year-old boys. Men, she amended. Feargal might have a boyish appearance but he was behaving like a man. Then she shrugged. She was thinking too much and enjoying too little. This time next Saturday she'd be sitting in the kitchen drinking tea and nibbling custard creams with her parents – and the Saturday after that. She may as well make the most of a night out.

Rose lifted her depleted glass. "Blue skies." She tipped it against his pint, chanting the first toast that entered her head.

"Blue skies," he agreed, holding her gaze for a moment longer than was strictly necessary.

Although necessity was relative, she was learning that.

He was close enough for his scent to drift into her nostrils, a seaside fragrance that reminded her of family holidays in Tramore. Feargal smelled of seaweed and slot-machines, of salt air and chips. Chips always tasted better by the sea. Rose remembered that smell from New Year's Eve, when it had twined around their kisses; it had left her wondering how a Londoner managed to reek of the shore. "Remind me why you're living in Dublin, Feargal?"

"I came over here to go to college and never went back. My parents had spent my entire life talking about Ireland. They still call it home nearly twenty-eight years after leaving the country. But they never brought my brother or sister or me here, so I took matters into my own hands and did a Masters at Trinity. One thing led to another and here I am, working at CityBeat FM, and not a notion of returning to Holloway."

"Oh yes, I remember you said you worked for a radio station." CityBeat FM was a new independent station catering for the capital, but she'd never listened to it – Rose had her dial permanently turned to the national broadcaster, RTÉ. She was always criticising its self-reverential tone but tuning in anyway. "What do you do?"

"Run errands, answer the phone, make coffee."

"Everyone has to start somewhere, I'm sure it's invaluable experience." Her expression was encouraging.

"Actually," he smiled, apologetic, "I was only joking. I do a bit more than that. To be honest, they let me present the morning phone-in show." Feargal warmed to his subject, enthusiasm rendering him garrulous. "It was brave of the station editor to take me on because English accents sometimes grate on Irish airwaves. But the presenter they'd lined up originally pulled out at the eleventh hour. I wasn't so much chosen as thrown in at the deep end on the basis that I was available, cheap and didn't have a stutter. Anyway, so far so good, we're hitting the audience reach we were aiming for – if we can just persuade the advertisers on board we're in clover. It targets a younger audience than the competitors – I imagine that's partly why they've taken a chance on letting me present it."

Wrong-footed, Rose hoped she hadn't sounded condescending. "I haven't heard it, I must listen out for you. What's the show called?"

He mimicked an exaggerated cringe. "*Issues Not Tissues.* Not my idea."

"So what do you do? Pick a topic and hope people will ring up to discuss it?"

"More or less. We usually have a few talking heads lined up to start the ball rolling, but whatever you say about Dubliners they're not short of opinions. The phone-lines are generally hopping within minutes and they text us incessantly. It keeps the discussion pumping." Feargal sloshed his beer around in its glass circumference, seeking to change the subject, keen to learn more about Rose. "What about you, how do you like working for the *Sunday Trumpet*? You're a photographer, right?"

"No, a picture-desk minion. Someone says 'Hunt out a shot of Cameron Diaz where she's showing plenty of leg' or 'Find us before and after pics of some celeb who's denying cosmetic surgery' and I trawl through computer files and download possibilities."

Feargal nodded, still without having a clear idea of what her job entailed, but loathe to appear ignorant.

That awkward pause which characterises most first dates reared its head. Both tried frantically to think of something to pierce it.

"Would you like to stay in Ireland?" Rose asked. "Do you feel at home here?"

"Certainly I do. I was conceived in Ireland. I worked that out from the dates."

"It seems strange your parents never brought the family over to visit. There was a London-Irish family who stayed in Slane every summer – we were always copying their accents. You could have gone to your cousins, the Garritys."

"Bad blood. But that's a story for another day, Rose."

She was about to inveigle him when a voice called across the room. "Whelan, hey, Whelan!" A young Bertie Ahern lookalike, face with that scrubbed raw texture only achieved with a flannel, waved from the far side of the bar. He fought his way across to them.

"All right, mate?" Feargal nodded.

"Heard the programme the other day, the one about public-transport subsidies. You had to do a bit of adjudicating there between the union man and the independent operator. Thought you might have to step in and separate them."

"That's the beauty of radio, you don't need to have them in the same studio. One was on a phone-line. All set for Ella's show?"

Young Bertie scratched his stubble. "Just been with her, holding her hand while she panics and gargles and panics some more."

"Nerves bad?" Feargal was sympathetic.

"Always are. The only way to shake her out of them is to tell her she should give up performing if it has that effect on her. That always puts her in such a temper she forgets she's about to be sick." He transferred his glance to Rose, then back to Feargal in a manner limpid with significance.

Feargal took the bait and performed the introductions.

Young Bertie, who was really called Ian Jackson but didn't look like either an Ian or a Jackson in Rose's view so her mind declined to remember his name, crushed up beside them. "I can't sit long, I have to manage the lights for Ella." He stayed to monopolise the conversation, however, chatting until a message was sent over the loudspeakers to remind him of his duties. Then he stood and lifted his almost full glass, emptying it without any evidence of pleasure.

"Better go handle the chanteuse." He winked as he pronounced it "shan-toozie", with a fake American accent.

A mauve beam shadowed Ella Jackson's face as she stepped onto the stage. She was one of those Irish women who looked as though they were born and reared in Seville; she even had a rose behind one ear and wore a ruffled skirt that smacked of the senorita. Rose wouldn't have been in the least surprised if she'd produced a cigar and rubbed it against her thigh. Ella stood motionless for a few moments, shrouded in her own construct of reality. Then she raised her face, throat throbbing, and released her voice into the audience. It was husky, pain-layered, a lamentation for weary years of solitude in a loveless vacuum. It stripped the onlookers of their desire to chatter – hands were suspended in mid-air as they held their drinks. The hush intensified as her song died away.

Young Bertie switched the lighting to golden, dust motes trembled in the orbit of its beam, and this time Ella was skittish, anticipating an assignation with her sweetheart. She swung her hips and scooped up the tail of her red and black skirt, swishing it against her calf. Rose knew she was in the presence of someone with an exceptional gift, even if she never had the chance to sing anywhere but pubs and coffee houses.

During the interval Rose met Feargal's eye. "Ay *caramba!*" she breathed. "That girl is the business. How come she's not rich and famous?"

Feargal shrugged. "Takes more than talent, I guess. She should be in West End or Broadway musicals, but maybe she isn't hungry enough. The cabaret act is only part-time for Ella – she works in the Clarence Hotel on reception."

Rose was curious. "Do you know her?"

Feargal shifted in his seat. "I met her through Ian. She's fairly volatile – it's the artistic temperament. You never know if she'll look straight through you as if you don't exist, or grab you by the hand and say 'Let's go for a midnight swim in the nip'. I'd guess her emotional maintenance bills are astronomical."

"I thought maybe you knew her through the radio station – she looks as if she should have her own show or regular guest spots on someone else's."

"Looks don't matter on radio, that's the beauty of it. You don't even have to dress well – in fact, half the station goes about like charity-shop rejects. It doesn't matter if you can't spell, either. Just so long as you can read, and even better, improvise."

Rose wanted to question him further about this unfamiliar world, but Young Bertie fiddled with his spotlights again and Ella stepped into the pool of light. She'd loosened her hair so that it surged down her back, and had moved the rose from her hair to a velvet band circling her throat. Every man in the room stretched his neck to bring himself a shade closer to her. Rose wondered at Ella's confidence on that makeshift wooden plinth – contrasting it with her brother's account of her nausea before the performance.

When the set ended Ella and Young Bertie joined them. While she had appeared ageless on stage, Rose judged that Ella was probably only in her late twenties. Imagine, she thought a heartbeat later, she'd used "only" and "late twenties" in the same sentence. Ella sat with a packet of cigarettes which she systematically emptied, jet-painted nails that seemed too large for her fingers tapping the table. Rose was surprised to see her smoke – not because it was illegal in pubs, since Faye's was a law unto itself, but because she thought singers were hysterical about pampering their vocal chords. She was even more disconcerted when Ella started blowing smoke-rings. Her mouth formed a scarlet pout and off they floated. Neither Feargal nor Young Bertie paid any attention even when she leaned forward and directed the smoke-rings towards them, and a nettled expression flashed across Ella's heavy-browed face.

Rose made an effort to draw her out, but she was monosyllabic. Compliments from people around Ella, halting on their way to the bar, generated no more than a regal inclination of the head. Perhaps, thought Rose, watching those nails harass the table, she was behaving this way from pent-up energy rather than boredom. Kitty's sister, Sunny, always maintained nobody could understand performers if they weren't in the business themselves. She should give Ella the benefit of the doubt.

Rose tried again. "How long have you been performing?" she asked.

"Since forever," Ella shrugged. Her treacle-coloured eyes flicked against Rose's, as indifferently as her fingertips disturbed flecks of ash from her clothes.

Fine, be like that, thought Rose. She disliked her on instinct and only her obvious talent made her tolerate her at all. She could sit there in a moody fog for all she cared.

Rose transferred her attention to Young Bertie. Ella's silence was in marked contrast to her brother's, who was capable of talking until the cows came home and milked themselves because nobody was paying any heed to them. He had hijacked her date, but she wasn't sorry – it gave her access to a let-out clause. Everyone knew dates didn't count if they were spent in the company of at least one other person. If Feargal objected to the hijacking, he disguised it well. He was probably relieved not to be stuck with someone as prehistoric as herself, thought Rose, dislodging a tube of Ella's cigarette ash from her lap. She abandoned Ella and joined in the conversation with Feargal and Young Bertie, leaving the prima donna to her own devices.

"Feargal." A sudden movement and a husky voice intruded on a story her brother was telling, spoiling the punch-line. In a single fluid movement, Ella perched herself on Feargal's lap, nails glinting against his skin as she trailed her fingers under his chin. "When are you going to get one of your radio friends to interview me, Feargal?"

Feargal let his hands rest by his side, careful not to touch her. "My friends are no good to you – none of them has an arts show. Rose is the woman you want to approach, Ella. She works for the *Sunday Trumpet*. One word from her and you can have a centre-spread with photographs." He swivelled an apologetic gaze towards Rose, trying to gauge her reaction to Ella sitting on his knees.

Naturally she was deadpan.

Naturally she was livid.

Naturally Ella could kiss goodbye to any chance of an appearance in the *Strumpet* while Rose had breath in her body. And she didn't need to know that an assistant picture editor had less influence than the contract window-cleaner when it came to deciding the newspaper's content. Just because Rose didn't know if she wanted Feargal Whelan didn't give another woman the right to muscle in.

Although, did her knee-jerk response mean Rose was competitive – or that Feargal Whelan, unsuitable boyfriend and no replacement for Damien, soon to be Father Damien, was burrowing under her skin? Panic blazed, as Rose suspected she knew the answer.

Ella contemplated Rose with the first hint of interest she'd betrayed all evening. "How do I persuade you to run an article on me?" Her smile was calculated – she held Rose's gaze with the force of her personality.

"Not by sitting on my knee." Rose matched Ella's smile, eyes wide open.

Feargal laughed and Young Bertie joined in.

"That's you told." Ella's brother slapped the table.

"I'm too much of a wimp for you, Ella, I can't take your weight." Feargal bumped her off his lap.

When the men were conversing again, Ella spoke to Rose sotto voce. "Sorry, didn't realise he was your boyfriend."

"He's not."

Ella lit another cigarette, wreathing herself in allure as hollows formed in her cheeks when she inhaled. A man at the table next to them was staring so fixedly that Rose expected his eyes to bore a hole in her face any second now. It wasn't that Ella was particularly striking, thought Rose, but she behaved as though she was. She had presence, which disguised a body that was a fraction too sturdy and a face with jowls a shade too prominent.

"Don't give up hope." Two inches of ash dangled on the end of Ella's cigarette. "Feargal's mother fixation is your best hope."

Rose could feel temper seeping through the skin on her breastbone, but she clung to the shreds of her composure. For a woman with a breathtaking gift, Ella hadn't the sense she was born with. If she'd only been civil to her, Rose might have had a word with Kitty who might have had a word with Des Redmond the features editor, who might have agreed to an article. Now she could whistle down the wind.

Feargal suggested they leave soon afterwards, finally sensing Rose would never strike up a lifelong rapport with Ella – men could be dense when it came to plumbing woman-to-woman chemistry. Feargal and Rose inhaled the cold, clear air gratefully as they turned onto Dame Street, en route to the taxi rank by the Bank of Ireland arts centre.

"How do you know you're ageing?" asked Feargal.

"It creeps up on you at first," Rose began, defensive.

"No, it's a joke. How do you know you're ageing?"

"I give in."

"You leave a concert before the last set to beat the rush."

"Right," she said. Not much of a joke; she and Father Damien had been doing that for years. Then she remembered she was on a date – she was supposed to laugh at his quips. "At least I haven't started pricing garden sheds," Rose pointed out.

"How about keeping old clothes for gardening instead of throwing them out?"

"I don't have a garden, I live in an apartment." But she probably would if she did, she admitted silently.

There was a queue of eight people ahead of them, but taxis were pulling up regularly. Feargal volunteered to keep her company during the wait and then walk home. She thought about offering to drop him off, even though it was in the opposite direction, but decided against it. He was only twenty-bloody-seven, he probably still watched *Top of the Pops*. A ten-minute walk to Liffey Street wouldn't bother him.

"Tell me again how you know Ella and her brother," Rose suggested, tacking on a smile. It was an order, but no point in letting him know that.

"Ian owns the flat I rent. He used to live there before me, but now he's moved in with his girlfriend. She couldn't come tonight, she's working – she manages an Asian fusion restaurant in Dawson Street. He's a sound man, we hit it off."

The woman in front dropped her umbrella and Feargal bent to retrieve it for her. Rose appreciated his courtesy and would have told him so, except it made her feel fossilised. There'd been a time when she wouldn't have noticed a man's manners, so long as his eyes crinkled at her. She and Feargal moved along the queue.

"Ella's what my mum calls a proper madam," he said. "But the lady can sing the blues, there's no taking that away from her. She hasn't had the break she deserves. Her manner is a little unfortunate, I suppose."

No need to tell me that, Rose thought, battling to keep her face blank.

"You're not really meant to have the artistic temperament until after you've notched up a few successes," continued Feargal, "but I guess it's frustrating when you have this undeniable talent and you're singing to a couple of hundred boozers on a Saturday night in a Dublin pub. They'd love her on the London scene."

He said London with an 'h' in the first syllable, Rose noticed. Lahn-dan.

By this stage there was only one other person ahead of them in the queue. Feargal grinned. "I'd feel safer escorting you home. Imagine if you were mugged between the taxi and the front door."

"I've no intention of being mugged – I'll ask the driver to wait until I'm indoors."

"I can't have it on my conscience. I should really go as far as Ranelagh with you."

"Then I'd have to invite you in for coffee." Rose kept her tone light, but she was guarded.

"Thanks, I'd love a coffee."

"I haven't invited you."

"I could have sworn there was an invitation in your voice." Feargal was impish under the streetlight.

She looked into his eyes and heard again that sound of silent laughter she associated with them. "Pushy," she chided. But her expression was far from reproachful – you couldn't fault a man for trying, although you could certainly fault him for not trying.

"Where to, love?" The taxi-driver chewed gum and twiddled his radio dial.

"Ranelagh, please." Rose turned back to Feargal. She ought to peck him on the cheek or something. Obviously he'd be disappointed that the evening should end so formally, but she couldn't help it. Kissing was dangerous. It led to more kissing. "Thank you for a lovely evening."

Feargal was reaching inside his jacket pocket and didn't notice her proffered cheek. "I have a present for you, I forgot to give it to you in the pub." He handed her a padded envelope. "It's a couple of days late, but Happy New Year." Then he turned away.

Without even kissing her.

Rose felt cheated as she wrestled with her seatbelt. He might have had the decency to try to kiss her. Just because she was forty didn't mean she was a hag – he had no problem with kissing her the other night. Now he was striding away without so much as an air-kiss. Restlessly she crossed and uncrossed her legs, and as she moved she felt the package on her lap. "Mind if I put on the light?" she asked the driver.

"Bulb's gone," he grunted.

These cabs were becoming increasingly decrepit. Rose hoped his brake-lights, at least, were working.

She tried to guess what was inside the envelope all the way back to her apartment in Clonliffe Square, at a slight remove from Ranelagh village, on the top floor of a redbrick house with a street-lamp that didn't work either in its gravelled forecourt. It was there for effect, a Victorian souvenir with more swirls and flourishes than a Christmas garland. She ran all the way upstairs, playing her usual game of competing with the timer on the landing-light switch, and fumbled at her own front door. The one she didn't have to share with three other flats. Once inside, she dropped her bag and coat in the hallway, incapable of waiting any longer, and ripped open the envelope.

A black and white print of a photograph by Ansel Adams confronted her, encased in a cardboard frame. It showed a stark vault of mountain, at once powerful and vulnerable, its fascia sliced open beneath a full moon. She flipped over the print and read two words on the back: *Half Dome.*

Rose trailed into her bedroom and perched on the bed, the moon playing peek-a-boo through the open curtains. The same moon that would be shining later that night on the Half Dome in Yosemite National Park in California. The same moon that was shining right now on Feargal Whelan. A photograph of a mountain was an unconventional present to give a near-stranger. She liked it.

The mystery of how Feargal had come to kiss her on New Year's Eve, and why she had kissed him back, was becoming less of a mystery to Rose.

Chapter 10

Kitty and Rose met by the ticket machine at Tara Street Station on Sunday evening and caught a northbound Dart train to Howth, a lovingly maintained station at the end of the line.

"I saw the twelve-year-old last night." Rose loosened her scarf and removed her gloves so she'd feel the benefit of both when she reached the seafront.

"You sly dog," Kitty prodded her. "First you meet a young lad on New Year's Eve and have what Sunny insists on calling 'deliciously repetitive, gloriously life-enhancing, casual sex with a stranger'. Then you're off meeting him again, obviously for more of the same. That must be what's putting a spring in your step."

Rose thought about admitting she hadn't indulged in casual sex, gloriously life-enhancing or otherwise, but felt she couldn't. Kitty seemed so pleased with her. "It'll go nowhere," Rose predicted.

"Relationships don't have to go anywhere, they're not trains." Kitty registered pride at the observation and made a mental note to use it in a column.

"Stop practising your columns on me, Kitty." Rose stuffed a leather glove into each pocket of her bouclé coat in case she lost them. "Anyway I probably won't be seeing him again, although he gave me a present."

"Really?" Kitty perked up. You could deduce a lot about a man by the gifts he bought.

"A framed photograph by Ansel Adams of some place called the Half Dome. It's a mountain in America."

Kitty fidgeted with the frogging on her coat and ruminated. She wasn't sure what you could construe from that about Feargal Whelan. Maybe she wasn't the only one who scavenged through Christmas presents for something to pass on.

"You do realise," Rose was crisp, "that being a mistress requires a certain amount of effort."

"In what way?"

"Keeping your legs and underarms shaved. Not draping damp tights about the bathroom in case he drops in. Buying uncomfortable underwear and, brace yourself, wearing it."

"Uncomfortable?"

"Impractical red and black stuff, basques and waspies and keyhole-cut briefs. Suspenders and stockings and baby-doll negligees in" – Rose smacked her lips –"diaphanous material with matching thongs. Your central heating bills will be astronomical or else you'll be permanently riddled with flu."

"Nobody ever cited expensive central heating bills as a reason not to become a mistress," objected Kitty, who felt Rose wasn't treating her strategy as seriously as it deserved.

"You have to be practical," Rose pointed out. "The mistress's job is to offer something a man can't find at home. Nobody wants a bit on the side in fleecy pyjamas, they have wives who wear those. I wonder if he'll ask you to shave your pubic hair into the shape of a heart or have your labia pierced?"

"Look," Kitty was huffy, "I'm not going to be anyone's bit on the side, and I'm certainly not having kinky piercings. I intend to be a mistress in the courtesan sense – this will be an entirely proper arrangement."

Rose whistled derisively.

"As for thong-things," continued Kitty, "sure, I wear those already."

"Suspender belts?"

"Well, no, the knobbly bits hurt my thighs."

"Baby dolls?"

"I find them draughty."

"Waspies and basques?

Kitty frowned. "Do they sell them in Clery's?"

"Not the sort you'll be expected to tog out in. I think you'll have to try Anne Summers or order your battledress from catalogues."

Kitty slanted an uncertain glance at Rose. She was fairly certain her friend was teasing her – but you never knew with Rose McBride. She trained her eyes on a row of telegraph wires, jittery at the undertone of impending sleaze. Why couldn't Rose understand how she intended to be a moral mistress?

Hubert de Paor's studio was in a converted Martello tower on the waterfront, a relic of the days when the British feared a Napoleonic invasion via Ireland and built strategic watch-posts. Little suspecting they'd be reinvented as restaurants, museums and artists' studios. Half the occupants of their carriage seemed destined for the tower, and Kitty and Rose straggled along in the wake of a prosperous couple whose woollen coats flapped in the breeze.

"I haven't really thought this through," Kitty admitted, pulling up her collar to shelter from the wind.

"How do you mean?" Rose sniffed the air.

"I'm not sure how to convey my availability as a mistress, should he catch my fancy and I catch his."

"Just wing it," advised Rose, who was doing something peculiar involving licking her forefinger and holding it up to the breeze, as though she were a ship's captain and needed to know from which direction the wind was blowing.

"That's a fat lot of use," Kitty muttered, but she could hardly blame Rose. She'd supplied the man, she wasn't obliged to provide the lines as well.

They were greeted in a concrete vestibule tacked onto the side of the Martello tower by a stately woman, dramatic silver streaks in her dark hair which folded like butterfly's wings along either side of her face. She radiated beatific peace and goodwill to all men, which may or may not have had something to do with the caftan she was wearing. On anyone else it would have looked borderline risible, but it suited her. She pressed glasses of mulled wine on them, admired Kitty's malachite choker and Rose's cobweb-fine scarf, called them both angel and nudged them in the direction of the throng. All executed with unhurried grace, despite the queue forming behind them.

Inside the tower their immediate impression was of a swarm of bodies, perhaps because there was nowhere for people to go except to funnel into the circular room occupying the entire ground floor.

"Which one is Hubert?" Kitty whispered to Rose.

"Can't see him. I don't recognise anyone here. Let's look at the paintings until we find someone to talk to."

The art, which was displayed on the unplastered walls of the tower, wasn't easy to assess – mainly because the multitude in the room meant it was impossible to step back and study it without jogging an elbow or treading on a toe. What was visible wasn't to Kitty's taste – stylised cartoon figures, all of them clutching glasses of alcohol with sausage-meat fingers. Most of the paintings were set in pub interiors and featured ugly, scrawny women spilling out of their dresses and uglier, scrawnier men staring at what was spilling out of the dresses. There was a joyless quality to each painting which proved more unsettling the longer it was scrutinised.

"I don't see why people need to be drinking in all the paintings," Kitty objected, swallowing most of her mulled wine in a gulp.

Rose narrowed her eyes, considering; she regarded herself as quite the art critic. "He's dabbling in the demi-monde," she interpreted, as though elucidating one of life's primal mysteries.

"I can see that for myself," complained Kitty.

It was hot in the room with so many bodies; Kitty fanned herself with her hand, while Rose had coloured up and was mottled pink.

"Such sly wit," enunciated a woman to their left.

Kitty turned to stare: surely she couldn't be describing one of Hubert de Paor's paintings? She noticed a man with cheeks as blue-veined as his damask waistcoat, his arm across the shoulders of another man with hairy ears – even at a distance. They were almost chin to chin, immersed in conversation.

"That's Hubert," hissed Rose.

"Which one?" Kitty hissed back.

"In the waistcoat."

Oh. Rose hadn't mentioned the broken veins when she'd described him.

"It's not too late to back out," weaselled Rose. "It doesn't have to be Hubert. You could go out on the town, assessing the talent, Dublin's full of married men on the look-out for a fine thing."

Kitty flinched. "I've told you, this isn't about being some bored chancer's one-night stand – I want a proper arrangement. Anyway I can't go hawking my wares around town – you'd be surprised how quickly you wear out your face. Now, introduce me."

"Fair enough, Calypso, on your own head be it."

Kitty found herself propelled towards Hubert de Paor. Up close, the gridwork of veins seemed less prominent. They would always be the most noticeable feature in his face, but they seemed to recede. Instead the eye was drawn to his splendid mane of silken white hair which he wore loose, almost touching his shoulders. Rose suffered herself to be kissed on either cheek, an affectation she didn't encourage, but Kitty was always telling her it was the price she had to pay for hovering around an arty crowd. In his exuberance, Hubert dislodged one of the clips that held her black hair in a loose knot.

"This is my friend, Kitty Kennedy," Rose introduced them, using her fingers to assess the damage to her hairstyle.

"Hubert de Paor," he boomed, squeezing Kitty's hand painfully.

"I know that name, Kitty Kennedy. Have we met before? Remind me, my sweet, my memory plays tricks on me."

She shook her head. "No, I don't believe –"

"I have it." His head snapped back. "You write a column in one of the Sunday newspapers – that's where I know your lovely face from."

Kitty was gratified, she never expected to be recognised from an inch-wide square of grey newsprint. "That's very kind of –"

"I'm not one for reading newspapers," he continued, "but I occasionally glance through the Sundays. They tend to have a more rounded arts section than the dailies."

"Well, that's –"

"I had a very favourable review in the *Tribune* last year – I felt the critic showed some grasp of what I was trying to achieve."

Kitty wondered if it was safe to chance a remark or would she be interrupted again? "It must be very rewarding, as an artist, creating something from nothing, you must –"

"Also very lonely," sighed Hubert. He stared at her lips.

Kitty realised he still had her hand and pulled gently, then a little harder, to extricate it.

Kitty felt Rose's elbow in the small of her back. She'd encountered that ridge of bone often enough to interpret its pressure: this was a nudge that read "Get in like Flynn, Kitty Kennedy".

"Better let the dog see the hare," murmured Rose.

"Sorry?" asked Kitty and Hubert in unison.

"I've just spotted someone I must have a word with." Rose disappeared into the crowd.

Kitty and Hubert locked eyes.

"Are you an art lover?" he asked.

"Adore it," she assured him. "I'm always loitering in the National Gallery, trying to –"

"My work will be hanging there one day." He was magisterial in his confidence.

Kitty stared at the flecks of dandruff on his waistcoat, while he listed all the famous people who'd bought his work. Harrison Ford had built a room onto his house especially for the paintings; Robert Redford had commissioned one after Bill Clinton had recommended it . . . she tuned out, wondering why nobody had warned her that being a mistress could be excruciatingly boring. Plus she hadn't even reached the mistress stage yet, they were still interviewing one another.

An unexpected pause. Kitty looked at Hubert looking at her. He was attracted to her, that much was obvious. Her mouth felt dry. "Is this where you work?" A whole sentence, unimpeded: they were making headway.

"No, on the next floor. There are only two. I have a skylight in the roof and the light floods through. I work off photographs and sketches, then I transfer my impressions to canvas." He smiled, unexpectedly less debauched.

Just then, Flora de Paor arrived with more mulled wine on a tray. "Why don't I take care of your young friend here" – she lingered over the word young – "while you do some meeting and greeting, Hubie."

He ran a finger delicately over an eyebrow, smoothing it. "Must I, Flora? You're so much more adept at social niceties than I am."

"Hubie," she pulled affectionately at his waistcoat, brushing off the dandruff, "I'm not the person they want to see – you're the famous artist in the family."

He lifted two glasses of mulled wine from the tray, scalded himself on one, bowed towards Kitty and trudged off.

Flora de Paor regarded Kitty across her tray, a resigned light in her eyes. "He's such a baby, my husband, you mustn't listen to a single word he says."

"He didn't really say anything." Kitty twined a strand of hair around her index finger, guilt and defensiveness bleeding into one another.

Flora's mouth twitched. "Such a piquant face you have, my dear.

I often wish I'd known how pretty I was when I was a girl. But then we never do, do we?" She moved off.

Kitty hesitated in the void left by Flora's departure. A prickle on the back of her neck caused her to whip about at a ninety-degrees angle, sensing that someone was watching her. She was right. A tall, copper-haired man with eyes a shade lighter than his hair, and skin a few shades paler again was studying Kitty. Someone buffeted against him, but he didn't flinch, keeping his gaze trained on Kitty's face. Sherry-gold eyes boring into hers. He pulsed with a concentrated energy, yet there was something slightly aloof about him – as though he resented being there but was making the best of it. Dressed entirely in black, in an unstructured suit and open-necked shirt, he was standing at ease, weight balanced evenly on both feet and his hands folded loosely in front.

Kitty expected him to lower his glance when she caught him scrutinising her so flagrantly, but he continued to appraise her with no hint of either embarrassment or apology. Kitty tilted her chin. Whoever the stranger was, he had no right to stare at her. It felt invasive. Almost as though he read her thoughts, a lopsided smile flickered across the man's countenance, immediately nullifying that detached air of his. Before she could help herself, Kitty responded to the smile. The stranger interpreted it as an invitation and started towards her, until a woman's command halted him in his tracks.

"Joe darling, I need you here."

Kitty's head swivelled in unison with Joe's in the direction of the voice. It came from a honey-tanned woman, with caramel streaks in her hair, talking to Hubert. The glitter of diamonds in her earlobes and on her fingers was visible across the room. Joe paused, as though tempted to ignore her, but the voice rang out again, more imperious than before.

"Joe darling!"

His shoulders shrugged their regret towards Kitty before he was swallowed up by the mass of bodies.

Rose reappeared. "Hubert's mad about you, isn't he? I knew you'd be right up his street. The last fling he had was with a petite blonde."

Kitty knitted her forehead, searching through the crowd for the copper-haired stranger. He had his profile to her, intent on Hubert's gesticulating explanation about a painting. "Who's that man, Rose, the one in black?"

Rose craned her neck. "No idea. So are you on for an affair with Hubert?"

Kitty saw Flora rescue a couple of empty glasses before they were toppled. "Did his wife know about his last relationship?"

"Certainly she did. Hubert's as discreet as a burst balloon."

Kitty was appalled; somehow she hadn't anticipated causing pain to a wife – especially not one as dignified and gracious as Flora de Paor. She'd assumed the mistress arrangement could be organised so that the wife was impervious. But Flora had tuned into Hubert and herself already and there hadn't been so much as an assignation mooted.

"Why on earth does she put up with it?" Kitty flushed with indignation on Flora's behalf.

"She must love him." A trace of envy crossed Rose's face as she dandled her glass through interlocking fingers. "It can't be for the money because she's wealthy in her own right – she inherited a huge farm in Kildare. In fact, without her financial support I doubt if Hubert would be as well-known as he is – she believes in him, always has. Right back when he was selling sketches of Celtic crosses to the tourists in Merrion Square."

Kitty – who'd already felt undersized alongside Flora de Paor – dwindled, as though she'd consumed the *drink me* bottle in *Alice In Wonderland*. "Maybe Hubert de Paor isn't the man for me," she muttered. "He seems to come with quite a lot of baggage."

"All men have baggage." Rose appeared inexorable, standing there with her wilfully badly dyed black hair; surely she wasn't going to force Kitty to have an affair with Hubert simply because she'd gone to the trouble of introducing them? "In fact," continued

Rose, "it's the ones without any obvious baggage you have to watch out for – chances are they've just checked it into a locker somewhere to confuse you." A smile lurked in her hazel-blue eyes.

Kitty was silenced. The ignominy of having her own column from several months ago quoted back at her was enough to silence anyone. Granted, she'd written that drivel about baggage; granted, she'd congratulated herself on a clever turn of phrase at the time; granted, her stalker had emailed her to tell her he had no baggage whatsoever and was therefore her alpha male. But she needed another glass of mulled wine if she was to take any more of this. Except she couldn't bring herself to approach Flora de Paor with her tray.

Suddenly Kitty understood Rose's tactics. "You knew," she taxed her friend.

Rose folded her arms. "Knew what?"

"That I'd meet his wife and not want to go through with it."

"Maybe."

"You did, admit it."

The smile expanded from Rose's eyes to the rest of her face. "Of course I knew. You're not mistress material, Kitty Kennedy, you're not selfish enough. Marianne O'Leary is mistress material, not you. Have you ever gone out with a man you weren't attracted to, specifically because he had a private plane?"

Kitty shook her head.

"Or a penthouse with a jacuzzi and a view of Leinster House?"

Kitty shook her head again.

"Have you ever dumped a man because he took you for pub grub instead of to a ritzy restaurant?"

Of course she hadn't.

"Or because he bought lager when you wanted Dom Perignon?"

Kitty pursed her lips and waited.

"Well, then, I have news for you, Kitty Kennedy. You have a heart. Or at least a conscience."

"I could work at being mistress material," wailed Kitty, her life-plan disintegrating in front of her.

"Trust me, you don't want to try. Now let's get out of here."

Kitty scanned the room one last time, hoping to make eye-contact with the Joe-darling stranger. He seemed to have disappeared. But as they winnowed through bodies towards the exit, Hubert materialised and bowed over Rose's hand and then Kitty's with exaggerated chivalry.

"Parting is such sweet sorrow – That I shall say goodnight till it be morrow," he chanted, and while Rose was distracted he slid something into the palm of Kitty's hand.

On instinct, she slipped it into a pocket before Rose noticed. A movement to the left brushed against the periphery of her vision. Kitty swivelled her head to find the copper-haired man digesting the scene, a faint frown beneath straight, dark-brown eyebrows. She tried to convey disassociation with her eyes – from Hubert de Paor in general and clandestine note-passing in particular – but his face froze and he turned his back on her.

Kitty trailed along beside Rose, feeling belittled. Which was ridiculous because Joe-darling was nothing to her and she was unlikely ever to lay eyes on him again. There was something familiar about him, all the same. She'd definitely seen him before, but she couldn't recall where. It distracted her all the way back to Pearse Station, where Rose hopped off the Dart to catch a bus to her apartment in Ranelagh. It was only then that Kitty dared put her hand in her pocket and withdraw a postcard showing one of Hubert's seedy demi-monde paintings. She flipped it over and saw he'd written a mobile phone number beside the words: *"Let's have one other gaudy night."*

Kitty cringed. Just because he'd memorised tracts of Shakespeare didn't lessen his inherent tackiness. There was no power on earth that could persuade her to call Hubert de Paor. Besides, the man with the challenging eyes had made her feel – she wrinkled her nose at the memory – tainted when he'd turned away from her. It had stung. It continued to sting.

Chapter 11

Sunny was feeling despondent. Mr Hollywood had turned up to the drinks party at the Four Seasons Hotel for all of six minutes, glad handed a few people, and retired from the fray before she'd realised there'd no chance to catch his attention, let alone monopolise it. Disappointed, she'd crashed a dress dinner at the Berkeley Court and had slept with a dentist from Lusk. He'd booked into the hotel overnight and there'd been a mini-bar in his room. She hadn't seen any reason to go home to her own bed while there were miniature Cointreaus and Kahluas to empty. Sunny didn't mind that foreplay hadn't been his forté, but she felt positively cheated that he'd broken her top-secret code of transposing the last two digits on her mobile phone number. Sunny always did this when she felt obliged to supply her number to men she never intended to see again. Now he kept ringing to arrange a date. Where was the point in wilfully giving men a wrong number if they deciphered it and harassed you anyhow?

She trailed downstairs to find her mother ironing. Perhaps she took in ironing from neighbours to earn pin money – one household of three adults couldn't generate so much laundry. Sunny checked the ironing-board and recognised a skirt; another theory bites the dust.

She filled a plastic jug and transferred water to the coffee percolator, noticing how her mother bent over the board, straining her back. Once, Dad had bought her an ironing-board with a seat attached, thinking to ease her backache, but Noreen-dear had refused to use it. She'd claimed she needed to stand to manipulate the iron properly – height lent her arm the pressure to eliminate creases. Sunny didn't know if this was a watertight scientific theory – and by God, she never intended to test it – but her mother believed it. The smart new ironing-board had been relocated to an Oxfam shop. Meanwhile, Sunny's mother continued to use her old board, loathe to buy it so much as a new cover for fear the symmetry between the two of them might be eroded.

"Will I make you a pot of tea while the coffee is perking?" Sunny's conscience was pricked by the thought of those strained back muscles.

"Sure I may as well take a cup in my hand. Call down to Denis in case he'll risk a cup, while you're about it."

Sunny decided to spare her father the character assassination that would follow his refusal. "Let's leave him in peace, it's cosy just the pair of us. Have you read the paper yet – what's Kitty hammering on about in this week's column?"

"Date rape." Noreen-dear deposited the words cautiously into her wholesome kitchen. "It sounds a desperate handling altogether. It was never heard tell of in my day."

"It was never spoken of in your day – that doesn't mean it never happened," Sunny corrected her, reaching for the teapot. Wouldn't it be great to be so rich, she thought, fishing out a pair of soggy teabags, that you could throw away teapots without dealing with loose leaves and other detritus. When she was a star she was going to enjoy her millions. Conspicuous consumption, I'm ready for you – I know you're ready for me.

"Don't forget to scald the pot." Her mother switched off the iron and sat at the kitchen table, fingering a scrapbook. Glue and scissors rested on top of it.

Sunny laid the teapot and a mug in front of her and flicked open the scrapbook. All of Kitty's columns were cut out and filed inside in chronological order.

"You must be Kitty's biggest fan – you should tell her sometime," remarked Sunny.

"And give the girl notions about herself?" scoffed her mother. "Besides, she knows how proud her father and I are of her – of both of you."

Sunny lowered her eyelids over blue eyes that were more bloodshot than was desirable if she had close-ups to prepare for. Chance would be a fine thing.

"I haven't done anything to make you proud – I'm barely scraping together a living."

"It's only a matter of time, Sunny. Anyway, aren't you living your dream?"

Sometimes it felt more aligned to a nightmare. Sunny never had any money, there was no job security and she competed with all her friends for every part they went after. She toyed with a mental vision of herself as a vet, say, or the manager of a health-food store. No, they didn't convince. Then she tried out an image of herself in a bronze sequinned gown with above-the-elbow gloves at an awards ceremony. Yes, that worked. "If you had your life over again, what would you do with it, Noreen-dear?"

"Go and live in Edinburgh." Her mother's response was decisive.

Sunny was dumbfounded. Noreen-dear had never expressed any interest in visiting Edinburgh, let alone living there. She was so amazed, she even called her "Mum". "Why, Mum? Doesn't Bray suit you?"

"It suits me well enough." Her mother's gaze travelled the circumference of her kitchen. "But I had the offer of a job as a nanny in Scotland nearly forty years ago and I've often wondered about the path my life would have taken if I'd gone."

"What stopped you?" Sunny thought she was au fait with

everything there was to know about her mother, but this was news to her.

"Denis. The job offer came through the day after he proposed. So I decided I'd honour my promise to your father instead of traipsing off to another country. I sometimes think if the job had materialised a day earlier he might never have asked me to marry him, and who knows how things could have turned out?" Her mother's mouth curved into a cryptic smile that imagined endless possibilities.

That's it, thought Sunny, she had to make the break from home. If even Noreen-dear had been willing to move to Edinburgh nearly four decades ago, there was no excuse for her to linger in Bray. She was never going to set the acting world alight from Number 16, Hunter Crescent. The Hollywood casting agent was her ticket out of Ireland. She wasn't going to give up on him so easily – she'd engineer a meeting, should she have to take a job as a chambermaid at his hotel to gain access.

Sunny carried her mug across to the sink, her mind buzzing with permutations. He'd be arranging auditions, that was one way, but half the country would be at those. Every stage school, every amateur dramatic society, every hopeful in Ireland would be hovering around him.

"How did you get on at the party last night? I didn't hear you come in," her mother's voice intervened. "Did any photographers take your picture in that lovely frock I ironed for you?" Before Sunny could answer, church bells started pealing, and her mother changed tack. "They'll be for one o'clock Mass. I'd better peel the potatoes. Your father doesn't like it if his Sunday lunch isn't on the table by two."

Sunny suppressed a smile; Denis Kennedy never seemed to notice what he ate, let alone the time he sat down to eat it. "The party was all right. I can't manage lunch at two, it's too early. Put something by for me on a plate. Oh, and I've made a decision, I'm leaving home."

Her mother, who was bent towards the vegetable rack, looked over her shoulder at Sunny, her expression deliberately neutral. Don't try and talk her out of it, the girl is headstrong, warned her brain. Noreen preferred having her daughter at home because it gave her someone to fuss over – her husband was difficult to pamper, indifferent to what he ate or wore and indeed to most classes of comfort. The house could be like a morgue and he'd never think to flick on the central heating, and if there was no cake in the tin he'd spread jam on a slice of bread without a word of complaint. All he cared about was buttoning on his overalls and going down to the basement to potter. It was his private fiefdom, for his wife had arthritic knees and couldn't easily follow him down. As for Sunny, she had no interest in subterranean dens. Life was for living in full public view as far as she was concerned – up on a platform with floodlights trained on her. "Have you been looking at flats again?" An involuntary frown chilled her mother's expression.

"No, when I say I'm leaving home I mean leaving Dublin, and Ireland too. I've got to go where the winners are, Noreen-dear – it's Hollywood or bust."

With that Sunny bounced upstairs, calculating how to meet Clarke T Maloney. If only her name was Maloney too, instead of Kennedy, she could claim a spurious kinship. Pretend they were second cousins once removed. Perhaps Kitty might have some bright ideas: Sunny unplugged her mobile from the charger, deleted another message from last night's dentist and rang Kitty's number, but it was engaged. She sent a text message instead instructing her sister to call, then contemplated a nap, but the caffeine from two mugs of coffee was rampaging through her system. So she lay on the duvet, indulging in some free-floating fretting.

* * *

An astonishing development intervened. For the first time, Sunny's agent phoned her on a Sunday. Normally Malachy Curran kept strict office hours – Sunny didn't have his home telephone number and he wasn't listed in the directory – and when she heard his voice on the line she assumed someone must have died. Malachy Curran had a sonorous, melancholy voice which permanently hinted at incurable disease and inescapable disappointment. "Sunniva," he dirged, "forgive this intrusion on your weekend."

"No worries, Malachy."

"I have some exciting news. I've just had a phone call from Mr Maloney's people. It seems he wants to meet some of the city's acting fraternity and was desolated" – he cleared his throat for emphasis – "desolated to find himself indisposed at the reception last night. A dubious seafood platter appears to be the culprit. However, I've been asked to round up a select group for dinner at the Unicorn tonight. Naturally, I thought of you at once – this could be a wonderful opportunity. I know it's short notice, but I recommend cancelling any clashing engagements and presenting yourself at the Unicorn at eight."

"Malachy, I'd cancel my granny's funeral for this. I'll be there."

"Excellent. Now, Sunniva, if I may make so bold, wear something elegant. There's only so much flesh a man needs to see on a first encounter."

Sunny rolled her eyes, but held her tongue. Malachy Curran would prefer all his actresses to attend their auditions as Grace Kelly clones, complete with pillbox hats and white gloves. He was a dapper man himself, who cycled about Dublin in a boiler suit to protect his bespoke suits from dust and puddles. Hearsay had it he also wore plastic bags tied with elastic bands on his feet to keep his shoes gleaming. Nobody had yet caught him wearing plastic bags – but his acting clientele clung to the rumour.

Sunny indulged in a cloud-floating reverie involving Mr Hollywood choosing her as his protégée, and her star eclipsing Pearl Roberge's by the time *The Quiet Man* was released. Then she realised the clock was ticking and ransacked her wardrobe.

* * *

It was Monday morning and a persistent shrilling was intruding on Kitty's sleep. She flailed at the alarm-clock until, realising that it wasn't going off, she concluded she must be hallucinating. She lay back, but the noise continued: it was her front doorbell. She opened one eye. It prickled so she shut it, but the buzzing sounded again more insistently. She prised up both eyes and squinted at the clock. Six a.m. on a Monday morning was no time for visitors. However the small square box in her hallway wouldn't call off its tumult. Bleary, she hauled herself out of bed and barked "yes" in the direction of the front door.

"Let me in, it's Sunny."

Kitty unlatched it, reversed into the living-room and sank onto the sofa, exhausted from so much effort.

Sunny swept in, effervescent. Her hair was slicked back with gel and she was wearing a black and silver spaghetti-strapped dress that was ankle-length at the back and knee-length at the front, teamed with Kitty's gossamer wrap. It looked better on her than it did on Kitty. Most of her clothes did, she'd already noticed. A fraction sourly.

"I'm on my way to Hollywood, Kitty-cat," Sunny sang. "I've been up all night, drinking daquiris and communing on an intensely personal level with Clarke T Maloney. He's gifted beyond compare. He says my face has character and the movie industry is tired of bland beauties with all the lines airbrushed from their faces. I'm a real woman, according to Clarke, and he's going to introduce the world to me." She hauled Kitty to her feet and waltzed her about the living-room. Sunny danced, Kitty sagged. "He's wonderful, I could have spread butter on him and eaten him on a slice of toast. My big break has just come knocking on the door and I'm throwing it wide open. I'm going to leave my foot and hand-prints in the cement outside Grauman's Chinese Theatre. I'm going to shop on Rodeo Drive. I'm going to have designers queuing to lend me their clothes. Sunny Kennedy's name will be up in neon lights as high as a house!"

She tripped and catapulted onto the sofa, where she exuded

bliss so beatific that Kitty hadn't the heart to prick it. It occurred to her that where drinking and that all-purpose night magic were in symbiosis, there was room for misunderstanding. Not that she underrated Sunny's acting abilities, but it seemed too good to be true that a casting director would take one look at her sister and pronounce her ripe for stardom. Especially as, by Hollywood standards, at twenty-nine she was overripe. "Congratulations, Sunny," she said. "I'll make coffee, I'm out of champagne."

Sunny nodded, compassionate. Inadequate housekeeping, but she'd overlook it. "Anyway I'm only going to drink pink fizz from now on."

Kitty hitched up the sleeves of her raucous-patterned heliotrope and gold dressing-gown and pushed through the saloon swing-doors to the kitchen. "Looks like rain, Sarge," she mumbled. Not loud enough for Sunny to hear; she didn't want to rain on her parade.

The clumping grains of the previous day's coffee still inside the percolator churned her stomach, as always. Kitty stepped on the pedal-bin and emptied the cone, glancing out of the window in the direction of Bumpermac's. Light shone from the supermarket as shelf-stackers set to work. She swung through the saloon doors again, the steady drip of percolating coffee in her ears, and regarded her sister. Sunny was humming to herself, still with that sublime grin that would crack her face apart if she stretched it any further. The central heating had only just switched itself on so it was still cool. Kitty threw her a hooded sweatshirt and Sunny tugged it over her party dress.

Kitty waited until each had a mug warming their hands before interrogating Sunny. "What exactly has Clarke Maloney –"

"Clarke T Maloney."

"Clarke T Maloney promised you?"

"That I'll be using valet parking at the post office for the rest of my life." Sunny was ecstatic.

Kitty blinked. This didn't sound much of an ambition realised. "Is that it or have I missed something?"

Sunny snuggled into Kitty's sweatshirt, tunnelling her hands into the front pocket. "Only those in the know get it. Beverley Hills post office is probably the only one in the world with valet parking. That's because all the stars live there. So it's Clarke's way of saying I'm going to end up with them as neighbours. On one street alone you have Eddie Murphy next door to Robert de Niro next door to Joe Pesci, with Brad Pitt and Jennifer Aniston on the corner. How neat is that?"

"Neat?" Kitty examined the word as she would an alien object trespassing in a bowl of soup.

Sunny blushed. "I mean fascinating. Clarke called it neat."

"What has he offered you?" Kitty tossed the query over one shoulder as she went back to the kitchen for a coffee top-up. She had a mental picture of her sister waiting on tables in Los Angeles to make ends meet, while Clarke kept her dangling for roles. There was no way a man called Clarke T Maloney could be trustworthy. People who used initials were inherently suspect. At least while she lived in Dublin the family could keep an eye on her – but in the City of Angels there were too many of the fallen variety.

"I'm booked for a reading for a small part in *The Quiet Man* remake. It's not much more than a walk-on part, just one line, but he's going to ask the script editors to flesh it out. He says we have to tread warily because Pearl Roberge is notorious for not wanting attractive women anywhere near her film sets – she's at the apex of insecurity in a profession riddled with doubt." Sunny's bluebird eyes fastened on Kitty's and a faltering quality surfaced in them. "You look worried, Kitty – aren't you happy for me?"

Kitty swept away her litter of neuroses. "Thilled, babe. You jet off to LA and twinkle like the star you are. I'll visit at least once a year and make you wangle me a pass for a film lot, embarrassing the actors by ogling them. You have to promise me we'll hit the tourist trail. I've always wanted to drive into the Hollywood Hills and see the sign. I read somewhere that when it's being painted, the workmen all wear white so that no-one can spot them in the distance."

Sunny relaxed. "Great plan, Kitty-cat. I'll have to wear sunglasses and a baseball cap while I'm showing you around, because I'll be such a celeb that otherwise I'll be mobbed by autograph-hunters."

Kitty stuffed a cushion in her face.

"Mmmf mmf cigarette mmf mmf," came Sunny's muffled voice from behind it.

"What was that?"

"Any chance of a cigarette indoors? It's freezing outside."

"No way. The last time I caved in to your blandishments the house reeked for days."

"Tyrant. People have been smoking since the Mayans latched onto nicotine fifteen hundred years ago. It'll take more than taxes, bans and sisters to stop us."

"I'm not stopping you, I just don't want to secondary inhale alongside you. Stop making me feel like a puritan, Sunny."

"Well, you stop making me feel like a pariah."

They had French bread with raspberry jam for breakfast and then Sunny borrowed jeans and trainers so she could go home to Bray on the Dart without looking like someone who'd been up all night. She was still floating on a nebula of expectation and showed no evidence of twenty-two hours without sleep.

"Wait till Noreen-dear hears." Sunny checked her watch and giggled. "She'll have left for Mass by the time I'm home. Bet you she claims this is all entirely due to the candles she's been lighting for my intentions."

Noreen-dear was a daily communicant – indeed, Kitty and Sunny sometimes worried that she showed Cathaholic tendencies. Denis Kennedy, by comparison, had spent a lifetime attempting to convince himself he believed in God. He tried not to let his wife know of his doubts, realising they would puzzle, then aggravate and ultimately terrify her.

Sunny hugged Kitty, enamoured with the world, and headed for the Dart station. As she checked the indicator board for the next southbound train to Bray, she had a last-minute change of heart and switched platforms. Instead she caught a northbound Dart to the city centre and deviated towards Grafton Street. Sometimes a girl just wanted to mingle with the crowd.

Kitty paced the floor when Sunny left, trying to convince herself that the foreboding threatening to erupt through her chest had no basis in fact. She was simply being hyper-protective of her younger sister. She stepped into the shower, dressed and left for work. She'd fit in a stroll by the Grand Canal close by her office, before allowing the day to make a start on her. Normally she didn't work on a Monday – the *Trumpet's* trade-off to staff for Saturday duties – but the interview with former Miss Ireland Puffin O'Mara had been rescheduled for that day and she needed to call by the office to check the library cuttings on her. All she could remember was that Puffin had a footballer boyfriend.

* * *

Kitty's feet led her away from the traffic towards a limpid stretch of water, where she peered among clumps of reeds for the swans. Last winter a new young cob had flown in from nearby Herbert Park, after his female partner had strayed outside and had been crushed beneath the wheels of a lorry. Everyone said swans mated for life, but the newcomer had driven off the older male, annexing both his territory and his companion. The female had seemed to settle down readily with the interloper.

"Why wouldn't she?" Rose had demanded, when Kitty had raised it with her.

Kitty preferred the received wisdom about swans mating for a lifetime and was disturbed by rents in the silken skein of the myth.

"It's disloyal," Kitty had complained.

"It's survival of the fittest, nature being red of tooth and claw the way it's intended," Rose had retorted. "Anyway, maybe she fancied a change."

"You're one to talk," Kitty had retorted. "How many years were you going out with Damien Crowe? Eight?"

"Exactly," Rose had shot back. "And where did all that loyalty leave me? Abandoned."

There was no sign of the swans. When you saw one the other wasn't far behind; they seemed joined by an underwater leash. But the swans obviously had more sense than to brave the elements in the hopes of some soggy bread. Kitty nibbled a corner of the wedge she'd brought in a plastic wrapper hoping to tempt them close, and a seed lodged between her teeth. It was tomato and fennel bread, the swans' favourite – the Grand Canal pair were gourmets. Kitty broke off another hunk and chewed. They didn't know and cared less that their lack of constancy had disappointed her.

She ambled a little further along the bank before sitting on a bench with a brass plate screwed onto its support. *In memory of my brother Edward Spillane, from his sister Alice Spillane*, it read. She always sat on this bench and the inscription always needled. Why had the dead man's sister felt it necessary to add her own name to the tribute? It detracted from the gesture. Like putting money in the St Vincent de Paul box only when you were certain of an audience. She should have paid the engravers to carve: *In memory of my brother Edward Spillane, who fed the swans and watched the world go by*. Anything but that vanity exercise – it was Alice Spillane's own epitaph dressed up as his.

She threw the remainder of the bread on the ground for the pigeons, shaking her head over her annoyance with a woman dead more than fifty years. Perhaps Alice Spillane had taken pleasure in her epitaph. Pleasure was, after all, a safer guide than either right or duty – someone wiser than her had worked that out centuries previously. If Sunny had an aptitude for seizing life by the throat, maybe she did too – perhaps she had an untapped talent for it. Only one way to find out.

Kitty left the tranquillity of the canal, heading for her office close to Charlotte Dock, where she decided to make a phone call. Hubert de Paor was about to win a second chance.

* * *

The phone call came as Kitty was preparing for bed. "Has something happened to Dad?" Kitty was unintentionally curt with her mother, who never rang so late.

"He's fine, still in the basement, pretending we don't always have our supper around now. There'd be trouble if it wasn't on the table at half ten, the same as always, though," predicted her mother.

Kitty ambushed a smile. "He's probably busy with his jigsaws, Mum."

"What am I supposed to do, rattling around here on my own while he futters with his jigsaws?" Her mother's sense of injury swelled. "If there was a sleeping bag in the basement he wouldn't bother coming upstairs to bed at all."

Kitty supposed life could be occasionally lonely for her mother – she went to Mass every morning, which occupied no more than an hour and a quarter of her time, including the walk to and from church and dallying to discuss the weather with other regulars in her circle. Small wonder she attempted to fill the vacuum with laundry. "I expect Sunny was out at work all day," she said, sympathetic to her mother's situation.

"No, she phoned in sick – she'll lose that job, mark my words – and took to her bed until late afternoon. Then she spent a couple of hours in the bathroom titivating herself, and sailed off about seven without so much as telling me she wouldn't be in for supper. Seeing that American fellow again, if I'm not mistaken."

"That's good, isn't it?" Kitty didn't want to discuss Sunny's American. She needed a full nine hours sleep that night so the area around her eyes wouldn't be gridlocked by pouches and crow's feet and all sorts of trespassers, before tomorrow's second-chance date with Hubert de Paor.

"It's not good, it's worrying," disputed her mother. "He'll whisk her off to America and we'll never see her again."

"Mum, it takes longer to drive from one end of the country to the other than it does to fly to the States. She's an actor, that's where the industry is based. If she's serious about breaking into films then she shouldn't be hanging around Bray making the odd commercial and selling timeshares in Spanish apartments to earn pocket money."

"She's happy here," wailed her mother. "At least she was until I told her about my silly ambition to be a nanny in Edinburgh. Now, nothing will do her but she has to take up with an American and talk about moving to Hollywood. It's all my fault."

"Sunny's always wanted to go and live there – you have nothing to do with it, Mum."

"Of course I do," her mother snorted. "Your sister's in a state of panic. She's going to charge off to America where she'll wind up a drug-addict, or a –" she searched for the word and pounced on it, triumphantly gloomy – "hooker, just because her thirtieth birthday is coming in August and she's afraid of failure."

Now Kitty was exasperated. "Mum, you're indulging in amateur psychology. Sunny has to live her own life."

"Don't you spout your ologies at me, young lady. You and your sister are each as bad as the other, both terrified under all that bravado." Noreen Kennedy was in full rant mode, unstoppable as a riot. "Sunny's scared to death of failure so she's determined to ruin her life by proving she's not. Rushing off to Los Angeles, where she'll be browbeaten into having plastic surgery and traduced into appearing in filthy films."

Kitty was left mute by her mother's imaginative gyrations, which whisked Sunny from a date with a casting director to surgical enhancement and a starring role in a pornographic movie. But Noreen-dear was still frothing.

"As for you, Kitty Kennedy, you're just as scared as your sister – petrified of making a commitment. That's why you rush around making commitments with all and sundry. You're allowed to refuse marriage proposals, you know. I turned down three before accepting your father."

Anger crunched through Kitty. "Who are you to pass judgement, Mum? It strikes me that a woman whose husband skulks in the basement all day and half the night has little room to manoeuvre when it comes to doling out criticism."

"I'm sure I don't know what you mean, Kitty."

"Are you, Mum? Are you sure?"

An austere pause intervened, as each woman considered whether another word from either would open up fissures in their relationship that could never be healed.

"I know what Dad does all day in the basement," Sunny's voice chirped over the extension, punctuating the tension.

"Sunny, I didn't hear you come in." Her mother's relief at the intrusion flooded her voice.

Kitty's racing pulse slowed as she, too, welcomed the encroachment on a conversation that needed to be scuttled.

"Obviously he has a still down there and is gulping down the home-brewed hooch behind Noreen-dear's back," said Sunny. "That's why he's never hungry – alcohol is a known appetite suppressant."

"I'm sure I would never stop your father taking a drink." Their mother was sulky. She regarded herself as a supremely tolerant woman, but with regard to alcohol she was inflexible. She was one of those teetotal Catholics who transferred their Pioneer Total Abstinence pin to every coat so there'd be no doubting their credentials.

"Before I move to Beverly Hills I'm going to organise a raid on his den, searching for evidence of moonshine activities," Sunny cackled. "He can't spend all day fixing broken handles on jugs and dismantling plugs to check fuses."

"And playing with jigsaws," contributed Noreen.

"And playing with jigsaws," agreed Sunny.

This sounded like ganging up on Denis Kennedy and Kitty's hackles did what they were accustomed to in such circumstances. "Leave Dad's basement alone, Sunny," she warned. "The poor man has enough on his hands, surrounded by a monstrous regiment of petticoats, without his basement being invaded. Anyway, why are you eavesdropping on my conversation?"

"Noreen-dear," remarked Sunny, "I have such a thirst on me I'd auction off the family silver for a cup of tea."

"I'll put the kettle on." Their mother replaced the receiver.

Sunny waited until she heard the click, before addressing her sister in an ingratiating tone. "Listen, Kitty, I'd like you to meet Mr Hollywood – he's mad into his ancestral roots and wants to be introduced to a real Irish family. Obviously I can't have him coming here to Bray to meet the deranged parents so I thought I might palm him off with you. What do you say? How about Saturday night? He'll treat us to a slap-up meal at Roly's or wherever you like."

"I don't know, Sunny, I'm always tired by Saturday night. I work on Saturdays."

"Please, Kitty-cat. He's seen your column in the newspaper and specifically asked after you. Come on, you're my claim to fame, you can't let me down. Think of all those Rodeo Drive shopping trips we can have."

Kitty vacillated. "I'm see what I can do."

* * *

Rest proved elusive for Kitty that night, cruciform-splayed under the duvet. She rolled onto her front, then tried her back again, watching the streetlight leach under the curtains. Exhausted but not sleepy, she adjusted her position to curl around a pillow. Then she counted sheep, monitoring each breath as the tally mounted to a hundred. That was supposed to be a foolproof way of nodding off. Some chance.

She decided to count her chickens instead of phantom sheep. This time next year she'd be limber enough to do as many positions in yoga as the instructor. That reminded her – she hadn't been to yoga in a month. Her mind flitted across the participants in her Sun Salute sessions – they were all women, female preserves don't come any more double X chromosome-jammed. In two years she'd encountered only one person of the male persuasion, a surveyor called

Shane who'd been shameless in admitting he'd taken up yoga lessons specifically to meet women. He hadn't been able to believe how well his wheeze was paying off: not only was he the sole man, which guaranteed him an excess of attention, he could check out potential girlfriends in their leotards without looking like a lecher.

"This won't do." Kitty retrieved a pillow from the floor, cantankerous at finding herself awake. Shane had dressed all in black, just like her copper-haired stranger. She found herself remembering the way the man – Joe, wasn't it? – had smiled at her, an asymmetrical grin that started as a gentle inclination at the left-hand side of his mouth and widened into a curve towards the right. She groaned and pulled the pillow over her face to blot out his image because it was pointless dwelling on an anonymous stranger. Especially since she suspected she was fixating on him as a way of distracting herself from the one topic she was disinclined to address.

Her mother had been absolutely right. For a much-married woman – granted, she wasn't in the Elizabeth Taylor bracket, but she'd married twice as many times as virtually everyone else she knew – Kitty had a deep-seated problem.

She couldn't handle commitment.

Chapter 12

Linus Bell was in an expansive mood. He swept through the office, panicking the staff by beaming at them indiscriminately, including people whose names he had never troubled to learn. The *Sunday Trumpet* had just won Newspaper of the Year – it was to be announced the following day, but he'd been tipped off in advance by a former colleague on the judging panel – and he was exultant. Oh yes, glitz and revelatory quotes paid off. This would show those other stuffed-shirt editors, who always recoiled slightly from him when they met. He was the one with his finger on the pulse, not those pro-Government lackeys who tried to dimiss the *Trumpet* as some girlie-gore-GAA comic. To celebrate, he intended to take his wife out to lunch and his girlfriend to dinner. The deputy editor would probably expect a meal as well, but he'd palm him off with a drink in the Treasury and leave some cash to cover a round for the staff. Linus Bell was convinced it was only a matter of time before he'd be offered the freedom of Dundalk, an honour he craved, not least because he was convinced Andrea Corr would form an intrinsic part of the ceremony.

He paused by his secretary's desk, instructing her to make lunch and dinner reservations. Nothing could dull the glaze on his universe. Until he caught sight of Marianne O'Leary dabbing cream into the smudged circles under her eyes. He frowned. The reason he'd bought her dinner at Patrick Guilbaud's the other night – charging it to the company – was because he wanted Marianne to find his wife a job. Linus's wife, Audrey Bell, was terminally bored and begrudged how much time he spent in the office since he was incapable of delegating. Her resentment translated into nagging which he was keen to assuage.

Even without a girlfriend on the side, Audrey Bell would have scarcely seen Linus, who believed home was somewhere you went to collect clean shirts. On balance, he'd prefer it if his wife didn't work: he liked knowing she was in situ, keeping milk in the fridge, feeding the tropical fish and arguing with the gardener. He didn't particularly mind that she spent his salary with a profligacy that was legendary in the more select boutiques about town, or that she complained to friends of neglect. But he was concerned that she might be bored enough to leave him, which meant his girlfriend might imagine he'd marry her, which meant rocking the status quo. Only Linus Bell was allowed to do that.

His solution was to find his wife a job, fending off her boredom. She'd always been interested in fashion, which was where Marianne O'Leary had a role to play.

Linus called to her. "Marianne – in my office."

The fashion editor snapped shut her pocket vanity mirror and smoothed her pencil skirt over emaciated hips, mentally rehearsing her excuses as to why she hadn't taken the editor's unsubtle hint and found his wife a job in one of the posh frock shops regularly featured in the newspaper. He seemed to think it was simply a matter of clicking his fingers. That might operate on Planet *Sunday Trumpet*, but in the real world it didn't signify.

Linus was sprawled behind his enormous mahogany desk. "Approach the bench." He said it for fun, but most of his staff felt they were in front of a hanging judge when they had those disconcerting one-on-one meetings with him. He smiled, a prodigal arc of teeth that occupied so much space his nose seemed to vanish altogether, then pressed ahead with a full-frontal attack. "So have you made any progress with that minor matter we discussed, Marianne?"

"I've asked around, but nobody seems to be hiring at the moment, Linus." She twisted a signet ring on her finger. "This is a busy time for retailers. All the shops can think about is the January sales – they haven't time to consider staffing."

Linus's grin faltered, but he stretched his muscles until it was bullied back into place. "Surely they need experienced staff now more than ever," he insisted.

"I understood your wife had no retail experience."

"She's a shopaholic. That should be experience enough for anyone, *capisce?*" he snapped, before remembering to ease back into a smile.

Marianne fantasised about responding that just because someone read a newspaper didn't mean they could edit it, but arguing with Linus Bell was an exercise in futility. He'd commanded her to find his wife a job and find her a job she must. It didn't matter a jot to him that Marianne's contract specified "fashion editor" and not "finder of jobs for the Exalted One's wife".

Linus flashed that alarm-inducing row of teeth again. "You'd be doing me a favour, Marianne." But he couldn't maintain his persuasive manner, it required too much effort. "Don't let the fact that your contract is due for renewal have any influence on your efforts," he added.

"I'll do another ring-around." She retreated to her desk, where she phoned for a taxi to take her to Brown Thomas. Marianne urgently needed a therapeutic wander through the handbags department – she'd call it research if anyone queried her.

Rose was tapping away at her computer as Marianne scurried past. An email had arrived from Feargal inviting her to see Bette Davies in *All About Eve* at the Irish Film Centre, part of its Screen

Divas series. She'd sloped off to a cubicle in the Ladies' to think of reasons for refusing but hadn't been able to devise any.

You're using him, warned her conscience.

He wants to be used, argued her ego.

It's unfair to date someone if you aren't sincere about him, counselled her conscience.

It's only manners to see him and say thank you for the Adams photograph, weaselled her ego.

You're doing this to get over Father Damien, cautioned her conscience.

It was the clinching argument – but it backfired.

Rose decided it was healthy to listen to the ego occasionally, it had an unjustified reputation for self-absorption. Actually, no, it deserved its reputation for self-absorption, but sometimes a girl had to think of herself. If Feargal could help her forget Father Damien she'd gladly spend time with him. This was one New Year's resolution she was determined to keep.

So now Rose was emailing Feargal, agreeing to meet him that night. She peeked over her shoulder, protective in case Kitty should spy her. She preferred to keep it to herself for now. Kitty, however, was not remotely interested in Rose's emails. Preoccupied with tonight's date with Hubert, she had a nasty feeling she was biting off more than she could chew. Her suspicions had been aroused the previous day, phoning Hubert de Paor from the deserted office.

"Kitty, how delightful, I hadn't expected to hear from you so soon." Hubert's voice had oozed down the phone, sticky in its consistency.

"I was afraid if I didn't ring you at once I'd lose courage and never do it," she'd lied.

It wasn't really a lie, just a slight distortion of the truth.

He'd been thrilled. "Do I intimidate you, Kitty? Does my reputation deter you?"

His reputation? God oh God oh God, was he known as a ladies' man the length and breadth of the country? "To be honest –"

"I know my paintings attract a lot of attention, and the cult of the personality means I'm becoming rather well known as a result, but underneath it all I'm still the same man I always was, before the fuss and fascination started up around me. An artist, searching for inspiration, hoping his work can reveal some of the eternal truths."

Kitty had silenced a groan; maybe she wasn't mistress material after all. She cast about for something to say. "Yes, your work is –"

Hubert had saved her from finishing the sentence, a mercy because she'd had no idea what she'd intended to tell him about his work.

"So, Kitty, will you meet me for dinner? Tomorrow night, perhaps? I know a cosy little place off the beaten track, close to Baggot Street. It's in St Mary's Road, the Expresso Bar."

She knew the Expresso Bar. So did half the staff of the *Strumpet*, which meant it wasn't nearly as discreet as he implied. Her brain waves had raced: she could insist on lunch, which gave her deniability if closer acquaintance revealed she couldn't stomach a relationship with him. Or she could accede to dinner but bail out if he carried on behaving like Toad of Toad Hall. "The Expresso Bar is perfect, I'll –"

"See you at eight, my sweet."

Kitty pursed her lips now, thinking about the date a matter of hours away. "New Year's Resolutions are dragon's lair territory," she muttered.

"Talking to yourself, Kitty," remarked Des Redmond, on his way to the fax machine. "That's dangerous."

"Arguing with myself," she sighed. "That's more dangerous again."

* * *

Commitment-phobes made ideal mistresses, right? Commitment-phobes didn't want to get married so husbands were safe with them. Relatively speaking. Kitty studied her reflection in the mirror of the Ladies' at work, convinced she'd rimmed her eyes with too much smoky eye-shadow. She checked her watch and bolted the door on one of the cubicles while she changed out of her lemon work suit with its cinched-in waist and into the fuchsia-pink velvet dress and boots she'd worn on New Year's Day.

On the floor below, Rose was acting out a similar rigmarole. However, she'd had the foresight to do it where half the editorial floor wouldn't be trooping in and out scudding knowing glances in her direction, because women can always detect other women on date-alert. She combed her black hair, arranging it over her shoulders, and checked her appearance in the mirror. Rose flinched – she wasn't so keen on mirrors as she'd once been, they had a tendency to show her a woman with blurred cheekbones and a certain crêpe-paper quality at the throat. She overlooked the eyes gleaming with inherent wit and the translucent skin. Still, she rallied herself, she was going to have fun. She might even allow herself a few more of those kisses which had transfixed her at the New Year's Eve party.

In the corridor she pressed the lift button; the doors opened to show Kitty, dressed for a night out.

"Where are you going?" they chorused.

"Out with an old schoolfriend," mumbled Rose.

"Seeing a contact," replied Kitty.

Neither was certain if they believed the other, but – conscious that people living in glass houses shouldn't aim their stilettos at them – they pretended to accept the explanation.

* * *

Leaving the cinema, Feargal suggested a drink.

"We could go back into the film centre," suggested Rose. "I like the bar in there."

"We could." He held the shoulder of her coat while she groped for the armhole. "Or we could walk over to my flat, it's only a few minutes away. Cross the Ha'penny Bridge and you're virtually there. I have a bottle of wine chilling in the fridge, waiting for you to say the word."

His flat. Rose paused.

"'Yes.' That's the word," he prompted. "'Yes, Feargal.'"

Bodies bumped against them, snatches of conversation drifting in their wake: "such a brittle actress . . . commentary on ambition . . . loved the *gúnas*."

"We could have the bottle open by now instead of standing here in the cold," he cajoled, chipping at her reticence.

Against her will Rose smiled.

It's only a glass of wine, she lied to herself.

I'm curious to see what his apartment is like. Another lie.

I want to prolong the sensation of his eyes caressing my face. That much was true.

"I feel the thwart melting," he murmured.

"What thwart?"

"The thwart inside you. All that grudging unwillingness to ease up on yourself and have fun without weighing the consequences. It's thwart."

"Oh." Rose managed a laugh, just a facsimile of one, for appearances. But she felt criticised. Exposed, too. She hadn't realised the demarcations of her life were so transparent.

It was in this state of vulnerability that she passed a newsagent's en route to his apartment and stealthily scrutinised their appearance in the plate glass, in case they looked ridiculous together.

"You're checking up on us," he challenged.

"Maybe."

"We make a handsome couple." He placed a companionable arm on her shoulder.

Rose glanced into the glass again and felt they looked inappropriate. Thirteen years' worth of inappropriate.

Feargal seemed to have a gift for reading her mind – or maybe it was her eyes. "The only couples who look daft are the ones who aren't enjoying one another's company." He pulled up her raincoat collar against a gust of wind and let his arm fall away.

It was then that she noticed a magazine on a rack near the

window, Princess Diana in her bridal gown on the cover. She was smiling as though the future had neither power nor desire to hurt her. As though the happily ever after each little girl is nurtured to expect for princesses was a foregone conclusion. Mostly Rose was able to keep her sceptical tank brimming over, but she was incapable of looking at these early photographs of Diana without a strap tightening around her chest.

"I spent that summer in Liverpool, staying with my aunt and doing a temporary job behind the haberdashery counter in John Lewis," she reminisced. "I had the day off work – it was a scorcher – because the wedding day was declared a national holiday. There were street parties everywhere. We watched television for hours and went to a barbecue near Lime Street station that evening. Everyone was sunburnt and all the women whispered about how crumpled Diana's dress had become from the heat. As though it might blight the fairytale to utter it aloud." They crossed onto Liffey Street, past the statue of the Hags With The Bags that tourists were always photographing. Rose's voice sounded unnaturally animated, startling the night air. "It was the first time I tasted champagne – it scratched my throat. What did you do?"

"I probably had fish fingers and was in bed by seven, Rose – I was only four years old in 1981," he smiled. Such an endearing smile.

Rose's innards deflated.

The temptation to hail a cab headed in the opposite direction assailed her. But even as she slowed, a downpour that had given no advance warning drenched them. It was as though the heavens were discharging their objections. "You're not alone on this one," Rose felt like shrieking. She knew he was younger than her, but she hadn't processed the extent of the gap. Thinking of him drinking Ribena while she tasted her first glass of champagne was alarming to the point of SOS signals.

"Quick, we'll have to make a run for it." Feargal grabbed her by the arm, mistaking the deluge as the cause of her inertia. "I can see my flat from here – look, it's the one above the optician's."

"Taxi . . . work tomorrow . . . later than I realised," Rose waffled, but he laughed and hustled her along, sheltering her with his body.

"It's not worth calling a taxi, it's only a few yards away. Besides, when did you ever see a cab in the rain?"

She allowed herself to be led into a hallway floored in orange linoleum with a bicycle blocking most of the space, up a flight of narrow stairs that creaked accusation at each step. However, the apartment when they reached it had light and space in its favour. Not to mention wine. She felt she not only needed but deserved a glass or two. No, just one, then she had to leave. Rose dripped on Feargal's seagrass carpet while he hunted out towels, then he peeled off her sodden coat and dabbed at a raindrop on her nose, all the while chuckling as though the evening had taken a turn for the better.

She looked about and had an impression of an expensive stereo system and a cheap sofa. It was untidy, but not so messy you'd consider calling in the Health and Safety Executive, and he seemed to like plants because there were at least three dotted around the room. Feargal interrupted Rose's mental scouting of her surroundings to position her near a heater that blew hot air onto her chilled skin. As she warmed up, Rose harried her powers of mental arithmetic: however she computed it, there was no disguising the fact that she was forty and Feargal was twenty-seven. It shouldn't have come as a shock, she'd known it from the outset. It was just that the image of Feargal tucked up in bed by seven on Princess Diana's wedding day, while she'd kissed a Greek waiter with the night off, was too graphic by far.

Rose had a tendency to forget she was forty. A youthful forty, she amended, vanity intruding on her self-flagellation. In truth, Rose wasn't fooling herself, for her long hair lent her a girlish quality and she was slim enough to fence off the years. She looked at Feargal, chafing floppy dark hair with a towel. He was a young man, there was no denying it. She had felt stirrings of self-consciousness earlier, observing people glance in their direction at the cinema. Imagining their . . . what? Censure, possibly. Surprise, certainly. Curiosity, undoubtedly. Such an age-gap when the years were carried in the gullies of the woman's face and the billowing softness of her body was still unusual enough to prompt others to pause and speculate. Well, age towed some compensations in its hoary wake. It taught her that she could drink a glass of wine in a man's home, engage in civilised conversation and then leave. No harm done, nobody compromised.

Yet there was something about finding herself with damp hair sticking to her face, leaking shoes separated from her feet and leading an independent existence on a mat by the front door, streaky tights drying on a radiator, that nibbled at her defences. She no longer felt mature and in control of the situation. Plus her toe-nail polish was chipped. That always put her on the defensive.

She considered Feargal. Rose sensed she should be circumspect about this boy-man whose candid face told her he had no defences. None against Rose or the pinch she would have to administer. The nip of rejection. It was for his own sake – there was no future for them.

"You look stunning," Feargal said.

"I look like a drowned rat."

"A stunning drowned rat," he corrected her.

She bathed in the admiration for a few moments, feeling it lap around her limbs and trickle across her sternly corseted self-esteem, for it had been some time since she had put herself in the path of flattery and Father Damien had never been one for the spontaneous compliment. Father Damien. Rose sighed: there he was, butting in again. "It would never work," she said. Feargal looked at her. "It could never work," she repeated, sensing the need for emphasis, unsettled by the way his eyes stroked hers.

"Would you like a glass of wine?" he asked.

Idiot that she was, she thought later, she accepted. Wine always made her want to embrace people, even the wine waiter, for it germinated a flowering of affection for strangers. With wine in her veins she adored the world; if she'd any sense she'd stick to whiskey, a solitary drink which helped her to hold it at arm's length.

"Blush." Feargal reached a wineglass to her.

"I'm not," Rose denied, shading to carmine on cue.

He laughed in that gentle way he had. "I meant the wine. It's rosé, but I've always liked the way Americans call it blush."

She hunched forward on his sofa, dandling the glass as though it was inconsequential instead of a lifebuoy, relieved he hadn't sat beside her. Disappointed he hadn't sat beside her. Acutely conscious of his proximity even though he wasn't sitting beside her.

He lounged opposite and smiled, so that she glimpsed the gap between his two front teeth. A seam of darkness between the sherbet pink and white. She sipped wine, holding it in her mouth before swallowing, and felt the years between them dissolve as his gaze softened into hers. "What do you like best about being a radio presenter?" She spoke to intercept the kisses that seemed, at that moment, inevitable.

"The adrenaline high. You're on air, juggling balls in all directions, interviewing someone about joyriding while your producer is bellowing into your ear-piece about a change to the running order because an item has fallen through, at the same time as you're squinting to decipher a text message from a listener flashing on your monitor. You're trying to wrap up and move on to the next guest while remembering you have an ad break in a couple of minutes, meantime wondering if you can slip out to the loo during the news headlines."

"Sounds frenetic." Rose swallowed some wine.

"It is." He pulled his chair close to her seat.

"Is there anything you dislike about the job?" she asked hastily.

He hesitated. "The cold," he admitted. "Ever noticed how radio presenters tend to have a taste for truly awful sweaters? Great woolly mammoths? It's partly because the studios are always freezing, something to do with keeping the microphones at the right temperature for sound quality. The fellow who's on before me wears silk polo necks inside his shirt." He shuddered. "You can't really go for jackets instead of jumpers – I tried that once and kept knocking the buttons against the microphone. It drove the sound engineer demented. But enough about work." Feargal stretched out a hand, touching the whorled tips of his fingers to hers.

"There's no way around the age-gap," Rose gasped, just before he captured her glass en route to her mouth and kissed her. She caught her breath after the kiss and tried again. "I'm too old for you. Trust me on this."

Feargal leaned his head to one side, admiring the curve of her throat. "It's only a handful of years." He extended his palm, fingers splayed, in a scattering motion.

She didn't contradict him, allowing the minor deception to curl roots into the shallow earth of their relationship.

"I'll finish this glass of wine and go home," Rose said.

"It's Californian wine," Feargal responded, listening to her tone and not the words. "We should go there, Rose, you'd love San Francisco. We could drive out to some of the vineyards in the Napa Valley and feel the same sun on our faces that ripens the grapes." In his exuberance a tongue of wine splashed from his glass onto his wrist and he lapped at the drops clinging to the lightly tanned skin. "But really," he continued, "I want to bring you to Yosemite. That's a national park. It's primal: you find yourself cupped in a valley surrounded by towering granite mountains and sequoia forests."

"Yosemite." Her hand flew to her mouth. "That's where my Ansel Adams photograph is from. Thank you again, I love it."

He nodded. "The Half Dome is ice-coated and unforgettable. The native Americans believe the mountain was once a woman." Feargal's eyes reassured Rose, easing her back into the sofa. Dissolving her tension. "They say a brave from another tribe came down from the mountains to her valley to marry her and bring back the woman to his people. The further they climbed, the more homesick she grew and she began crying. They argued and the gods grew angry at such disharmony amid beauty. They turned him into a mountain called the North Dome and the woman became the Half Dome. It has fissures the length of its face and the native Americans say they're the tracks of her tears." Beguiled, Rose, relaxed into Chinese cushions, squashing miniature pagodas. "We could sleep in a log cabin at the foot of the Half Dome and trek around her base during the day." Feargal's laughter rumbled, subterranean. "It strikes me it might be discourteous to climb her. On a clear night, when the stars are so close you imagine you could stretch out a hand to touch them, we'll go to a waterfall in search of moonbows. I promise you, Rose, you'll be enchanted by them – money back guarantee. They're like nothing I've ever seen before, a fusion of moonlight and spray from the falls. Rainbows with the colour seeped out, but something ethereal taking its place."

For a few kaleidoscopic moments, Rose felt she was being offered the chance to close her eyes and take a leap of faith, leaving the consequences to care for themselves. Consequences were well able to do that, given a free hand. She imagined a woman in buckskins and plaits, tears coursing down her cheeks, solidifying to granite and merging into the landscape. It was a mountain in whose shadow she'd like to stand, craning her neck to glimpse the peak.

"Will I check the Internet for flights? My computer's in the corner." Feargal rose and the spell was fragmented into shards; she was too sensible to play at being carefree.

"You sound as though it's a foregone conclusion we'll be going there," Rose sniffed. "Don't I have a say?"

"Of course." He was grave, enthusiasm stilled. "You have the final say. It doesn't happen without you."

His spontaneity unnerved her. "Feargal, you haven't been listening." Agitated, her tone was more harsh than she realised.

He sat back, piqued. "You haven't been saying anything worth listening to."

Then he finished his wine and she emptied her glass, and when he offered to refill it she acquiesced. Halfway down the second glass he kissed her again. No noses in eyes, no spectator versus participant, no Father Damien trespassing. He kissed her until she forgot about the age difference and it was a struggle to remember to call a cab.

That was how it started with them. With Rose in denial about the degree to which he moved her and Feargal refusing to consider that years lived by one and not by another could have a bearing.

"Would you refuse to see me if I were black?" he confronted her, while she buckled on her shoes and the taxi-driver waited.

"No, that would be racist."

"If I were Muslim?"

"No, that would be sectarian."

"If I were in a wheelchair?"

"That would be an advantage – you'd be easier to run away from."

Feargal laughed, but his eyebrows bristled with determination. "How can you allow age to be a barrier?" he contended.

She had no answer to give him and his dark eyes glowed, scenting a dissolution of reservations.

"I don't want this," Rose thought, retreating downstairs towards the decrepit Toyota Corolla waiting to take her home. Its clock was ticking and so was hers. Not her biological clock, that belonged to the Father Damien phase, but the knowledge that she'd never be twenty-seven again. Life had left her fearful; she no longer wanted to take chances. Her trepidation angered her yet she knew it had her best interests at heart. It could spare her pain.

Feargal mouthed against the window of the car just before it pulled away. "The Half Dome is waiting for us."

Rose waved, pretending not to hear, but already she felt a stab of disloyalty. He was growing on her.

Like a carbuncle. Or a luscious pre-Raphaelite curve. She couldn't tell which.

Chapter 13

Hubert de Paor flicked a few flecks of dandruff off the shoulders of his butter-yellow corduroy jacket with leather elbow patches, as he waited for Kitty in the Expresso Bar. He'd already ordered a bottle of red wine, a meaty Cabernet Sauvignon, and was about to start on his second glass when she arrived. Hubert was always early for everything, undermining preconceptions about absentminded artistic types. He realised he had a shambling walk and preferred not to be seen making his way into the restaurant. Hubert was at his best seated, where his shapely head and leonine sweep of hair lent him a patrician air. He had made up his mind to sleep with Kitty, if she'd allow it, and his guess was that she would. Maybe not tonight, but soon. He wasn't planning on offering her a position anywhere near as permanent as a mistress, although Hubert believed it was appropriate for great artists to keep them. He imagined keeping a mistress meant, literally, paying her bills and he couldn't do that without Flora discovering it. His wife handled all their financial affairs. Convenient though this was for a man who never liked to be troubled by household economies, it left little room to manoeuvre for renting love nests. He hadn't tuned into Kitty's version of the mistress arrangement, predicated on sharing dwindling resources – i.e. men – rather than using it as a pension scheme. But he'd certainly have approved of it.

Hubert dipped his nose into the glass, inhaling the grapes. Blackcurrant undertones, if he wasn't mistaken. He fancied the idea of a young mistress who could stir his blood in a way Flora no longer managed. She'd spread considerably more than was desirable about the hips and had thickened in the waistline since the boys' arrival. Even her breasts, once his favourite feature, had been flattened by feeding the children and had never regained their globular lushness. His wife was loyal, competent, caring . . . but she no longer excited him. He still made love to her, but arousal was taking longer to achieve. There had even been one or two – it chilled him to dwell on them – abortive attempts.

Lately, Hubert had found himself appraising girls: waitresses who arched their swan necks as they stooped to refill his coffee; two students who shared a house near his studio and whose bare navels were festooned with a tantalising collection of tattoos and jewels; the New Zealand-born barmaid in his local pub, whose underarm hair he had glimpsed as she had reached for a glass. Girls, in all their dewy freshness, were reducing him to the state of a callow youth. He had trouble regulating his breathing in their indifferent presence.

He scrolled through the restaurants he patronised, selecting several with basement dining-rooms ideal for meeting a woman who wasn't his wife. The Expresso Bar was far enough off the beaten track to be safe, but even so, he shouldn't take chances, for an artist of his stature could easily wind up in the gossip columns. The next time he and Kitty met, he must ensure he wasn't exposed to discovery with a window seat. Delighted by his foresight, Hubert smiled at the waitress as she squeezed past with menus to reach the table next to him. Her mouth made a dutiful bow back, but her eyes were unresponsive. She thinks I'm an age-encrusted fogey, he realised, conscious that his chest had migrated to his stomach. Hubert swallowed another mouthful of Cabernet Sauvignon and brightened as Kitty pushed through the glass entrance door. She was every iota as pretty as he remembered. Feminine, too; he appreciated that in a woman. That pink velvet suited her blonde hair. Best of all, she was young enough to stimulate him – but old enough to be acclimatised to the ways of the world.

Hubert de Paor stood with extravagant gallantry and bent his mouth over her hand. *"O! she doth teach the torches to burn bright,"* he boomed.

Kitty regarded him warily. Flattery was welcome, although she wished he'd compliment her a little more discreetly – the diners at adjoining tables were tittering. She was uncertain how to respond. "Hi" seemed pedestrian by comparison with his profligate eloquence. She settled for formality and said, "Good evening, Hubert, I hope I haven't kept –"

"Not at all, I was early, called in to see an old friend in Raglan Road and then sauntered across to the restaurant."

Kitty exhaled slowly and decided to leave most of the talking to him – that way she wouldn't be galled if he continued to chime in every time she opened her mouth.

Hubert was unfazed by her reserve, accustomed to dominating conversations. He was keen on overt displays of manners, fussing about pulling out her chair, loudly enquiring whether she was sitting in a draught and offering to hang up her coat. However he didn't establish whether she preferred red wine or white, assuming she'd drink what he had already chosen.

Initially the meal was strained, as Hubert concentrated on impressing Kitty and she concentrated on being impressed, a state of affairs tailored to create tension. Their table was soon littered with the name of every famous person who had ever drawn breath in the vicinity of one of his paintings.

Hubert ordered quails' eggs as a starter and scrutinised his plate with a portentous expression. *"Ex ovo omnia,"* he announced. "Ovid."

Pretentious, thought Kitty, slathering butter on a slice of onion bread.

"That's Latin for –"

"The answer to the great imponderable: which comes first, the chicken or the egg?" Kitty managed an interruption of her own.

Hubert frowned, lifted his fork, detected a minuscule blemish and called to the waitress for clean cutlery.

Kitty was imperturbable as she watched the hollandaise sauce on her asparagus spears cool; he needn't think he could have everything his own way, just because one of his paintings was hanging in the President's husband's brother's study.

By the time they'd reached their main course of cod in parmesan batter for her and lamb couscous for him, Hubert had progressed to sharing his opinions on New World versus French wines, left-wing propaganda dressed up as newspaper editorials and his top ten city-breaks. Meanwhile Kitty nursed her first glass of Cabernet Sauvignon and noticed his teeth were wine-stained.

Unexpectedly, just as she was wondering whether she should go to the Ladies' and forget to return, he stopped being opinionated. Instead he became knowledgeable, speaking fluently about art, leaning across the table to touch Kitty's forearm as he emphasised the single-point linear perspective rule, the vanishing point in any painting. No longer listening with detachment, she was enthralled. Perhaps he'd been holding forth in such a didactic fashion earlier because he was nervous. With that her reserve thawed and she smiled. Encouraged, he smiled back. She really was quite a fetching little creature, he thought – shame her breasts were under-developed.

Just then the door was thrown open, with a flourish owing more to the grand entrance and less to consideration for diners who might be averse to icy air. The newcomer looked as though she were born and reared in Seville; she even had a rose behind one ear and wore a ruffled skirt that smacked of the senorita under her astrakhan coat.

"It's Ella Jackson!" Hubert stood and bowed from the waist towards Ella. "You look enchanting, my dear – *a rose by any other name would smell as sweet.*"

Ella touched the bloom in her hair, charmed, while Kitty wondered if Hubert intended to regurgitate every Shakespearean line in his repertoire that evening. Shouldn't he be comparing the waitress to a summer's day? "Come and join us, Ella," he invited. He turned to Kitty. "Ella is a wonderful singer, she has a rare gift." His eyes slewed back to Ella's. "Were you performing locally tonight?"

"I was at Jury's Hotel, singing at a sixtieth birthday party – that's why I'm finished so early." Ella Jackson radiated moodiness. "They booked me from seven until nine-thirty so they could squeeze in a few foxtrots and still be home for eleven." She lit up a cigarette.

"This is a non-smoking establishment." Kitty had contracted an instant dislike for Ella Jackson, from the sleek coils of her inky hair to the spotted ribbons on her strapped flamenco shoes.

Ella's eyes under their pelmet of false lashes considered Kitty. "I'll just finish this one cigarette, then."

Kitty arched an eyebrow, but decided to let it pass.

Hubert missed their exchange, preoccupied with ordering another bottle of wine. He returned his attention to the women. "Ella is my wife's half-sister. Flora was disappointed you didn't come to my exhibition, Ella – we don't see enough of you."

She shrugged, insouciant. "I was working. Anyway, the wine you serve at your exhibitions gives me indigestion."

He lifted her free hand and tapped the wrist, the motion causing the ash trembling on the cigarette end in her other hand to fall onto the tablecloth. Kitty itched to relocate it to the floor.

"Bold girl," chided Hubert. "I know you're only trying to be provocative."

Ella inhaled on her cigarette, angles appearing all over her face.

"No smoking," interjected the waitress, uncorking the wine.

Ella glared at her, but flipped her cigarette into the mouth of the empty bottle.

Hubert kept hold of her hand, his square-tipped thumb stroking the wrist almost absentmindedly. Ella looked at the thumb and said nothing, although a flicker of inner amusement tiptoed across her face. "You must sit for me, my dear," said Hubert. "I'd love to capture the imperious vault of those eyebrows and the slender arch of your instep."

His voice altered when he addressed Ella, Kitty noticed, its timbre undulating around her.

"You know I couldn't sit still long enough, Hubert." Ella was impatient. "The last time I tried it was a disaster."

"I'll risk it if you will," he cajoled her, but she pulled away her hand.

Kitty felt like a voyeur. However she was grateful to Ella and the effect she had on Hubert, because it had emphasised what she'd known in her heart already. There was no way Kitty was prepared to become Hubert de Paor's mistress: even if she could disregard the broken veins in his cheeks, she couldn't blank out the sheer carnal lechery of the man. No chance of being a moral mistress with him; it would be a tawdry liaison from start to finish. She cleared her throat, preparing to make her excuses and flee.

Kitty was in the process of pulling back her chair when the door opened again. Framed in the doorway stood a copper-haired man in his thirties, wearing a dinner suit and a white shirt that was conspicuous against his lightly-tanned skin. An energy charge enveloped him. Yet Kitty had the sense that the stranger's gaze relaxed and mellowed when it fixed on her. She returned his stare. It was one she knew well.

"You took your time, Joe," complained Ella.

He placed the long, narrow leather case he was holding on the floor alongside their table and grinned to encompass the trio. Kitty noticed he had a dimple in his chin which blurred when he smiled.

"Anyone mind if I sit down?" He pulled up a chair alongside Kitty and spun it around, so that his elbows leaned on the back as he straddled it.

155

Kitty had never seen anyone with such crystal concentration in their eyes. They latched onto her again, golden-brown and intense. She felt a compulsion to lean forward and touch him – just to lay her hand on his arm for a second, or brush some lint from a lapel. Anything to make physical contact. Kitty sat on her hands before they moved towards him of their own accord.

"I'm Joe French." He unhooked his bow tie and jammed it in a pocket. "I work as a bouncer."

There was something familiar about that name – the face, too; she'd thought it before, at Hubert's exhibition. "I'm Kitty Kennedy. You don't look like a bouncer."

"Too pretty, eh?" His crooked grin blurred the dimple again. "You're right, I'm not a bouncer. I toot my horn occasionally in Ella's backing band."

"My trumpet player. He's not reliable." Ella was languid. "He's always jetting off somewhere, regardless of whether we have a gig or not. Music is only a hobby to Joe – he saves his true ardour for making money."

Joe French laughed. "Making money isn't what it's about, Ella, that's only a by-product. Cutting the deal is the sweet part." He winked at Kitty, implicating her in his world.

"I was in school with your sister, Sunny," Ella addressed Kitty.

"Were you friends?" Kitty didn't remember Sunny mentioning Ella.

"Not really. We didn't have any classes in common, we were only in the same year. She went into acting, didn't she?"

Hubert decided the group had lasted too long without the benefit of his conversational skills and didn't wait for Kitty's reply. "Joe, it was good of you to take time to come to my exhibition on Sunday. I know how frenzied your schedule is."

Joe was non-committal. "It was Emma's idea. She has a couple of your paintings."

"Yes, I spoke to your delectable wife at the exhibition. She has a commendable interest in art."

"Paid for by Joe's commendable talent for commerce," drawled Ella.

His wife. His delectable wife, Emma. The woman in diamonds with the caramel-streaked hair was Joe's wife. Kitty felt a rush of emotion: unadulterated jealousy. It swooped through her body and came to rest in her throat, restricting her breathing. *No, this is excellent,* she reassured herself. *He's a married man, exactly what I want.* But the throttling sensation refused to budge. Her eyes were wary as they travelled across his face. If a married man was exactly what she wanted, why wasn't she happier to discover Joe French was spoken for?

Joe and Hubert were still discussing his work.

"Emma wanted to keep it, she's a fan of your red series, but I sold it to an Egyptian collector who bought it over the Internet, sight unseen," said Joe.

"I hope it fetched a good price." Hubert looked as though he didn't know whether to feel wounded that his painting had been sold instead of retained in Joe French's collection, or flattered it had been bought sight unseen.

"I made a tidy profit. But don't let's mix business and pleasure." Joe returned his attention to Kitty and lowered his voice to a confidential undertone. "Tell me about yourself. None of the mundane stuff about where you work or live. Tell me things nobody else knows about you."

Kitty was charmed.

Hubert monopolised Ella, which left Kitty and Joe free for one of those conversations where the subtext is more riveting than any words spoken. She felt an instantaneous rapport with him. He had that most beguiling of habits; he listened carefully to everything she said, and under his gaze Kitty felt herself grow enthralling. Sunny had told her once that the secret of being found charming was to find others charming first. Joe obviously shared the secret.

"Are you with Hubert?" asked Joe unexpectedly. He turned away his head, speaking in an undertone.

"No."

"I thought you might be."

"Hubert's a friend of a friend. Nothing more. I was on the brink of leaving when you arrived."

"Did you stay because of me?" Joe's voice was still low, so they couldn't be overheard.

Kitty dipped her eyes to the table, wondering how honest she should be. "Yes," she admitted, "I stayed because of you."

It silenced both of them.

Joe recovered first. "There's something I've noticed about you – you're a woman with opinions." Joe was approving.

She rested her chin on her hand, their faces inches apart. "Doesn't everyone have opinions?"

"Not everyone. At least not so quickly. I could say, 'Give me your opinion on Third World debt' and you'd have a quick-fire one. Or Marx Brothers films. Or why it was women who invented windscreen wipers and laser printers. I feel like testing you."

"Go on then." Kitty was tickled by the game.

He pretended to consider. "Marriage," he said. "How do you feel about that?"

This was easy, she'd written a column about it recently. "Marriage. Well now, that's a tricky one. I see it as a control mechanism established by men to safeguard their own interests." Kitty warmed to her theme. "You see, single women threaten them in a way the married version doesn't: single women are independent, self-sufficient, autonomous. Also terrifying. That's why unmarried women are belittled – called spinster, lesbian, and most scornful of all, feminist."

Joe's eyes gleamed. "You don't pull your punches, lady. Do you really believe this?"

"Those are my opinions." She was regal as she lifted her chin. "And if you don't like them, I can change them."

His gaze wavered, uncertain. Kitty snuffled, which gave him permission to chuckle too. It was only a string of opinions, for goodness sake, no more valid than the next person's – people treated them so seriously.

"Don't you believe in falling in love, settling down and living happily ever after, Kitty?" He squinted, trying to read her eyes. He liked their blue-grey colour, which sang out from her face.

"Absolutely, if your name is Snow White or Cinderella." She pushed her fair hair behind her ears. "I used to believe in fairytales. Then I saw sense." Kitty knew she sounded cynical but couldn't help herself.

Joe leaned forward and caught her by both hands, in that single impulsive gesture purging the bitterness that was starting to build between them. Rancour because he was married to someone else and she resented his Emma. Joe, too, for being a husband. Unavailable. Or only available in doled-out slivers.

"It sounds like you've been hurt, Kitty Kennedy."

She was soothed by the feeling of her hands in his. "I suppose I've done my share of hurting back too. You don't walk away from two marriages without taking a few pot-shots."

Joe was checked. A segment of hair at his crown detached itself from the mass and spiked up. He noticed Ella watching them and dropped Kitty's hands.

"That's right." For the first time Kitty relished her status as a much-divorced woman. By Irish standards, anyway. "Two broken marriages by the time I was thirty-three. I'm a walking disaster area when it comes to men." She lolled back, complacent; this was one of those times when it struck her there was something rather louche about her track record. "I had this vision of myself with a husband who adored me, the two of us living a gilded existence in a cottage with a rose garden. So I married a man who worshipped me – and before long it struck me as an inherently unhealthy way to live." She studied her left hand, where one of the fingers still had a wedding-band indentation. "Then I married a man who didn't worship me, which was healthy, but he didn't seem to like me either, which wasn't. That's why, Joe, I'm a doubting Thomas when it comes to the miracle of love and marriage."

"What about the rose garden? Did that come with either of the husbands?" His voice was compassionate – supportive, she fancied.

"The rose bushes rotted. They had to be uprooted."

Ella yawned, interrupting them. "I'm ready for that lift now, Joe." Her jet nails glinted against the wineglass as she drained it.

Hubert stood to pull out her chair. "Promise you'll call Flora soon. She'll scold me for not pinning you down to a definite arrangement."

Ella tossed her head, setting her garnet drop-earrings jangling, neither rejecting nor complying with the request.

Joe bent to lift his trumpet case from the floor with his right hand and reached out his left hand to shake Kitty's. As she grasped the hand she felt the warm smoothness of his wedding ring.

"I hope we meet again," she said, wishing she'd asked for his card when neither Ella nor Hubert was listening. Wishing he'd asked for her telephone number. Wishing Ella hadn't called a halt to their conversation, although without Ella Jackson they might never have met.

He smiled without replying, the grin that turned up one corner of his mouth and lent him a quirky air.

Kitty felt a sense of loss in his absence.

Hubert returned his attention to Kitty. "Ella is much younger than Flora. Flora's mother died and her father remarried and had a second family. Now then, here's a menu, why don't we choose some dessert?"

Preoccupied by Joe French, Kitty set down the laminated card without glancing at it. She had never met anyone with such capacity to suck in every morsel of attention in the vicinity. He was magnetic.

"That French is a bright fellow. Chief executive of Bumpermac's, the supermarket chain – he's worth millions. Or at least his shares are. I believe I'll have the pecan pie."

Of course, that's where she recognised the name from. He was always heading lists of dynamic captains of industry. Nobody knew much about him, however, because he lived quietly and avoided the social columns.

Hubert rattled on. "The Doyle brothers were running their father's business into the ground until Joe French came on board and dragged it by the scruff of the neck into the twenty-first century." Hubert touched the lipstick stain on Ella's glass, transferring a little of the rouge to a finger-tip, where he rubbed at it speculatively, assessing the colour. "He married a prominent horse-trainer's daughter a few years ago. Stunning girl, Emma. They had a baby daughter last year."

Kitty gazed at him, aghast. A baby. That meant he was passionately in love with his wife. She'd been fooling herself to believe there was any rumble of chemistry between herself and Joe French.

"You're taking a long time to decide on a pudding, Kitty." Hubert stroked a hand over his mane of silver hair, smoothing it back. "Too many temptations?"

"Actually, Hubert, there's too little here to tempt me." She scraped her chair legs against the floor as she stood, selected a couple of notes from her purse to cover most of the meal, laid them on the table and walked out. The blood pounded in her ears and her heels punished the floor; she was conscious of Hubert's dumbfounded gape and of the need to bank down a giggle which threatened to quiver from her throat. It was all so impossibly theatrical.

On Baggot Street she hailed a taxi and sank into the seat, expecting to laugh until the tears flowed over at her silliness in imagining she could have become Hubert's mistress. Except, Kitty discovered, she couldn't even smile. Indeed, she was seized by something akin to regret. Sorrow that she hadn't met Joe French when he'd been single – because she knew that she'd just encountered the one man she could spend a lifetime with. Becoming his mistress would be an inadequate substitute. Indeed, it didn't even seem to be an option.

Chapter 14

Sunny inhaled the scent of freshly-baked bread from the Bumpermac's supermarket near Kitty's house as she walked along her sister's street. If she lived here, she'd be forever running into the store's bakery for a loaf – she didn't know how Kitty had the willpower to resist. She let herself into the house, for Sunny went there sometimes during the day when she knew Kitty would be at work. Her sister didn't mind, so long as she never emptied the milk carton without replacing it. Sunny had decided not to return to her telephone sales job. Granted, the money was handy, but soon she'd be high on the hog in California: charge accounts, chauffeur-driven transport, designers lending her clothes. The life she'd been born for was so close that Sunny could almost stretch out her fingers to trace its spun-sugar perfection. She could easily afford a week or two off work. Still, Sunny knew how her parents worried, so it was less complicated to slope off to Kitty's house than explain she didn't need that fatuous job any more. The good times were about to start rolling and Sunny was ready to surf that wave.

She lifted a letter lying on the mat – an electricity bill, post had stopped being interesting around the time email had become commonplace – and threw it on the hall table. Then she flicked on the central heating and went into the kitchen, pouring herself some sparkling water from a bottle of Ballygowan in the fridge. As the radiators crackled into life, she carried the glass into Kitty's spare room. Sunny uncoiled the cable at the back of the computer and stretched it out to the phone-socket in Kitty's bedroom, ready to access the Internet.

While the computer warmed up, Sunny sipped her water and reviewed her plans for the new life that awaited her. Clarke T Maloney would find her other roles, maybe a television series that would become cult viewing. She felt a surge of confidence – the inner voice in optimistic mood – that her acting career was finally about to blossom, but it all hinged on keeping Clarke interested in her. The land of sunshine and sitcoms could turn overcast if she found herself alone.

Her mobile phone beeped with a text message and she pressed her thumb against a couple of buttons. *Dinner 2nite? Catch repaired on LCs.* She checked the number it was sent from, but it meant nothing. What on earth were LCs? Oh no, it was that lab technician with the widow's peak and a pair of leopardskin love-cuffs he'd fiddled with so long, trying to fix the safety mechanism on the lock, that she'd fallen asleep waiting to be titillated. The phone message meant he'd unscrambled her mobile phone code too, just like the dentist. Perhaps she should start giving her pick-ups the number for Bray Garda station.

Sunny erased the message, thinking she really should cut back on her drinking, maybe have a month off to give her liver a fighting chance. Not January, though, it was too long a month – she'd re-consider in February. Then she logged on to the Internet, using a search engine to check out Los Angeles – it was going to be her new home soon, after all, she should familiarise herself with it. Sunny called up a street map and studied the place names – Rodeo Drive, Sunset Boulevard, the Walk of Fame. Hollywood Boulevard ran for miles – no wonder everyone drove there. She giggled as a random memory struck her; an ex-boyfriend had attempted to walk around a small town in Washington State once and a cruising police car had slowed to enquire his business. Pedestrian alert: must be a suspicious character.

Sunny tapped on the keyboard and a map of California appeared; she was surprised by how close Las Vegas was to LA – she could easily cross into Nevada for weekend junkets with Clarke. They could stay in Caesar's Palace, take in a show and play a hand of blackjack. Sunny had never actually played the card game; when she thought of it she was reminded of the liquorice-flavoured blackjack sweets she'd eaten as a child. Never had there been such telltale sweets: her tongue, teeth and a halo of skin around her mouth had been dark grey by the time she'd finished a bag. Clarke could explain the rules of blackjack to her as they sat there attracting all eyes, Clarke in a cream tuxedo and Sunny in an evening gown. Something in satin that rippled when she moved.

She stalled, fingers resting on the mouse-pad. Clarke was a strange sort of name for a man who wasn't a superhero, she reflected. But he was interested in her, she sensed that, although he had a reserve she had yet to breach. Still, he'd promised to find her a role. Naturally that was fantastic, but Sunny instinctively knew their relationship could progress further. Her career would prosper as a result – everyone needed a sponsor, mentor, facilitator, sugar daddy, call him what you like. And it was always a "him".

Sunny yawned, stretched and continued to read up on Los Angeles in a state of ripening contentment, acquiring a mélange of fascinating but superfluous information. The letters in the Hollywood hills were five storeys high and an unknown actress had flung herself off one in 1932. John Wayne was evicted from the Argyle Hotel for riding his horse through the lobby. Tour guides showed tourists the green electricity box outside Johnny Depp's Viper Room club, beside which River Phoenix died, as well as the park where George Michael was arrested for making an indiscreet approach to an undercover cop. What a country – there was no ethical distinction between fame and infamy. Sunny loved the sheer amorality of it.

The print started ghosting in front of her, each line of type with its unfocused twin, as her lack of sleep began to catch up; she pressed her fingers into the base of her taut neck. "Might not do any harm to lie down on top of Kitty's bed for an hour," she mumbled, jaw clicking as another yawn rippled through her. These late nights with Clarke were tiring, especially when he still hadn't tried to take advantage of her. Sunny was very keen to be taken advantage of – in fact, she'd gone to meet him last night positively determined on it. But nothing had happened apart from an excess of soulful staring and a few fumbled moments when parts of their bodies had touched, although she couldn't honestly say they had been engineered by him. Sunny assumed it could only be old-fashioned courtesy holding him back; maybe he had Bible Belt principles despite living on the West Coast. "If he doesn't make a move soon, I'm going to take the initiative," Sunny confided in Kitty's cream lace pillow. She stretched languorously and within seconds was sound asleep, dreaming about driving along Sunset Strip in a bubble-gum-pink Cadillac with the roof down and the palm-trees waving at her as she passed. "You're one of us now," they cooed.

* * *

"Sunny!" exclaimed Kitty.

Sunny opened her eyes and winced. Kitty was standing by the side of the bed and the overhead light was on. She glanced at the alarm-clock on the bedside table – surely it couldn't be after midnight already? If it was, it meant she'd slept for six hours.

"Coffee," she whimpered.

Kitty looked at her for a moment, concern moulding her features into something approaching Noreen-dear's face, then headed for the kitchen. The kettle was boiling when Sunny trailed in, having detoured to the bathroom to splash water on her face and scrub at her teeth with Kitty's toothbrush.

"Instant all right?" asked Kitty.

Sunny nodded, raking her fingers along her hairline, still groggy. "I just lay down for half an hour. I dropped in to use your Internet and suddenly felt tired. Did you know that Cary Grant died six months after moving from Los Angeles to Iowa? They said he missed the smog."

"No, I didn't know." Kitty removed her coat and draped it on over a stool. "Bring your coffee through to the living-room, we'll be more comfortable there."

They sat alongside each other on the sofa, stretching their feet towards the coffee table in identical movements.

"It's fantastic coming home to a warm house. It must be like having a wife," remarked Kitty.

"You could always set the central heating on timer."

"I do. Obviously I don't give it long enough. It's a shame you're going off to Los Angeles to be a star – I could employ you to turn on my central heating and have dinner ready in the evening. Maybe I could even train you to know at a glance whether you should pour me a gin and tonic or make me a pot of tea, depending on the day I've had. Des Redmond, the features editor, claims his wife can do that."

"That's called a housekeeper, not a wife," Sunny corrected her. "I expect I'll have one of those myself when I'm the toast of Hollywood. I suppose I'm still not allowed to smoke in your house?"

"Absolutely not. Even stars have to go out to the backyard if they want to light up." Kitty trailed her fingers along the wine-dark glaze of the pottery mug, twisting her neck to regard her sister. "So you're really going off to make movies, then, Sunny? It's a done deal?"

"Absolutely – Clarke's mad keen on me. Both as an actor and as a woman, if you catch my drift."

Kitty had something she needed to tell Sunny, something she was certain would tarnish her effervescence. She selected her words with care. "I heard some news in the office today, Sunny. It was about a film premiere in Dublin at the end of January."

Sunny tipped her face towards Kitty, cheeks concave as she sucked in her breath.

"It was mentioned to me in passing by the fashion editor, Marianne O'Leary. She's heard a Welsh actor is flying in to do publicity for it." The pain-laced attention in her sister's eyes left her stammering. "I think, maybe, you know who I mean."

"Nick Shooter." Sunny was monotone.

"Yes," acquiesced Kitty, miserable. "I didn't take Marianne's word for it – I put in a call to the film's publicity department and they confirmed it. Marianne's information was right on the money." She eased closer to Sunny, their outstretched legs resting against each other.

"You know," Sunny was conversational, "having sex with someone you love ruins casual sex for you. I mean, you still do it, you'd be stupid not to, but it's never the same. There's always something missing after that. They spoil it for you, because they show you how it could be and then they take it away from you."

"I see." Kitty wondered where this was leading.

"Nick Shooter is the only man I ever loved, and he treated me with disdain. But you know something, Kitty? I still love the bastard. I go to see every film he appears in, I buy them when they're released on video, I freeze-frame his face and stare at it until the video recorder unclicks and moves on." Sunny ground a knuckle into the corner of each eye. "I sleep with any man who bears a passing resemblance to him, hoping to transfer what I feel for Nick, but it never happens. I feel nothing for any of them, and contempt for myself, but it doesn't stop me. I'm hoping with Clarke it can be different."

Kitty was moved. "How long is it," her voice croaked, "since you were last together?"

"One year, ten months, seventeen days. It was a Sunday afternoon and I'd just spotted a rainbow. I was expecting something wonderful to happen and then it did: I saw Nick's face. Except I also saw the faces of his wife and daughters. His face, which always welcomed me into it before, retreated from me. He looked" – Sunny considered – "displeased to see me. Distinctly displeased."

Kitty stood and padded into the kitchen, thinking about Joe French. Remembering how he'd looked when he'd seen her in the restaurant earlier that evening – there had been a spark of recognition when his eyes had rested on hers. A sensation of homecoming. But she mustn't allow herself to be distracted by Joe French; Sunny needed her and it was a rare enough occurrence. Kitty rattled through a cupboard and found what she was searching for, added ice to two glasses and returned. "Got them from Christmas crackers." She brandished two miniatures of Baileys. "Infinitely more useful than sewing kits and tiny screwdrivers. I've been saving them for an emergency." She handed a glass to Sunny, who accepted with a nod, cobalt eyes almost obliterated by the encroaching darkness of her pupils.

Sunny gulped a swallow. "In case of emergency empty into glass. I'd call Nick Shooter an emergency – I'd call him a crisis."

"I've met a man," Kitty ventured, after a time.

"Married?"

Kitty nodded slowly. "He has a baby girl."

"He'll never leave his wife for you, Kitty-cat."

"I don't want him to." Kitty crossed her fingers behind her back.

"Anyone I know?"

"I wouldn't think so. His name is Joe French, he runs a chain of supermarkets."

Momentarily, Sunny was startled. Her path had crossed with Emma French's a couple of times at social events. She looked as though she had life all wrapped up. With shiny paper and a real ribbon bow. But she had a cheating husband. Sunny rattled the ice-cubes in her tumbler; you never knew what lay behind the façade. "I have a theory about adulterous men." She spoke softly, reflective. "They convince themselves that by confessing they'll never leave their wives, they're exonerated from what subsequently happens. It's the Pontius Pilate approach: they've given you fair warning and everything's above board. If you imagine there's more to a relationship after that, you only have yourself to blame and they'll point out – excruciatingly reasonable – that you knew the score, even as they dice your heart and feed it to the waste disposal."

Kitty shivered. Then she cast about for words of comfort for her sister, uncharacteristically showing her vulnerable side. "You can smoke indoors if you like, Sunny," was the best she could manage.

It prompted a half-smile. "Finally, she makes a massive concession, on the one day I'm out of smokes."

Another pause straddled the conversation.

"So what next?" asked Kitty.

"You tell me," Sunny shrugged. "I don't suppose you'll learn from my mistakes since I seem incapable of it."

Kitty frowned, twirling a strand of fair hair around her forefinger. "Brace yourself, Sunny, I feel a big-sister moment approaching. You have two options regarding Nick Shooter. Option one is to ignore the fact he's going to be in town, let bygones be bygones. You don't need to see him if you don't want to – he's an A-list star these days, it's doubtful if you'll bump into him hiking up Bray Head. Option two is to arrange to meet up with him so you can throw a glass of red wine in his face – it looks so much more dramatic than white. It's possibly not the most mature response. Then again, it may be a mental-health essential."

"Which would you do?"

Sunny sounded so plaintive, Kitty slid a finger into hers for their wishbone caress.

"Option one, Sunniva. He's not worth losing another minute's peace of mind over, no man's worth that. Especially not a former lover, who may not mean that much to you when you finally meet him face to face. Maybe you're only in love with the memory of Nick Shooter, not the reality of him."

Sunny's gaze flickered to their fingers, entwined on the sofa. "Maybe." She was doubtful. "Bogeymen are often just shadows on

169

the wall caused by the furniture, isn't that what you used to tell me, Kitty?"

"That's right, Sunny."

She mulled over Kitty's advice. "When did you get to be so grown up, Kitty Kennedy?"

"Just crept up on me, I guess," she smiled. "Now, I'm going to boil you some pasta for a late supper since you're probably starving. It's Penne Puttanesca: the aspirational pasta, for girls whose meals are – sadly – spicier than their love lives."

"Speak for yourself, Kitty-cat." Sunny yawned, recovering already. "A man with the good taste to dry-clean his leopardskin love-cuffs between users invited me to dinner tonight."

Kitty mimed distaste. "Leopardskin love-cuffs, supremely shoddy. I'd only consider men who use Burberry-print ones."

As Sunny listened to Kitty clatter about the kitchen, her mind grappled with the prospect of seeing Nick Shooter again. It was clear he had absolutely no respect for her and had lied throughout their time together, yet if he crooked his finger she'd come running. Knowing he'd discard her again as readily as he had before. Which was still not deterrent enough, thought Sunny, lips puckered as though she'd swallowed something tart, to safeguard her from Nick Shooter if he chose to target her a second time. She needed Clarke T Maloney – he was her best hope. A mentor and a protector.

Nevertheless, something warned her she'd be seeing Nick Shooter again, one way or another. "Looks like rain, Sarge." Sunny bit her lip.

Chapter 15

Rose risked a thrashing from Linus Bell's cat-o'-nine-tails tongue to linger by Kitty's desk. "I've just heard you went on a date with Hubert de Paor and it was a wash-out."

Kitty shrugged to imply he only had himself to blame.

Rose's mouth twitched at the corners, amusement overcoming her disapproval. "Not that I have a morsel of sympathy for him. I'm glad someone had the taste to turn him down. He's overweight, under-talented despite the hype, and married. I don't know what gives him the right to imagine he can pick and choose."

"That'd be the male hormones." Kitty raised dark-ringed eyes to meet Rose's, for she and Sunny had sat up into the wee small hours the previous night.

"Male hormones are extraordinarily accommodating and always imagine they're housed in a body that's at least twice as alluring as the reality." Rose spewed out her earthy laugh. "Anyway, I came across to tell you that Hubert is extremely hurt by the cavalier way you treated him. He left an irate message on my voice mail accusing you of being a tease."

Kitty worried at a staple on a press release. "Nobody warned me how shabby I'd feel trying to become a mistress. I think I should do this with someone whose wife I haven't met and liked. I couldn't stop feeling guilty about Flora de Paor." Emma French was a convenient oversight. Besides, they hadn't been introduced.

Compassion and exasperation battled within Rose. "You didn't really think this through, did you?"

"No." Kitty's neck drooped under the weight of her head.

"You must realise it's irrelevant whether or not you meet the man's wife – she still exists, she can still hurt."

Kitty's entire body sagged. "You're right, Rose."

"So you're going to abandon this daft notion of becoming a mistress, aren't you?"

"I suppose I should. I didn't think about how it would impact on other people's lives, only how it might improve my own. I was being selfish."

Rose scented victory and became unguarded. "Mistresses aren't exotic, Kitty, they're morally bankrupt. Just like the opportunistic men who keep them."

Irene from reception arrived at Kitty's desk. Her mournful face peeked around an etiolated bloom which was milk-white, sheathed in cellophane. "This arrived for you. You seem to have an admirer." The information was delivered in the doom-laden tone of one who viewed admirers as an unnecessary evil.

Kitty accepted the orchid with surprise. A faint whiff of its delicate scent wafted towards her nostrils as she felt for the card. She checked the signature first: *Joe*. A shimmer of pleasure suffused Kitty. Then she read on. *Please meet me tomorrow. 10.30 a.m. in the James Joyce Room in Bewley's on Grafton Street. Wear comfortable shoes. Joe.*

Rose, assuming the gift was from Hubert, emitted a low whistle. "Stylish of the old goat."

Kitty didn't correct her. She was too busy feeling pursued, and a heady sensation it was. She hadn't told Joe French where she worked but he'd made it his business to find out. She was bewildered by the footwear advice, though.

Rose hoped Kitty wasn't going to be swayed by a flower into giving Hubert another chance. She stretched her lips tight against her teeth before a word of criticism leaked out. She couldn't help herself, however. "You should think very carefully before seeing Hubert again."

"Of course I'm not going to see Hubert again." Kitty was absentminded, wondering whether to feign illness or claim she was meeting a contact at ten thirty a.m. so she could keep the date.

The door of Linus Bell's office slammed open, its frame quivering from the impact.

"It's like a bad soap-opera set," whispered Rose, as Linus stalked down the editorial floor.

He'd learned that one of the newspaper's most important advertisers had scrapped a series of ads, because the company's managing director had been featured in an unflattering profile. Since Linus had authorised the profile there was no minion he could heap blame on, but he needed to offload his ire. His fretful gaze fell on Rose and Kitty, having what was clearly a personal conversation during working hours. Almost as much as losing lucrative advertising revenue, Linus loathed employees having personal conversations – he was convinced he always figured in them.

"Kitty," he barked, since he hadn't yet bothered to learn Rose's name, "we need more glitz this week. I want you to crack on with finding me five top women executives who run their own companies, drive sports cars and have had boob jobs. Make sure they're all blondes."

Rose gave Kitty a sympathetic glance as Kitty lifted the phone to begin attempting the impossible, all the while clutching the bloom from Joe, a porcelain-white barricade against a grey day. Life was amazing: it could be transformed in a matter of moments. In the length of time it took for a receptionist to glide from her desk to yours with a white orchid in her hand.

"Linus is obsessed with breast-enhancement stories." Rose began to move away.

"Tell me about it," Kitty muttered, covering the mouthpiece. "I wouldn't mind, but he calls them all dogs however well-endowed they are. If they could hear what he says about them, there isn't a woman in Ireland who'd agree to be photographed for our paper."

* * *

"It's too soon to see him again," Rose reprimanded herself, on the pavement outside her Clonliffe Square apartment. Although late for her date with Feargal, she hesitated to hail a taxi – it was an extravagance she indulged in rarely, out of deference to her hefty mortgage repayments. A plump droplet of rain landing on her forehead, swiftly followed by another, decided her. A cab approached, yellow light shining, and she extended her arm: "Shelbourne Road, please."

As she fumbled for her purse while the engine idled outside the French Paradox, Rose glanced upwards and noticed Feargal's anxious face at the first-floor window scouring the street. Then he spied her stepping from the taxi and his frown evaporated. He was waiting at the top banister as she mounted the stairs, in one of his characteristic T-shirts advertising some product or band or other. One day, thought Rose, she was going to buy him a plain T-shirt.

"You looked so worried when I saw you at the window." Rose laughed gently at his eagerness.

"I was afraid you'd get wet, the rain's pelting down." Feargal leaned forward and dabbed with a tissue at a trace of moisture on her forehead.

Rose allowed the warm waters of his solicitude to lap against her. It had been so long since a man had been anxious to please her: the early years with Father Damien, before their love had been calcified by habit. She smiled and found herself hugging Feargal, although she was unsure if he had put his arms around her, or she had to succumbed to instinct and stretched hers about him.

"Coming through," called a waiter with a prominent Adam's apple, and they disentangled. Feargal threaded his way past the bar, leading her to the table by the window that he'd reserved, where an unopened bottle of champagne rested inside an ice bucket.

Rose's eyes widened. "Are we celebrating?"

"Absolutely."

"Anything in particular?"

"Me persuading you to come out on another date, when it's 100 per cent apparent you feel you're about to be handcuffed and charged with corruption of a minor."

His beam was so brash that Rose had to giggle, even though he was uncomfortably near the mark.

"Of course," Feargal leaned forward, confessional, "there's something crucial you haven't learned to take into consideration when dealing with me." He waited, dark grey eyes glistering.

"What's that?" Rose obliged.

"I'm a bit of an operator." He lifted the champagne and eased out the cork, vapour rushing from the neck of the bottle but not a drop of the foaming liquid wasted.

"I'm impressed – where did you learn to do that?" Rose extended her glass while he filled it, noticing how a swirl of the haze that had emerged with the cork was still suspended in the air above the bottle.

"All part of an operator's tricks of the trade," he assured her, solemn as he tended to his own flute.

"Here's to operators." Rose clinked her glass against his, feeling a giddy whoosh of elation before she'd taken so much as a sip.

"I'd have preferred a more romantic toast for our first bottle of champagne together," he objected.

Rose paused with the glass resting against her mouth.

"On the other hand, I can't think of anything soppy at this precise moment," he confessed. "Maybe I'm not that great an operator."

He looked woebegone and Rose felt a band of pressure squeeze her diaphragm. "To the sweetest operator I've ever met." She clinked her glass against his again and this time drank, bubbles prickling her throat.

They ordered a cheese plate to share and, engrossed in one another's company, grew oblivious to the other diners in the elongated room. A businesswoman seated at the bar, briefcase knocking against shoes that pinched each big toe, glanced in their direction. It was almost worth falling in love for. She sighed and returned her attention to the Latvian factory owner with whom she was meant to be striking a deal.

"I heard your show this morning," said Rose.

His smile flashed and she noticed once again the schoolboy gap between his two front teeth.

"At least, I heard part of it, before the *Sunday Trumpet* intervened and I had to switch off my pocket radio because I'd arrived at the office. It's sinful how much of your life is occupied by work. Anyway, the discussion about mandatory recycling sounded interesting, but I don't know how you'd police it."

Feargal's narrow face became animated. "Recycling's a passion of mine. We're all incredibly wasteful and running out of natural resources at a lightning rate. I was determined to set up a panel discussion about it on the show – it was quite a coup luring on the environment minister. My producer spotted her at a party, rang me and then cornered the minister until I turned up and talked her into it. Once we had her on air I think we pinned her down to one or two commitments that she hadn't intended to make on the recycling front." There was a hiatus. "Listen to me droning on about my job. What did you get up to today, Rose?"

Just then their waiter with the enlarged and now frantically bobbing Adam's apple arrived. "I have terrible news." He was wringing his hands in misery.

Both faces were upturned towards him, wondering at the nature of the calamity.

"That's the last bottle of Veuve Cliquot in the building – if you want to carry on drinking champagne you will have to switch to Moet et Chandon." The waiter was all but weeping with mortification.

"We'll bear it in mind." Feargal was grave.

Rose kept her eyes clamped on her glass for fear she'd betray herself.

They waited until the waiter had gone downstairs before their snuffles erupted into full-scale laughter.

"I was afraid you were going to tell him if we couldn't have Veuve Cliquot we weren't prepared to drink any more champagne in this establishment," choked Rose.

"I was even more afraid he'd see how my credit card was trembling in my wallet at the thought of being forced to buy another bottle of champagne," Feargal guffawed.

After they'd recovered, Feargal topped up their flutes. Rose pinged a nail against the glass, to hear its ringing note, and admired the way his thick, dark brown hair covered his head. Father Damien's had started thinning – and for a man secretly planning to defect to the spiritual life, he'd demonstrated a worldly hunger for reassurance about the patches where his scalp was peeking through.

"Penny for them," prompted Feargal.

"I was wondering about the paradox in the French Paradox."

"We could quiz the waiter, but he still looks distraught about running out of Veuve."

"Let's risk it." Rose beckoned and the waiter rolled as though on castors towards them.

"More champagne?" He patted down his striped apron.

"Not just yet," said Rose. "We were wondering if you could explain the name of your wine bar."

He beamed, exposing a fleshy pink tongue. "The paradox is that French people eat and drink like kings and yet they remain relatively healthy. Everything in moderation, right?"

"Right," chorused Rose and Feargal.

"I thought the French were prone to heart disease," whispered Feargal, as soon as the coast was clear.

"Only the immoderate ones," Rose hissed back, and they collapsed in giggles, convinced they were the wittiest couple in Dublin.

Later as they waited to cross the main road gouged through Ballsbridge, a steady stream of traffic whizzing by, Rose debated inviting him home for a nightcap. "It's a clear night, a stretch of the legs might be pleasant. It's less than half an hour by foot to my place from here." She cleared her throat, diffident.

Feargal, who was guiding her across the dual carriageway during a lull, turned towards her. "Don't you want a taxi?"

Then his gaze met hers and it hammered a tattoo in her ears.

"Would you like me to walk with you? I could keep you company."

"Yes," agreed Rose, "you could keep me company."

Chapter 16

Kitty didn't want to wear comfortable footwear to meet Joe French. She yearned to turn up in spindly heels to lend her leg-length and allure. She longed to arrive looking more desirable than any woman had before, so he'd be tempted by her as she was tempted by him. No, no, no, this was all wrong. She was supposed to be the source of temptation, not him – being a mistress was about seizing control, not relinquishing it. She chewed the fleshy ball of her thumb in consternation: Joe French was muddling her. What on earth could he have in mind for them at ten thirty a.m. that required flat shoes? Come to think of it, ten thirty a.m. was a strange time for a date. But he was a busy tycoon – she must remember to look him up in the office cuttings library – perhaps he was squeezing her in between meetings. Kitty didn't mind that, she was grateful to figure in his schedule at all. It hadn't been easy, juggling her work to create the space to meet him. She'd worked late the previous night to give herself a head-start, but she knew she'd have trouble meeting her deadline and Linus would be incandescent.

She dawdled along Nassau Street, trying not to arrive at Bewley's too early. But it was only ten twenty-five as she walked past the gift-packaged tins of tea. That was the trouble with comfortable shoes, your progress was too quick in them. Joe was there already in the James Joyce Room, studying a vibrant oil painting on one of the walls. He had his back to Kitty, hands clasped behind, and she stepped unobtrusively to his side. The top of her head barely skimmed his shoulder.

"Orange, isn't it," he remarked.

"Not as orange as the one behind us."

Joe turned and checked. "You're right. That's more orange again." His eyes tangled with hers and he smiled that lazy smile of his, only one corner of his mouth quirking upwards. "Perfect, you're exactly the way I remembered you." A cocoon of intimacy was generated between them.

A woman in hiking boots and a tartan wool lumberjack's coat clapped her hands. "Has everyone bought tickets for the Georgian Dublin walk? Anyone who needs one can buy it from me now. The price includes a cup of tea or coffee at the end. Our tour will last around two hours, weather permitting, and take us through the superb architecture of Georgian Dublin, where the famous Irish writers including Wilde, Joyce, Yeats and Shaw lived and worked."

"Ready?" Joe nudged Kitty.

"Ready for what?"

"The walking tour. I've been meaning to do it for ages. I made a New Year's resolution that I'd mop up all those 'I've been meaning to's' and this is number one on the list. How does it feel to help a man keep his New Year's resolution, Kitty Kennedy?" He paused. "That's a Mona Lisa smile if ever I saw one – share the joke."

"I'll help you keep yours if you help me keep mine." Kitty laced her fingers demurely in front.

"You'll have to tell me what it is."

"All in good time."

Joe laughed. "Come on, Mona, the tour's about to leave. I've cancelled a meeting with our biggest bread supplier for this."

"I've invented a visit to the dentist," said Kitty.

"Stolen time. The best kind of all." His golden eyes were conspiratorial.

To fend off the cold, Joe lent Kitty his silvery cashmere scarf, wrapping it around her neck and tying it in a lavish pussycat bow that made her look either faintly ridiculous (her opinion) or enormously fetching (his). Their walk took them along the stately rows of Merrion Square, past Oscar Wilde's former home – now the American College – and looped round to Parnell Square. Kitty and Joe giggled throughout the tour, complicit in their mutual absorption. All he had to do was intercept one of her glances and the pair of them were trying to suffocate their laughter so hard that she developed a stitch in her side. His sotto voce interpretation of the guide's commentary was hilarious. If Kitty were to repeat back to a third party what it was Joe said, it wouldn't sound in the least amusing, but it had Kitty snuffling and the woman in the tartan jacket throwing them suspicious looks.

An hour into the tour, a white Mercedes slowed to the kerbside and a man in an immaculately tailored suit, with hair the colour of unbaked dough, leaned from the passenger window. "Joe, still playing your aggressive expansion games, I see. How many stores is it now – eighteen? Better be careful you don't over-extend."

"It's twenty-one stores, Bill, but we're not stopping there. I hear the insurance business is on a go-slow. Be a shame if you had to start downsizing, wouldn't it? Still, might free up more time for the golf-course."

"Let's do lunch soon," snarled Bill, grinding the gears as he pulled away.

Joe grinned at Kitty. "Your man is managing director of the second-largest insurance company in the country. He's narked with Bumpermac's because we've started selling travel insurance in-store, undercutting his lowest offer by five per cent."

"Are you a shark, Joe French?" Kitty noticed his animation as he relished the cut and thrust of competition.

"It has been said of me." He radiated complacency. "But I'm a shark who likes Georgian architecture – and beautiful newspaper columnists. Does that make it all right?"

"I'll have to get back to you on that," Kitty quibbled, although her instinct was to say yes, oh yes, and once more with feeling – yes. Nevertheless, she wondered at him, strolling about town so openly with her. What if word wended its way back to Emma French? "Don't you worry what people might think, being seen with a woman who's not your wife?" she challenged him.

"What could be more innocent than two 'colleagues' checking out potential city-centre locations for a scaled-down version of Bumpermac's?" Joe responded. "We need to think about opening some convenience shops for the affluent-singles brigade."

Oh good, he had a cover story. A sensible precaution. Kitty frowned, unwilling to examine why she was vexed by his commendable prudence.

There were five other people on the tour, all of them tourists. One had a picture-messaging phone and every time the woman in the tartan jacket pointed out a location of note, he snapped himself in front of the building and then clicked away busily on his keyboard sending it to someone.

"I have one of those phones." Joe produced it from an inner pocket.

Kitty glanced at the phone casually, then more attentively. His screensaver showed a gurgling baby of a few months old, dressed in a romper suit with a hood and Winnie the Pooh ears protruding from either side.

He followed her eye-line. "My daughter, Clodagh. The prettiest little girl in the whole wide world. Everyone says that about their child, but I know for a fact that it's true about Clodagh."

Kitty's face was impassive, but her emotions were churning. Mistresses have to learn to deal with feeling guilty occasionally – it goes with the territory, she told herself. It wasn't just guilt nipping at her, however, but a trace of aversion to Joe French. What was he thinking of, risking that baby girl's happiness? The antipathy receded almost the instant she became conscious of it. "How old is Clodagh?" Kitty kept her voice monotone.

"Ten months. She took her first steps last week. I held out my arms and said 'Come to Daddy' and she did. Well, almost." His voice was swollen with pride.

"To the left is the house where James Joyce . . ." The guide's explanation bisected their conversation and Kitty concentrated on what she was saying, refusing to be lured into Joe's impudent asides. He sensed her withdrawal and quietened too. Finally they were back at their starting point.

"Shall we avail of our free cup of coffee? If you smile I'll buy you a sandwich to go with it." Joe stood on the pavement, rocking slightly on his heels. The wind whipped a high colour into his cheeks and she saw a glimmer of gold bristle on the underside of his chin where he'd missed a patch shaving.

Kitty was tempted. God oh God oh God was she tempted.

But an element in the attraction of being a mistress was the prospect of freedom within a relationship. She'd have a man in her life, but she'd stay in charge. With Joe French, Kitty knew that was not an option. He had the potential to transform her life into a snow-globe and give it a shake whenever he liked – because everything would be on his terms. She saw, as surely as though a mirror into the future was held before her eyes, that with him on the scene she'd spend evenings by the phone willing it to ring. She'd cancel other arrangements at zero hours' notice to accommodate him, turn away other men with whom she might be happy. There'd be the candlelit suppers she'd anticipated, certainly, the romance and the excitement, and yes, if she was honest, the thrill of the illicit. Reddest stolen cherries. But a void would yawn inside her during the times Joe was with his family. She'd have to learn to live with a sense of exclusion: her nose would be pressed to the window of his real life. This wasn't freedom, it was incarceration.

Kitty took the one course of action she recognised would save her from making a profound mistake. She turned away. "I can't manage coffee, I'm due in the office. Thanks for the walk."

She was at the corner of South Anne Street before he caught up with her. "Hey, come back here. I'm not going to let you disappear that easily. For starters, you have my scarf."

Kitty was mortified and uncoiled it.

"Only kidding, you're welcome to keep it." He smiled into her eyes, trying to charm an answering one. When it didn't materialise, his expression became grave. "Where did I go wrong, Kitty? We were doing so well. I've never felt this level of connection with anyone before."

"Not even your wife?" Fury coursed through her. Irrational wrath that he'd married someone else instead of waiting for her. Then sealed it by having a baby, an infant whose photograph he'd been careless enough to let her see.

"Not even my wife. Especially not my wife."

Their breath hung in frosted clouds before them for the space of four or five heart-beats, an oasis of indecision for Kitty. Joe wasn't touching her and yet she felt detained by him – as surely as though his arms restrained her. She wrenched herself away and, head lowered, walked quickly towards Pearse Street Dart station. This time, he didn't chase after her.

Chapter 17

It was after ten o'clock that evening as Kitty turned the key on her parents' front door. She hadn't wanted to go there; she was feeling flayed since her date with Joe. She'd have preferred to drag herself home and run a bath, moping over why she seemed unable to become Joe French's mistress when he fulfilled every specification – including the marital status one.

It seemed weeks since she'd met him instead of only that morning. Her column had been predictably late and Linus's response had been blistering. His criticism had been so barbarous that Kitty had been tempted to play her trump card. Tears. They were the only weapon known to reduce Linus to incoherence, because female emotion horrified him. It was an antidote that only worked once, however, and Kitty was saving it for a truly dire emergency, so she'd accepted his censure in silence. Then, just as she'd been leaving, he'd dropped a few words of praise regarding the column's content. Typical of him: he played good cop, bad cop all by himself.

Her plans to brood in bubble-bath had been derailed by a phone call to work from her father saying Noreen-dear was feeling low and would appreciate a visit. Since her father never used the telephone, Kitty had immediately grasped the importance of making the effort.

Kitty halted now in the hallway and listened to the stillness. Despite the lack of noise she knew Number 16 Hunter Crescent was occupied, for it was a silence of presence. She continued to use her key to walk in, a privilege she didn't intend to have foreclosed as readily as she'd yielded the lilac bedroom to Sunny. Although she hadn't so much surrendered it as lost it in a flagrant act of occupation. At least, she consoled herself, it was still a bedroom – she knew a woman whose parents had barely waited for her to move before selling her bedroom furniture and turning the room into a gym. Kitty inhaled extravagantly, slid the key back into her handbag and instinct directed her to the kitchen.

Her father was dismantling a radio at the kitchen table, a sight indicative of mayhem on the domestic front. Under normal circumstances her mother would never have permitted such disorder in the heart of her fiefdom – and her father wouldn't have wanted to do it there, too close to the kettle for comfort. Her mother's telltale forehead ran the gamut of emotions when she saw Kitty, but the predominant one was relief. A troublesome development. Since when had Kitty become the fixer in the family? She felt a twinge of unease.

"I'll put the kettle on," said Noreen-dear. She rattled crockery and muttered about surprises being sprung on her at this stage of her life. Kitty never could understand how her mother made so much racket setting the table. It was as if inanimate objects were enemies, to be thumped down with a vengeful crash – even when she was in a cheerful mood. Kitty exchanged surreptitious glances with her father, before his gaze strayed longingly towards the hall, beyond which lay his basement. What was this all about?

She watched the teacups being matched to their saucers, the pot scalded, the caddy opened. Tea was used to pour oil on troubled waters at Number 16 Hunter Crescent; also to celebrate, commiserate and circulate news within the family grid. If Kitty closed her eyes she could picture every teapot they'd ever had, from the white one with the blue stripes and a precarious handle to the brown one with the eggshell glaze that dribbled unless it was held it at a certain angle. Then there was the ancient metal one Dad kept throwing out and Noreen-dear persistently rescued from the bin – allegedly because tea tasted better from it, but Kitty suspected it was a power struggle. The tea-making ritual kept her mother's mental health tuned, although sometimes she feared it might tinker with her father's. "Your mother can't reconcile herself to Sunny going off to Hollywood, chicken," explained Kitty's father, hands too cumbersome for the handle on the cup he was reached, like it or not. "We have to remember it could be the start of something big, Noreen-dear."

"Or the start of something sordid," snapped her mother. A renegade curl vaulted out of its hairspray corral and landed on her forehead.

"I don't see why she has to be an actress anyhow," muttered her father, forgetting milk had been added and splashing in another waterfall. "She had the grades to do accountancy."

"Actor," his wife corrected him, sidetracking her animosity in his direction. He didn't understand the reference. "Sunny's an actor." Noreen-dear was spiky as she spelled it out – Sunny had obviously been preaching at her about this. "Kitty's not a journalistess so why should Sunny be labelled an actress?"

Her poor father continued to look bemused so Kitty whipped in to save him a lecture. "Where is she anyway?"

"She went out for brunch with some fellow by the name of Clarke and hasn't come home since. Elevenses aren't good enough for people any more." Noreen-dear quivered with indignation.

"There's always a chance this could be Sunny's diamond-studded opportunity," Kitty suggested. "Picture it: your little girl flies out to Hollywood a nobody and returns to Bray a star."

Her mother quelled her with a look so melancholy it could have been worn by a medieval Madonna at the foot of the Crucifix.

"Your mother didn't spend two seasons with the Kilmacanogue

Players in our courting days for nothing." Her father defined the malaise. "It's from Noreen-dear that Sunny inherited her love of performing."

"Sunny's like me," said Noreen. "She enjoys an audience but she's not a star. Except I realised it early on – she's still in denial. The truth is she'll never make a living from it." She swapped a look with Kitty's father, a united front of parenthood. "If she didn't live here rent-free she'd never survive in the outside world. Acting provides Sunniva with pocket money, but it would never put food on the table for her."

Her husband patted her hand. "You're right, Noreen-dear. She's a home bird, for all her fancy talk about spreading her wings. She could never bring herself to move to London, let alone Los Angeles."

Kitty's mother picked up his dangling thread, for once both of them in rapport. "We know what happens to girls there – they end up in slap-dancing clubs."

Kitty had a graphic image of flesh thumping against flesh.

"We could always make sure she has a return ticket." Her father rattled the change in his pocket.

Her mother considered, tapping the side of her china cup patterned with forget-me-nots. All her china had flora and fauna on it. "Yes, a return ticket could keep the toads in their holes."

"Stop it the pair of you." Kitty had to intervene. They were infantilising Sunny; it was degrading. "She's a twenty-nine-year-old woman. We can't hold her hand and bribe her with lollipops."

"Really, Kitty, I can't imagine what you mean." Her mother reacted as though she'd said something uncouth.

"Kitty's right, Noreen-dear, Sunny's not a child," said her father, their alliance faltering already.

Its evaporation reassured Kitty – it was unsettling to have her parents in harmony.

"I might have expected you to side with Kitty, she can do no wrong in your eyes, Denis." Her mother clattered the saucers on top of one another and turned towards the sink.

This was riveting – Kitty had never thought of her father as her defender before. He just skulked in his bunker as far as she was concerned.

"Be reasonable," urged her father.

Her mother tossed her head, sloughing at least four decades.

Suddenly Kitty understood. This had nothing to do with Sunny being exposed to white slave traders in Los Angeles – and everything to do with her mother's reluctance to have her last chick fly the nest. She and her husband might be obliged to communicate directly, face to face, man to woman, instead of using their daughters as intermediaries.

Her mother was petrified of it.

Compassion welled inside Kitty and spilled into words. "How about inviting Clarke T Maloney over for dinner? You can check him out under cover of hospitality. Sunny's already asked me to meet him tomorrow night – we could introduce him to all the Kennedys instead."

She could tell the idea appealed to both parents, even as they scrutinised it for flaws. If nothing else, Kitty reasoned, the American would find it difficult to treat Sunny like a disposable commodity if he'd been welcomed into the bosom of her family.

"Why would a hotshot Hollywood casting director bother coming to Bray?" asked her mother, although Kitty could tell she was already trawling through cookery books in her mind's eye.

"It's the race card," Kitty explained. "Don't underrate yourself – you're a genuine Irish mammy. He'll turn all dewy-eyed just looking at you." She remembered Sunny's description of Mr Hollywood as a man smitten by his roots.

Her mother was beguiled by the notion of reducing a Hollywood mogul to sniffling sentimentality. She turned to her husband. "It might be worth a try, Denis. It couldn't do any harm to give that Clarke T Baloney character the once-over."

"Whatever you think, Noreen-dear, but I'm not eating cabbage and bacon for anyone. It plays havoc with my digestive system."

"There's just one snag," Kitty pointed out, as her father started for the basement and her mother plugged in the iron. They paused. "We have to persuade Sunny to invite him."

Her mother sent Kitty a measured look. "We'll leave that to you, lovie. I don't know where you think you're going, Denis Kennedy – your daughter needs a lift home."

* * *

On the Dart into the office the next morning, her nostrils filled with the scent of pine-needles from the Christmas-tree recycling dump she'd passed near the station, Kitty wrestled with the conundrum of how to deal with Sunny. At least it had the merit of distracting her from Joe French. She'd tried to throw away his orchid last night except her hand wouldn't obey her. So it was still sitting on her coffee table in Blackrock. Reminding her of her stupidity. She should have grabbed what he had to offer with both hands when she had the chance. Joe Frenches were thin on the ground – perhaps they had to be shared. But she'd lost her chance.

Kitty's head was throbbing. With an effort she re-focused on Sunny and her Mr Hollywood. Her sister had made it clear she didn't want him exposed to Bray – implying that the combined impact of all the Kennedys on home territory would somehow sabotage her big chance. All she'd wanted was Kitty, on neutral terrain. But now she had to persuade Sunny to unleash every member of the Kennedy clan on him. Just because there were only four of them didn't make it any less overwhelming.

At Sydney Parade station a youth wearing eyeliner and cut-off trousers to his shins stepped on the Dart and leaned against the glass in front of her seat. An elderly passenger was mesmerised, reviewing this parallel universe – taking in the teenager's light brown dreadlocks, the deliberately frayed edges of his trousers, the barbed-wire tattoo circling an ankle. The older man's response was as transparent as if he had a bubble floating above his head with the words inked in. Kitty could tell he was sorry he hadn't fought in a war so he'd have the consolation of demanding, "Was it for scruffs like this pup that I risked my life?" At least the British senior citizen had that consolation. The sixteen-year-old was conscious of the scrutiny, but resigned to it. Which was all very distracting, but here she was at Grand Canal Dock, her station, and she still hadn't calculated how to persuade Sunny to bring home her Yank.

* * *

Shortly before that time of day when Kitty's eyes started stinging from the combination of cheap overhead lighting and computer screen glare, a text message flashed on her mobile phone from Sunny. "Call me," it ordered. She dialled her sister's mobile.

"Are you in on this conspiracy?" Sunny demanded.

So the Clarke T Maloney plan had been revealed – Kitty should have known Noreen-dear would be incapable of leaving it to her to persuade Sunny to invite him. "I'm knee-deep in on so many cabals I've lost count, Sunny. Which particular one did you have in mind?"

"The plot in which our mother lures a certain Hollywood casting agent to Hunter Crescent, plies him with cabbage and bacon and is offered a walk-on part in *The Quiet Man* remake so I have a built-in chaperone."

"Oh, that plot. Sure, she's demented, it has no chance of success."

"That's where you're wrong, Kitty. Step one has already been accomplished. She phoned him up and invited him to dinner tonight. He said yes. So consider our prior engagement cancelled."

"How could she have phoned him up? Mum wouldn't know where to begin tracking down a Hollywood casting agent."

"Noreen-dear was a bloodhound in a previous existence." Sunny was gloomy. "She rang the Merrion and the Four Seasons, asking for Mr Clarke Tea, and finally struck gold at the Clarence. They put her through from reception and would you believe it, the sap happened to be in his suite and answered the phone. He said he'd be honoured to accept. He's just rung to congratulate me on having such a peachy mom." Sunny spluttered, but wasn't ready to draw breath yet. "She's not peachy. She's Lady Macbeth, she's Hecuba, she's Medusa. She'd bent on ruining my one chance in life."

"Maybe she has your best interests at heart." Kitty was tentative, for Sunny in juggernaut mode was not easily steered onto the hard shoulder.

"Hah!" Sunny spat down the phone – Kitty could almost feel the phlegm land on her cheek. "I knew you were on their side."

"I'm not on anyone's side," she protested, knowing how it felt to run with the hare and hunt with the hounds. "What are you frightened of? It might be the fuse to send your career sky-rocketing into orbit."

"I can just see Denis inviting Clarke down to his basement to do one of his trillion-piece jigsaws with him, *Snowstorm in the Arctic* or some other riveting exercise in futility. Meanwhile Noreen-dear's producing every embroidered tray-cloth she has in the coffers, hinting about the largesse of linen for the man who manages to overturn my spinster status. She'll be changing the tablecloth after every course so he can admire the full panoply of my hope chest. She'll force-feed him tea and make him look at those old photographs of me on the potty. Mark my words, Kitty, this will be a disaster. She'll stymie my one shot at the big time."

"Sunny, I really think you're overreacting. By the time Mum's finished with Clarke he'll be champing at the bit to jettison Pearl Roberge and offer you the starring role on a platter."

Sunny hung up.

Before Kitty could replace her mobile in her bag, it shrilled again. "Make sure you're there tonight. It's at seven o'clock sharp," ordered Sunny.

"But the Exalted One throws wobblers if anyone leaves the office before eight p.m. – it shows a lack of commitment," Kitty bleated.

"Irish-Americans eat early so it's seven p.m. sharp for a seven thirty sit-down, Kitty. No excuses. Jam a fist down your throat and throw up in the wastepaper bin if necessary so you're sent home sick."

"You don't know the Exalted One. He'd tell his clamshell-faced secretary Valerie to make me a cup of sugary tea and then it's on with the show."

"There'll be show time out in Bray, too, and I need you there. You're to stop Noreen-dear collaring Clarke and spoiling everything for me – we all know she's capable of it. My future depends on this, Kitty. I'll never forgive you if it falls apart."

Chapter 18

Kitty and Rose didn't have much time to talk, with the Saturday deadline epidemic gripping the office, apart from a snatched minute by the water cooler.

"We should take up smoking, then we could sneak out for cigarettes," said Rose. "I'm always envious of that impression of belonging to a secret club smokers exude, huddled in the basement carpark inhaling and then coughing out their entrails."

"I doubt if I could spare a minute for a smoke today, even if I was a forty-a-day woman. I have to be on the 6.19p.m. Dart to Bray for a Clarke-vetting exercise."

"What's a Clarke-vetting exercise?" Rose's black fringe was in her eyes and she swiped at it impatiently.

"Family emergency." Kitty lowered her tone, conscious of bored colleagues nearby. "My twenty-nine-year-old sister, who's regarded as too immature by my parents to make her bed let alone a decision, needs my moral support. Meanwhile my parents think they need it too. It's all a bit complicated. I'll bring you up to date on the festering Kennedy insanity another time."

"Look forward to it – festering Kennedy insanity sounds

promising," grinned Rose, several decibels louder than Kitty felt necessary in view of an entire sports department a few feet away.

* * *

As the Dart rattled towards Bray, Kitty sank her head gratefully on the carriage window without noticing the scimitar sweep of coastline to the left of her or the pink ribbons streaking the skyline over the Pigeon House. She had draped her raincoat across the back of her office chair so the Exalted One, should he stroll through her department surveying his bailiwick, would imagine she was in the Ladies'. A pathetic ruse, Kitty acknowledged, especially as she'd worked a few hours on Monday, her day off, doing the Puffin O'Mara interview, so it wasn't as though she was pulling a fast one. But how that editor hated to see people go home.

The woman beside Kitty was rolling her wedding ring round on her finger, an unconscious gesture as she counted stations on the overhead map. A column of light picked up the movement of the gold band, forward and back. Kitty found herself looking at her and thinking, "What have you got that I don't? How come you can make it work? Do you settle for things or am I too demanding?" The woman stood at Booterstown station and a man took her vacant seat.

"Sloping off early?"

Kitty started at the Dundalk accent – God oh God oh God, it was the Exalted One. On the Dart. Sitting beside her on the Dart, instead of being chauffeur-driven around town in his belching, twin-exhaust, ozone layer-depleting executive's Jaguar.

"I had to leave on urgent family business, but I worked through my lunch-break and was owed time from Monday," she stuttered, a wayward ten-year-old caught with her hand in the *Trócaire* box.

"Families are a desperate handling." He snapped open his Gucci briefcase. "Boarding-schools and old people's homes are the only way to deal with them."

Kitty craned to see what was inside the legendary Linus Bell briefcase, source of fevered speculation in *Sunday Trumpet* circles. P45s and brochures for plastic surgery clinics were favourite suggestions. It was something of a jolt to encounter bank upon bank of Rothmans cigarettes and cans of Diet Coke. Nothing else, not so much as a newspaper. Linus Bell extracted a silver and red can, offered it to Kitty and when she declined pulled open the metal ring for himself.

She chanced a remark. "It's a little unexpected to see you on public transport."

"Motor's off the road. My driver had a mishap this morning – swerved to avoid a cyclist and pranged the Jaguar. The garage was supposed to supply a replacement, but Gary can't collect it until tomorrow, as he's stuck in Casualty. Hadn't much choice but to give him the day off." Linus sniffed and adjusted the lapel of his pin-striped suit. He always wore suits with broad stripes, while his minions favoured ones with narrow pin-stripes in keeping with their lesser rank. "I'll tell you this, Kitty, I'm scrapping that editorial calling for more cycle paths through the city – we want less of those suicidal feckers on wheels, not more. I don't know what I was thinking of, agreeing to run it in the first place. It's not as if cyclists are glitzy. Some of the birds are all right if they wear those Lycra shorts, but the men? Do me a favour."

While he held forth, Kitty checked his left hand again. Still no wedding band. She knew it was totalitarian to believe all married people should wear them, but it always struck her as dishonest when some didn't. She wouldn't have felt comfortable married to a man who refused to wear a ring. On the other hand, she hadn't felt comfortable married to two men who did wear rings.

It seemed unreal to encounter the Exalted One on a Dart, almost as bizarre as standing behind a member of royalty in a bus queue. Kitty felt tongue-tied. Fortunately the Exalted One didn't believe in listening when he could be talking so he maintained a monologue that would have made a taxi-driver proud. To pass the time, Kitty kept an expletives-tally.

Suddenly he shot her a veiled glance. "What was that column of yours all about the other week, saying relationships were power struggles? You claimed women in their twenties had the upper hand and lost it in their thirties."

Kitty shrugged. "It's true, although I find the notion of snaring and keeping a man as the route to happiness for a woman profoundly depressing. But it's a myth that's peddled relentlessly. What's wrong with deciding to be on your own, with occasional male company as and when it suits you?"

Linus stood, as the train slowed for its creaking entrance into Dún Laoghaire station. "Here's my stop," he announced. "You want to watch that cynical streak, Kitty. You'll never find true love with that attitude, *capisce*? Be seeing you, babes." He nodded at her and stepped off the train, while Kitty grappled with the dichotomy that her adulterous editor was advising her on affairs of the heart – and God oh God, oh God, he'd called her babes. Wait until Rose heard.

A Filipino woman with the round, trusting face of a child was waiting on the platform. She gave Linus Bell something his shoes with elevated insteps could never achieve – alongside her he had height. He leaned in and nuzzled her nose, oblivious of the crowd surging around them.

Well, who'd have thought it, Kitty marvelled. The Exalted One was in love.

* * *

There was something peculiar about their house, it seemed to Kitty, as she walked along Hunter Crescent, past the small black van driven by their miserly neighbours two doors down because its insurance was cheaper than a car's. Then it struck her and she cringed: someone – and Noreen-dear was the likeliest culprit – had hung a jaunty triangular Stars and Stripes flag from the front bedroom window.

"It's only me," Kitty sang out as she opened the door. Sunny was always complaining about people saying that – she insisted it was too abject. "But what am I supposed to call? It's wonderful me?" Kitty would remonstrate.

Her mother's flustered face appeared in the hallway. "Kitty, thank heavens. Your father won't come out of the basement and Sunny's locked herself in the bathroom. She's like that Macavity the Mystery Cat she played at the Pavilion years ago, never there when you're looking for her. The table hasn't been set yet, I still haven't changed because I didn't want to get boiling bacon splatters on my clothes and the Yank is due at any minute."

"I'll set the table, Mum. Why is Sunny locked in the bathroom? Is she having doubts?"

"No, she's taking an eternity to get ready. I was banking on her to lend a hand, but she's too busy with her pearl shimmer illuminator, whatever that is. Meanwhile your father's been ready for the past hour and is lurking in the basement doing a crossword puzzle to pass the time. He offered to lay the table, but I couldn't risk it – he always sets the knives facing the wrong way and spills salt, guaranteeing bad luck."

"Offer it up for the suffering souls in Purgatory, Mum." Kitty tittered, to show she was only teasing, although her mother always meant it when she said it. "By the way, I see you're going all out to welcome Clarke with the flag."

Noreen-dear had the grace to redden. "I found it lying in the bottom of the coats-cupboard – your cousin Justine brought it back from her honeymoon in Disneyworld. Americans go in for flags. They call it Old Gory or something."

Kitty checked to see if she was joking and couldn't decide. "I'll press on with setting the table."

"We're using your Great-aunt Agnes's cream damask cloth and napkins," Noreen-dear cried from the bottom rung of the stairs. "I've left them on the table."

The dining-room was used no more than half a dozen times a year, and Kitty and Sunny were always trying to persuade their parents to knock the wall through to the sitting-room and create more space. Noreen-dear wouldn't hear of it. Throughout her childhood she'd aspired to a house with a dining-room, and she wasn't about to let builders with sledgehammers flatten her pretensions. Kitty gazed around the over-furnished room, wondering what Joe French would make of it all. He lived in a converted eighteenth century coach-house in Malahide, probably in palatial splendour if he was as wealthy as Hubert had implied. She remembered Joe mentioning that the estuary lay at the bottom of his garden; Emma French didn't look the type to roll up her trouser bottoms for a paddle. Kitty didn't suppose Joe would ever meet her parents – mistresses didn't usually introduce their lovers to the family. She made an involuntary moue. She'd have liked Joe to know her father, at least.

The doorbell rang and Kitty walked through to the hallway to answer it, as Sunny materialised on the landing and hissed "Leave it for me". Kitty shrugged. Sunny wafted – it was the only word for it, Kitty decided, watching in horrified fascination down the stairs, in an apricot pyjama suit and mules with maribou feathers fluttering at the toes. She looked like a sophisticated invalid. Noreen-dear was seconds behind her in the coral two-piece she'd worn for cousin Justine's wedding. At least she'd left the matching hat at the bottom of the wardrobe. Kitty snatched at small mercies.

As the door opened, her father emerged from the basement, still in his overalls.

"Denis!" shrieked Mum.

"Clarke," cooed Sunny.

"Kitty," stumbled Clarke.

Who wasn't Clarke at all, but the first boy Kitty had ever kissed. Slack-jawed, Kitty gaped at him. No wonder all those clever scientific people maintained the universe was curved. Her past had just boomeranged into her present.

"Tim?" she checked, scarcely able to believe the evidence of her eyes.

"Clarke," he corrected her. "Clarke Timothy Maloney. I was too embarrassed to use my full name when I was a teenager. You remember how shy I was."

"But you were Tim Newman when I knew you," Kitty persisted.

"That's true." He cleared his throat. "I decided to revert to my father's name when I left home. Newman was my stepfather's name and my mother more or less forced it on me after she remarried."

Sunny looked from one to the other, compressing her scarlet lips in a mannerism inherited directly from Noreen-dear, and curtly suggested to Clarke that he might like to vacate the doorstep. Meanwhile their mother had missed the exchange because she'd steered sideways towards her husband, making face and hand signals that suggested he take off his overalls right now this minute if he knew what was good for him. Once she had his boiler suit kicked down a flight of stairs, Noreen-dear turned her attention to the visitor. "Mr Maloney, you're welcome to our home. What are you thinking of, girls, leaving him to stand in the hallway? Come into the lounge, come in at once out of the cold."

Kitty tried to make eye contact with Sunny because they always wriggled their eyebrows at one another when Noreen-dear called the sitting-room the lounge, another one of her affectations. Sunny wouldn't meet her halfway. Her body language signalled suspicion that Kitty knew her Hollywood casting director already. Worse, Kitty appeared to have a history with him.

Clarke had come bearing gifts and was no sooner in the sitting-room than he distributed them with grave courtesy. There was a bottle of Black Bush for Dad – Noreen-dear frowned, but couldn't complain in front of a visitor – perfume for her and champagne for Kitty with two free glasses taped to the side in a presentation box. Sunny's present was the only one that didn't come in a bottle: it was a Tony Bennett double CD, her favourite singer. A lavish haul for a simple cabbage and bacon dinner, especially one where there'd be no wine served because Noreen-dear didn't believe in people drinking in the home. She didn't believe in them drinking outside the home either.

Their father was feeling confident, perhaps due to another man in the vicinity instead of the usual double-X-chromosome tyranny. "I'll crack open this and we'll have a snifter each before dinner," he told Clarke, cradling his whiskey.

"Shoot, I won't say no."

Noreen-dear followed Denis out to the kitchen to make sure he used the Waterford crystal glasses instead of the tumblers that came free with petrol, while Sunny smoothed a silken sleeve between her fingers and considered Clarke and Kitty with wounded eyes. How dare they know each other?

Clarke had grown from a lugubrious boy who reminded Kitty of Eeyore to a lugubrious man who reminded her of Eeyore. He was tall, rangy and brown all over, from hair to skin to eyes. Even his shoes were dun-coloured.

"How have you been?" she asked.

"Good. You?"

"No complaints." Actually, Kitty had masses, but she wasn't about to share them with the first boy she'd ever dumped.

"I'd recognise you anywhere," he said, "you haven't changed a bit. No, ma'am, not one bit."

"Tim, I mean Clarke," Kitty protested, "it's been twenty years. I'm amazed you recognised me so quickly."

"We-ell," he elongated the syllable, "I knew I'd be seeing you. I remembered you had a baby sister called Sunny and when she told me about her big sister Kitty I decided it had to be the same family. You're the reason I'm here in, what's the name of this place – is it really as simple and straightforward as Bray? Oh, OK, you never know with Irish towns, long words are pronounced in a short way leaving out half the letters and short words are the exact opposite. Anyways, I couldn't resist the chance to meet up with you again, Kitty Kennedy – you were the first woman to break my heart."

"Steady on," Sunny intervened, unaccustomed to being reduced to audience status. "I'm not sure if I'm following you, Clarke – are you suggesting there was something romantic between you and my sister?"

Clarke realised she was still standing and guided her to a seat, gangling arms and legs flapping around her. "Yes, ma'am, I fell in love with her when I was a boy of seventeen. Shoot, I went into decline when she left me."

"Tim, I mean Clarke," Kitty objected, "I was only sixteen and I didn't leave you. I was on an exchange holiday to Boston and when the three weeks were up I went home."

"You promised to write, you vowed you'd come back." He was accusatory.

"I'm sure I did write."

"Twice, then I never heard from you again. I wrote to say I'd spend the next summer in Dublin, but you sent back my letter with 'not known at this address' scrawled across it. Except I see you're still living at the same address. I've never forgotten it. Sixteen, Hunter Crescent, Bray, County Wicklow, Ireland. Sixteen. The same age you were when you danced across my heart."

They say your sins will find you out. It hadn't even been much of a sin – teenage girls were supposed to play fast and loose with teenage boys, how else were they meant to test their power parameters? Kitty had only kissed him a few times, it had been fun, but she hadn't wanted this lanky American teenager landing on the doorstep and cramping her style all summer long. Not when she'd been fairly sure Ronan, who had a motorbike, a diamond stud in one ear and a job in the amusement arcade on Bray seafront, would ask her out if she loitered about the one-armed bandits long enough. Ronan wore leathers, whereas Tim – make that Clarke – had asthma and a predilection for baggy T-shirts, and had wanted her to wear his hulking great class ring. Even the exoticism of an American twang hadn't been sufficient to disguise his nerd tendencies.

"I'm sorry if I was cruel – it goes with the territory when you're a teenage girl," Kitty muttered. "I've improved since then, I'm hardly ever cruel to men," she felt compelled to tack on, but he didn't react.

Sunny did, though – she snorted. It was a "chance would be a fine thing" class of snort.

Noreen-dear sailed in with a tray containing two glasses of whiskey for the men, three tumblers of fizzy water for the women, a bowl of peanuts and another one of ice because everyone knew Americans were compulsive about adding ice to their drinks. She'd enhanced her ensemble with a frilly white apron in the style of an Edwardian parlour maid, with pleats ironed in.

"I'll have a whiskey too," snarled Sunny, stamping off to pour herself one.

"So," her mother smiled from Clarke to Kitty, "have you two been having a lovely sociable chat? My elder daughter is a prominent journalist, Mr Maloney."

Kitty groaned; before the night was over she'd have her reinvented as the Irish Woodward and Bernstein rolled into one.

"Call me Clarke, ma'am," he urged.

"You'll have ice with that, Clarke." Complacency screeched from her countenance: we know a thing or two about refinement in these parts. She'd unearthed some silver-plated ice-tongs and was clicking them at him.

"Not for me, thank you, ma'am. I'll go native and have it neat." He nodded at Kitty's father, who nodded back, and swallowed half his drink.

Kitty sat there with her Ballygowan, wishing it were a gin and tonic, and found herself wondering what the Exalted One was up to with his nurse in Dún Laoghaire. Were they emptying his briefcase of packets of Rothmans and cans of Coke? Maybe they were adding rum to the Coke and having Cuba Libres. Or she could be rustling up a Filipino delicacy, although the only one that sprang to mind was Bang Bang Chicken and involved doing something inhumane with a large thumping implement and a live fowl suspended upside down. Not that the Exalted One would be bothered by bloodthirsty behaviour towards chickens when he didn't believe in treating humans with consideration.

"What do you think, Kitty?" asked her mother.

Four pairs of eyes slewed towards her.

Caught not paying attention, she played for time and muttered, "I'd need to give that some thought."

"Trust Kitty not to commit herself," brayed Sunny.

It was unfair that Sunny was irked with her, thought Kitty. How was she supposed to know twenty years ago that she should steer clear of an American boy who bought her candy and wanted her to wear his class ring? The sisters locked eyes, Sunny's adversarial and Kitty's defensive.

Clarke rode to the rescue, and yes, of course it made Kitty think of Eeyore again.

"We're discussing whether I should make time to do the Ring of Kerry – your mother says it's the one part of Ireland no American should miss seeing. Of course I'm an Irish-American" – this was uttered with some reproof – "but I think maybe I'll try to swing by and fit it in."

"You don't swing by Kerry, it's at the far end of country. You have to be going there for its own sake," snapped Sunny, who was in a lather with Clarke as well as Kitty. He might have told her he knew her sister; she felt diminished.

Kitty stood and walked with decisive strides to where Sunny was leaning against the mantelpiece, too moody to sit. She held her by the shoulders and spoke with quiet authority. "I wouldn't have courted your future beau if I'd known you were going to take a shine to him, but at sixteen my clairvoyance skills weren't honed."

Of course she didn't, she only fantasised about it. Instead she called, from the safety of ten feet away, "Will I fix you another drink, Sunny?"

"I'd prefer it if you fixed me another life," fired the response.

"The cabbage will be boiled dry," exclaimed their mother, fleeing to the kitchen.

Their father was on his feet seconds after her. "I'll give Noreen-dear a hand."

Never in the history of the Kennedy family had their father helped their mother with the cooking; obviously the tension between Sunny and Kitty was affecting him. Noreen-dear took pity on her husband and let him stay in the kitchen instead of exiling him to the sitting-room.

"So what's the story with you and Clarke?" Sunny asked Kitty. The American visitor was resolutely ignored as she turned her back on him. Discomforted, although unsurprised by Sunny's hostility – he should have prepared her, but he had wanted to surprise Kitty – Clarke drained his glass and ran his thumbnail along the slashed indentations of the tumbler's surface

"Teenage romance." Kitty aimed for a blithe note. "Handful of kisses and it was all over. It was the summer I went to Boston with the exchange programme. Our hosts were expecting deprived kids from war-torn Derry, but none of them wanted to go in case they missed any rioting, so they had to make do with a consignment from Bray instead. They kept asking us about the Troubles and we knew less than they did."

Clarke, who'd made a snuffling noise when she'd dismissed their liaison as a handful of kisses, intervened. "It was a lot more than that, Kitty. I measured every woman afterwards against you and they all fell short."

He was ribbing her, thought Kitty. He had to be ribbing her. God oh God oh God, look at the face on him, he wasn't kidding. Clarke T Maloney, or Tim Newman, or Mr Hollywood, or whoever this emotionally stunted American chose to style himself, was giving her that intensive look she'd found preposterous as a teenager, never mind as a thirty-six-year-old woman. "That was a long time ago, Clarke. A lot of water has passed under the bridge since then." Kitty kept her eyelids at half-mast, to shirk his glance.

Noreen-dear made another entrance, face heated from the kitchen and lipstick renewed with more panache than expertise. She banged a little gong and trilled, "Dinner is served!"

This time Sunny and Kitty did suspend hostilities long enough to exchange eyebrow-raised glances – where did she find her accoutrements?

"Noel Coward said some women should be beaten regularly, like dinner gongs," remarked Sunny, setting her glass on the mantelpiece where it would leave a ring and annoy Noreen-dear.

"Surely not," protested Clarke.

"Absolutely." Sunny hitched up the waistband of her trousers and swaggered out ahead of him.

Clarke abandoned his empty glass and followed Kitty, who'd cantered after Sunny because she didn't want to be left alone with him.

Just as soldiers were fired for battle by a ration of rum before the charge, Denis Kennedy had been emancipated by his pre-prandial tot of Black Bush. He brandished a bottle of white wine – a Christmas offering from a neighbour who'd dropped in for mince pies – which had been exiled to the depths of the larder. It was unchilled, it was Riesling, but it was alcoholic. Kitty and Sunny brightened while their mother glowered.

"Everyone except Noreen-dear for a drop of wine?" he inquired needlessly.

Everyone except Noreen-dear nodded enthusiastically.

"My wife's a Pioneer," he explained to Clarke, while Noreen-dear fussed about finding the tulip-shaped wine glasses that matched the tumblers.

It was clear from Clarke's mystified reaction that he pictured someone in a covered wagon boldly heading west into hostile territory.

"Teetotal," interpreted Sunny.

"Right." Clarke still looked at a loss. "I thought the Irish loved to drink."

"We do," Kitty assured him. "Apart from the ones who don't."

Clarke was sidetracked from pursuing this conundrum by Denis, who placed him ceremoniously at the head of the table. He demurred, then accepted the seat, a vein throbbing in his left temple.

The dining-room smelled of furniture polish, shag-pile carpet and Brussels sprouts. It always smelled of sprouts, although they were only served once a year. A framed family photograph of the four Kennedys taken twenty-five years previously – each of them rivalling Cheshire cats with the circumference of their grins – had pole position on the chimney breast, beneath which glowed an imitation fire. On the sideboard stood Noreen Kennedy's collection of Belleek china vases, each one more lavishly shamrocked than the last. Kitty was thankful to see both her wedding photographs had been removed, finally, although the frames were pressed into service showing cousin Justine's nuptials and Sunny in her first stage appearance at the age of eight, dressed as a flower with a halo of stiff yellow petals radiating from her skull. The stark remnants of the garden, settled into winter hibernation, could be glimpsed through French windows whose velvet curtains remained open.

"Curtains, Denis," protested their mother.

"Sorry, Noreen-dear." He kept his wineglass in his hand as he drew them, in case of summary confiscation.

Leek and potato soup was served from a tureen on a tea trolley. Noreen-dear urged Lilt on everyone, but they turned it down in favour of Riesling refills. At which stage the bottle was empty, with Kitty and Sunny both wondering whether they could skedaddle to the off-licence between courses. Their father felt he'd chanced his luck enough for one night and was privately jubilant as he drank the wine he thought tasted diabolical. Wine buffs made too much of a song and dance about the stuff. Give him a decent whiskey or a pint of stout any day.

Clarke was an appreciative guest. He had a second helping of Noreen-dear's home-made soup and three slices of her speciality wheaten bread. He even submitted to her repeated offers of a glass of Lilt although his grimace, on sipping it, betrayed that it wasn't the funky fruit-juice his taste-buds had been expecting.

"Will I go to the off-licence?" volunteered Kitty, as the soup bowls were cleared away.

"You will not," countermanded her mother, "the cabbage will be soggy if it's kept waiting to be eaten any longer."

"You shouldn't have asked, you ought to have stood up and gone," seethed Sunny.

"I didn't see you leaping to your feet," retorted Kitty.

"Sunny," intervened Noreen-dear, "I need your help with slicing the boiling bacon."

Sunny was sullen as she left the room, scuffing her mules against the carpet.

Denis looked from Kitty to Clarke and back to Kitty. "I'll fetch the whiskey," he said.

Alone momentarily, Clarke leaned toward Kitty, his frame trembling with urgency. "I must see you on your own."

Kitty was apprehensive that Sunny would burst in and deposit the boiling bacon in her lap. "Why?" she panted, watching the door.

"We have to talk." He crowded her with his gaze.

"There's nothing to talk about," objected Kitty. "We don't know each other."

"I have photographs of you."

For one heady moment, Kitty thought he meant compromising photographs and he was intent on blackmailing her.

"Don't try telling me I don't know you," continued Clarke. "We're arm in arm in those photographs – we look like a couple in them."

"We're kids in them, for goodness sake."

Kitty's father arrived with the bottle of Black Bush tracked down to the drum of the washing-machine, although Noreen-dear claimed she had no idea how it ended up there. "Now, Clarke, we're not supposed to mix the grape and the grain but, sure, I'll risk it if you will. Anyway the damage is done already." Denis Kennedy was jovial, for contrary to his expectations he was enjoying the evening. He recognised there was a degree of tension in the air and had detected the nuances of sibling rivalry, but that was women for you. Noreen-dear was in high spirits, elated at playing hostess, and it wasn't every day he had a few Black Bushes with his dinner.

Clarke accepted his whiskey with the gratitude of a drowning man grasping a life-jacket. He asked for water in it, which sent Denis back to the kitchen, and immediately Clarke fastened those mournful eyes on Kitty.

"Would you stop hounding me – you're my sister's boyfriend." She was accusatory.

"I am not," he spluttered.

"You danced the night away with her." Kitty folded her arms, implacable.

"That's hardly grounds for breach of promise."

"But you did make her promises."

"I did?" Clarke looked bewildered.

"About a part in the new film you're casting," Kitty prompted him.

"Well, sure I did, but that doesn't make me her boyfriend. Come on, Kitty, gimme a break, I haven't laid a finger on your sister. I mean, I might have kissed her hand at the end of a dance, but that's the limit. Look, we haven't much time, say you'll stop by my suite in the Clarence for a nightcap. I can give you a lift there in my limo – it's swinging by here at eleven."

"That'll look great, me heading into town with you in your fancy car. Sunny will love that."

"Gee, I never thought of that. Leave it with me, we'll work something out. I'm determined to see you, Kitty. I've waited twenty years for this and I'm not about to let you slip through my fingers again."

Chapter 19

Noreen-dear paced ceremonially into the dining-room, a platter between her hands. "A traditional Irish dish for our visitor," she announced, "cabbage and bacon. Generations have been reared on it. I was reared on it, Denis was reared on it, the girls were – well, no, they never cared for it. It's food fit for a high king. I hope you brought your hunger with you, Clarke."

"Yes, ma'am." Reverential, he volunteered, "When I was a kid I heard my grandpa talk about cabbage and bacon."

Noreen-dear nodded. "There's nothing to match it for lining the stomach."

Now that she had the meal served, Noreen-dear was ready to relax into her role as inquisitor. Between mouthfuls, he was subjected to an intensive grilling about his Irish roots – distant, but try telling Clarke that; his marital status – divorced, with a five-year-old son; and his CV as a casting agent – two films, four sitcoms and a mini-series.

"And do you really have a part for our Sunny in your new film?" Their mother heaped another mound of mashed potato on his plate, ignoring her husband's empty one.

"Sure." Clarke gamely tackled the never-ending stream of food.

"With lines and everything?" insisted Noreen-dear, spearing a slice of bacon and depositing it beside the potato.

"Sure do. Just a couple, but it's a start." Clarke picked up his knife and began cutting the meat. "She's one of the village girls, right, Sunny?"

"I am. I show the American newcomer where to find his cottage when he steps off the train." Sunny looked mollified as she reflected on what she'd already achieved with Mr Hollywood.

"I loved that film – Maureen O'Hara was only gorgeous in it." Noreen-dear sighed, then chased it away with a frown. "I hope you fellows don't go making a mess of the new version. Leave well enough alone, that's what I say."

"I don't want them to leave well enough alone, I want to be in the new film," protested Sunny.

"Still," Noreen-dear was Cassandra-like, "people will never forgive the Yanks" – she coughed – "the Americans, if they make a banjax of it. That film is loved, Sunny, loved. Am I right, Denis?"

"You're right, Noreen-dear."

They were in the sitting-room with cups of tea and rectangles of her mother's chocolate-coated shortbread when the doorbell shrilled.

"That'll be my driver." Clarke surged to his feet. He pumped Denis's hand, one manicured hand cupping the older man's elbow, next taking Noreen-dear's hand with the veneration he'd show a sacred relic. When he reached Sunny he bobbed down and kissed one cheek, then he was finally standing before Kitty. She thrust her hand at him before he got any notions, but Clarke took it and held on firmly. "Say," he drawled, as though suddenly struck by an idea, "don't you live just off the main drag back into town? How about I drop you off?"

"There's no need." Kitty injected a sliver of ice into her tone, but Clarke was impervious.

"No problem, we're going that direction anyways. Makes sense, doesn't it, Noreen?"

"It certainly does," said Noreen-dear. "Don't be ungracious, Kitty, accept the young man's offer of a lift. It will save your father taking the car out of the garage – anyway, he's over the limit, aren't you, Denis?"

"I seem to be," agreed Kitty's father, delighted by such an unfamiliar set of circumstances. "Will you have one for the road, Clarke?"

"No, thanks, sir, I have a breakfast meeting in the morning so I should head for the hills. But you can rest assured I'll see to it that this little lady of yours reaches home safe and sound."

"Meetings on Sunday mornings – you Americans have a tremendous work ethic," marvelled Denis.

Clarke shrugged. "Somebody's gotta bring home the bacon."

"I'm not ready to leave yet, I want to stay on," wailed Kitty, but it was too late. Her mother was bundling her into her coat and Sunny was glowering.

Before she knew it, she was sitting in the back seat of a stretch limousine with smoked glass windows and a mini-bar. Clarke saw her glance dally along the length of the mini-bar, for she'd always fancied trying one out. It had to be even more fun than hotel mini-bars and they were addictive.

"Shall we?" Without waiting for an answer he poured a couple of inches of Jack Daniels into two glasses, ice added before the car had turned out of Hunter Crescent.

So that's why they have smoked-glass windows in limousines, thought Kitty. She sipped cautiously, half-expecting the car to take a bend and send her drink flying, but the ride was smooth.

"I was crazy about you, Kitty Kennedy." Clarke was reflective.

"So how come," Kitty rolled the bourbon around her tongue, feeling it shoot straight to her nose, "it took you so long to find me again?"

"I meant to a hundred times, I almost did, and then before I knew it I was married – to the wrong girl – and I never had the chance to visit Ireland. But when the opportunity came up to do casting for this movie in Dublin I seized it with both hands, and part of the reason I did was the hope of catching up with you again." Three beads of sweat swelled above Clarke's upper lip.

Kitty supposed she should feel flattered, and she did a bit to be honest, but he'd been a summer romance, he wasn't meant to reappear. Besides, her sister would never forgive her if anything happened between her and Clarke.

"Listen, Clarke, Sunny is keen on you and she doesn't just latch on to people without any encouragement. It wasn't fair of you to use her to reach me."

"I didn't do it deliberately, Kitty. Shoot, it was only in the last day or so I put two and two together and worked out the connection between you. I'd intended to get the job done and then see if I could find you – I never imagined I'd be auditioning your sister."

She glanced out of the window and saw Montrose looming ahead to the right of the dual carriageway, the television pylon reminding her of a skeletal Eiffel Tower. "We've overshot my turning. Please ask your driver to take the next turn-off and double back to Blackrock."

"Won't you come to the Clarence with me and get reacquainted?" His brown eyes were appealing. "I have a view across the river – it looks real pretty at night with all the lights twinkling. Just for an hour, I'll have my driver run you home as soon as you say the word."

"I'd like to go home now. It's been a long day and I'm tired."

He nodded, resigned. "Sure thing. But how about I buy you lunch tomorrow?"

"I never get up before lunchtime on a Sunday."

"Afternoon tea, then. I hear you Irish like it almost as much as the British. Please. There's something I want to tell you."

Probably more drivel about teenage romance. "Give me your number and I'll phone you." Kitty postponed the decision.

He scribbled on a business card. "Have the hotel page me if I'm not on this number, I don't want to miss your call. What I need to let you know is real important."

* * *

Next morning Kitty lay in bed wondering why so many unsuitable men were currently cluttering up her life. She must be emitting pheromones to indicate availability. If only she could have been more pragmatic about Joe French. He was married and that was what she wanted, wasn't it? So why had she developed scruples? She was baffled by her response to him. Kitty threw on some clothes and wandered into the living-room, where she noticed Joe's orchid was wilting. A parable, she supposed.

Kitty flopped on the sofa and text-messaged Rose: *"Met blast from past last night."* She knew true text-fiends dropped consonants and used shortcut spellings, but she couldn't bring herself to do it – she'd spent her working life as a journalist learning how to spell and texting risked unstitching all her good work.

Back whizzed the reply: *"Think you've got problems? Try my life."*

Kitty clicked busily: *"Date disaster?"*

"Worst kind, said it was serious."

This was too exciting to rely on text messages for the next instalment; Kitty rang Rose. "You told Feargal you were serious about him?" She was incredulous.

"No," Rose wailed, "he told me. Obviously I can't see him again."

"Obviously," Kitty agreed. A lull ensued. "Why not?"

"People want readymade intimacy without the trouble of building up to it. It's impossible, but it's typical of today's instant gratification fixation. Anyway, Feargal's enamoured with the idea of being serious about me, not with the reality," Rose explained, in a temper, as though it were Kitty's fault a man was professing devotion to her.

"Reality's overrated," Kitty suggested.

"That's where you're wrong, Kitty, reality is all that's certain. These guys who talk about permanence right from the start aren't interested in who you are – only who they want you to be. Their love object. They should be avoided at all costs because sooner or later reality catches up with them and they can't handle it. I have to go, my toast has popped and I don't like it cold."

I can't even talk to her about Joe French, Kitty thought, piqued, as the disconnect tone sounded. She'll just say of course I shouldn't get involved with him and my instincts are right. Which wasn't what Kitty wanted to hear at all.

The land-line rang two minutes later. "It's madness," Rose expostulated. "When I'm sixty he'll be forty-seven. But I probably won't know him when I'm forty-one let alone sixty because he'll win me over and then, just as my guard slips, he'll leave me high and dry for some fresh-faced twenty-year-old."

"George Eliot married a man twenty years younger than her when she was sixty," Kitty observed.

"That's right, and he jumped into a canal on their honeymoon in Venice."

Static crackled on the line.

"Feargal panics me," Rose admitted. "Father Damien is the only man I want to love me, even though I know there's no chance of that any more." She adopted a Deep South evangelical minister's voice. *"Why, honey, the truth is he loves Jesus more."* She sighed. "I still want him back, Kitty, we were together too long for me to start over with someone else."

"Maybe you could just practise on Feargal for a while," suggested Kitty, thinking it was high time they discussed her own predicament with Joe. Who hadn't even tried particularly hard to pursue her when she'd left him, so he probably didn't care one way or the other. "What does Feargal do, anyway?"

"Radio show. He has a morning phone-in slot five days a week on CityBeat FM. *Issues Not Tissues*, with Feargal Whelan."

"Oh yes, I've heard him." Kitty's interest-levels cranked up. "He has a kind voice."

"You see what I'm reduced to? Kindness."

"Kindness is the most important quality there is, much more reliable than charm or a handsome face." A seam of steel filaments threaded Kitty's voice. "The older I grow, the less I'm sure of, but I know this with absolute certainty. Ultimately, kindness is all that matters."

Kitty was right, thought Rose. But why couldn't she find a kind man who was closer to her in age?

"You know, Rose, if you were a man the age-gap wouldn't be relevant," continued Kitty.

"True. But I'm not a man." Rose became heated, voice rising an octave. "I'm a woman with crow's feet and a belly that no amount of exercise will flatten. I find pubs too crowded and most live music too raucous. I've learned my legs are best covered up, whatever the fashionable length of this season's skirts, and that skin-tight jeans flatter only the very young."

"Middle-aged people wearing jeans have ruined them for the young anyhow."

"Pay attention, Kitty, I'm baring my soul here. I don't want to have to start again and build a history with someone new."

"But that's exactly what you must do, Rose." Kitty was sympathetic but uncompromising.

Her friend recognised the sting of truth. Truth didn't ring like a bell, it lacerated the top layer of skin. "I know, Kitty." She spoke quietly, resignation permeating her voice. "It's not that I care about raised eyebrows when I'm with Feargal, it's that I feel the age gap already. Sometimes I feel infinitely older and wiser than him when we're talking, and it leaves me uncomfortable in my own skin."

"Perhaps that feeling will fade. It can't be there all the time or you wouldn't have befriended him."

Rose considered. It was true – most of the time she found herself compatible with Feargal. It was just now and then that she cringed.

"There were twelve years between my grandparents," said Kitty.

"Let me guess. She was nineteen and he was thirty-one and nobody batted an eyelid."

"Twenty and thirty-two, actually."

"Exactly." Rose swished lukewarm tea against china and felt persecuted. "The twelve extra years were on his side – that makes all the difference."

"The last time I checked the calendar we were living in the twenty-first century. I was under the impression I had a friend who owned her apartment, had a pension plan so she wouldn't be reliant on someone else's, made her own decisions – and wasn't limited by outmoded notions of what other people consider appropriate. Have a bit of fun with him, Rose. Nobody's asking you to darn his socks and bake his bread."

Rose realised she had been holding her breath and exhaled. "All right then," she agreed, unexpectedly meek. "Maybe a bit of fun wouldn't hurt too much."

"Good woman. My sister maintains a little temptation is healthy. And a lot is healthier again. Mind you, I've always suspected she reads these globules of wisdom over someone's shoulder on public transport."

Kitty, who hadn't the energy to angst to Rose about Joe after all, replaced the receiver in its cradle and trailed off to brush her teeth.

* * *

Rose loaded up her washing-machine and wondered how to mend fences with Feargal, whom she hadn't heard from since he'd walked her home from the French Paradox earlier in the week. They'd held hands strolling along the side of Herbert Park, cutting through Donnybrook to Ranelagh, while Feargal had named the stars in the night sky and Rose had admired his upraised profile. At Clonliffe Square she had invited him in – intending to allow him to persuade her he should spend the night. For during that walk home, Rose had decided to sleep with Feargal.

While she had hunted out a corkscrew, he had drifted around her cream-painted living-room, assimilating everything – almost as though memorising it. The Ansel Adams print had charmed him.

217

"You had it framed," he'd exclaimed, coming up behind her and catching her around the waist. Rose, wrestling with a slippery bottle, had found herself frog-marched across to the print, where he'd kissed her with so much passion that she'd thought they might end up coupling on the floor beneath the Half Dome. That was all right, that was gratifyingly spur of the moment, the last functioning fragment of her brain had decided. Spontaneity was allowed because you could deny intent afterwards.

Then Feargal had spoiled everything. He had lowered her gently onto the rug, cradling her head in the crook of his arm, and polluted the moment with three words that sizzled through her with the grace of a cattle-prod. "I love you."

She'd thrown him out.

* * *

As Rose separated the whites and coloureds of her laundry into two separate piles on her kitchen floor – stonily determined not to acknowledge the tendril of doubt which suggested she might have treated Feargal contemptuously – a knock was sounding on Kitty's door a few miles away.

If that's a pizza delivery for next door I'm having it, my conscience can look the other way, decided Kitty, whose cupboard was bare. She was starving. She'd been under so much pressure last night, between Sunny mentally sticking pins in a waxen image of her, and Clarke mooning like a lovestruck calf, that she had only moved her dinner from one side of the plate to the other. Now she had high hopes of some breakfast pizza. The delivery company, which dropped off jumbo-sized quattro stagioni pizzas at all hours of the day and night to the firemen on the left side of Kitty's party wall – the side not occupied by a squalling baby – was always confusing the houses.

Joe French stood on her doorstep. At least I'm dressed, was Kitty's first thought.

I wish he'd undress me, was her second.

Chapter 20

"I came to make amends." Joe was subdued, his characteristic aura of barely contained energy restrained. His hair was damp, the copper dimmed to a reddish-brown and curling at the temples as though he'd recently stepped from the shower.

"How did you know where to find me?" Kitty held onto the door-snib for balance, winded by his unexpected appearance.

"You're in the phone book, Kitty. I didn't need to hire a private detective. Although obviously" – his teeth flashed against the arc of his mouth – "that was plan B. I know this part of town. In case you hadn't noticed, one of our biggest stores is in the next street." He nodded towards Bumpermac's. "I thought about ringing, but couldn't take the risk you'd hang up. You looked so desolate the last time I saw you. My head tells me it was two days ago, but my heart flatly refuses to believe it." Joe rubbed the palm of his hand against his cheek, at once pleading and sheepish. "Whatever chance I stood with you, I realised it had to be face to face."

"How did you know you'd even find me in?"

"I didn't. But I knew I could always go away and come back. May I come in? Or would you like to step outside and take a walk with me? There's something I want to tell you." His eyes shimmered with entreaty.

Kitty found herself unclenching. "Just a minute." She retreated into the house for a coat and keys, then joined him on the pavement. "Where to?"

"This is your territory, you decide."

Kitty shivered, turning over the possibilities, and before she knew it his cashmere scarf was tied at her neck, pussycat bow in place. One of their traditions already. It was too soon for traditions; it was too dangerous for traditions.

They walked towards a park overlooking the sea. Joe's eyes were fastened on the bulbous jut of Howth on the far side of the bay, as they paced a downward sloping path and he rehearsed his overture to this woman who was preoccupying his every waking thought.

He risked a glance at Kitty, fumbling for an opening. "I know hardly anything about you, yet I know I don't want to lose you." Joe's voice was cracked. He cleared his throat and Kitty waited, sensing there was more. "I wish it could be possible to have more than one life. To have an alternative life. Instead of being forced to slot into the uncompromising grooves of the first life you've chosen. A life which you now see is impossible to satisfy you. But equally impossible to walk away from." He turned to face Kitty, who was weighing his words – trying to draw some hope from them but aware that, the more he said, the less prospect there was for any. "If I could have met you before, Kitty, it might have been a different story. But I'll never leave my daughter, which means I'll never leave my wife. I'm selfish enough to still want you, even though I know I have so little to offer." He hunched his shoulders, downcast, and she had a craving to comfort him.

But there it was: the caveat. Sunny had warned her Joe would confess he could never end his marriage, but would still hope for a no-blame relationship. She'd called it the Pontius Pilate approach.

"I respect your candour." Kitty was studiously bland. It allowed her to mask a plethora of conflicting emotions swirling inside her.

She pitied Joe. She resented him. And she desired him. She wanted him to say "I choose you," illogical though it was. Especially as they'd only just met. They were virtual strangers – she knew so little about the contours of his life. She had no idea which side of the bed he slept on, whether he kept a pool of change in his car for toll roads, if he wet-shaved or used an electric razor. Perhaps he was one of those high-octane businessmen who shaved in the car to save time as they raced from one meeting to the next.

Joe's eyes hadn't left Kitty's face for a second since making his speech. Now his hand reached out and, tentative, took hers, flitting his lips against the pulse-point on her wrist. Kitty started. He may be a stranger, but some strangers were as familiar as a ring never left off the finger. His hand fell away, although his gaze stayed on her, and she was acutely conscious of his physical presence.

"What are you thinking, Kitty?"

"I'm wondering about your life – and how I could fit into it. Whether it's possible for me to fit into it."

"It's possible, yes." Joe took a step closer to her, then another step, until he was so near his features blurred before her eyes.

Kitty's eyelids drifted down as she waited for his kiss. This was exactly what she wanted, a no-strings attached arrangement with a man she could share. Learn to share. It might be difficult at first. Joe French was telling her plainly that she could become his mistress and there was absolutely no danger of his wanting to marry her. She should thank her lucky stars. Then she should let him kiss her.

The kiss didn't come. Kitty opened her eyes to find Joe had turned away and was gazing across the chilly grey expanse of the Irish Sea.

"You probably think I'm the most immoral bastard you've ever met." The tip of his nose had turned pink with the cold.

"Maybe that's how you succeeded in business?" she suggested.

"Maybe." He laughed and the mood, which had been dense with emotion, lightened. "My forté is take-overs. I suppose you believe I'm bent on taking over your life."

"I might not mind. I might welcome a take-over bid. So long as it wasn't a hostile one."

"How about an extremely friendly take-over bid, would you be interested in one of those?" He pretended to be engrossed in the tail-chasing antics of a dog let off the leash at the far end of the park, but Kitty could see he was waiting for her answer. This was it, her chance to fulfil her New Year's resolution. So why was she vacillating?

He understood the hesitation. "Listen, I expect you're wondering what sort of arrangement I have in mind. The truth is I'm unsure. I've never found myself in this situation before. We've only just met and yet it seems imperative that I keep you in my life somehow. I've never experienced such an instantaneous rapport with anyone. I have a whole set of feelings for you – inconvenient ones, maybe, but I can't deny they're there, clamouring inside me. I've never been so uncertain about the future. All I know with absolute conviction is that I don't want to lose you, although there's no way I can keep you against your will. I don't even know how you feel about any this, Kitty – you could be on the brink of shrieking for the guards."

He looked so doleful at this point that Kitty took pity on him. "Tempted," she confessed. "I feel supremely tempted by you."

Reassured, Joe caught her by the elbows, pulling her towards him in one fluid motion. Kitty found herself nestled beneath his shoulder, cheek pressed against the gabardine cloth of his raincoat and head cradled in his hand. She felt soothed there and they rested in silence for a time. Trains careered on the railway track below them, but it seemed peaceful nonetheless.

By and by Joe slid a forefinger under her chin, tilting it upwards until their eyes collided. The air around them stirred and grew engorged with expectation, and Kitty felt the hum of life sound insistently within her.

"Come home with me, Joe," she invited.

Chapter 21

"I brought bagels." Clarke waved a brown-paper bag in front of Kitty's nose.

She fantasised about taking it from him and closing the front door in his face. It was such a satisfying image that Kitty was smiling as she stepped back to allow him in.

"I gave up waiting for your call." He seemed to swell to fill every square inch of her narrow hallway, which dwindled to Lilliputian dimensions in his presence.

"I had chores to do," Kitty protested. Not that you'd call Joe French a chore – he was a pleasure. A pleasure forestalled, unfortunately, by a call from his office just as he and Kitty had arrived at the corner of her street.

As his mobile phone had shrilled, she'd averted her eyes from the infant image on his screen-saver. Joe had dashed off, promising to come to her that night. "Ring me when you're on your way," she'd suggested, scribbling her phone number on his wrist, admiring how the spray of fine gilt hairs curled in the same direction. He'd explained something about a glitch in a property deal for a new store in Monaghan. She hadn't been listening, however. Just watching how his mouth formed the words.

"I'll drop by tonight, if I may, Kitty – it could be late though, I should warn you. This business in Monaghan could drag on."

She'd nodded wordlessly. He could arrive on her doorstep at any time of the day or night.

"I'll bring my horn and play you my Louis Armstrong tribute, 'What A Wonderful World' – because it is," Joe had smiled. Then he'd taken her in his arms before rushing off. Kitty had let herself into the house in a trance, convinced there was something unique between herself and Joe French. Something that superseded traditional notions of morality.

Now here was Clarke, whining about bagels.

"You weren't going to call, were you?" asked Clarke.

A layer of guilt, topped by one of defensiveness, and a final coating of hostility oozed up in Kitty. "I hadn't decided," she muttered.

"Never mind." Clarke was breezy, his morose features arranged into an expression of cautious triumph. "I was prepared for the worst so I took precautions. I had my driver make a note of your address last night, my personal assistant track down some fresh bagels this morning and here we are, ready for an afternoon snack." He stepped forward, so that Kitty was obliged to retreat or find herself in exceptionally close proximity to him. "I sent the driver on an errand for an hour – I hope that wasn't too presumptuous of me."

Presumptuous exactly summed it up. For some reason Kitty didn't feel like remonstrating – maybe it was the smell of the bagels through the paper bag he was brandishing and the lack of food in her house. "I suppose I could manage a bagel – I hope you brought cinnamon and raisin ones." She led the way into the kitchen, grudging but resigned.

Clarke perched on a stool at the counter, chin wedged on a palm, while she set out mugs and produced a canister of coffee from the freezer.

"Is that decaff?" He tensed.

"No, when I don't want caffeine I drink herbal tea."

"It's just that I've already had a mug of caffeinated coffee today."

"A second one won't hurt you." Kitty spooned two scoops into the cafetiere.

"Oh, but it will, my nutritionist only allows me one serving of coffee a day. I get hyper if I exceed that."

"Will I make you a cup of tea, so?"

"I'd prefer a cup of decaff."

"You see, Tim, I mean Clarke, I don't have any decaff." Kitty's voice was conversational, but her temper was unravelling.

He looked bewildered. "No decaff?"

"No. So will I make you a pot of tea?"

"Gee, I could have brought some if I'd realised you didn't have any."

"So you could," she agreed, splashing the teapot under the hot-water tap. "Don't worry," she reassured him. "There's soap in the bathroom and all the light bulbs work, we're not complete savages."

"I didn't mean to suggest you were." Clarke rubbed his hand across his scalp, the heavy silver of the class ring on his pinkie finger catching the light. The same ring he'd offered once to Kitty. "I guess you just have a different idea about what constitutes necessities in Ireland."

"We do," agreed Kitty, temper continuing to fray as she tore the paper bag to access the bagels. "Now, do you want these fellows toasted?"

"Sure do. There's a pot of cream cheese in the bottom of the bag to go with them."

She occupied herself with preparing their food, trying not to dwell on how Sunny would be incandescent if she knew the American was in her kitchen – and Kitty would be held to blame. Clarke T Maloney, sitting there with his over-sized feet and his knobbly joints, reinforced her sense of having taken a wrong turn way back when – she squinted, trying to work it out – when she was twenty. If she hadn't married Ryan she'd never had dropped out of college, and if she hadn't dropped out of college she'd never have needed to go back and finish her degree, so she wouldn't have met Benjamin. She might never have married anyone, which struck her as a more satisfactory arrangement than choosing wrongly. Twice. Involuntarily, her eyes strayed to a cork notice-board above her fridge, where a newspaper clipping she'd cut out in a fit of self-flagellation was pinned. *"St Gregory Nazianzus, who lived 1,600 years ago, had this to say about multiple marriages: once is in conformity with the law, twice is tolerated, a third marriage is harmful and a fourth makes one resemble a pig."*

"Food's ready." Kitty directed a dazzling smile at Clarke to compensate for the negative thoughts she'd been pumping in his direction.

"Smells good. I sure like a woman who can bake. It's such a feminine skill." He pronounced it to rhyme with porcupine.

"Is it, indeed? What about embroidery and painting watercolour miniatures? Are they femin-nine skills too?"

"Absolutely." Clarke was stifling his chuckles as Kitty rose to the bait she knew was being dangled deliberately.

"Well then, Clarke, I have to tell you I'm a fine example of the femin-nine female because there's nothing I like better than baking and needlepoint and labouring over exquisite miniatures, unless it's massaging my man's temples in rose water."

By this stage they were both chortling openly.

"That's why we liked each other," reflected Kitty, after the snuffling fit had died away. "We shared a sense of humour."

"And a liking for mint-chocolate ice cream."

"I've moved on to honeycomb crisp." Kitty aped condescension. "Only babies bother with mint chocolate now."

Clarke slapped his palm to his forehead. "D'oh! Why does nobody tell me anything?" He produced a minuscule tape recorder from his pocket and clicked the play button. "Memo to self: sack lifestyle coach."

"So, you said last night you had a particular reason for seeing

226

me," hinted Kitty, after they'd eaten the bagels and she was making more tea and coffee to pass the time.

"I do. I have some money for you, quite a lot of money, in fact." Kitty wrinkled her brow.

"Remember how you left me a State lottery ticket when you flew back to Ireland? You don't? OK, Kitty, take it from me, you left me a lottery ticket with a romantic note attached. It said: 'This is an investment in our future. If it comes up trumps we can buy plane tickets every month to see each other.' Well, I thought it was a romantic note – obviously it didn't mean much to you if you can't even remember it."

"I remember now," Kitty placated him. "Sort of. Did my lottery ticket win a fortune?"

"No, it won two hundred and six dollars and forty-seven cents. That wasn't enough for a plane ticket, so I bought some shares in a little technology company, a lucky fluke, I guess, because the company was taken over by a bigger one, which was taken over by Microsoft. Our $200 worth of shares are now worth significantly more than the original investment. I've come to give you half."

"I'm dazed," breathed Kitty. "Are you telling me I'm rich?" Excitement ratcheted.

"Depends on your definition. You're rich by Third World standards, but probably not by Irish ones. You've got a tidy investment. I owe you a little over ninety thousand dollars. I believe I'll make out the cheque for ninety thousand, two hundred and six dollars, forty-seven cents. I have a sentimental streak."

Ninety thousand dollars out of the blue – now that's what Kitty called a cracking start to the year. She groped her way to a seat opposite Clarke. "I don't understand why you're giving me all this money. I never knew about it – you don't have to do it. You're the one who made the investment, not me. The credit's due to you. Back then, I'd probably have bought a stereo and some new clothes with my share."

"I don't know about credit, I just struck lucky," Clarke shrugged.

"It doesn't matter that you knew nothing about the money, I knew about it. I knew its origins." Clarke folded his arms. "That lottery ticket helped me start my own business. I used my share of the cash as a deposit on my first office. It brought me luck – you brought me luck, Kitty. It's how I'm a Hollywood casting agent today. Well, that and my eye for talent."

"Is Sunny talented?" Kitty was momentarily diverted from the main item on the agenda, which was to sit there mentally spending her windfall.

"Some." He massaged his knuckles in the palm of a hand, meditative. "She'd never be an above-the-titles draw, but there's something to her, I'm not sure what. Our people could get to work on her, tone her up, maybe tint her hair a different shade. She has possibilities."

"Truly?"

Clarke pulled a face. "Maybe not great ones. I'll level with you, Kitty, she's late starting out in this business. Julia Roberts, Nicole Kidman – they were already huge stars by her age."

"She's not starting out, she's been acting all her life," protested Kitty.

"Some straight-to-video releases in Ireland and the UK don't count. Your baby sis is a newcomer, Kitty, that's how it is. Now, I brought my chequebook, do you want your cheque made out to Kitty Kennedy or Kathryn Kennedy?"

At that, the doorbell rang and Kitty sprang up. "Let me get rid of whoever this is. I want to concentrate on that line of noughts as you write them, Clarke." The cheque was going to look beguiling lodged in her bank account. Even more bewitching converted into a racy little car and a long-haul luxury holiday, with enough left over for a deposit on a house with a garden somewhere not quite so close to a dual carriageway. The possibilities were as intoxicating as they were limitless. Kitty pattered out to the hallway, brain whirring.

Sunny stood on the doorstep, a basilisk cast to her demeanour.

"Kitty, I believe you owe me an explanation. Exactly what is going on between you and Clarke?"

* * *

Rose had fed her washing-machine with two loads, cleaned her skirting-boards, phoned home, dusted the Ansel Adams print, and could delay the inevitable no longer. Her conscience was gnawing at her; she rang Feargal. Not to see him, only to be polite – he had told her he loved her, after all, and she'd responded by showing him the door. The least she could do was put in a call to check his feelings weren't utterly vaporised. But there was no way she was meeting him. Absolutely not.

Feargal said he'd be at her apartment in half an hour if she reminded him of the address. She did.

He was in her sitting-room twenty-seven minutes later. "Good job it's a Sunday," he panted, "otherwise there'd be no presenter for the morning phone-in show."

"Why not?"

"Because I'm in Ranelagh instead of the Dorset Street studio."

"Oh, right. But you wouldn't be in Ranelagh if you were meant to be on air."

"Wouldn't I?"

She glanced at him doubtfully. She could never tell when Feargal was teasing and when he was serious. "Tell me about growing up in London," she suggested.

"Noisier than Dublin, wider range of ethnic restaurants, more job opportunities." He rubbed the bridge of his nose. "If you stand on a London pavement you'll see virtually every skin-colour walk by, but in Dublin people are still mostly white. Or freckled, I should say."

"Do you think you'll go back one day?"

"I don't know," Feargal shrugged. "I like it here, I'm starting to feel I belong. I think I mentioned my parents are Irish; both of them come from Cavan. But staying with the Garritys over New Year was my first meeting with any Irish relatives. Shocking omission. Down to Mum and Dad, of course, but they had their reasons. Anyway, after college I decided it was time to give the motherland the once-over, so that's why I did my Masters in Dublin."

"And you're still here, five years later."

"I'm still here, five years later," he agreed. "My folks think I'm unhinged. They took the boat to Liverpool, caught the train to London, lived the rest of their lives in Holloway and never looked back. You'd imagine Ireland was the dark side of the moon the way they carry on. But I like it here. It feels," he reflected, "familiar to me. Of course I'll always be an Englishman to the Irish." He smiled, realigning the sombre silhouette of his face. "Then again, no harm in being an outsider, it saves you from being drawn into that club mentality. Now, isn't it time you honoured the legendary Irish reputation for hospitality, Rose, and offered me a cup of tea?"

Feargal and she ate a toasted sandwich apiece and then, as though nothing could be more natural, he caught hold of her hand and led her into her bedroom, where they lay on her creaky brass bed. Giving it more reasons to creak.

"I'm not ready to make love," she murmured, as he lowered her bra-strap and kissed the camber of a shoulder.

"Me neither," he fibbed, easing the garment back into its original position.

But it was comforting to lie within the circumference of his arms and Rose didn't worry, even fleetingly, that her body might be too world-weary for him.

"Let's loll on the sofa and watch the streetlights come on," Feargal suggested. They carried the duvet through from the bedroom and cuddled under it, not quite naked, but definitely not fully clothed.

"You're gorgeous." He settled her against a cushion and kissed the base of her neck.

"You should see me first thing in the morning."

"Is that an invitation?"

"You're embarrassing me," she remonstrated.

"There's no need to be embarrassed. Although you know, Rose, I can't be responsible for your feelings – only my own."

They gazed in companionable silence towards the green in the middle of Clonliffe Square, where an au pair was pushing a double buggy.

"Perhaps we should put the rest of our clothes back on," Rose suggested.

"Waste of effort, I'd only take them off again," he warned.

"But we haven't done anything," protested Rose, feeling ridiculous, because lovemaking didn't have to take a physical form. She'd shared more intimacy with Feargal that afternoon than she had in a long time with Damien. Such intimacy, in fact, that she was induced towards more.

"There's so much we could do together if only you'd let us, Rose. We could travel, see sights, build a store of memories to share." He transferred his gaze to the starkly atmospheric Ansel Adams print and she followed his eye-line. The Half Dome seemed to glimmer at her, urging her to agree. "Say yes," smiled Feargal.

"I can't," resisted Rose.

"You can."

Temptation tweaked at Rose. It started as a tickling sensation and billowed as Feargal outlined the pleasures of a trip to Yosemite National Park, until it became impossible to deny herself this indulgence. That's how it felt to Rose, an indulgence, but one she craved. Still, she suspended a decision. She stood abruptly, throwing off the duvet, and went into the bedroom for a sweater. She offered one to Feargal – "in case you're cold" – but he patted the sofa. "You keep me warm," he invited. Instead she walked across the living-room and leaned on the windowsill, watching a fat robin perched on the ornamental lamppost in the forecourt. His neat head jerked this way and that, assessing the lie of the land. She smiled at his bombastic self-confidence and the smile lingered on her lips as she turned back to Feargal.

He was so persuasive, grey eyes glowing in his thin face, that it was impossible not to be stimulated by his description of a valley of lush meadows and forests of towering sequoia trees, girdled by 3,000 feet high sheer granite walls. He tossed names at her feet that bewitched Rose: Happy Isles, Mirror Lake, Sweetwater Creek and best of all, Bridalveil Fall.

"What's Bridalveil Fall?" She was charmed.

"The Ahwahnee people, that's a tribe of native Americans who lived there, called it Spirit of the Puffing Wind." Feargal left the squashy oatmeal sofa to join her on the windowsill, willing Rose to share his passion for Yosemite. "It's a spectacular waterfall. You walk along a spongy path in the forest to reach it, following the sound of thundering water, until you step into a clearing and you're upon it, almost drenched by the spray. It's magnificent, powerful and breathtaking and totally primal."

He smiled, and Rose no longer thought the gap between his teeth stripped years from him. It simply suited him.

"I imagine its name may come from the fact there's so much mist frothing around that it looks like a bride's net veil," Feargal continued. "I sat at the viewing point, on a length of tree-trunk with hearts and initials carved along it, and knew I had to bring back someone with me to share those falls."

Rose felt breathless, as though she too had risen early one morning and climbed the forest track through thinning air to reach Bridalveil. "Let's do it," she cried, impulse fusing with temptation. "I have a fortnight's holiday to take before the end of March."

Feargal laughed. "Is that a promise, Rose McBride?"

"It's a promise, Feargal Whelan."

"I'm going to hold you to it," he threatened. "Now, we'll need to fly to San Francisco and hire a car to drive out to Yosemite. You can't fly direct from Dublin, you have to change either in London or Los Angeles and pick up a connecting flight. Any preference?"

"You decide." Rose wanted him to book quickly before doubts set in and she regretted her spontaneity.

"Depends on availability." He was businesslike, reaching to his jacket thrown over an armchair and producing a diary. "Are there any dates you can't manage? No? Fine, let's go on the Internet and see what we can rustle up. It'll be cold there at this time of year. You're thousands of feet above sea level and the log cabins aren't designed for central heating. But if you wear the right clothing you should be fine – thermal underwear is a must. You're not one of these women who need comfort on holidays, are you?"

Rose smothered a smile. If his mind was on thermal long johns, Feargal clearly wasn't attempting to set up a sensual holiday. Maybe that was the generation gap in operation again: young men may have become more interested in adventures than in seduction since she'd last noticed.

"Where's your computer?" He levered himself up from the windowsill. "Will we log on? I can check American Airlines."

"My Internet has crashed, I need to have it fixed."

"No problem, I'll shoot off home and make a start there." Feargal was pulsing with energy – Rose could see him mentally ticking off items on a list already: winter woollies, check; long johns, check; dollars, check; guidebook, check. "I'll give you a ring later on as soon as I have some news to report."

He was already halfway to the door; he was always so exuberant about everything, it would wear you out. She'd have needed another cup of tea before she could have contemplated checking out flight availability. Rose realised with dismay that her energy reserves had petered out in the past few years. Once, she too would have been ricocheting about making arrangements.

On the saddleboard, Feargal realised he hadn't kissed Rose goodbye and sprinted back, sweeping her into his arms with an exaggerated flourish that had both of them giggling.

"See you, gorgeous," he beamed. "You've just turned January into my favourite month."

Chapter 22

"This isn't a good time," Kitty prevaricated, as Sunny loomed on her doorstep.

Sunny was merciless. "We can talk about it on the street or we can talk about it indoors. Clarke may not realise this yet but he's mine, Kitty, and there's nothing you can do about it. I don't care how many letters you sent each other with SWALK on the envelope when you were teenagers."

"Let's go for a walk and discuss this," murmured Kitty weakly, aware that Clarke T Maloney was inside and the sight of him would loosen the already tenuous grasp Sunny had on her temper.

"It's raining."

Kitty could almost see the drops sizzle where they hit her sister's forehead. Sunny tucked her hands inside armpits and Kitty realised she was playing her no-nonsense detective from *Beat It*, the pilot that had never made it past a solo run.

Kitty caved in, stepping aside, and Sunny pushed past her and into the kitchen. Kitty leaned against the doorframe, braced for belligerence as her sister encountered Clarke. Suddenly she realised silence reigned in the house – more ominous again than broken crockery.

She awarded herself a couple of steadying breaths and followed Sunny through to the kitchen at the rear of the house, a low, rectangular extension which sliced through her back yard. There was no sign of Clarke. Only Sunny was in the room and she was striding its length, treading mud into Kitty's clean floor and defiantly smoking.

"So what have you got to say for yourself?" demanded Sunny, blonde hair spiked by restless fingers.

Kitty was circumspect. Best not say anything which might incriminate her. "About what?" She had her back to Sunny as she deftly binned the empty paper bag which had contained the bagels and set the mugs she and Clarke had used into the sink.

"About what?" mimicked Sunny, agitated, twisting a button on her shirt until it popped off. "About who, more like."

"Oh, you mean Clarke." Kitty wondered where on earth he could be. He couldn't have slipped upstairs out of the way because he'd have had to go through the hall to access the stairs, and the same applied to hiding in the living-room. The only explanation was that he had slunk out by the back door into the lane.

"Yes, I mean Clarke," Sunny parroted, coming to an abrupt halt in front of Kitty. "Is there something going on between you? He was particularly tenacious about wanting to take you home."

"That's hardly my fault. The last time I saw him I had a poster of Roxy Music on my bedroom wall and a bag of chips and a walk on the pier was my idea of a hot date. Come on, Sunny, be reasonable, I didn't have a notion that your Mr Hollywood was my American boyfriend when I was sixteen." Kitty began to feel cautiously optimistic, as though she'd been offered a whopping great reprieve. Maybe Clarke T Maloney had had the tact to vanish off the face of the earth. Preferably leaving a signed cheque in his wake.

"But why would he be so determined to meet you again after twenty years?" persisted Sunny. "It doesn't make sense."

"He wasn't determined, he just happened to be in Dublin on

business and thought he might as well look up an old acquaintance." Kitty was tired of Sunny towering over her and sat on a stool at the breakfast bar, hoping her sister would follow suit. "I don't know why you imagine he's interested in me – all he did was give me a lift home in his limousine. Which meant we were chaperoned, because he has a chauffeur. I'll probably never see him again; we're nothing more than ships passing in the night."

"Really?" Sunny faltered. Kitty saw the whites of her eyes were tinged pink from sleeplessness.

"Really."

Sunny realised her cigarette had burned to a stub and ran water from the tap over it. "You must think I'm deranged, Kitty. I was tossing and turning last night trying to make sense of it all, and the more I puzzled, the less I understood. I'm sorry for barging in on you like this."

"No problem." Kitty was magnanimous. Not to mention swamped with relief that she'd been able to reassure Sunny so readily.

"But," Sunny clicked the flint on her lighter on and off repeatedly, "he was strangely insistent about sweeping you off in his car. What did he want to talk about?" Her eyes were navy with mistrust.

"Sentimentality," Kitty ad-libbed. "He wanted to reminisce about the good old days. He had all sorts of questions about people in the group from Bray who'd gone on that exchange programme to Boston."

Sunny relaxed. "He is quite sentimental, isn't he – he told me his son was called Brocton, Brock for short, because that's the name of the small town in upstate New York where he met his wife. Ex-wife," she amended.

"See? You know more about him than I do. I hardly know anything about him any more." Kitty seized on the information to allay her sister's misgivings.

Sunny smiled. "I suppose we do have a rapport, Clarke and I –

we talked the night away at that dinner in the Unicorn. I've never experienced such an immediate feeling of compatibility with anyone. Well, not since Nick Shooter. But I don't know how sincere Nick was about anything. Clarke, on the other hand, is sincerity personified." She reached for the kettle. "I may as well have a coffee before I hit the road."

"No!" Kitty expostulated, with more venom than seemed appropriate – both to her and to a surprised Sunny. She wanted to usher out Sunny as precipitately as possible. She still hadn't reconciled herself to the fear that Clarke could pop out of a kitchen appliance at any moment.

"I can't have a coffee?"

"Of course you can. It's just that I thought we could stroll down to the village and check out a new café near the Ulster Bank. I'm bored with these four walls."

As Kitty was frisking the coat-rack to find her umbrella, the doorbell rang. Sunny had walked into the hallway ahead of her and was closest, so she opened it. On the road was a matt black machine, while Clarke's driver stood outside Kitty's front door. "I'm here to collect Mr Maloney," he explained.

Kitty froze.

"Why are you collecting Mr Maloney from this address?" asked Sunny.

"I dropped him here, miss. He asked me to call back later."

"When did you drop him?" Sunny was puzzled and hadn't yet jumped to any conclusions, although Kitty knew it was only a matter of time.

"Earlier today, miss." The driver was expressionless, hands folded in front of him.

Sunny turned and looked at Kitty, who was braced for rage or accusation. But not for the sorrow oozing from her sister's eyes.

"Perhaps you'd tell Clarke his car is here," Sunny was mild, "and then the pair of you can carry on where you left off. Laughing like hyenas at my expense."

"I don't know where he is." Kitty spread her arms, palms outwards, in a gesture at once helpless and pleading.

Sunny stepped across the threshold and walked away, her back ramrod straight.

Kitty moved her eyes from Sunny's rapidly moving form to meet the driver's curious gaze.

"If you could tell Mr Maloney I'm here?" he prompted her.

"Mr Maloney left some time ago," said Kitty.

The driver was perturbed. "Mr Maloney isn't familiar with the city, he'll end up lost."

"Not while he has a tongue in his head to ask for directions and money in his pocket for a taxi." Kitty retreated to the kitchen and slumped on a stool. She lacked even the energy to close the front door, although she heard it slam as the driver pulled it shut from outside.

Everything was in disarray. All she needed was for Joe French's wife to turn up and denounce her on the revolving stage for farce that was her doorstep, and her day would be complete. The phone rang and she lifted the receiver listlessly. It was probably the Exalted One telling her he'd replaced her with a cheap school-leaver.

"Kitty, it's your mother here, Noreen. That lovely American of yours has just sent me a box of chocolates the size of a bathtub."

"He's not my American."

"Isn't he? Sunny said he was. I don't know whether I'm coming or going between the pair of you and your men. I'm going to save my chocolates for Mother's Day. I have them displayed on the sideboard in the dining-room. Did you say you were coming home for Sunday dinner this evening?"

"No, I didn't, Mum."

"I could have sworn you said it last night as you were leaving, Kitty."

"No, I didn't, Mum."

"Well, that's very disappointing, lovie, and me with a hand-delivered box of chocolates, sent all the way out to Bray with that chauffeur fellow of his. Just himself and the box of chocolates in the car. Would you credit it? 'Compliments of Mr Maloney,' he said, and gave a little bow. Put your sister on to me."

"She's not here." Kitty held the receiver away from her ear and noticed her back door was unlocked. She trailed her glance along the back yard, with its motley collection of pots sprouting semi-moribund plants, and checked the gate on the outer wall. A gust of wind rattled its hinges – yes, it was open. At least that explained how Clarke had vacated the premises, and the certainty was better than wondering if he might be huddled inside her fridge with an icicle forming on his nose.

"How can she not be with you?" Noreen-dear tsked her tongue against her teeth. "She said she was on her way to Blackrock. Well, tell her to call me when you see her, but don't mention the chocolates. I want to see the surprise on her face when she opens the door and thinks she's wandered into one of those Butler's chocolate shops by mistake." Her mother chuckled. "I might even pretend Denis has developed a romantic streak and that he bought them."

* * *

Clarke wandered along the lane behind Kitty's house, feeling guiltily conspicuous, even though the only creature he met was a haughty cat. Finally he decided that Irish weather wasn't conducive to open-air loitering and stumbled off, all his extremities turning blue, in the direction of Blackrock village. He wound up at the café where Kitty had intended taking Sunny, unthawing his fingers round a glass of decaffeinated latte. Instinct told him he'd be safer going back to the Clarence, but he still had that cheque to give Kitty. Perhaps he should just slide it through her letterbox.

After a decent interval he set off to do that. Navigation, however, wasn't one of Clarke T Maloney's skills, and these terraced streets of doll's houses all looked identical to him. It was Saint-Something street, he remembered that much, but he'd already paced up one side and down the other of St Attracta's Street, St Eugene's Street and St Patrick's Street. They all looked familiar, uniform in colour, with decorated wooden eaves protruding above the front doors. That was a drawback with having a driver, you tended not to pay attention to routes. Where in heck was his driver, come to that? If he'd any sense he'd be cruising the block looking for him.

"Do you know a lady called Kitty Kennedy?" he asked a couple of nine-year-olds plotting where to lay their hands on the money for cigarettes.

"Buy us ten Majors and we'll show you where she lives, mistuh," bargained the shorter of the two.

Clarke didn't know what ten Majors were, but he had the impression they weren't candy bars. He tried another of those identikit streets, feeling a distinct sense of what Feargal Whelan would call "thwart" building within him.

By chance Kitty was in her living-room, watching the phone and wondering at what time Joe French intended visiting her. Perhaps she should chill the bottle of champagne Clarke had presented her with – or was it Joe's role to provide the bubbles? Distracted from the niceties of mistress-lover demarcations by voices outside, she did a double-take and realised that Clarke's was one of them. He was a-hump with the cold in his inadequate navy blazer and flannels and, tempting though it was to pretend she wasn't at home and leave him outside, she really had no choice but to admit him. Kitty opened the front door in time to hear Mrs McGill's grandson from the bottom of the street barter, "How about if you keep the packet and just give us one smoke each from it?"

"Stop hustling for cigarettes or I'll tell your granny on you, Jake," she cried.

At the sound of her voice, Clarke turned, relief flooding his morose features so that he almost looked animated. "Kitty, thank God. I couldn't remember where you lived."

"Come in, you must be frozen," she invited through gritted teeth.

He crossed the street in a couple of strides.

"Your driver called for you," she said, after she'd settled him beside the gas fire in the sitting-room.

"Where is he now?" Clarke had a striped rug draped around his shoulders and was almost squatting in the fireplace.

Kitty shrugged. "Probably back at the Clarence, unless he's been on to the American Embassy and persuaded them to issue a missing person's alert."

"I'd better ring my personal assistant and –" Whatever instructions he had in mind were ambushed by a great whooping sneeze which left him gasping for breath. "I seem to be coming down with a cold," he announced. "Colds always cripple me, I can't function with them."

"You need vitamin C." Kitty returned from the kitchen a few moments later with a glass of orange juice. "That should head it off at the pass."

"I doubt it – my colds are never deterred by anything." Clarke was glumly exultant as he made his prediction, but he drank the orange juice anyhow. "Not freshly squeezed," he noted, handing back the glass. Another sneeze waylaid him.

"Bless you," said Kitty automatically. "I'll fetch a box of tissues." Now, how could she raise the subject of the cheque and arrange for him to vacate the premises without looking like a heartless baggage? "Clarke, you're welcome to stay here until you feel well enough to go back to your hotel," Kitty began, after rustling up a honey and lemon drink and listening to the tribulations of his last cold, which it had taken a week to shake off.

"Thanks, Kitty. Appreciate it."

"But wouldn't you be more comfortable in your suite, with room service on the end of a telephone line?" she pressed on.

"I guess." He seemed dubious. "Shoot, it's kind of cosy here, but I'm taking up too much of your time. I suppose you have other plans."

"No, you're fine," – she felt mean, but she didn't want him there when Joe arrived – "but this house is prone to draughts. I'd hate to be responsible for your cold deteriorating into something more serious."

Clarke registered alarm. This certainly was an inadequately insulated country and he had a weak chest, despite his strapping build. "Gee, maybe I would be better in the Clarence."

"Do you think so?" Kitty reacted as though it was his idea. "Well, if you insist, perhaps I should ring your driver. I could tell him to heap some rugs in the car so you're snug as a bug all the way into town."

Clarke dictated the telephone number, then asked Kitty for a thermometer so he could check his temperature while they waited for his lift. Kitty seized the moment. "Listen, I've been thinking about what I should do with that ninety thousand dollars you mentioned." She was reluctant to bring up the subject of money – but even more reluctant to let him leave without mentioning it.

"I didn't write out your cheque." Clarke half-rose to his feet and then fell back onto the mint green two-seater sofa.

"No rush," lied Kitty, who wished he'd get a move on and sign it so she could believe it was real.

"My chequebook's in my jacket." He reached into an inner pocket, frowning. "I must have forgotten it, it's not here." He patted his wallet in the back pocket of his trousers. "That's safe enough, but no chequebook."

"When did you last see it?" asked Kitty.

"Did I take it out in your kitchen to start writing the cheque?"

"I don't think so."

"Maybe I left it in my hotel room; I know I had it there this morning before I set off for Blackrock. Gee, Kitty," he beamed for the first time since his sneezes had shattered the peace, "I'm real sorry about this, but I believe we may have to meet again so I can give you the cheque."

"You could always post it." Kitty knew she was fighting a losing battle, but was unwilling to concede without one last try.

"I promised myself I'd hand over that money to you personally."

Clarke's face acquired a patina of manly determination. "I have a whole bunch of meetings scheduled, but I'll call you and set up something later in the week."

Kitty finally bundled him out and adjourned to the bedroom to change the sheets in preparation for Joe's visit. Then she cast a carping eye around the room: it was comfortable and practical but lacked that boudoir feel. She scavenged in a drawer and scattered a few scarves across surfaces, grimacing at the result. They looked messy rather than seductive. She bundled them back in the drawer and cleaned the bath instead, exfoliated into it and had to clean it again, then started wondering why Joe hadn't been in touch yet. Surely he wasn't going to develop misgivings after kissing away her reservations?

She savaged her lower lip. Perhaps he'd taken out his phone to tell Kitty he was on his way, looked at the screensaver of his baby daughter in her Winnie the Pooh suit – and changed his mind.

Chapter 23

Sunny's heart was set on Clarke, and not just because he could further her career, although that certainly buffed up his allure. Clarke personified celluloid success to her. He represented everything she aspired to in life. Superstitiously, she believed acceptance by him – not just into the film he was casting but into his private life as well – would guarantee the stardom she coveted. He'd described his shingled house near the oceanfront in the picturesque town of Carmel, where even the litter-bins were reinvented as works of art, and where surfers gambolled along the turquoise swell of the Pacific. It was within commuting distance of Los Angeles and Sunny's facility for imaginative pirouettes – inherited from her mother – pictured herself ensconced there, a permanent house-guest. Not freeloading, exactly. Her gratitude would take a particularly corporeal form.

Sunny mooched along Kitty's street. Clarke didn't seem to want her gratitude and certainly not the kind she was intent on offering. She was overtaken on her way to the Dart by Clarke's limousine, as the driver headed towards the Clarence, compounding her sour temper. She hadn't even set foot inside the car and her sister had been ferried around in it. Clarke had probably invited Kitty to Carmel too.

Sunny wasn't just latching on to Clarke as her password to Hollywood. He was her amnesty from Nick Shooter too. With Clarke by her side, she was convinced she could overcome her addiction to Nick Shooter, which meant she could slough off her addiction to casual sex – which was becoming progressively less glorious and life-enhancing, in truth. Furthermore it was diverting her energies from the business of pursuing stardom. So she had reassembled Clarke as the ultimate facilitator, her open sesame to a shinier life.

A breeze riffled her platinum hair and she hunched her shoulders against its draught. Sunny perceived herself to be the victim of a gross miscarriage of justice. It rankled that Clarke seemed to prefer Kitty and Sunny, transcendentally illogical in her persecution fixation, blamed her sister for this. Sunny was weary of Kitty being the high achiever in the Kennedy family, with herself lagging behind. All her life she'd been trailing in her older sibling's footsteps. Kitty had always managed better exam results, been offered jobs that paid more money – she'd even notched up more proposals of marriage.

Sunny was the beauty of the family and Kitty was the brains. That was the map of their family geography. Beauties were supposed to be free to pick and choose, weren't they? The sisters had never competed for the same man before, but if they had, Sunny would have felt confident that she'd emerge victor. Her looks were her foremost asset, after all. Sunny paused to crumple her empty carton of cigarettes into a litter-bin, checking that her inner certainty was in place. She was going to be a star, wasn't she? Nothing. Her name would go up in lights, wouldn't it? Still nothing. Fear lanced Sunny. Damn Kitty – she'd stolen Sunny's man and her inner certainty.

Fright was replaced by a scalding gush of fury at her unscrupulous sister. Kitty had lied to her, tricked her and made a fool of her. That drivel about being interested in a married man and wanting to become a mistress was nothing more than a charade. Clarke had been her target all along. Unless she was so unprincipled she wanted both of them. Kitty was treacherous, devious and corrupt: she deserved to be punished.

* * *

After Feargal's precipitate departure to check travelling arrangements to Yosemite, Rose glanced at her wall-clock – for the first time not dejected about its status as a gift from Father Damien in his pre-Father Damien guise. She decided to go to Slane for an overnight stay with her parents. Rose hadn't intended visiting them until the following day, but her mother and father would be glad of the company. Besides, she needed a break from this puppy of a boyfriend she seemed to have acquired.

She loaded up her aged silver Honda Civic, which rattled but was essentially sound, to drive the familiar groove of the N2 northwards to Slane. The first person Rose saw, after driving over the winding bridge and chugging uphill at the approach to the village crossroads, was Alan Garrity – Feargal's cousin. As her engine idled behind a car waiting to turn left towards the castle, Rose studied Alan, hands in his pockets as he stood on the pavement, engaged in conversation with someone she didn't recognise. Alan Garrity had a slight build similar to Feargal's, and his head was cocked on one side in the identical mannerism she'd noticed in her flat a couple of hours earlier. He was a year older than Rose and married to a girl she'd gone to National School with. She'd known both of them all her life. Alan saluted as he recognised the Honda Civic and she nodded back. Whoever had coined the phrase about six degrees of separation hadn't reckoned with small-town Ireland, which speeded up the process.

"You're late, Rose." Her mother was stooped over the fire in the kitchen, poking at the heart of the blaze. Hannah McBride always liked to give the coals a couple of jabs with the poker when her husband was out of the house – it was her only opportunity because Kevin tended to monopolise it. He fussed with it constantly.

"Traffic." Rose dropped her overnight bag on the floor beside the scrubbed deal table and hugged her mother.

Hannah had the staccato movements of a squirrel, the beady dark eyes of one too, and she bustled about preparing something for her daughter to eat. At seventy-seven she was still sprightly and took pride in baking her own bread, but last year Rose had overruled her and employed someone to call twice a week to take care of the cleaning and ironing. Rose was chewing a slice of soda bread and home-made blackberry jam when her mother dropped the bombshell.

"Damien was in looking for you earlier," she said.

"Father Damien?" Rose's mouth plopped open like a trout on the fishmonger's marble slab, while her face drained of colour until it resembled the stippled white of the counter. She hadn't spoken to him since August, when they'd managed a stilted two-minute chat on the pavement outside the corner shop, as Rose had held a dripping ice cream cone. The last time she'd seen him had been leaving church after Midnight Mass on Christmas Eve, when she'd deliberately scurried out of his path.

Her mother nodded, sympathetic to Rose's distress but uncertain how to demonstrate it. Her daughter was so prickly where Damien Crowe was concerned. Admittedly they had been courting for a long time, but wasn't it better that he'd called it off before the wedding day rather than press ahead with doubts? Everything had been honest and above board. The way Rose carried on, you'd think he'd done a moonlight flit with her best friend.

Rose braced herself. "What did he want, Mam?"

"To see you, girl, not to spend time with old folk like your father and me, that's for sure – although Kevin collared the poor man and kept him talking for three-quarters of an hour about John Treacy's greyhounds. I said to him, I said, 'Kevin, the good Father's not interested in John Treacy's greyhounds – would you give the man peace.' But did he pay a blind bit of heed to me? Of course he didn't."

"All part of Damien's training for parish work," spat Rose. "He's supposed to visit the old and infirm and have the ears talked off him."

"He looked a bit peaky, I thought," continued her mother, ignoring the interruption as she disregarded all of Rose's temper flashes. "I hope they're feeding him properly below in Maynooth. I asked him if the seminarians ate fish on Fridays, or if they took a bit of meat these days, and he told me it was optional." Hannah McBride paused, her round face radiating wonder. "Imagine, now, all these years when we ate fish on Fridays, or maybe just a boiled egg with our potatoes if there was no fish to be had, and then the Church went and changed its mind. Optional, he said." She shook her head slowly from side to side, setting the extra layer of flesh beneath her chin trembling.

Rose struggled to contain her impatience. Her mother had an increasing tendency to stray off the point, but trying to nudge her back onto it had to be managed with tact or she'd clam up altogether. "How is he finding it in the seminary?" Rose was studiously casual.

"He said it agrees with him, but sometimes he feels old compared with his classmates – he's twenty years senior to some of them." Her mother cut her bread into eight rectangles and popped one in her mouth.

Rose was shaken by a spurt of rage. Father Damien should try going on dates with people twenty years younger than him, then he'd know all about it. Yes, she realised Feargal was only thirteen years behind her, but it might as well be twenty.

"But I said to him, I said, 'Damien – you don't mind me calling you Damien? It's just I have the habit, you see – Damien, nobody wants a priest who's wet behind the ears. A mature man who's lived a little and knows the workings of the world, that's what's needed.'"

Hannah smacked her lips against her dentures. "I think I set his mind at rest, indeed I do."

Rose debated asking why Father Damien had visited, but decided it wasn't worth the effort. The mood her mother was in, she'd hear a re-run of the entire conversation with the student priest. "Where's Dad?"

"Above with John Treacy, discussing greyhounds. He said he'd be back before dark, but it's not far off now. I said to him, I said, 'Kevin, I don't like you crossing that road except in daylight. The speed those cars travel at, they'll have you knocked to kingdom come.' Naturally he accused me of fussing."

Rose sighed. "I brought you that tweed skirt you asked me to look out for in Clery's sale. They didn't have it in grey so I chanced it in olive green. I kept the receipt in case you don't like it."

Her mother perked up. "I'll just wash my hands and then I'll try it on, girl. I suppose I'll have to get a foot chopped off the end, they make skirts very long these days. They must imagine we're all giants." En route to the sink, she paused. "Father Damien said he'd drop by again this evening – there was something particular he wanted to ask you. Most particular, he said."

Rose mauled the ball of her thumb, speculating. It couldn't be a request for the return of the engagement ring he'd given her, because she'd already hurled it at him. She'd never been particularly attached to the pinprick solitaire, a cheapskate token tricked out as a romantic one because he'd palmed her off with his granny's diamond. She'd understood only cads and skinflints accepted back their rings – surely there was some sort of tradition whereby a woman's jewellery was sacrosanct? However Damien, heart set on becoming Father Damien, had bent and retrieved the ring, dusting it off against his sleeve, and had slipped it in his pocket.

Rose couldn't imagine what he might want to say to her; she'd just have to wait. She began to clear the table of dishes, trying not to notice how her heart whirred against her ribcage. Life was just about becoming manageable again, but Father Damien still had the capacity to rock her equilibrium. She felt breathless as she ran the hot water, testing its temperature for washing the dishes. A man's face oscillated in front of her eyes – and it wasn't Feargal's.

* * *

Damien Crowe was an exceptionally beautiful man. It struck Rose afresh as she sat opposite him while her mother chattered, thrilled to have a priest in her house, even a fledgling cleric, and her father heaped coals on the fire until it roared up the chimney. Damien was in his early forties, although there was an ageless quality to his face – perhaps because it exuded serenity. He had strawberry-blond hair, whisper-soft skin faintly dappled with freckles and a long, straight mouth suggestive of melancholy. He would have been sublime for film, with his head too large for its average-sized body. But if he couldn't play a president with his profile on a bank note, or a Roman general subjugating barbarian tribes, then a priest was a fair substitute.

As Rose looked at him she realised – with a sense of something deflating inside her – that it would take more than a New Year's resolution to uproot Father Damien from her mind.

She had been on edge listening for his footsteps outside her parents' slate-grey three-storey home. The front door of the elongated house opened onto the pavement, and she'd tensed every time feet had passed in front of the kitchen window. Her hair had been combed and re-combed in readiness for his arrival, because he'd always admired the black length of it, and she'd forcibly quelled the urge to change her clothes into something more flattering than taupe canvas trousers. Damien had never noticed what she was wearing when he was courting her – why should it be any different now?

He'd arrived after dinner in a flurry of civilities, apologising for intruding and bombarded with assurances from her parents that it was always a pleasure to see him. He'd driven over from Collon, the next village along on the main road, and had been quizzed about the amount of traffic he'd encountered. Rose had kept her distance, watchful.

It was easier for Rose, with her parents in the room, to mime polite exchanges. To take his outstretched hand, feeling the habitual dry warmth of his touch without flinching – to look him in the eye, noticing the disappearance of the troubled expression which had become synonymous with his dealings with her. No doubt about it, concluded Rose, bile rising in her throat, the priesthood agreed with the man she'd been due to marry. He had the look of someone who'd chosen the right path in life.

"Rose, you're blooming, as ever," he said.

"So are you." She called him nothing, neither Damien nor Father Damien, for now that he was sitting a couple of feet away from her, one leg crossed over the other, he seemed less real than at any time in the past twelve months.

"The new job suits you, I'd say," he continued.

"Hardly new, it's been almost a year," she contradicted him.

"Doesn't time fly," he marvelled.

Banalities, she fumed silently, was that what they were reduced to? Once they'd meant everything to each other, they'd planned a life together, maybe children, and now they couldn't manage more than the chit-chat of strangers. The whirligig of time had much to answer for.

"How are all the family?" She adopted her cue from him.

"Grand, Rose, grand, thank God. My mother suffers from a shortness of breath going uphill, but other than that she's fine."

Rose thought of his three sisters, all teachers, and of his mother, a hearty woman who'd patted her hand and said "What's past mending is past minding" – as though that could possibly comfort her. Splitting up with Damien meant losing his family too, regardless of the platitudes people trotted out about keeping in touch; Rose had been close to the Crowes, but severance from Damien had meant the womenfolk were lost to her too. She embarrassed them, with her ringless finger.

251

Rose fidgeted, wondering what he wanted with her, while her father clattered about the fireplace attempting to roast them all and her mother eavesdropped shamelessly. Only Father Damien seemed completely at ease. He cast a sedative spell with his Buddha demeanour, hands plaited in front.

Tea had been offered and rejected twice before Father Damien cleared his throat. "I'm sure you're wondering why I came to see you."

Rose observed her father lay aside the poker and her mother, who had been pretending to flick through the *Meath Chronicle*, set down the newspaper.

"It occurred to me to wonder," Rose agreed. "We've not seen much of each other this past while, on account of your going off to Maynooth." Round about the time you should have been honeymooning in the Seychelles with me, she thought. Pride prevented her from delivering the barb.

Father Damien's face under its cap of strawberry-blonde waves, still without a trace of grey, irradiated at the mention of Maynooth. "I can't tell you how glad I am to be there, Rose, it's like a homecoming to me. Naturally the work is intensive, and at times I have a sense of being unworthy, but I always pray until that feeling passes. You see, I've never had a moment's doubt since I walked through those gates: this is what God wants me to do with my life."

"That's marvellous for you," Rose managed through gritted teeth, "but imagine, now, if you'd heard the call to God two months after the wedding, instead of two months before it. That might have been awkward."

Damien's eyes bored into Rose's and a flicker of remorse dulled them. "I've caused you grief, Rose, and I'm genuinely sorry for that. I care for you, of course I do, but I'd have been no good for you as a husband. No good at all."

It was too hot by the fire, her left side was scorching. She moved her chair, dragging it along the floor-tiles, unconsciously putting distance between herself and Father Damien. "No point in crying over spilt milk." The cliché tripped from her tongue unexpectedly. They had their uses. She needed to change this conversation quickly, or else she'd be across the room and hammering her fists against his chest, screeching, "Why, Damien? Why did you stop loving me?" An audience of her parents wouldn't stop her – she hadn't cared that strangers had been staring that last time they'd talked about his call to the priesthood. Indifferent to onlookers, she'd hurled his ring at him and it had glanced off his cheekbone, scratching the skin. Rose inhaled cautiously, rationing the breath. "Anyway," she aimed for a bright tone, "how can I help you?"

His blue-green glance remained steady, but one thumb began circumnavigating the other, three rotations one way, three rotations the other. "I wanted a word about your apartment in Dublin, Rose."

She forced herself to hold his candid gaze. "Yes?"

"I need the money that I lent you for a deposit. There's a project in Uganda I'm involved with, a village we've adopted at the seminary. A whole generation of parents has been wiped out by AIDS and children are being raised by grandparents. They need help desperately – grandparents can't go out to work to feed and clothe children the way parents can. My money could build a school, equip a hospital, enhance people's lives."

Rose digested his words. "You said there was no hurry with paying you back." She was perplexed, for how could her apartment overhanging a private park, with shady benches and clematis-covered arches, help Ugandan orphans?

"I need the money I lent you," he replied, patient but correspondingly inflexible. "We're raising funds for the village, buying a pig for each family, helping them plant crops, trying to construct a future for the children."

Anxiety corroded Rose. She was already mortgaged to the hilt, paying for the luxury of living close to work. She couldn't easily lay her hands on the cash he wanted. Yet, how could she refuse him, dangling Ugandan orphans before her? "You told me you regarded the loan as an investment. We agreed it entitled you to a percentage of whatever I sold the apartment for eventually. It's still a sound investment – your money's safe. Safe as houses."

"The best investment is in people's lives, not property." Father Damien's voice was mild, the expression in his eyes milder again. "What's a share of a flat compared with giving children schoolbooks and medicine right now, when they need it?"

It was an irrefutable argument; Rose laced her hands tightly and fretted about how she was going to pay him back. She should never have accepted that loan, but house prices were so astronomical she'd been left with no choice. She'd delayed scrabbling for a toehold on that infernal property ladder referred to by everyone in hushed tones – now she was paying the price. She should have done it years ago, but when she'd worked in the arts her salary had been unimpressive. Besides, there hadn't seemed to be any urgency. Taking out a mortgage was something married couples did, or so she'd thought then. But as prices had mounted and Damien had resisted setting a wedding date, she'd started to reconsider.

Buying a home had proved expensive. Cripplingly so. Her parents had been without savings they could offer, and her own had been gobbled up by legal fees and stamp duty connected with the purchase. So when her fiancé had suggested advancing her the money in return for a share of the place, it had made perfect sense. They were going to be married, after all, they'd be pooling their resources one way or another. It would be an investment in the future – their future. When they'd parted, Rose had been so shell-shocked that she hadn't paused to wonder how she'd pay back Damien. She'd been grateful for his offer that it could continue to act as an investment until he needed some capital.

"There's no hurry," Father Damien soothed. "I understand it takes time to arrange these matters. But the sooner I have the money, the sooner we can help the orphans." He delivered that beatific smile Rose recognised from eight years of being on the receiving end of it. Then he turned to Rose's mother. "Do you know, Mrs McBride, I might take you up on that offer of a cup of tea after all. Especially if there's any of your home-made cherry cake to go with it. You have a light hand with cake batter that's second to none."

After Father Damien had gone, scattering "God blesses" with profligate largesse, Rose's father turned his head from the fire and studied her with a compassionate eye. "Will it be a problem for you finding the money, Rose?"

"How could it be a problem?" demanded her mother. "Isn't her flat worth a fortune above in Dublin, the way prices keep rocketing there."

"I'll manage." Rose spoke with more conviction than she felt, reluctant to worry her parents. "I'm sure I can raise something on the mortgage or organise a short-term loan. First of all it's a question of working out how much I owe him, so I suppose on Monday I'd best contact an estate agent and establish what Clonliffe Square is worth."

Her mother and father nodded, satisfied. Their clever, capable daughter would be able to handle it. Besides, those orphans in Uganda could do with a helping hand. Rose's mother had slipped a note from her purse into Father Damien's pocket as he'd left, whispering it was for the poor motherless children in Africa.

While Rose brushed her teeth, against a backdrop of creaking springs from next door as her parents lowered themselves gingerly into bed, she felt Someone Up There was having fun at her expense. Periodically, over the year since she'd split with Father Damien, she'd fantasised about the time when they'd be able to sit down together and have a rational conversation. Never, in all the scenarios she'd played out in her head, had she envisaged him asking for money. Pleading for her to take him back, yes; confessing that the seminary had been a mistake, yes; recalling his loan, no.

But there was no avoiding the reality that she owed him the money, and his intention to pass it on to Ugandan orphans meant Rose was honour-bound to repay it as promptly as possible. She should have bought an apartment somewhere more affordable than Clonliffe Square. She'd been acquisitive for that second-floor flat in its elegant terraced shell, Victorian fireplaces and mouldings intact, and now she was paying the price of temptation. She'd have to hamstring herself with a personal loan on top of a mortgage and see if the *Sunday Trumpet* had any overtime shifts to offer.

Then another problem occurred to Rose. There was no way she could afford to go to Yosemite with Feargal now, which meant breaking her promise to him. She knew he'd take it amiss. Trust Father Damien to hijack her plans – that man was destined to overshadow her life.

She only hoped Feargal hadn't booked something already, because it would have to be unbooked. Intending to brood over her own penniless state, with an additional mope about how well prayer and celibacy were agreeing with Father Damien – his skin was glowing, his incipient pot belly had receded – Rose found herself dwelling instead on Feargal's inevitable disappointment. She should have known better than to become involved with him. Already she was making herself responsible for his feelings.

Rose sighed. If anyone had told her twenty years ago that life grew more complicated, not less, she'd have diagnosed exaggeration. Yet here she was at forty and the way ahead wound like a mountain path. Why couldn't she be married with a parcel of children like most of her classmates, instead of being juggled about by a couple of men? Both of them, to add insult to injury, purporting to care for her.

Chapter 24

Sunny was indifferent to Noreen-dear's chocolate-box extravaganza. She didn't even sympathise with her mother when she complained about how few of the neighbours had been on the street when the chauffeur had arrived with them, and what a pity it was he didn't wear a uniform.

"Imagine a liveried man bringing chocolates to your door," Noreen-dear was wistful. "Still, at least he bowed as he handed them over."

Sunny clenched her teeth, declined to indulge her mother, tramped upstairs and flung herself on the bed. The unfairness of life crowded in on her, causing spots to cartwheel across her vision, followed by the onset of tears.

She abandoned herself to the luxury of grief. Sobbing when a person is lying on their back, however, is less rewarding than it ought to be, because tears dribble into the ears and eventually serve as a distraction. After a while Sunny became bored and pulled off her socks, wriggling her toes experimentally, before adjusting her toe-ring. Finally, with nothing better to do, she descended the stairs. "Why does everything always work out right for Kitty and wrong for me?" she wailed to Noreen-dear, who was folding and stacking towels.

"I wouldn't say that, lovie, she hasn't had a lot of luck with men."

"Ryan was a pet, Benjamin was a pain," sniffed Sunny. "One out of two isn't bad."

"But she left both of them." Noreen-dear was still folding busily. "You don't think," a thought struck her with such impact that her hands stilled, "there's a chance Kitty and Ryan could get back together?"

"He has twins with someone else. Anyway Kitty's self-sufficient, she doesn't need anybody." Sunny was dismissive before her mother hatched some improbable matchmaking plan. Although it would serve her sister right if she did. But if anyone was going to hatch a plan involving Kitty it was going to be Sunny. Something to penalise her for having Clarke at her beck and call when he should be at Sunny's. She'd already ruled out vandalism inside her house, because she'd be the prime suspect as the only other key-holder. She might persuade one of her actor friends to stage a scene at work – something to embarrass Kitty in front of Linus Bell. She watched her mother, lulled by the towel-folding repetition. "What do you think of Clarke?"

"A gentleman," pronounced her mother. "I'll be able to sleep easy at night knowing he's watching out for your best interests when you go to Hollywood, Sunny. When is that happening, anyway?"

"Don't know." Sunny was dismal. "Suppose I should ring my agent and check if the contract has arrived. Then I might give the gang a shout and see if there's any action tonight."

"Good idea, lovie. Did Kitty mention coming home for lunch tomorrow? Monday's her day off."

"I'd say Kitty is far too occupied with snatching Clarke from under my nose to bother about lunch in Bray," Sunny muttered. "She has a predatory streak the Great White Shark would envy."

"Must come from your father's side," Noreen-dear said automatically. "Wait a minute, what do you mean about your sister snatching that nice young man of yours?"

Sunny gave her mother the benefit of her over-cooked theory, which threw a distinctly unflattering light on her sister. She was wary of heaping opprobrium on Clarke, still her best chance of a job in Hollywood. It came as a revelation to Noreen-dear, who had been so preoccupied with impressing her American guest that she hadn't plumbed the undercurrents.

"So he's the same boy who wrote those letters to Kitty after she came home from Boston?" Noreen-dear checked, still slightly confused.

"That's the one." Exasperated, Sunny waited for her mother to share her sense of outrage.

"Such a lot of letters he used to write, and in beautiful penmanship." Noreen dimpled. "Do you remember how we used to tease her about him? You were only a little girl, Sunny, not much more than eight or nine. You were upset that nobody sent you letters so you started writing some to yourself, from your doll, and leaving them under your pillow."

Provoked by her mother's jaunt down memory lane, and her inability to share her vision of Kitty as a traitor, Sunny went for a walk.

She idled down to the seafront, pausing to check her balance in an NIB cash machine. Thirty-four euro and ninety-one cent. Even allowing for free rent, she wouldn't make much progress on that. Why did she never have any money? It's not as if she was spendthrift. She bought quite a few clothes, but she needed them, with auditions to attend – she had to look the part to have a chance of winning the part, that was the cardinal rule. Her hair cost a fortune to maintain at this shade of platinum – dark roots colonised the blonde overnight if she wasn't vigilant – but appearances were pivotal in her profession. She did spend a fair amount at the beautician's, between facials, manicures and those

Brazilian waxes that made her wince, however often the beautician claimed she'd become inured to them. Nobody could pluck eyebrows like Tanya; she could take years off a woman with a pair of tweezers. Her fees were exorbitant, but it was all an investment in the future. Her future. When Sunny was a Hollywood star the studio would pick up the tab for such sundries.

"You've given yourself a year," Sunny psyched herself. "By this time next January you're either Hollywood's hottest discovery or you're signed up for drama teaching." She reached the promenade where she'd walked with Kitty on New Year's Day. Three Eskimo-wrapped children with buckets and spades were attacking the shingled beach. Sunny tried to remember why she'd become an actor. What her motivation was, to parrot a teacher from more than a decade ago, preparing her for a production of Hamlet. Sunny had yearned to play Ophelia, but she'd towered over Hamlet and had been cast instead as the Ghost, the part taken by Shakespeare. "For the applause," she told a seagull perched on the orange and turquoise railings, which cawed in response and wheeled off. "I became an actor for the applause."

All the effort and anguish – learning lines, fighting nausea in the prelude to a performance, watching roles she coveted go to someone else, earning minimum wage rates for dead-end jobs she could walk away from if a part came up, being paid a similar pittance for stage productions in leaky halls with inadequate dressing-room facilities – were worth it for that glorious upsurge of elation as an audience showered her in love. She'd helped divert them for a couple of hours: they had bills they couldn't pay, relationships they couldn't make work, problems they couldn't solve. But she'd transported them for a sliver of time.

"Thought I'd find you here, chicken," said Sunny's father. He'd thrown a battered Harris tweed coat over his boiler suit and was sucking a Fox's Glacier Mint.

"Hello, Dad, out for a constitutional?"

"I had my walk this morning, but Noreen-dear insisted I come out again to look for you. It was either that or sit in the kitchen and drink tea with her, so here I am." He rotated the sweet in his mouth. "Will we take a turn?" He jerked his head along the pier, in the direction of Bray Head.

"Why not?" Sunny slotted her hand into the crook of her father's arm.

They strolled in easy silence, Denis nodding at people he recognised, his coat flapping open. The jangle of the amusement arcade and the rustle of the waves segued into one another, and the wind whipped colour into their cheeks. Sunny's phone pipped in her pocket, a text message from one of her friends no doubt rounding her up for a drinking session later, but she ignored it. Her father only reached up to the top of her ear, yet she felt protected by the spreading warmth of his body.

"What do you think of acting, Dad?"

"Do you mean as a job or a hobby?" He passed her the blue and white bag of Fox's Glacier Mints and she popped one into the hollow of her cheek.

"As a job."

Denis Kennedy sucked thoughtfully. "You'd want to really love it."

"Why's that?"

"There's no security, the financial rewards apply only to the very few and the older you become, the less they want you." He gave her a sidelong look. "Sorry, chicken, I don't suppose that's what you wanted to hear."

"I asked you a question and you answered truthfully, Dad. It's fair enough."

They circled around at the end of the pier and walked back under gathering shadows.

"Your mother seems to think you're a bit disgruntled with Kitty over that American fellow," said her father.

"Everything comes easy to Kitty. I have to tussle for what I want."

"Nonsense." Denis realised his daughter was on the outside of the pavement since they'd turned, an unacceptable arrangement in his rulebook, and swapped places. "You're as pretty as a picture, look at you – half the men in the country would give their eye teeth to have your hand on their arm the way it's hooked into mine."

Sunny smiled. "You've no idea the effort that goes into maintaining these looks, Dad. I was totting it up before you came along and it's a scary figure."

"Don't be silly, you take after your mother and she was the best-looking girl in town. Who else do you get that lovely blonde hair from but her?" He tapped the hand closest to him. "I don't like to see you on unfriendly terms with your sister, Sunny. There's only the two of you. Take it from a man – there's not one of us worth squabbling over."

"Clarke T Maloney's worth it." Sunny huddled nearer to her father's body heat. "There's something special about him; I've never felt about any man the way I do about him. Well, maybe one other man." She shivered, determined not to allow Nick Shooter space inside her head. "That's all in the past, whereas I hoped Clarke could be my future."

"Would you be so interested in him if he wasn't a Hollywood hotshot?" asked her father. "Imagine if he was a plumber or an estate agent, or if you'd met him in a queue for the bank instead of at a fancy-pants party. Would you still think he was worth it then?" His shrewd blue eyes darted over her face.

Sunny didn't know what the truth was. But she still resented Kitty.

They walked in silence until they reached Barracuda, where she and Kitty had shared New Year's Day drinks.

"I've often wondered what that place is like." Her father paused, stomach bulging from his grey tweed jacket.

"Have you never been inside?"

"Noreen-dear isn't one for pubs."

"You only live once, Dad. Come on, I'll buy you a drink." Half pushing, half pulling, Sunny dragged him towards the door.

"It's a bit early in the day to be hitting the hard stuff." Denis Kennedy looked thrilled at the prospect.

"It's the weekend, the sun is wherever it should be in relation to the yard arm and we're both consenting adults." Sunny was tickled by the idea of teaching her father wicked habits.

"It's tempting. But your mother won't like it, chicken," he warned.

They hooted in unison. "That settles it," they chorused, and walked into the ground-floor bar.

Sunny had forgotten about Karl, whose face lit up when he saw her. "You grab that table and I'll order some drinks," she told her father. "Do you want a pint, or will you live dangerously and try a cocktail? A cocktail it is – I'll start you off with a chocolate Martini."

At the bar, she smiled in a distant way at Karl who was grinning so widely it was a mercy his teeth didn't drop out. "Sunny, always I try to ring you, but the person who answers says she's never heard of you."

"Maybe you took down my number wrong," she suggested, racking her brains for his name.

"Maybe." His shaven skull winked under the electric light. "So perhaps you could write it down again?"

"Listen, this isn't a good time for me. I'll talk to you later. I'm here with my father and we'd like two chocolate Martinis. Could you drop them down to us, please?"

Her father had removed his coat and was sucking on another mint. "The barman seems fairly smitten with you."

Sunny shrugged.

"Foreign-looking individual. He's not from these parts, I take it?"

"I think he's Polish." Sunny was starting to wish they'd gone elsewhere for a drink.

Karl arrived with a tray and a pair of chocolate Martinis. He unloaded the tray with a flourish, clicked his heels together as he shook Denis's hand and announced the cocktails were on the house. His eyes lingered on the crimson crescent of Sunny's mouth as he turned away.

"I said he was taken with you," chuckled her father.

Sunny drank her Martini, ignoring how Karl was staring. "What do you think of it?" she asked, after her father's first cautious sip.

"Like a runny bar of Dairy Milk with a kick in the tail." He smacked his lips. "I wouldn't want to drink more than nine or ten of them, but it makes a change from a cup of tea."

They stayed for an hour, managing another round of drinks, and Sunny ended up scribbling her telephone number on a beer mat at Karl's pleading. Except it wasn't really her telephone number but her date of birth with another digit added to pad it out.

As they reached 16 Hunter Close, a little giddy because Karl had been generous with the spirits, the front door was flung open.

"I've been worried half to death, you've been gone so long. I nearly called the coastguard in case you'd been washed out to sea," exclaimed Sunny's mother.

"We just stopped off for some chocolate, Noreen-dear," said Denis.

Sunny thought she would implode from choked giggles.

"Imagine thinking about chocolate at a time like this." Noreen-dear was at her most imperious. "Sunny, your agent's been on the phone, he says it's urgent. Some hiccup over this part you have in the American film. It's all off."

Chapter 25

"Kitty Kennedy, I've made a decision. It's time I did something to court you." The voice on the line was Joe's – he didn't need to identify himself.

"You don't have to court me." Kitty was swamped with relief that he'd finally called. "What time are you arriving, Joe?" It was already ten p.m. on Sunday night and she'd started imagining doomsday scenarios because there'd been neither sight nor sound of him.

"Well then, I'd like to do something to court you," insisted Joe, ignoring her question.

"Can't we talk about this when you arrive?"

"No, let's talk about it now, it can't wait a minute longer." His voice was lower than she remembered, deepened by the echo from his mobile phone.

"All right then." She was laughing, prepared to be indulgent. "What did you have in mind?"

"Would dinner be too obvious? Is it up there with red roses and heart-shaped balloons and sonnets to my lady's elbow?"

"I don't know how obvious sonnets to my lady's elbow are, but dinner would be perfect. Not tonight, though, I gave up waiting for you to arrive about nine and microwaved something. Are you still driving back from Monaghan? I have champagne in the fridge for us." Static crackled. Kitty heard Joe speak, but couldn't determine the words. "You're breaking up, Joe." A ripple of foreboding vibrated within Kitty.

"I'm sorry, Kitty. I'm only leaving Monaghan now, it will take me a couple of hours to get back. Maybe it would be better to do this another day. Let me make it up to you. I'll whisk you out to dinner – anywhere you like. You choose."

Kitty was disappointed, but tried to stifle it. "I don't work on Mondays so you could wine and dine me tomorrow, if you like."

Joe hesitated. "That could be a problem. I'm supposed to fly to London for a meeting in the morning. Then it's on to Frankfurt and a couple of east European cities."

"When will you be back?"

"I'll be gone until Saturday. The trouble is," – he floundered, trying not to alienate her – "I can't turn up, dump my suitcase and go straight out again. I need to spend time with my daughter."

"Your wife, too," noted Kitty, icy. Detesting him. Detesting Emma French. Detesting herself.

Joe ignored the barb. "Can we meet for dinner next Sunday? I really want to see you, Kitty. I know this situation isn't ideal, but I'll make it up to you, I promise."

Kitty held the receiver away from her ear and studied its sleek curve. She had a straight choice: she could either replace it in its cradle now, or stay on the line and accept that cancellation and disappointment were the inevitable corollaries of becoming Joe French's mistress. So much for the carefree confidence of her New Year's Day plans. "This is going to be hell," she whispered. It wasn't a disclaimer but an acknowledgement, for she was already enmeshed in Joe French's life and could not free herself.

"Kitty?" Did you say something?"

Still she held the receiver suspended in mid-air. Then she watched her hand move in slow motion, bringing it back to her ear, and heard herself speak. "Sunday it is, Joe."

"It will be worth it, Kitty. Cross my heart and hope to die. We're really busy at Bumpermac's right now with acquisitions and a new computerised system for tagging stock, but I plan to take time off soon. I'll spend it with you, if you'll let me."

Joe was persuasive, Kitty acknowledged. Although her desire to be persuaded made it easy for him. "Call me again," she suggested, and hung up.

* * *

Sunny clicked metal-tipped heels on the floor as she waited, nervous energy keeping her on the move. She knew she was unlikely to achieve anything by bursting in on Clarke, but she had nothing to lose. The phone call from her agent had been to tell her the remake of *The Quiet Man* was off the radar screen because its funding package had collapsed. She was incensed that Clarke hadn't bothered to tell her himself – clearly she meant nothing to him. Sunny had fumed, painted her toenails, then gone out with some of her acting friends for a session that was supposed to help her take the blow pragmatically. Her crew were past masters at dealing with dashed hopes – they were bound to be able to rustle up a few platitudes between them. "We're all the walking wounded when it comes to rejection," her friend Quentin had consoled, but Sunny hadn't been convinced. Quentin looked far too healthy, a little smug, even. He'd just landed the part of Lucky in *Waiting for Godot* at The Abbey. Even if he wound up with chronic backache from crawling around on all fours by the end of the run, it was a boost to his career.

Nothing for it but to drink. Sunny had wound up in The Sugar Club, cornering a scrawny fellow who looked so underfed she'd believed him when he'd said he was musician. He had invited her back to his flat in Collins Avenue, rolled a massive joint, smoked two drags, given her a love bite and passed out. Sunny had sat up for the rest of the night talking to the drummer, who wanted to be a beekeeper in his spare time and had borrowed a book from the library about it. Whole chapters of that book had been committed to memory and he had proceeded to regurgitate them for Sunny. It had not been a satisfactory evening. She could have left earlier, but going home before daybreak had seemed defeatist.

It was now Tuesday afternoon, however, and she was determined to confront Clarke. He owed he: he had danced and flirted with her, eaten dinner in her home – then shown every sign of preferring her sister to Sunny. Now came the final ignominy. Her part in his film had vanished in a puff of smoke. But he couldn't simply relay a message via her agent, she was entitled to an explanation.

Sunny paced the length of the foyer in the Clarence.

"Be with you as soon as I take care of something," he'd assured her on the internal phone, leaving her to fester.

"It's Sunny Kennedy," called a dark-haired figure from behind the reception desk. Sunny paused in her striding. "Ella Jackson," prompted the woman.

"Of course, Ella, you were in the same year as me at Loreto Convent in Bray, weren't you? Stupid of me not to recognise you, it must be the uniform. How are you? Still singing?"

"Still singing, still waiting to be discovered," agreed Ella. "A write-up in one of the papers would help raise my profile. But it's all promises, promises. How about you? Still appearing in pantomimes?"

"From time to time," acknowledged Sunny through clenched teeth. She couldn't even flaunt *The Quiet Man* remake because it had been shelved.

Ella arched an eyebrow. One that would benefit from a pair of tweezers being let loose on it, thought Sunny. "I saw your sister the other day, she was having dinner with . . . a gentleman." Ella hesitated to identify Hubert, her brother-in-law, out of loyalty to Flora.

Exasperation flashed through Sunny. Kitty was obviously still carrying on with that Joe French fellow she'd told her about. The married man. But he wasn't enough for her, oh no, she had to keep Clarke dangling too.

Ella couldn't resist adding, "I wouldn't have thought he was your sister's type."

"Everybody's Kitty's type," grumbled Sunny. "Especially the married ones. The more married the better as far as she's concerned. She's remorseless."

Poor Flora, Ella reflected. She always knew about Hubert's philandering; there was no point in alerting her to the latest episode. Love stripped you of your defences. Ella never intended to care for anyone the way Flora cared for Hubert. "It's a shame, all the same," Ella spoke aloud, thinking of her half-sister. "If he does it right under his wife's nose, I mean. I don't mind what anyone does as long as they're discreet. That's only fair. For his wife's sake."

"Emma French never struck me as one of life's victims." Sunny checked her watch, not realising what she'd let slip. She had more pressing matters on her mind than Kitty's affair. Sunny's career needed her attention.

Emma French? Ella was nonplussed. Then she recalled the rapport between Joe and Kitty when she'd introduced them at the Expresso Bar. Hadn't Joe held Kitty's hands at one stage and spoken to her in an urgent way? It all made sense now. Her eyes gleamed. This gobbet of information could be extremely valuable; she should consider carefully how to make the most profitable use of it. The phone near Ella's hand rang. "Of course, Mr Maloney, right away." She replaced the receiver. "He'll see you now, Sunny."

She was ushered into Clarke's suite, his hand resting on the small of her back in a way which, if she weren't convinced he was snagged in a liaison with her sister, Sunny would have read as a promising omen. There was a definite frisson between them. Clarke was simply in denial. A woman in her early twenties, light brown hair skewered in a bun, was typing on a laptop by the window.

"You may as well take a break now, Barbara – you didn't get out this morning, did you? Go breathe some fresh air into your lungs." Clarke extended his hands, distributing largesse.

The woman flashed him a resentful look, but pressed *save* on her computer and gathered her bag and coat.

"Shall I ring down for some sodas or coffee?" Clarke fumbled a smile at Sunny.

Sunny shook her head, rooting in her pocket for her packet of Silk Cut. "Do you mind if I smoke?"

"Cigarettes?" His bulging eyes conveyed his horror.

"No, Cuban cigars."

His eyes were ready to vacate their sockets.

"Yes, cigarettes," she sighed.

"Sunny, this is a smoke-free suite." His gaze darted nervously behind her. "Rules are rules, you know – they're not my rules, but it wouldn't do to go breaking them. They have a sign on the door."

"No, it wouldn't do," agreed Sunny. "There'd be anarchy if people went around lighting up under *no smoking* signs. The social fabric would disintegrate."

"Exactly. How about a pretzel instead?" Clarke reached for a cracked-glaze porcelain bowl and she accepted it, sinking into a sofa.

"So, how's your mom?" Clarke rotated the initial cufflink on his blue Brooks Brothers button-down shirt.

"Grand." Sunny munched a pretzel and wondered what Clarke would look like without the shirt. Or the beige trousers. Or the striped boxer shorts she guessed he was wearing under them – he didn't strike her as a Y-fronts man. "She's your number-one fan since you sent her those chocolates. She has them on display in the dining-room, all but genuflecting as she dusts past them. You'd swear they were sacred relics."

"Gee, that's cool. Your mom's a great lady. She's" – he searched for the appropriate word and seized on it – "authentic."

That was enough small talk. Sunny hadn't come to debate Noreen-dear's authenticity. "I had a disappointing phone call from my agent about the film."

Clarke perched on the edge of a desk and steepled his fingers.

"Disappointing, yes. But we mustn't give up hope: When you've been involved with as many productions as I have, you'll know if the finances aren't hammered into place everything can collapse like a house of cards. But I hear from my office in LA that a new deal may be put together – it's just a case of bringing the right folk into the same room for some heavy-duty jaw-jaw." He transfixed Sunny with a disconcerting stare, intended as reassuring. "I'm going back home to horn in there and do my bit."

"You're going back to the States?" A worm of disappointment burrowed inside Sunny.

"Shoot, I certainly am. I can't stand idly by while *The Quiet Man* project flails to get airborne. I believe in this movie, Sunny, I'm going to make it happen. And you know what will keep me going? Your faith. Don't lose faith in me, Sunny, and I won't let you down." His face was bathed in an evangelistic glow by the time he'd finished his speech.

Sunny smothered a guffaw. She'd lost more parts than Clarke T Maloney had taken hot showers – and he looked like a twice-a-day man. He was behaving as though civilisation's future rested on his shoulders. Since Clarke still had his achingly earnest brown eyes fastened on her, she felt obliged to say something. "I certainly appreciate it, Clarke."

He nodded, sincerity radiating from him in great glooping waves. But he still looked expectant; hyperbole seemed to be required.

"It means the world to me," she added, anticipating a snort of derision. It didn't come – instead his head continued its dipping movement.

At which point Sunny grasped that it didn't mean the world to her at all. A realisation so shocking that she staggered to her feet and out to the lift, mumbling her farewells, without trying to discover what exactly was bubbling away between Clarke and Kitty. Anyway she had a fair idea, she didn't need diagrams. Instead, the mind-numbing comprehension that she was indifferent about

271

moving to Hollywood and becoming a star seeped through her. It was immaterial that she'd never be photographed by paparazzi wherever she went. Or have designers queue to lend her their clothes. Or be swept about in limousines.

Sunny didn't care.

Clarke followed her to the lift to wave her off. The sight of that lugubrious face she'd never see again penetrated the lacquer of her shellshock. Sunny paused before pressing the button. She stretched out her hand to his face. "It could have been fabulous," she whispered, cupping her palm around his chin.

The door closed between them.

Clarke frowned. She'd meant working on the film, hadn't she?

During the descent in the lift, a welter of emotions jostled Sunny. There was regret that what she'd hoped for with Clarke had failed to materialise. There was also a tender zone where her inner certainty used to live. But that would heal over in time, she was convinced of it. In any case her inner certainty had been taking leaves of absence lately. By the time the lift doors opened on the foyer, elation was her predominant response. This was liberating. All her life she'd wanted to be a star and now that she didn't, she felt lighter than gravity. An eddy of wind would send her sailing above the roof-tops.

She lurched towards the door, freed from the tyranny of craving fame, and waved to Ella. "Isn't life amazing?" she trilled.

Ella, who had to be at a fortieth birthday party in Balbriggan by eight p.m. and who felt Atlas had transferred his load to her shoulders, didn't find it particularly so. Exhausting and only occasionally rewarding was closer to her interpretation. She glowered.

Sunny reeled out of the Clarence, stunned by the wonder of no longer being shackled to the drive for fame. "Anonymity's fine by me," she felt like explaining to a couple in waxed jackets, returning to the hotel after an afternoon's mooch around the shops. Instead, she stopped them in their tracks with an arc of a smile.

Her mobile phone rang. Unguarded, Sunny answered it, to find the dentist from Lusk attempting to make a date. "Where are you right now?"

"In the surgery, I'm between appointments," he stuttered, unaccustomed to dealing with Sunny instead of her voicemail.

"Haul yourself into town, I feel like celebrating."

Chapter 26

Rose arrived back at Clonliffe Square late on Monday evening to a succession of messages on the answerphone from Feargal, followed by a series of clicks, indicating someone who'd started hanging up rather than leave yet another message. She unpacked her overnight bag to delay the inevitable, then lifted her receiver to call him. But she couldn't go through with it. She knew he'd be aggrieved by her decision to cancel the trip to Yosemite. Rose really didn't like maltreating him – but what choice did she have? She couldn't afford it, which was probably fate intervening to tell her she shouldn't have said she'd go in the first place.

It was Tuesday night after work before she could bring herself to ring him.

"I've been worried about you," he complained. "You vanished off the face of the earth. Did I do something to offend you?"

"No, it was nothing like that, something unexpected cropped up."

"I came hurtling back to your place on Sunday, Rose, after checking the Internet and printing off timetables and prices and special offers. But you weren't in. I had all the details about our trip and nobody to discuss them with."

Rose began plaiting her hair, fingers working methodically as she cradled the phone between ear and shoulder. "I was in Slane with my parents. I go there most weekends, Feargal."

"Right." Brief interval. "It's just that you didn't say you were going."

"I didn't know I needed permission."

His hurt crawled out from the receiver and reproached her.

Rose regretted her brusque tone as soon as the words left her lips, but it was too late to recall them. "They're old," she continued, conciliatory now. "My father's nearly eighty and my mother's not far behind. They rely on my visits. I try to spend at least one night every week with them."

"Of course, I understand completely." His voice was stiff, her acidity stinging still.

"I'm sorry if there was a misunderstanding and you believed I'd be waiting in for you. Even if I hadn't gone to Slane I could have been anywhere. I could have been meeting friends or stocking up at the supermarket — what were the chances of finding me in?'"

"I didn't think," Feargal admitted, miserable.

"I'm at home now. You could drop by if you like, or I could meet you in town." She was tired, but knew she should see him sooner rather than later and call a halt to the Half Dome expedition.

"I'll bring a bottle to your place. I wouldn't mind a drink. I had coffee with my producer this afternoon and she was cross with me. She had a list of mistakes I keep making on air."

"Such as?" Any time Rose had tuned in to check out Feargal's airside manner, he'd sounded competent and relaxed.

"I didn't remember to trail what was coming up next. I have to stop saying 'welcome back' after a commercial break, it implies the listeners have pottered off to make a cup of tea or switched stations. Which they're not supposed to do — they're meant to stay tuned to CityBeat FM."

"That's not too hard to fix; it sounds nothing more than a bit of fine-tuning to me. Just stick a few Post-It notes on your desk and they'll soon become second nature."

"True." Feargal reflected. "She wasn't really tetchy with me, just trying to help me improve. It's my first presenting job and I've a lot to learn – I should be grateful there's someone on my team willing to share their experience. It's just that my producer has a slightly hectoring tone and she leaves me feeling inept. Anyway, that's enough obsessing about work, I'm on my way to Clonliffe Square to obsess about holidays."

Guilt coagulated within Rose as she disconnected. She reached for her spectacles for armoury because she needed to look serious here.

* * *

Breaking the news to Feargal that she couldn't afford to go away with him was more of a burden than she'd anticipated. He was so decent, so hopeful of finding a solution.

"I'll lend you the cash for the trip," he volunteered.

"You don't understand, I must raise a large sum quickly. That means taking out a loan which I'll need to repay. I won't have any spare money for holidays for a couple of years." Rose swallowed some of the Pinot Grigio he'd brought with him, wishing he wouldn't add impediments by being so reluctant to abandon the Yosemite adventure. "Go yourself, send me a postcard. I'll be green with envy, but I'll pin it to my notice-board."

"I wanted to show it you." His eyes were scalded.

She almost reached out to hug him.

"Rose, I wanted you to discover for yourself what it's like to be somewhere so unspoiled that the clean air slices through your lungs, and the clouds hang low enough in the sky to touch. Where you can see as far as forever because you're 4,000 feet above sea level, way above the snowline. It won't be the same on my own." He indicated a pile of computer printouts on her coffee table. "I brought these for you."

She lifted the top sheet and found a bear warning: no food to be left in cars, no bears to be fed, no matter how appealing the cubs. "I'm sorry, Feargal," she said simply.

"I'm sorrier. I know what you're missing. I know how much it would have moved you – the sense of wellbeing that would have enveloped you."

"It can't be helped." Rose sighed. "We'll go together one day."

"You don't mean that. Stop treating me like a child, promising treats you have no intention of delivering." A trapped nerve twitched in his left cheek and his face was clenched.

Rose cut her glance away, then back to him. Realisation hovered along the hairs on the back of her neck – as though, if it were stealthy enough, it could navigate past without her noticing. But she did notice. And all at once it changed everything.

Rose realised she had become accustomed to Feargal's partisan stance towards her, the internal laughter behind his eyes when he watched her, that knack he had of conveying preference entirely for her; she disliked this withdrawal of indulgence. Its loss left a chill.

Acting purely on instinct Rose walked up to Feargal and, taking his dear face with its aquiline nose between her hands, she kissed it. His lips were warm and moist and they parted at the pressure from hers. As they embraced she observed that he was on a level with her, only the difference of an inch in height between them. At which point Rose no longer noticed anything because she was immersed in his kisses, feeling his wine-scented breath on her neck and at her throat as his lips moved across her face, then back to her mouth. Next he was leading her – or she was leading him, she couldn't tell which – to the bedroom.

* * *

Rose studied Feargal's dozing form, narrow-hipped, an almost hairless chest. Nude, he appeared more boyish than when fully clothed. Tentatively she twined a tendril of his hair from the base of his neck around her forefinger and felt a swelling of affection for this impulsive, uncomplicated young man. Of course they had no future, but the present had its compensations. She lay propped against the headboard, loose-limbed, the sweet weight of his head resting on her stomach.

Feargal shifted, murmuring in his sleep, and Rose waited for him to waken, hankering after reassurance. Just a caress. He was the first man she'd shared a bed with since Father Damien and she yearned for a smattering of comfort, ridiculous though it sounded. She understood that she'd let go of her former fiancé now, it was irretrievable; regardless of what happened with Feargal she had finally moved on. But the recognition left her rudderless in the ink of the night, for she and Damien Crowe had spent eight years together. A spike of loss jabbed her. If only Feargal would rouse and sense that emptiness. She rasped a nail along the stubble on his jaw, hoping the slight disturbance would waken him, but he rolled off her lap and burrowed into the pillow.

At this, a rush of panic welled inside Rose. She forgot the tenderness of their lovemaking, the way Feargal had held her and murmured endearments, and thought only of the impossibility of their relationship. It had taken her a year to find her equilibrium – did she really want to risk it again? It was flattering that a twenty-seven-year-old man wanted to be with her, and yes, if she was honest, she enjoyed the envious glances of girls so much younger than her. But sooner or later she would wind up hurt, as Feargal's attention drifted to someone nearer to him in age.

Someone who hadn't started plucking at the excess skin on her throat, feeling cheated by the creeping corrosion of her body. Who didn't wince because the white of her eyes was shading to yellow. Or because she'd discovered pads of fat on her previously skinny upper arms. Someone who hadn't learned to fear the vulnerability of loving.

Rose was a realist. She recognised that, however well disguised her years, the signs of decay were surfacing. She was on the turn, it was as brutal as that. She had taken her youthfulness for granted all her life – now it was decomposing when she needed it most, and how she resented it. She'd never thought there was anything special about looking fresh-faced, shrugging when friends had cracked jokes about portraits in attics. Then her youthfulness started crumbling and she didn't feel grateful to have had a good run for her money, she wanted to holler, "Give it back, I'll start appreciating it!"

Rose lay awake for another hour, marvelling at how soundly Feargal slept in a strange bed. Men had an innate capacity for confidence; it probably hadn't occurred to him to feel uncomfortable. Finally she reached out to her bedside locker and slid her Guatemalan Worry People under the pillow. These totems fashioned from pipe-cleaners were meant to transfer an owner's problems onto their own shoulders and give a decent night's rest. While they had never yet managed to siphon off her woes, Rose still had faith in them. Let's see what the Guatemalans can pull off, she thought.

* * *

"We've overslept."

Feargal's voice startled a sleep-fuddled Rose.

"I'm late for work, I'll have to dash. Is it all right if I jump in your shower?"

His tapered, light brown body was already flashing out of bed as Rose yawned agreement. He might have overslept, but she didn't have to be in work for another two hours. While the water thundered and he sang tunelessly above it, she pulled a kimono over her head and trailed into the kitchen to fill the kettle. The roar of the shower stopped and the door cracked open, followed by pounding footsteps along the floorboards. She plunged a pot of coffee, ear cocked, and when his footsteps exited the bedroom she poured him a mug.

"Isn't it hilarious when you have to go into work in the clothes you were wearing the previous day?" Feargal tousled his wet hair, laughing.

No, Rose didn't find it hilarious, she found it inconvenient. Must be another of the differences between twenty-seven and forty.

"What a star, you've made coffee – but I've no time for breakfast." Feargal was cheerful, noisily so, it seemed to Rose. He lifted one of the speckled green pottery mugs from the worktop and gulped. Then he snaked a hand around Rose's waist, pulled her towards him and smacked a coffee-flavoured kiss on her mouth. "Ring you later, gorgeous."

She nodded dumbly, sapped by this whirlwind of energy in her apartment. Rose was accustomed to silence in the morning, perhaps the thrum of a discussion programme on the radio in the background. She was uncertain how to handle someone who whizzed through her rooms chanting snatches of a rock song she didn't recognise. He managed another mouthful of coffee and lunged for his coat, heading towards the door. She pushed her fringe out of her eyes and raised a hand in farewell. Feargal paused to blow her a kiss, good humour leeching from every pore.

Rose brought her mug to bed with her, noticing the damp towel trailing on her wicker laundry basket. She pulled back the duvet, nose wrinkling at the odour of male body, and climbed in. A Latin phrase landed noiselessly in her mind, parachuted in from schooldays several decades ago. *Ceteris paribus*. She didn't know where it floated in from or why that tag. It could as readily have been *nil desperandum* or *mutatis mutandis* or any one of the others drummed into her by the Homer-worshipping Miss Stewart. But it was *ceteris paribus*. Other things being equal. Other things being equal she'd have liked to know Feargal Whelan better.

Rose peered under the bed and saw that Feargal had removed the two used condoms he'd thrown there. He deserved some credit for that. Then she lifted the phone by her bedside and called Kitty. "I did it, I slept with him."

Kitty, whose alarm had only just sounded, was confused. "I thought you did that on New Year's Eve."

Detected in her fib. She'd just have to be brazen. "I was

exaggerating. I thought it was the sort of thing I should have done at the party if I weren't so Father Damien-fixated. Which I'm not any more. I slept with Feargal and it's flushed Father Damien out of my system."

"Sound woman." Kitty was approving. "Deliciously repetitive, gloriously life-enhancing, casual sex with a stranger – there's nothing like it." She didn't add that it was Sunny's mission statement, not hers. Anyway, it was only a matter of time before she did it herself with Joe French, who had been ringing her nightly from hotel rooms in London, Frankfurt, Sarajevo and Riga. Prolonged, revelatory chats which put them on a courtship footing.

Rose savaged a rag nail and didn't like to admit there had been nothing casual about it from her perspective, although she couldn't speak for Feargal.

"What's Feargal like?" asked Kitty.

Rose reflected for so long Kitty thought she had no answer to give. "He's not someone to be valued adequately at first sight," said Rose finally.

"I'm dying to meet him."

There was a hiatus during which Rose pondered introducing the two, conscious of a certain reluctance. Her connection with Feargal was such a tender shoot that she wanted to protect it from outsiders. Even Kitty.

Meanwhile Kitty was tempted to confide in Rose about Joe French but held back. She was wary of Rose dissuading her. Her friend was transparent in her disapproval of Kitty's moral mistress machinations – she refused to see the benefits to everyone concerned. She'd never become a mistress if she listened to Rose McBride.

"I'm glad you're over Father Damien," said Kitty.

Rose thought about trying to raise thousands of euro at short notice. "The cure may have been worse than the disease. There's a good chance it may cost me my home."

Chapter 27

Anticipation was always the part of the dating ritual Kitty loved best. Sometimes she prolonged the preparations, sipping on a steadying glass of crème de menthe, her secret indulgence, because she knew in her heart that the reality wouldn't compare with the prospect. But she had no such reservations as she readied herself to meet Joe French, after his week in transit across Europe. They had passed the flirtation stage and were ready for a more concrete statement of intent.

The phone rang several times while she was reassembling her appearance, but she left the machine to monitor the calls.

Her mother's voice upbraided her. "Kitty this is your mother, Noreen. Ring me at once."

Rose followed. "Give me a call, Kitty, it's fairly urgent. There's something you should know."

Nothing could be as vital as a lover-in-waiting at the Clarence Hotel. Kitty decided she'd leave Rose until the following day.

Twenty minutes later, on the brink of departure, there was another call. "Kitty, it's your mother here, Noreen. I insist on speaking to you immediately. I'm very disturbed by something in the newspaper."

Noreen-dear probably just wanted to complain about her column.

When her opinions didn't tally with her mother's, she usually took issue with her. Kitty was too intent on meeting Joe to deal with it. That could wait until the next day as well. Only Joe mattered.

Except the man she met in the Clarence was a pale imitation of the one she'd been expecting, sustained by the intimacy of those late-night calls. They sat facing one another in the Tea Room restaurant, art on the walls, artifice in the air. Kitty was near-speechless with desolation. None of this felt right. There was no chemistry, no collusion, no collision of sexual intent. Joe was uptight, even defensive, body language rigid. He said almost at once that he couldn't stay long. In a functional manner, as though this was a duty dinner. Joe had kissed her on the cheek when she'd arrived, not even bothering to comment on her appearance, although she'd spent half an hour pinning up her hair and was wearing a jet bead choker that you couldn't fail to admire. Unless you were Joe French. He'd mumbled something about needing to be home early to take a call from Australia, but Kitty knew he was lying. He was regretting this – wishing he'd never embarked on their feeble excuse for an affair.

Kitty let her gaze rove around the room rather than risk eye-contact with this ill-at-ease stranger. She was wounded and didn't want him to read the reproach in her face. She wasn't going to force the man to take her as his mistress; there was no need for him to conduct himself as though she was being coercive. The hotel's dining-room was minimalist and high-ceilinged, with a soothing atmosphere. The adjoining table seemed to be miles away across the wooden floor, a pleasant change from restaurants where a forkful of food intended for your own mouth risked ending up in a neighbour's. But there appeared to be twice as many waiters as diners, a situation which always left Kitty feeling exposed to more attention than was ideal. On the other hand, since Joe was monosyllabic, at least there might be some communication with one of the waiters. All her attempts to initiate conversation with him had been rebuffed.

The specials were recited by one waiter, drinks orders taken by another, and their starched napkins draped in their laps by a third. Number one wheeled back with the bread basket, but it was removed after a slice each, when Kitty would have preferred it left on the table because it gave her something to fidget with. This was ludicrous, Kitty decided, with a snap of her head that set her earrings bobbing. Even if he was preoccupied by high finance, consumed by guilt, or had simply realised she didn't interest him, he should have the manners to make an effort and talk to her. She excused herself and went to the Ladies', where she touched up her lipstick and sniffed a square of perfumed soap. Hopefully her absence would have invigorated Joe.

It hadn't. His face lengthened as he stared towards one of the sexagonal windows, and Kitty observed how his arrow-straight eyebrows halted abruptly at either side of the dip leading into the bridge of his nose. Almost as though he'd taken a razor to the patch of hairs in-between.

"I have something here we should discuss."

With a start, she realised he'd just broken the silence. Joe reached into the breast pocket of his midnight-blue linen jacket and produced a sheet of newspaper methodically folded into squares. It was the gossip column from the *Sunday Globe*, the *Trumpet*'s main rival. "There's a story that concerns both of us in today's paper. I suppose you know about it?"

"No, I didn't find time to read the *Globe* today." Kitty was perplexed.

"This sort of publicity is not something I welcome, Kitty, and not something the Bumpermac's board of directors is likely to welcome either." His eyes darkened, accusatory.

A kernel of dismay tapped against Kitty's chest cavity. Joe seemed to be blaming her for a crime she was ignorant of committing. How fair was that? "Perhaps you might let me know what I'm charged with," she prompted.

A furrow indented between those horizontal eyebrows. "It's short, acerbic and goes straight for the jugular. Have you really not seen it? I'll read it to you: *"The* Sunday Trumpet's *columnist, blonde divorcée Kitty Kennedy, has carved a niche for herself sermonising to readers week after week. Yet some might suggest she's hardly a fit person to preach. She's been spotted around town with a prominent married businessman who's forever singing the praises of his baby daughter. But let's just say, when Kitty and her new admirer were overheard deep in conversation, they weren't discussing the price of nappies. The Diary hears she was too busy giving him something to blow his trumpet about."* He folded it up and replaced it in his breast pocket. "I know this doesn't name me, Kitty, but it's too close for comfort. I can't afford to be tainted by scandal. I'm in the process of negotiating to buy a small chain of eight properties in the south-west from an arch-conservative family, active in the Catholic Church. They'll refuse to deal with Bumpermac's if they connect me to this."

Kitty took a sip of water, the incense from a nearby vase of arum lilies permeating her nostrils and overpowering her so that her vision blurred. This had to come from Sunny, she was the only person to whom Kitty had divulged Joe's identity. How could her sister stoop so low? She'd told her in confidence that Joe had a baby girl – now Sunny was using it against her. Kitty's innards convulsed. She realised Sunny was furious with her over her imagined liaison with Clarke, but she had no idea her sister could be quite so vindictive. No wonder Joe had been wooden all evening. He probably thought she was lethal. Deadly nightshade tricked out as a dinner companion.

"My sister and I had a misunderstanding," she faltered.

"So your sister is responsible for that poisonous article? If that's what a misunderstanding generates, I wouldn't like to cross her in a full-scale row."

Kitty laddered her eyes upwards to Joe's face. It was impenetrable. Suddenly she remembered those phone calls as she'd been preparing for the date. Her mother and Rose had both tried to warn her. She sucked in a steadying breath. "I'm as horrified as you are, Joe, probably more so – I'm identified, after all. It's my reputation being trampled. I have to go into work tomorrow and face my colleagues. I can't begin to imagine the commentary I'll be subjected to as I walk though the newsroom." She felt the prickle of moisture in her eyes and clamped down on her lip to quell it. She wasn't going to descend into tears, she was determined to maintain her dignity. God oh God oh God, Sunny was a law unto herself. It was an appalling betrayal.

Joe knew it was excessive of him to blame Kitty for this, but he couldn't risk his life becoming gossip-column fodder. It could have a catastrophic impact on his business transactions – he'd lose all status if people were sniggering about him. Those properties in the south-west weren't the only deal that could be scuppered. And then there was Emma to consider; she could take away his child if he wasn't careful. Joe felt a charge of antagonism towards Kitty. Everything had been manageable before she'd arrived on the scene, making his life – a perfectly adequate one until then – appear sterile and two-dimensional.

But honesty obliged Joe to acknowledge that it had been him pursuing Kitty, not the other way round. He'd sent her an orchid, had invited her to walk around Dublin city-centre with him in broad daylight, had turned up on her doorstep after she'd attempted to have no more to do with him. Anyone could have seen them during their Georgian stroll and tipped off the *Globe*. It might have been Bill, from the insurance company, who had lost business to Bumpermac's. Joe had given him the ammunition, after all, by behaving indiscreetly. He'd have to be more circumspect in future. If there was to be any future between himself and Kitty . . .

Joe felt a belated gouge of shame at his chilliness towards Kitty, and his knee-jerk attempt to foist all culpability onto her. He'd been seized by panic and he wasn't proud of it. Then Joe looked at Kitty more closely and saw how she was struggling to control her emotions. The stab of shame was doubled. Quite simply, she affected him, however inconvenient he found it. He reached across the table to cover her hand with his. "Are you all right?"

She dipped her head, still devastated by Sunny's perfidy. Her sister's duplicity consumed her, so that she overlooked the injustice of Joe's earlier hostility towards her.

His grip on her hand tightened. "This will be a storm in the teacup," he comforted. "It might be embarrassing tomorrow, but deny everything and it will soon be forgotten. Nobody can prove anything, Kitty. We're the only two who know the truth of the situation."

A waiter arrived with her mushroom and bacon risotto and his Dublin Bay Prawns, proceeding to describe what was on their plates as though they had no eyes to see for themselves. Even though the atmosphere had relented between them, Kitty thought she would choke if she ate a mouthful. The waiter hovered, however, making it plain he wouldn't leave until they tasted the food. He was anxious for reassurance that the food which somebody else had cooked, and somebody else again had arranged on oversized plates, was to their satisfaction. Kitty banked down the urge to say "Scat!". "Delicious," she announced instead after a nibble, which did the trick.

"We're going to work through this together." The jut of Joe's jaw was supportive. "I'm not prepared to lose you because of someone else's spite." He smiled for the first time that evening, blurring the dimple in his chin.

He seemed so certain, so determined to be with her, that Kitty's gratitude swelled, his earlier harshness forgotten. In that moment Joe French seemed worth any amount of trouble. As she gazed at him, the terrain of desire stretched promisingly before her.

"Is your sister a rabid supporter of marriage?" asked Joe.

"Not particularly – she's just using any weapon that comes to hand to punish me. I think she feels more or less the way I do about it, that it works for some people but not for others. Yet it's supposed to be a one-size-fits-all recipe for eternal bliss."

He nodded, jerking movements that set sections of his hair

standing on end. It looked engaging, stripping him of years' worth of gravitas. "I remember standing at the altar rails wondering how I'd ended up there – and more to the point, why. I looked at Emma and wondered who this stranger was." His face softened. "But then Clodagh was born and it made sense of everything. Emma isn't a natural mother, she doesn't particularly like babies. We have a nanny and she's heavily reliant on her. Emma says it'll be better when Clodagh is older and she can take her to ballet classes or a pony club. She feels panicked because Clodagh can't communicate with her – Emma doesn't know what the baby wants when she wails. But I know what all the different cries mean. She has a different sound for when she's hungry or wet or fractious, or when she just wants to be picked up and cuddled."

Obviously Joe and Emma didn't have much of a relationship, thought Kitty, but she hoped he wasn't going to be one of these people who were compulsive about sharing every detail of its deterioration. Sometimes she wished men and women embarking on a new relationship were obliged to fit all their gripes about the ex – or even the current – on a postcard and swap it, after which further complaints were banned. Still, she was curious. He'd been the one to raise the subject so she might as well take advantage of it. "Don't you love your wife?"

He moved his neck around on its axle, as though easing a strain. "Yes, I love her, but I'm not in love with her."

That old chestnut. Kitty stifled her impatience. "How long have you been married?"

"Three years."

"Not long to lose the 'in love' feeling, Joe."

Now it was his shoulder-blades which troubled him. He rotated first one shoulder, then the other. "She suffered post-natal depression and didn't really bond properly with Clodagh. I suppose I picked up the slack and over-compensated."

Kitty lifted her glass of Pouilly Fumé and emptied it. She knew it was expensive and should be savoured, but she transferred it from glass to throat without tasting its smoked sweetness. He was ducking the subject of why he was no longer in love with his wife. But was it really any of her business? If he could compartmentalise, she could too. She wanted a married a man and now she had one. But it was supposed to be fun, that's what she'd believed on New Year's Day. Being a mistress was meant to pivot on embracing the present. *Carpe diem*-ing. When was the merriment due to start for her and Joe?

Joe beat three waiters to the wine cooler and refilled her glass. "Remember what it was like to be nineteen? Remember how you intended to reach out with both hands and grab the world by the throat?"

Kitty didn't remember wanting to throttle the world, although she smiled dutifully. "I watched my father spend a lifetime running a sub-post office in Ardee," continued Joe, "hardly able to afford a holiday, scrimping and saving to put us through school, and for what? To die of a heart attack at sixty-three. He never lived to enjoy his retirement. I wanted to be one of the winners – I suppose I am, by most people's standards. I thought part of the prize was a house with the right address, a wife with the right face, a parcel of kids with the right stuff in them." He sipped a mouthful. "Emma can't have any more children – there'll only be Clodagh. That makes her all the more precious. When I cut a deal, I do it for her. When I bank a cheque, I do it for her. When I win, I win for her."

Kitty cocked her head, jet beads lustrous in the candlelight. "What do you have for yourself from all this, Joe French?"

He pushed aside his plate, which prompted a brace of waiters to materialise at his elbow, offering dessert menus, and attempting to add water to their already brimming tumblers. His eyes brooded into hers while the bustle fretted around them. When they were alone Joe answered Kitty. "I know what I'd like to have. But it's not mine yet."

She understood him at once, but made him say it, for the giddy pleasure of hearing it spoken aloud.

"You. I want you, Kitty Kennedy."

Chapter 28

Joe caved in to the beseeching eyes of a waiter and ordered a couple of cappuccinos.

He dipped his forefinger into the froth clinging to the side of his cup, studiously casual, and asked, "Would you ever consider getting married again?"

Kitty knew instinctively that Joe was on tenterhooks for the answer. This was her audition.

She shook her head. "Marriage doesn't agree with me."

"Maybe you never met the right man."

"No, Joe, I prefer the single state. Don't go taking away my sense of having achieved something, if only a pattern of failed marriages."

"Even so-called successful marriage can be failures. Fundamentally, marriage changes nothing between two people." He was pensive.

"I don't agree. People are fond of claiming marriage changes nothing, but it's one of those profound statements that leak like a sieve as soon as it's examined." Marriage had altered everything between her and Benjamin.

Benjamin joined Kitty and Joe at the table. He was there as bodily as though he'd pulled up a chair; look at him, eyeing the remnants of her risotto with distaste. "You shouldn't eat bacon, Kitty," he reproved her, "it gives you the hiccups." She lifted a rectangle of meat and popped it between her teeth – there, that showed him.

"Would you like to go on somewhere for a nightcap?" asked Joe.

"Did you bring your trumpet? You promised me some Louis Armstrong."

"You mean my horn," he corrected her. "Well, let's see, do I have a pocket horn about my person?" He patted his pockets.

"What's a pocket horn?"

"The tubing's twisted so it's only eight inches long, but it has the same sound as a normal horn. No, don't seem to have it. Next time I'll serenade you, Kitty. For now you just get me."

"That'll do for me," she thought.

He smiled as he translated it in her eyes.

"Come home with me for a nightcap," she invited.

"I'd love to." He paused. "Could you excuse me while I make one quick call?"

"The Australian matter?"

"Oh, that was a big fat lie. My escape hatch. I just want to see how Clodagh is – the nanny thought she might be coming down with chickenpox. I need a condition-check to set my mind at rest and then I'm all yours."

All hers. The atmosphere grew charged in a way that made Kitty catch her breath. This was going to be so fine between her and Joe.

As he stood a waiter pre-empted him and shot across the room, moving his napkin from his lap and positioning it in a graceful sweep on the arm of his chair. Joe came across to her side of the table and leaned in towards Kitty, his lips brushing her earlobe. "Sorry to leave you alone, even for a minute. I promise there'll be no more phone calls after this."

"How can I be alone with that squadron of waiters poised to pander to me?" She hummed contentedly while she waited. I'm giving myself permission to do anything I like tonight with Joe French. Anything at all. A tingle of anticipation skipped up her spine.

Joe was back moments later. "I'm so sorry, Kitty, the timing is all off, but there's a pressing matter I must attend to. It's a union problem, it won't wait."

"But it's after eleven," she wailed, all her delicious anticipation ebbing.

"If I don't sort it we could have a strike on our hands. My deputy has been trying to get hold of me for hours – I had my mobile switched off. Look, you have no idea how much I regret this, Kitty, truly I do, but it's an emergency. Let me help you to a cab." He ushered her outside and had her bundled into a taxi within seconds, hailing one as it sailed along the quays towards Heuston train station. Kitty felt the pressure of his lips against hers, a fleeting intensity which seemed to signify a covenant between them. *Our time will come.*

She wished it would get a move on.

"I'll call you tomorrow, you can sue me if I don't." He tried to coax a smile.

Kitty made an indistinct movement with her head. Their evening wasn't supposed to end this way.

* * *

"Are you married?" Kitty asked the taxi-driver abruptly, cutting across his conversation. He was attempting to discuss recent by-election results, relating them to his theory about a pan-Marxist government infiltration plot.

"Women always want to talk about relationships." He changed from third gear to fourth. "Yes, thirty-one years, she was my first sweetheart. I've known her since we were both at school. We have three daughters and five grandchildren. The mortgage will be paid off in two years' time, then we plan to retire to Dunmore East."

Kitty relaxed into the seat, consoled. She liked hearing how other people could make their marriages work, even if she couldn't. Sometimes all the unhappy marriages she was aware of depressed her: her own two had been dismal, her parents' was gouged from habit and Joe's was clearly stagnating. Although maybe his workaholic tendencies were as much a contributor as his wife's peculiarities – whatever they were. All he'd said was that she wasn't a natural mother and had suffered from post-natal depression. Hardly grounds for an affair.

Stop right there, Kitty Kennedy, she ordered herself. She mustn't lose sight of her objective. She couldn't start feeling an affinity with Emma French or she'd never go through with this. She wanted an affair, she needed an affair, she *deserved* an affair. And she was damn well going to have one.

Joe. She whispered the name, noticing how her mouth pursed into a kiss to pronounce it. Joe was the best thing to happen to Kitty in ages. He was attractive, successful, charming, he had a dimple and made Kitty feel like a vibrant woman. What more could she ask for? She settled back in the taxi, determined to be upbeat.

However, upbeat was hard to maintain when he wasn't exactly wooing her in the fashion she'd hoped for. There was euphoria, undoubtedly, but so far it was all promises and no passion. Where were the weekends in country house hotels? The afternoon sessions in four-poster beds? The toe-sucking, tummy-button-licking and bottom-nibbling mistresses were entitled to? He hadn't even ordered champagne with their dinner.

Joe French would need to shape up.

* * *

Noreen-dear studied Kitty suspiciously. "So you're absolutely positively not having an affair with a married man. I have to warn you, Kitty, if you were misbehaving in that fashion your father and I would be bitterly disappointed in you." She lashed off a warning glance at Denis, requiring his corroboration.

"We would, Kitty." Denis shuffled, mortified by the conversation. "But I never believed it for a second."

"Thanks, Dad. Mum" – Kitty met her eye and told her what she wanted to hear – "of course I'm not having an affair. I have an email stalker who keeps trying to make dates with me. He probably planted the story from some twisted sense of revenge because I've been ignoring him."

Noreen-dear wavered. "There are some very odd folk about. I hope you remember to lock your doors at night before going to bed."

Kitty wanted to throttle her sister rather than cover up for her, but if she told her parents the article had originated with Sunny it wouldn't be so easy to deny her relationship with Joe. Sunny was in trouble, though. She'd been ducking Kitty's calls, but she'd catch up with her viper of a sister sooner or later. "Now, never mind that spiteful article, Mum. What do you think I should do with ninety thousand dollars?"

Noreen-dear held the cheque gingerly by a corner. "That's a lot of money."

"A heck of a lot, chicken," confirmed Kitty's father.

"But how should I spend it?" Kitty didn't imagine for one second she'd want to take her parents' advice, but it was entertaining to solicit it. Clarke had sent the cheque to her office that afternoon by courier, with an apology that he couldn't deliver it in person because he had to fly to Los Angeles to cope with an emergency.

"Top up your pension." Her father's was a predictable offering.

"It doesn't take ninety thousand, two hundred and six dollars forty-seven cents to do that," chided Noreen-dear. "Kitty, have you admired my box of chocolates from Clarke yet?"

"No, Mum, I'll do it now." She was back a couple of seconds later. "You could plant a flag on them and claim them as a colony. Any advice about what I should spend my windfall on? Would you and Dad like a winter break at my expense? Tenerife is supposed to be lovely at this time of year."

Noreen-dear allowed herself a moment to daydream about the

neighbours' faces if she mentioned that she and Denis were jetting off for some winter sunshine. Then commonsense, of which she had more than her fair share, intervened. "No, Kitty, don't go frittering bits of that money here and there, it'll all be squandered before you know it. Use it to change your life." She caught her daughter by the wrist, to lend emphasis to her words. "Hand in your notice and start work on that travel book you've always said you wanted to write."

Kitty leaned towards her teacup, vapour from the hot liquid tickling her cheek. Even if he was a workaholic, there was no way she was going to jet off around the world and leave the extraordinary Joe French behind her. Still . . . it could have been wonderful. She'd often fantasised about kicking over the traces of work and strapping on a rucksack. She'd frequently complained about being a wage slave, rambling on to friends and family about writing a guide book on how the single woman could safely negotiate the world's more inaccessible reaches. Timbuktu, say, or Bora Bora.

Her mother watched the equivocation chase across Kitty's face. When her husband opened his mouth to register an objection to his daughter haring around the world, she jabbed him in the ribs.

"What about my job?" Kitty was thinking aloud, but Noreen-dear answered.

"Leave of absence, that sabbath thing I hear them talking about.

"Sabbatical. What about my house?"

"Rent it out. Your father and I can keep an eye on the tenants."

"What about my –" Kitty stopped short. She had been about to say "mistress scheme", but remembered in time that she hadn't confided her intentions in her parents. "What about my life here?" she managed lamely. *What about Joe French?*

"Your life will still be waiting for you when you come home again." Noreen-dear was beginning to feel chafed by her daughter's caution, and a curl flopped onto her forehead, sharing her impatience.

"I'll think it over." Kitty stood up from the kitchen table and reached for the kettle to cause a diversion. "Who's for a fresh pot of tea?"

Denis Kennedy delivered a reproachful glance to his daughter. "I'll just check on whether that stool I was trying to glue back together is fixed." He slid from the room, his mind full of a Gobi Desert jigsaw.

"We'll throw your name in the pot," called Noreen-dear, but he was already on the basement stairs. "He won't be back," she sniffed. Kitty played mute. "Just as well, he was worse than useless, trying to persuade you to spend that money on a pension."

"What money?" The front door banged and Sunny kicked off her shoes and dropped her shoulder-bag on the floor. Her white-blonde hair glinted in the leaky remains of the sunlight. "Leave some hot water in the kettle and I'll make myself a coffee, Kitty-cat."

Kitty, no longer playing mute, was now struck dumb. Her sister had some cheek. A few days ago Sunny had held her up as a laughing-stock, announcing to the world that she was having an affair. Now she was calling her Kitty-cat and beaming that Oscar-acceptance grin in a circumference that appeared to include her.

"I'll rustle you up a mug of coffee if you like." With arsenic in it, she mouthed. "Fantastic." Sunny stretched out her long legs in their knee-high toffee suede boots, looking at peace with the world. Not a bit like someone who'd treated Kitty as public enemy number one.

Sunny, however, was considering whether to commiserate with Kitty over the story in the *Sunday Globe*, but decided to leave well alone. She couldn't imagine who'd spoken to the newspaper, but it wasn't surprising that the word was out – she'd warned her sister there'd be trouble if she tangled herself up with a married man.

Noreen-dear carried the teapot and a plate of home-made shortcake biscuits to the table. "Kitty's had a stroke of fortune," she said.

Don't mention Clarke's name, shrieked Kitty internally.

"She's just been given a cheque for more than ninety thousand dollars," continued her mother. "From that American gentleman with the beautiful manners, the one who sent over his chauffeur with the chocolates for me." She nodded towards the cheque lying on the table.

Kitty groaned; now she was in for it. Sunny's rampant jealousy would spoil everything for her.

Sunny lifted the cheque and studied it, prepared to be gracious. To hell with it, she wasn't. "Bribe? Payment for services rendered? Kiss-off? Tell me, Kitty, I'm intrigued." Anger mounted within Sunny. She may have decided to concede defeat with regard to Clarke and her ambitions, she may have forgotten to devise a punishment for Kitty, and she probably wouldn't bother now, since she'd been humiliated enough, but that didn't mean she was ready to forgive her sister. Especially when she had the Midas touch.

"Actually, the cheque's an honourable settlement of an account." Kitty sketched out its history.

Sunny drank from her coffee mug, fuming internally, but leaving a scarlet smile imprinted on the rim. Men didn't give women a nest-egg unless they planned to share the nest. "So what are you going to do with it?"

"That's the million-dollar question," responded Noreen-dear.

"Or even the ninety thousand-dollar question." Sunny gritted her teeth. "Spend and enjoy, that's my advice. Are you headed for Paris and the couture houses? South Africa and the diamond mines?"

"Maybe Easter Island and the giant carved heads. But not to buy them, just to admire them." Wagon, Kitty thought. Just wait till I get her on her own – twisting the knife by making me take part in polite chit-chat.

Wagon, Sunny thought. This is just a cover. She's relocating to Carmel, California, as surely as I'm destined for teacher-training college.

"Kitty's going to research that travel book she used to talk about writing," burst in Noreen-dear, who felt entitled to some credit for the plan.

"Maybe," prevaricated Kitty.

"A travel book – you used to talk about doing one years ago." Sunny slanted a glance at Kitty: let's see how adept her sister was at lying. "Will you be going to California as part of your research?"

"Definitely not. If I were to do it – and there's a great deal to take into consideration first – I'd only go to places with unpronounceable names, after trekking across mountains by llama for three days to reach them."

Very accomplished, she didn't flinch, thought Sunny. "An adventure," interpreted Sunny, "that's what you're going to have. Here am I, deciding I'm not cut out for stardom and I want a quiet life after all, and there you are throwing caution to the winds and hitching up your skirts to ride llamas and yaks. Who'd have thought it?"

"The day you settle for a quiet life, Sunniva Kennedy, is the day I give up the ghost," scoffed Noreen-dear.

"Nevertheless, I'm not going to America to make my fame and fortune after all, now that the financing for the film has fallen through." Sunny curled the palm of her hand around the mug, a pang prickling her. Not a very large pang, just enough for a needle-point pain.

Serves you right, Sunny, Kitty rejoiced. Since she couldn't say it aloud, she concentrated on thinking it. A tear bleared in each of Sunny's true-blue eyes, but she blinked them away. Kitty was jubilant. Sunny deserved everything she had coming to her. She'd nearly subverted Kitty's relationship with Joe, thanks to that meddlesome leak to the *Sunday Globe*.

Looks like rain, Sarge, thought Sunny. Then she shook her head, clutching at that sense of liberation she'd experienced at the Clarence with Clarke. No, it would be sunshine all the way, and she didn't have to go to the Sunshine State to find it. Anyway, she'd have been no better off there than she was in Bray. She'd have spent all her free time cruising Rodeo Drive, spending money like devaluation was just around the corner. She flashed that awards ceremony smile she hadn't yet reassigned to more pedestrian events. "Must hotfoot it upstairs to transform myself. There's an engineer I'm seeing tonight who doesn't know it yet but who's going to buy me Kir Royales. We're starting in Café en Seine and who knows where we'll end up? St Tropez, with any luck. I'll bring my passport just in case."

Kitty followed Sunny upstairs and confronted her in her bedroom. "Tipping off the *Globe* about Joe and me was a barbarous betrayal. Ever heard of a little more than kin and a little less than kind? You've redefined it, you absolute madam."

Sunny was puzzled. What on earth was Kitty ranting about?

"As far as I'm concerned, I don't have a sister any more," continued Kitty. Her fingers itched to slap Sunny, but relinquished the idea with a certain amount of regret. Her sister would slap back – harder.

Suddenly Sunny grasped what Kitty was bleating about. "You can't believe I phoned up a newspaper to tittle-tattle about you!"

"Who else knew? You had the information and you had the motive, your pathetic jealousy over Clarke. But there's nothing between Clarke and me, Sunny, and even if there was you still had no right to broadcast my affairs."

Enraged at her sister for jumping to conclusions, Sunny declined to defend herself. Let Kitty think what she liked. She wasn't going to dignify such a ridiculous accusation by denying it any further. "Broadcasting your affairs? So there's more than one." Sunny yawned. "My, my, what a busy girl! You're a late developer, but they tend to be the ones to watch."

"You've caused me no end of trouble, you malevolent freeloader," Kitty hissed, keeping her voice low in case Noreen-dear overheard. "Thanks to you I've had to endure a succession of suggestive remarks from my colleagues, some very odd looks from

Rose and a couple of nutters emerging from the woodwork to demand my sacking. But it's all been in vain, Sunny. You haven't managed to split up me and Joe. All you've done is show yourself in your true colours. Petty, self-obsessed and vindictive."

"Run along, Kitty, you're not welcome in my bedroom."

"It was my bedroom before it was yours." Kitty knew it was a puerile jibe, but it shot out before she could stop herself. Sunny laughed aloud, which left Kitty seething. "You're unprincipled – but you're not the only one capable of serving up revenge on a slab. You seem to have forgotten Nick Shooter is coming to town." The words were spur-of-the-moment – she didn't really intend using Nick to hurt her sister.

But Sunny stilled, her face emptied of expression. Then there was a spasm and her features twisted as though she was inhaling a foetid stench. "What's happened to you, Kitty? You used to have such a sweet nature before you started your ridiculous moral-mistress scheming. You've changed – coarsened. I don't recognise you any more." She pushed past Kitty.

Chapter 29

Joe phoned Kitty that night. He had a gift for her, he said. Compensation for the unromantic foreclosure on their date.

"Post it to me," she deflected him, loathe to appear a pushover.

"This is a present I want to give you personally," he insisted, a throb of something promising in his voice. "Say you'll meet me."

"I'll think about it." She'd already decided to agree, however: refusing would be counter-productive. But he didn't need to know that yet. She'd leave him to plead a little more. Finally she agreed to meet him in the Gresham for a drink the following night at nine. Kitty diverted herself for ages speculating on what the gift might be. A puppy? He'd said he worried about her living alone. A diamond bracelet to clasp around her wrist? Shares in his company? Maybe those last two possibilities verged on the extravagant – she wasn't a gold-digger. She'd settle for a heart-shaped balloon and an ode to his lady's elbow.

* * *

The next morning Kitty was in a vivacious mood as she hunted for an ironed shirt to wear to work. Joe's intentions definitely weren't honourable if he planned to meet her in the Gresham bearing presents. Since Kitty's certainly weren't honourable either, that suited her. She snatched up her briefcase, indulging in an accommodating fantasy whereby instead of catching the Dart into work, she turned up on Joe's doorstep and they spent the day together. Except, she gnawed her lip, she didn't know his address, only that he lived in Malahide. Furthermore, Joe was probably already in his office so it would be Emma French answering the door instead of him. Probably holding their baby in her arms, another twist of the knife.

On balance, Kitty deemed it safer to strike out for the *Sunday Trumpet* building. But she intended to look up Joe French's library file as soon as she arrived. It offended her sense of protocol that she didn't even know his home address. Kitty and Rose met at the lift in the foyer.

"Rose, you look shattered," exclaimed Kitty.

Rose shrugged. "Worrying does that to you. I didn't want to come in, but the Exalted One will stop my pay cheques unless I turn up. And I have financial problems that definitely require a salary to be lodged in my account on a monthly basis. I saw an estate agent last week and my bank manager yesterday. Guess it's only a matter of time before a sale board goes up on Clonliffe Square."

"Rose, I'm so sorry, I'd forgotten you thought you might have to move. Surely your finances aren't that grim?"

"Unfortunately they are." Rose grimaced. Then she remembered she'd promised herself to stop doing anything that would score deeper the lines that were already on her face. It was her new policy and had nothing to do with finding herself interested in a twenty-seven-year-old man. Absolutely not. It was simply sound practice.

They walked along the newsroom floor. "This week you're having the sports editor to fancy and I'm having the new circulation manager." Rose tried to distract herself from her money worries.

"No way," wailed Kitty. "I can't take on Darren from sport. He's – he's – he's from the Midlands!"

"It's only for a week. You don't have to do any more than flirt. It can even be non-verbal flirting."

"I'd like to know," Kitty was bitter, "whose idea this game was in the first place and why I ever agreed to play it."

"It's a reminder that we still have a pulse, ninny. Anyway the new circulation manager isn't exactly a catch – have you heard how bossy he is? He's living proof that men shouldn't be let near clipboards – the power goes to their heads."

"OK. Now, do me a favour and look up the picture file for me, Rose. I need anything we have on a hotshot businessman called Joe French. I'm supposed to be compiling a profile of him."

Rose peeled off, while Kitty made for her desk and flicked onto the newspaper library on her computer system. Most of the stories saved for reference about Joe were business reports. Dull-dull-dull. Nothing that breathed life into the man: just formulaic quotes from him about the battle to win the hearts and minds of Irish shoppers and the need to lure customers from Bumpermac's competitors. She was almost ready to call a halt when she struck gold. The article was dated four years ago, but described him as the country's most dynamic entrepreneur. She read it avidly, scanning through arid business-speak for nuggets of personal information. He was six-foot-one, thirty-two – that made him thirty-six now, the same age as Kitty – with two sisters and a brother, had studied accountancy at University College Dublin, had wanted to be an airline pilot growing up, played the trumpet in his spare time, insisted all the staff at Bumpermac's call him Joe, had a pet dog called Louis, a penthouse apartment in Christchurch and a girlfriend called Emma. Now his wife, clearly. Presumably the penthouse had been traded in for his house in Malahide. Kitty's phone rang.

"It's Rose. I've pulled up some pictures onto my screen if you want to take a look."

Kitty was there in seconds. Rose's computer screen was divided into a bank of tiny boxes, each one showing a different image of Joe French. Joe grinning in a pair of Bumpermac's overalls at the topping-out ceremony for a new store; Joe looking quizzical as he answered a question at a press conference; Joe huddled in conversation with one of the Doyle brothers, who owned the chain.

"Here's a good shot." Rose rapped a command on her keyboard and one of the photographs engulfed the screen, eclipsing the others.

It showed Joe with his arm protectively circling the shoulders of a striking woman with caramel-streaked hair, immaculately made-up, who was holding a pale pink blanket in her arms. From the uppermost tip of the blanket, a tiny nose and chin peeked.

"A family shot – that would be ideal for your piece, Kitty." Rose was approving. "Shame we can't see more of the baby. The caption says: *'Proud father, Bumpermac's chief executive Joe French, collects his wife Emma and their new baby daughter from hospital.'* It doesn't give the little girl's name."

"Clodagh." Kitty couldn't wrench her eyes off the image. They looked like a family in it. They looked complete. "The baby's name is Clodagh."

Kitty dragged her lethargic legs back to her desk, where she frittered away the next hour. She felt so many responses it was impossible to disengage one from the other. Among them were self-disgust, jealousy and disappointment – yes, disappointment – in Joe French. Imagine having his own slice of heaven and being prepared to risk it. Did he believe himself inviolable? Or did he think he was entitled to all that – and a mistress besides? Why wouldn't he, with women such as her prepared to accommodate him?

"I thought you were my friend!" A voice intruded on Kitty's reverie. It was the former Miss Ireland, Puffin O'Mara, oozing reproach.

"How did you get in?" stuttered Kitty. This was a nightmare: she'd mocked the beauty queen, an easy target, in the celebrity profile run last Sunday.

Puffin O'Mara shrugged. "I told the security guard you were expecting me and he waved me through. Kitty, how could you have written that about me? We had Tia Maria and Pepsi together." A luscious lower lip outlined and filled in with MAC products – and a squirt of collagen to plump it up – wobbled.

Kitty decided this was no time to remind Puffin that she'd been the one drinking Tia Maria and Pepsi combinations – Kitty had stuck to fizzy water because she'd been working. She squirmed. "It was nothing personal, Puffin."

"I let you try on my new faux fur." Now the lip was caught between teeth.

Kitty scanned the room for someone to rescue her. Where was Des Redmond, the features editor? He was an executive, he should be here making executive noises. Or what about Linus Bell? The way he carried on, handling a distraught beauty queen would be child's play to him.

"Could somebody call security?" Kitty implored. Nobody moved – her colleagues were afraid of missing the show.

"Why did you do it?" Puffin slumped against the side of Kitty's desk. "You said I thought sushi was a martial art."

Kitty's eyes darted around, looking for the security guards. Surely someone had called them?

"My boyfriend's dumped me and it's your fault. He claims all his friends on the soccer squad are laughing at him." Puffin's face crumpled.

This couldn't be happening to her, Kitty groaned. She had no alternative but to trot out the number one cliché in the journalist's manual. "I'm sorry, I was only doing my job."

Puffin reached into her bag and produced a bottle of perfume, squirting a cloud at her.

"You just missed my eyes," howled Kitty. "You could have blinded me." She coughed, throat burning and nose streaming.

"How about a mug of coffee?" Rose appeared at Puffin's side. "I've made some for all three of us, it's waiting in the kitchen." She steered away Puffin from Kitty's desk. "Coming, Kitty?" Rose called over her shoulder.

Kitty lumbered to her feet and followed.

In the kitchen, Puffin's enormous hazel eyes were reproving as they fastened on Kitty. "You journalists should realise how hurtful your stories are – you're writing about people's lives."

Kitty nodded, contrite despite the perfume attack.

"My little girl will have all this repeated to her in the playground, you know."

"I'm sure you're overreacting," soothed Rose. "I read the piece and thought you came across really well – a strong, single mother who's not afraid to let down her hair and party, but who works hard to pay her daughter's school fees."

Puffin turned to Rose, avid for reassurance. "You think I sounded strong?"

"As a rock. Anyway, nobody reads those articles to the end, they just flick through the first couple of paragraphs and admire the pics." Rose pushed the mug of coffee towards Puffin, whose hands accepted it mechanically. "Isn't that right, Kitty?"

"Absolutely, and you looked fabulous in the photographs. They'll really have raised your profile, Puffin. I'm surprised the London modelling agencies haven't been on to you already."

Puffin sniffed, slightly mollified. "All the same, I thought you were my friend. You spent hours talking to me. How could you write those mean things?"

"It's journalism, not friendship." Kitty propped a hand against her cheek. "I wasn't sitting in the Westbury to become bosom buddies with you. I was working. I'm sorry if you had the wrong impression."

"But you were so interested in everything I had to say," wailed Puffin, hair sticking to damp patches on her face. "I trusted you."

Kitty exchanged a look with Rose. "Sometimes I don't like my job very much," she admitted.

Puffin rooted for her make-up purse and produced a canvas container so crammed with tubes and pots it had burst a section of its seams. She began dabbing at her blurred eye make-up. "You have to realise I'm a single mother," she explained, intent on her pocket mirror. "That's a job I take seriously. But you make me sound as if I'm always on the town guzzling Tia Maria and Pepsi and hitting on men."

"I was just trying to show that you know how to enjoy yourself." Shame prodded Kitty.

Puffin teased up her hair with her fingers. "Apart from the fact you cause people pain, there are consequences when you write sneering stories. I don't care about Ray dumping me, he was only looking for an excuse, but I do care about my daughter. Her father could sue for custody, using your story as evidence that I'm an unfit mother."

"Kitty did portray you as a responsible parent. She mentioned you rang home twice on your mobile to say goodnight and check she wasn't watching too much television," interjected Rose.

"That's true, I said you were obviously devoted to her," tacked on a chastened Kitty, for she didn't often come face to face with the repercussions of her celebrity profiles. If it happened on a regular basis, she'd have to earn her living some less stressful way.

"My Jade means the world to me." Puffin's expression grew gentle beneath her renewed mask of make-up. "I want her to be a ballet dancer when she grows up – she goes to lessons twice a week. She's a little fairy in her tutu."

After she had left, Kitty made a beeline for Des Redmond. "Where were you when I needed you?"

He twitched. "I thought it best to leave you to talk over your problems, woman to woman. No point in everyone wading in there, muddying the water."

"What if she'd turned violent? I didn't see you spring into action when she sprayed me with perfume," Kitty stormed.

Des sniggered. 'Don't be such a drama queen, Kitty – a bottle of

Chanel doesn't count as an offensive weapon. She's a fine-looking woman, that Puffin O'Mara. But I'll speak to the security people about how she got in."

He lifted his phone, wanting her to leave him alone, embarrassed by the contretemps he had lacked the courage to intervene in. "Buy Rose a decent meal on expenses, she deserves it."

Kitty returned to Rose's desk, glancing towards Linus Bell's office door. "Typical that the Exalted One disappears for a long lunch the one day we actually need him."

Rose was pensive. "You did a fairly vindictive hatchet-job on Puffin in that article, all the same. I didn't know you had it in you. You never used to be so cutting, Kitty."

Kitty was dismayed. It reminded her of what Sunny had said about no longer recognising her. Could it be that she was changing – becoming a shade more brittle, a touch more relentless?

Chapter 30

Joe was standing just inside the revolving door of the Gresham Hotel, vigilant for Kitty's arrival. He touched her on the shoulder, standing so close that she had to crane her neck right back to meet his eye.

"You look radiant, Kitty." His smile reached out to stroke her. "How's the newspaper business?"

"Gets me out of the house. How's the supermarket business?"

"Gets me out of the house."

They laughed, oblivious to the crowds swirling through the foyer of the O'Connell Street hotel.

Joe dropped his voice an octave. "I'm so glad you could come." He bent and brushed his lips against the tip of her nose.

Kitty felt something liquefy. Her bones, she presumed. Her resistance had long since turned to mush.

As Joe guided her towards a table – behind a pillar, at the back of the lounge where they couldn't be seen – it struck Kitty that there was an inner seam of excitement threaded through each of them, kindled by the other's presence. He settled her into her seat and raised his hand at a passing waiter. "What would you like to drink?"

"A gin and tonic, please."

"A gin and tonic for the lady and a glass of red lemonade for me." He intercepted Kitty's tremor of amusement. "I've always loved red lemonade since I was a boy. White lemonade doesn't compare with it. Besides, I'm driving. Now, I want you to do all the talking this evening. I need to know everything about your day. Start at the beginning, leave nothing out."

Faced with that instruction, Kitty was flummoxed. She considered her contretemps with Puffin O'Mara – the entire episode from start to finish didn't reflect well on Kitty, and she knew it. "I fixed up an interview with Lola Dunne," she managed at last, naming the latest pop sensation.

Joe looked blank. Kitty, thinking she was boring him, drained her gin and tonic in a fit of nerves and he instantly signalled for another. "What did you do today, Joe?"

He smiled. "Up at six. Played with Clodagh. Read her *The Princess And The Pea* – it's her favourite story. I know she understands it, even if she is less than a year old. Met an architect to discuss plans for a new store. Never mind any more of that, I have something for you." He produced a small package.

Kitty thrummed with pleasure as she traced her fingers across its outer surface – it felt like jewellery. She fondled it a little longer before unwrapping it. To find a packet of glow-stars. Disconcerted, she turned them over in her hand.

"I have a nephew who has them on the ceiling above his bed," explained Joe. "They glow for ages after you turn out the light. I hoped – if it wasn't too presumptuous – you might let me come to your house and stick them on your bedroom ceiling. I have a book of constellations, I thought maybe I'd take a crack at Venus."

Venus, the goddess of love. Kitty was charmed. This was better than a diamond bracelet, this was commitment. She looked at him, uncharacteristically fidgety as he waited for her answer. "Perfect, Joe, we can go and do it now if you like."

"Well . . ." he hesitated.

What? God oh God oh God, surely he wasn't going to tell her he needed to nip home first and tuck in his baby daughter.

"It's just that . . ."

"Yes?" snapped Kitty.

"It's not very romantic, but my stomach thinks my throat's been cut. I haven't eaten since a sandwich at lunchtime and if I don't cram some food down my throat in the next five minutes I'll collapse on the spot. I don't suppose you'd care to join me for supper here?"

Kitty laughed, relieved. "Of course. Regard it as an open invitation to drop by and get creative with the glow-stars."

"It's an invitation I plan to take you up on very soon." Joe sent a meaningful glance winging Kitty's way. It almost scorched her cheek. "Let me talk to the manager and see if there's a table free in the dining-room."

Kitty fingered her glow-stars in his absence, thinking how unusual Joe French was. Of all the gifts he could have chosen for her, a packet of plastic stars was by far and away the most beguiling

Joe was smoothing down a wayward tuft of his copper hair as he returned to Kitty. "Unfortunately the kitchen has just closed, but if we check in to the hotel we can order room service." He paused. "We don't have to stay the night – but it might be, ah, congenial to eat in private. Just the two of us. They say they can set up a table and supply us with a waiter."

As realisation overtook her, Kitty felt colour well from her collarbone along her neck.

"Forget it," rushed Joe. "I'll pick up a burger and chips in a takeaway."

"No," Kitty forestalled him. "A private dinner sounds perfect." She drained the dregs of her second gin and tonic, exhilarated and just a fraction nervous. She was about to become a mistress at last. The die was cast.

* * *

A bottle of Bollinger was cooling in an ice bucket when they arrived in the room. It overlooked the street and, by craning at a certain angle, you could pick out the metallic length of the Millennium Spire in the middle of O'Connell Street. A sentinel waiter stood by a small table draped in white linen. Joe removed Kitty's coat and suit jacket, hanging them up in the wardrobe, while she smiled uncertainly at the obelisk-faced attendant.

"Would you like the champagne opened now, sir?" he asked Joe.

"Yes, please."

The waiter handed her a flute, then one to Joe.

"I can't have more than one of these because I'm driving." He clinked the glass against hers.

As the liquid scratched against her throat, Kitty felt the vestigial shreds of her inhibitions recede. Its impact was dramatic, in pursuit of a pair of gin and tonics taken on an empty stomach, for she'd been too keyed up at the prospect of meeting Joe to eat dinner. She drank deeply, a spiral of flightiness eddying through her, not noticing when the waiter excused himself to fetch their meal.

"How many times have you been in love, Kitty?" Joe reached down to push a stray lock of hair behind her ear.

"Twice, I suppose." Kitty watched the play of light against the crystal glass.

Joe refilled it, but not his own. "Someone once told me that everyone should love three times: first passionately, second disastrously and, finally, looking before you leap. But leaping anyway."

Kitty glowed. It made absolute sense: Ryan had been her passionate love, Benjamin her disastrous one – and with Joe she felt ready to leap. She faced him squarely, digesting the sherry eyes with their dark brown lashes, the dimple in his chin, the impact of authority. Yes, she believed she was ready for Joe French. "Here's to love's leap." Kitty raised her glass level with her head, held it suspended for a second, then emptied it at a swallow.

A knock tapped on the door and their waiter returned wheeling a trolley. Cutlery was already on the table by the window, and inside its parameters he placed two plates with silver domes covering their contents. "May I refresh your glasses, sir?" he asked Joe.

"No, thank you, I believe we can manage from here." Joe felt in his pocket for a tip.

"Have a pleasant evening, sir, madam." The waiter bowed and withdrew.

"I took the liberty of ordering for you," said Joe.

Kitty was thrilled. This was straight out of a 1950s film like *The Seven-Year Itch*, masterful men choosing what their women would eat. She didn't care if he'd ordered something she didn't like; this was so beautifully old-fashioned she'd forgive him anything. Even a predictable steak.

It was Salad Niçoise, followed by salmon in filo pastry with rosemary potatoes, and a cheese plate to finish off; Kitty couldn't have chosen better herself. Except she didn't fancy any food with this wonderfully addictive champagne to drink. Kitty realised she should moderate the rate at which she was emptying the bottle. But it was impossible to cover the top of her glass with her hand when Joe was fulfilling her New Year's Day fantasy – a man who would whisk her off to hotels and buy her Bollinger. She kicked off her shoes and wriggled her toes beneath the table, replete.

After picking at dinner, coquettish under the champagne's influence – for which she had limited tolerance – she indicated the sofa. "That looks comfortable."

Joe grinned, teeth gleaming against his skin. "It does. Would you like to move there? I'll see if I can find some music on the radio."

Kitty stood. This was it. A new phase of her life was about to begin. She loved Joe French – probably – and she was going to do something about it. Unexpectedly she tottered as she walked towards the sofa, ankles woolly, and crash-landed on the side of the bed. Oops. She really needed another sip of champagne to steady herself. Kitty put a hand to her forehead, suddenly over-heated. "It's a bit warm," she mumbled.

Joe was across to her in an instant. "Are you all right, Kitty? Can I fetch you a glass of water?"

"I feel a little woozy. I'm so sorry, Joe, I'm such an idiot. I think I overdid it with the bubbly."

"Don't worry, Kitty, I'll take care of you." He returned from the bathroom with a beaker of tap water, holding to her mouth while he stroked her hair back from her sticky forehead.

Kitty finished it and then rested her face gratefully against his shirt front. After a time Kitty rallied and raised her head. "Thank you, Joe. You've been spectacular."

He nuzzled the top of her head. "No, it's you that's spectacular."

She snuggled in against him and he massaged her shoulders, kneading away knots of tension. Then he grazed his lips down her cheek and along her neck, lodging in the soft hollow where her neck met her shoulder. Kitty waited, expecting a surge of passion to ignite her at any moment. She'd been angling towards this, hadn't she? Everything was progressing exactly as she'd anticipated. But she felt clammy and the sensation of stifling airlessness returned to her. Joe's bulk beside her was blocking her oxygen supply. Kitty realised she needed air or she'd pass out.

"Just have to use the bathroom, be back in a jiffy," she mumbled, tacking on the facsimile of a smile. The corner of her brain still able to discern such details noticed that he looked a little surprised as she staggered towards the bathroom, but she was incapable of caring.

She locked the door behind her and ran the cold-water tap, splashing her face. That was better. Kitty sank onto the lavatory seat, forehead against the cooling porcelain of the sink, heart hammering amid the residue of relief and revulsion which marked the ebb of a nausea attack. She was an idiot – two gin and tonics followed by the best part of a bottle of champagne. It was a mercy she hadn't thrown up all over Joe. She had no tolerance for bubbly.

Gradually her pulse slowed and she began to feel somewhat better.

Joe knocked on the bathroom door. "Is everything all right, Kitty?"

"Fine, thanks, I just need to catch my breath, I'll be out directly." She ran the cold-water tap again and trailed her fingers in the stream, feeling them turn numb. Then she spied a face flannel, soaked it in cold water and pressed it to her forehead. A few moments later Kitty passed out, still perched on the lavatory seat.

It was four a.m. when she roused, realising with mounting horror what had happened. She opened the door, scarcely knowing what to expect, and found Joe on top of the bed, fully dressed and sound asleep. His eyelashes formed dark crescents on either side of his face. God oh God oh God he was perfect – and she'd lost him by her stupid behaviour. He must despise her. Although not as much as she despised herself. Her best bet was to slip out quietly. Maybe later she could try to find some way of making him understand it had been an aberration and she wasn't really a lush.

Kitty tiptoed past the bed, wobbling as she stooped for her handbag, heart-stoppingly close to Joe's dangling right hand. She inched on towards the wardrobe, paralysed as the door rattled, then her jacket and raincoat were in her hand and she was almost home and dry. In the corridor she realised she had forgotten her shoes. She looked at her stockinged feet, which should be wearing suede pumps to match her shell-pink suit. She thought of the pink kitten-heels she loved lying under the table where she and Joe had dined. Kitty weighed up the repercussions of returning to the room. She abandoned the shoes.

The night porter was impassive as she walked through the foyer, carefully not looking at her feet. "Can I help you, miss?"

"Could you call a cab for me, please? Kitty held her handbag protectively across her front.

He lifted the phone and spoke to a taxi firm controller. "Couple of minutes, miss."

"I suppose you're wondering why I'm not wearing any shoes," began Kitty.

He shook his head, a shock of grey against the coal black of his eyebrows. "I see all sorts in this line of business. Losing your shoes is only the tip of the iceberg. Could be worse, miss, could be wet out, then you'd know all about it."

Kitty giggled, gripped by the ludicrous nature of her situation. "Looks like rain, Sarge," she spluttered.

The night porter set down the pen he'd been doodling with. "How did you know I'd been in the Army?"

Chapter 31

The estate agent had given Rose good news and the bank manager interviewing her about a loan had offset it with bad; unfortunately, one didn't cancel out the other. On the positive side, the apartment in Clonliffe Square was saleable; in fact, the agent had clients interested in the area and the property had increased in value. But she'd need to raise a crippling sum of money to buy out Father Damien – and the bank manager wasn't willing to lend it to her, based on her current salary and out-goings. Somewhat daunted, she'd approached her building society about re-mortgaging, but the equity in the flat wasn't enough to raise what she needed.

Her mind ricocheted, considering and discarding solutions. The sums might have added up if she took in a tenant, but since there was only one bedroom it wasn't viable; she could ask Linus Bell for a pay rise, but unless he was willing to double her salary it wouldn't make enough difference; she could take on a part-time job at weekends – but how would she see her parents? Rose allowed her eyes to roam the serene cream space she had created for herself. The solution was to sell the apartment, pay off Father Damien and move somewhere cheaper. A knot of rebellion tensed in the pit of her stomach: Clonliffe Square was her home and she had no desire to leave it. She didn't want to dismantle the framework of the life she had constructed for herself there. She liked being able to pad about in the dark in the middle of the night, knowing instinctively where to avoid outcrops of furniture and which cupboard door to open to find a mug. Of course she'd eventually achieve familiarity with another home, but Rose felt jaded at the prospect.

"You wouldn't be in this position if you'd stood on your own two feet and bought what you could afford," ridiculed a traitor voice inside her skull. "You were a fool to take Father Damien's cash in the first place."

"We were engaged to be married," Rose wailed aloud. "It was supposed to be a partnership."

"Remember that former Corporation house in Ringsend, you could have managed the mortgage on that by yourself," continued the inexorable voice. "But no, you fancied Clonliffe Square, it appealed to your notion of gracious living. You were reaching for the moon, Rose McBride, just like you always do."

She switched on the radio and searched for CityBeat FM. Feargal's voice filled the room, crystalline and rational. It struck Rose as inherently ludicrous that she should be listening to the man who had recently touched his lips to her naked skin adjudicate a radio debate. She turned off the radio and left for work.

Rose's phone was ringing as she reached her desk.

"Hey, gorgeous, it's the man in your life!"

"It's not the men in your life, it's the life in your men," she responded automatically.

Feargal was impressed. "Did you just make that up off the top of your head?"

"No, Feargal, a blonde bombshell movie star beat me to it."

"Uma Thurman? Wait a minute, I know, Marilyn Monroe."

Rose felt ineffably ancient. "Mae West. A long, long time before Marilyn."

"Cool, we'll have to rent some of her films on video. I've just come off air, I'm about to go into a production meeting, but I wanted to tell you I miss you and ask what you'd like to do for Valentine's Day."

"That's weeks away. Besides, aren't men supposed to organise surprise treats for Valentine's Day? It's not the same when I demand a dozen red roses and dinner at an island hideaway – it lacks the element of surprise if that's what I wind up with."

"You're right, Rose, I'll give it some thought. How about meeting me for a drink tonight? I'll collect you from work."

"I –" began Rose.

"Production meeting's started, got to dash. See you sevenish, gorgeous."

Rose sat at her desk and switched on her computer, feeling vaguely uneasy. It was reassuring he wasn't treating what had happened between them as a one-night stand, but disturbing he was so confident that he assumed she'd be his Valentine's date.

"You're being inconsistent," accused the meddler inside her head again. "You're afraid of becoming involved with a younger man because you don't see how it can last – yet when he shows he's serious about you, you feel affronted that he's taking you for granted."

"Rose, we need to arrange a photo shoot with the President." Gerry Harty, the picture editor, scratched his beard. "Can you call her office? It has to happen by Thursday at the latest."

Rose nodded, glad of the distraction from that busybody inside her skull.

Later she rang across to Kitty's extension to suggest a coffee in the staff kitchen.

"My email stalker's been on again," complained Kitty. "Listen to this message: he says my opinions are worthless, my line of reasoning is defective and my frame of reference limited, then expects me to meet him for dinner."

"Where does he want to take you?" Rose was interested in spite of herself.

"Abrakebabra, for a dose of realism. He says I'm probably

spoiled with men sweeping me off to expensive restaurants and pandering to my every desire."

"Psychic as well, you can certainly attract them, Kitty Kennedy. Do you have time for a coffee?"

Just then Linus Bell volleyed through Editorial. His wife had made his life a misery last night, nagging about the hours he worked. He'd tried to meet his Filipino girlfriend, but Imelda had been on night duty so he'd flounced off to Lillies Bordello – where he had free membership as befitted his senior status in the media – and had drunk himself comatose in the Library Bar.

"I want to see some commitment from you people today," he snarled to nobody in particular. "Sunday's paper was a dog's dinner. Coffee, Valerie, plenty of sugar in it."

Rose, who had quickly replaced the receiver in view of Linus's psychic abilities regarding personal calls, peered over her shoulder and giggled at Kitty. "Hangover," she mouthed.

Kitty was delighted she wasn't the only victim – she was still suffering the effects of last night's over-indulgence at the Gresham. "Unless it's the clap," Kitty mouthed back, but Rose couldn't decipher it, so she clapped her hands together instead.

Linus re-emerged from his office, caught Kitty clapping, and glowered. But he had more important matters on his mind. "Marianne!" he bellowed. "In my office – now."

The fashion editor tensed. She knew he was going to denounce her for using the model with swimmer's shoulders in last week's shoot; he'd complained about her before, but there had been no-one else available at short notice.

Linus was slouched at his desk nursing a can of Diet Coke. Last night's screaming match had been as a direct result of his wife's boredom; Audrey had sacked the gardener and then started on him. He wasn't able to fire anybody – the union and the State's employment laws had him in a pincer movement between them – but his wife could click her fingers and do as she liked.

"What's the progress on finding a job for my wife?" Linus

demanded without preamble. No frightening display of teeth or attempt to humour her.

Marianne had been hoping he'd lose interest in the project, but it was clear the Exalted One was determined to set his wife to work. She resigned herself to calling in a favour and only hoped it didn't rebound on her. "Caroline White-Hegarty is looking for an assistant for her flagship shop on Fitzwilliam Square, someone who'll wear her clothes with panache and converse with the customers on their level. It's as much an ornamental as a saleswoman role."

"My wife knows all about being ornamental. Isn't Caroline White-Hegarty that fashion designer who had a sex change?"

"No, Linus, she's Ireland's leading couturier." Marianne's eyes prickled with the effort of not allowing them to roll skywards. "As far as I'm aware, she was born female and intends to die female."

He sniffed. "Set it up. I want my wife in gainful employment by the end of the week, *capisce?*"

Marianne almost collided with Valerie carrying in a mug of coffee as she left the office.

"Good work," Linus called after her, a shade grudgingly.

Valerie shot the fashion editor a look of unpolluted jealousy.

Marianne wasn't given to theorising, but if she were Buddhist she'd speculate that Valerie was being punished for victimising peasants in a previous life. Even without Buddhism in the frame she was being penalised for something; imagine eking out an existence making coffee for Linus Bell. Marianne shuddered and wondered if she should engineer a marriage proposal from her boyfriend. He was a barrister, he could afford a wife with costly tastes.

Rose and Kitty decided to risk sliding out of the office for a coffee and dodged the traffic, finding a corner table in Café Society. Kitty's hangover demanded a caffeine injection.

"Anything happening your end?" asked Rose, who thought Kitty was looking waxen.

"*Lechery, lechery, still wars and lechery, nothing else holds fashion,*" quoted Kitty.

Rose widened her eyes. "You don't mean you've found someone to be mistress to? I thought you'd abandoned that madcap idea."

Oops, now was no time to confess about Joe French. Besides, she'd been such a twit she'd never hear from him again. She honestly didn't know if anything could be salvaged. "I didn't mean it literally," Kitty said hurriedly.

"You must have been giving it welly last night. You look like a three-day-old corpse."

Kitty groaned. "I should never drink champagne, it doesn't agree with me. I managed about two hours' sleep before I had to leave for work, and my feet are in ribbons – it's a long story. Luckily Linus is preoccupied with a domestic situation. He's been invited to a glitzy film premiere party tonight and wanted to bring his girlfriend, because she's a massive Nick Shooter fan. But his wife is determined to go. I heard Valerie talking to Mrs Exalted One about it, claiming Linus would be too busy working the room to take her, something to do with schmoozing advertisers. She spins a convincing story, Valerie. Anyway, Audrey Bell wasn't falling for it. This is the party of the year and she would prefer to curl up and die rather than fail to figure on the guest list. I could hear her screeching down the phone that either she went to the showbiz gala with Linus or she'd have a barring order taken out against him and he'd never set foot in their house again."

"Linus wouldn't want to lose their place on Shrewsbury Road – he loves having an address in Dublin Four," said Rose. "He lives for the chance to give visitors directions – 'Left at the Haitian Embassy, straight past the Icelandic Consulate, then we're the first mansion on the right'."

"Absolutely. So Audrey gets to pose at the post-premiere party in the Gravity Bar, while Imelda has to stay at home with the TV guide."

"Mistresses must become used to disappointment." Rose gave Kitty one of her significant looks.

Kitty, riddled with hangover, let it pass. She still hadn't worked out if Joe was due an apology, but she didn't think she could face it. Anyway, what would she say? I intended to sleep with you but got too drunk to follow through. She flinched as her dehydrated body punished her with a throbbing ache in her temples. "What's happening with you, Rose? Is Father Damien still putting the welfare of Ugandan orphans above yours?"

She was reassuringly partisan, which allowed Rose to be magnanimous. "It *is* life and death as far as they're concerned, whereas with me it's only a matter of debt. Father Damien is simply prioritising."

"You're having to sell your home." Kitty's eyes flashed, more grey than blue.

"Only if I can't arrange a loan."

"There may be other financial institutions you can turn to – you shouldn't become downhearted after one refusal. Banks are notoriously cautious," urged Kitty.

"Tried a couple more already; it's the same story everywhere. They only lend money to people who don't need it."

"This is all wrong. I feel so outraged for you, Rose."

The more affronted Kitty became, the more tolerant a stance Rose felt able to adopt. She sipped her espresso and shrugged.

"What does Feargal say? He must think your ex is inhumane. Father Damien's charity should begin closer to home." Kitty crumbled her crusts, too agitated to concentrate on food. Part of what was disturbing her, however, was the realisation that she could lend Rose the money from her cheque. But that ninety thousand dollars could buy her so many luxuries. If she gave it to her friend she might never be re-paid – she shouldn't make any rash promises.

"I haven't gone into the details with Feargal. I just explained I had some debts I needed to clear quickly and that meant I couldn't go on holiday with him." Rose remembered she was still wearing her spectacles and removed them, in case of accidentally becoming over-dependent. "I'm seeing him tonight. I might explain the background then."

"It's becoming serious between the two of you, isn't it?" divined Kitty, trying to distract herself from the mental accusation that she was being selfish. A true friend wouldn't hesitate to lend the cash.

"Serious? No. But I like him. Mainly," Rose's lips twitched, "because he's not asking for a large sum of money from me."

"How much do you need, Rose?"

"Forty-five thousand euro. It might as well be forty-five million."

Half of her cheque; Kitty winced. She definitely couldn't spare that amount.

Rose misinterpreted her cringe and reached across to pat her hand. "Don't look so distraught – every cloud has a silver lining. I just haven't identified it yet."

* * *

Rose encountered delays leaving the office and Feargal was shaking with the cold by the time she met him after work.

"You shouldn't have stood about in this weather, you'll get your death," she chided gently.

"They wouldn't let me into the building. I don't have a security pass." His teeth were chattering and he burrowed his hands deeper into his pocket.

"They're suddenly become strict about security in this building since a certain incident with a former Miss Ireland," Rose admitted, feeling an uncharacteristic desire to touch her warm nose to his pinched one, even though it was starting to run. "Come on." She threaded her arm through his. "Let's get you home to Clonliffe Square. I'll rustle up a hot whiskey and you can thaw out."

It was then that she knew, walking along the side of Herbert Park towards Donnybrook, ducking from dripping tree branches, that she didn't want this fitful beginning with Feargal to reach an end just yet. Oh, it had to happen, she was certain of that. But she didn't want to precipitate it. Rose was prepared to see if their clumsily kissed merger could totter forward towards some sort of partnership.

Rose had finally succumbed to temptation and was willing to take a chance on Feargal Whelan. She cuddled her body against his, the lamplight lending their faces a yellow glow.

"You're quiet," he remarked.

"Counting my blessings," she responded, tucking the scarf into his jacket and reaching him a tissue.

She wasn't twenty any more, that was the reality. But she had notched up a host of accomplishments by forty that had been pipe dreams at twenty. Granted, she wasn't as pretty as she had been, but all those twenty-year-olds labelled rivals by her insecurity had nothing more than fresh-faced youth to recommend them. Rose had driven on the other side of the road, eaten curry from a palm leaf, gone deep-sea diving through a coral reef. In her forties she knew who she was, whereas in her twenties she had still been defining herself.

"I'm broke," Rose announced, halfway down Appian Way with its imposing sweep of houses, their footsteps wakening the concrete.

"Me too." Feargal chuckled. "Although I thought you older women were supposed to have money. Does that mean I won't be on the receiving end of lavish hospitality?"

"You won't be on the receiving end of a hot whiskey if you carry on calling me an older woman," threatened Rose.

"You wouldn't withhold medication from a sick man," cajoled Feargal. "You're not older, you're more sophisticated."

"Good answer. Sophisticated definitely earns you that hot whiskey." Rose hesitated, indecision etched on her face in the beam of an oncoming car. "But I really am broke, you know, Feargal. I have to sell my apartment – it's the only way to repay my debt."

"Is there no chance of a stay of execution?" he frowned.

She shook her head wordlessly.

"Why not take in a tenant?"

"It's only a one-bedroom place."

"How about re-mortgaging?" Feargal searched for a solution.

"There isn't enough equity in it to raise the sum I need."

His grave face lightened. "It's only bricks and mortar, you know, it's not where you live but who you live with that counts. Sell up and move in with me – that way you can afford to go to Bridalveil Fall."

"Feargal, I met you a month ago. I'm not going to move into Liffey Street with you."

"I could move into Clonliffe Square with you. Wouldn't that solve your money worries?" A half-smile licked along his features.

Rose paused. The bank manager had made it clear that he'd have advanced her the money if she'd owned a two-bedroom place and had been in a position to take in a tenant. She'd discounted it because there was no space for a tenant, but a lover . . .

Feargal watched the shadows flail across her hazel-blue eyes. Tempted to press home his advantage, he left her in peace to think.

They turned off the main road and into Clonliffe Square, past houses with curtains open and lights blazing, their inhabitants careless of their visibility in the early evening. They mounted the steps to the front door of Rose's building.

"I always wanted a home with steps," she confided. "I think it's because our house in Slane opens onto the street. I liked the notion of a place that was set back and you climbed up to it."

"Don't laugh, but I always wanted a cottage with a thatched roof. It sprang from my idealised view of Ireland, being London-Irish."

Later, after they'd shared a pizza and watched an episode of *The Simpsons*, Feargal returned to the subject of living together. "So which side of the wardrobe am I having for my clothes?"

"Are you always this presumptuous?" Rose was evasive.

"The Irish generally answer a question with another question – no wonder you're such a slippery race."

"Don't you consider yourself Irish then? Even with that London accent?"

"I'm neither fish nor fowl. I know I don't belong in England, but

I don't feel one hundred per cent at home in Ireland either. I guess I'm an outsider."

"Don't take it personally, Feargal. Dubliners make Tyrone people feel like outsiders, Cork folk make anyone from Galway feel like outsiders, and southside Dubliners make northsiders feel like outsiders. We have a village mentality, for all our self-aggrandising talk about being natural-born Europeans."

Fergal was pensive. "My parents always said Ireland was parochial. That's when they mentioned it at all – they didn't often talk about the homeland. They never went to those social clubs in places like Kilburn or Camden where other Irish people spent their weekends. Being Irish was incidental to their lives. They never lost the accent, and they called myself and my brother and sister Mick names, but there was no warmth in their voices for Ireland or their families here. I was amazed when I contacted the Garritys and they were so friendly, inviting me to Slane for New Year. They didn't mention the bad blood with Mum and Dad. It's all water under the bridge now, my aunt said. She's Dad's younger sister." He paused, suddenly self-conscious. "You have me talking the hind leg off a donkey – isn't that an Irish expression? It's one of my mum's."

"Why did your parents lose touch with their families?" Rose pushed her black fringe out of her eyes, curious.

"They ran off together. It caused something of a stir in Kingscourt, County Cavan, where they were both from, because my father was a married man and my mother was half his age. He'd known her all her life; in fact, he delivered her because he was the local doctor. The general consensus was that he should have known better – and as for her, she was a siren." Feargal laughed. "I've never met a siren so dedicated to doing novenas."

"So do you have half-brothers and half-sisters in Kingscourt?"

"No, my father had no children with his first wife. I expect that's partly why he chose my mother over her. She was carrying me when they did their moonlight flit. My mother left home with only the clothes she stood up in and my father hadn't much more. He felt guilty and wanted to leave everything to the woman he was deserting."

Rose registered envy of any woman so much in love that she'd hitch up her petticoats and go.

"They weren't able to get married for years and years, which used to bother my mother," Feargal continued. "Dad told her it was irrelevant, and she always called herself Mrs Whelan and wore his ring, but it niggled all the same. Then as soon as divorce was introduced in Ireland – that was about the mid-1990s, right? – Dad filed for a petition. His first wife wasn't too pleased and claimed it was against her religion and she'd prefer to be a deserted wife than a divorcée, although they'd been separated for twenty years by this stage, but the court overruled her. So Mum had her wedding day at last. I was Dad's best man, my sister Patricia was bridesmaid and my brother Aidan took the wedding photographs." Feargal's smile illuminated his face.

"So have you grandparents in Kingscourt?" asked Rose.

"Only aunts and uncles. The last of the grandparents died before the divorce came through. I think Mum nursed fantasies about walking along the main street of her small town with a bona fide wedding ring on her finger and the husband who'd given it to her on her arm, but it seemed pointless after her mother died. I can't see them ever going back. Not that anyone could care about past scandals after more than a quarter of a century. My aunt in Slane said she'd love to see Dad again. I suspect he's willing, but Mum's the reluctant one."

They sat in a comfortable reverie for a time. Its pleasure was tinged with a tart quality for Rose, realising she would not enjoy many more such evenings in Clonliffe Square. Feargal roused himself and bent towards Rose, lifting her hand to stroke her wrist, where the pulse beat its faint tattoo. "You still haven't answered my question," he taxed her.

"Which question?" Rose prevaricated, knowing only too well.

"Shall I help to solve your money worries by moving in with you?" Feargal's grey eyes watched her, unblinking.

She was silent. She prized her independence. Nor did she want someone to move in with her because it made financial sense – especially so soon into this tentative relationship. Then again, maybe she should stop looking and try leaping.

"Let me move in," coaxed Feargal.

His face swam before her eyes. Now he was kissing her and she'd never be able to think logically.

"Let me move in," repeated Feargal, breath honey-scented from the whiskey.

Rose swallowed. Her heart told her to agree, but her head warned against it. She was torn . . .

Chapter 32

Nick Shooter's face dominated the front page of Dublin's *Evening Herald*. On the plane to Ireland he'd given emergency resuscitation to a woman who'd collapsed in the seat behind him. *In The Nick Of Time*, ran the headline. The Aer Lingus staff had radioed ahead to the airport and by the time the plane had touched down, a media scrum was developing. It was a slow news day and a have-a-go-hero, especially a film star, was infinitely preferable to another political wrangle.

Sunny looked at the grainy black and white image of Nick Shooter in the newspaper seller's hand. He was as photogenic as ever. No, that was begrudging, he was as handsome as ever. Her heart flipped its customary somersault when she saw his features.

"Do you want a *Herald?*" The seller rattled his change, thinking about the pint of Guinness he planned to have with his toasted sandwich in half an hour.

Sunny produced a couple of coins from her pocket and carried away the paper.

Her mother was ironing as she walked into the kitchen. "Fancy a cuppa, Sunny?"

Sunny filled the kettle.

"You'll have coffee, I suppose." Her mother unplugged the iron.

Sunny nodded, distracted. She'd known Nick Shooter was coming to Dublin for the premiere of his film, that he played a gangster in it who was redeemed by his love for a blind girl, and that he was lined up to appear on *The Late Late Show* and act as master of ceremonies at a charity auction in the Merrion. What she didn't know, however, was that she'd be walking along Westmoreland Street and the sight of his face on a newspaper would reduce her to an automaton.

"Is that the evening paper?" Noreen-dear lifted it, not even glancing at the front page. She turned straight to the television page. "Oh good, Nigella Lawson is on tonight. I enjoy a decent cookery programme." She sighed. "It's earlier than suits me, though. I'll have to make sure the dinner is on the table twenty minutes sooner than usual and your father won't like it. He's a creature of routine."

"Denis won't mind." Sunny's voice was wooden, preoccupied by how Nick Shooter was in Dublin within easy reach. Except there'd be nothing easy about reaching out to him. He'd hurt her again, just as carelessly as he'd done before.

Noreen-dear radiated incredulity. "Denis won't mind? Of course he'll mind. We always eat at six-thirty on the button." She reached for the Barry's Gold and splashed hot water into the teapot. Neither Sunny nor Kitty, and definitely not Denis, could tell the difference between one blend and another, but Noreen-dear was a connoisseur and could spot a counterfeit at the first sip. She carried the teapot across to the table, along with a mug of instant coffee.

Sunny folded back the newspaper to the front page and studied Nick Shooter. Was that a bruise on his temple or a smudge of ink? She'd heard he'd taken a fall from a horse, insisting on performing his own stunts.

"I suppose I could ask your father to tape Nigella while we ate dinner at the usual time, but then I'd miss *Who Wants To Be A Millionaire?* on the other side," Noreen-dear strategised, sipping her tea.

"Turn the clocks forward by twenty minutes, he'll never notice," suggested Sunny, forefinger stretching out to stroke the length of Nick's newsprint face.

Her mother snorted.

"Bribe him with a drink with his dinner, then." Sunny was losing the limited interest she had in their conversation. She wondered if she should go into town and join the mob on the pavement outside the Savoy cinema, waiting for a glimpse of Nick Shooter. She knew it was pathetic, but she wanted to gaze into his eyes again – a glance would tell her if that chemical spark which had blazed between them was still dormant within him.

"Sunniva, you know how I feel about intoxicating beverages. I made an exception for your young man Clarke, on account of his being a guest, but I simply can't condone drinking in the house. It cheapens a home." Noreen-dear's forehead bristled with indignation.

Sunny shrugged – her supply of ideas had dried up. Her mother would just have to accept that Denis Kennedy couldn't care less about the time he ate his dinner, and it was futile inventing arbitrary preferences for him.

She'd asked her father once why her mother was so anti-alcohol, imagining it might be due to religious fervour. He'd said it wasn't, although whispering that Noreen-dear did go a bit overboard in that direction.

"It was because her father was an alcoholic and she's never forgotten the misery he subjected the family to – her own mother in particular," Denis had told her. "He could sniff out any spare cash your granny managed to save up. Once she squirrelled away enough to buy winter shoes for the children and he found it hidden in the butter-dish and converted into a three-day session. Your poor granny couldn't hold up her head in front of the neighbours after the scams he pulled. He'd borrow tools from the people next-door and sell them for drinking money. The year after your mother and I started courting he was found dead in a ditch, a handful of loose coins and a bus ticket to Omagh in his pocket, and your granny wore black for the rest of her life. There's no accounting for love, chicken."

Sunny had galloped to tell Kitty about their alcoholic grandfather, and Kitty had been so worried about inheriting his genes that she'd refused to drink anything stronger than Lucozade for two months. It had certainly explained to the sisters why their mother wouldn't accept a drink and thought their father was on the high road to perdition if he indulged in a second pint. Noreen-dear had tried to pressurise Sunny and Kitty into taking "the pledge" when they had made their confirmations, but there had been enough of their grandfather's blood in them to enjoy a drop – and enough of their mother's to prevent extremes.

"I think I'll take a nap." Sunny stood, reaching for the newspaper, while her mother lifted the lid of the teapot.

"Leave the *Herald* for your father, would you, lovie? There's another cup of tea in the pot he might come up from the basement and have it with me if there's a newspaper to look at."

Sunny dropped the paper reluctantly. Then, with a sudden, violent movement, she lifted her mug and set it squarely on Nick Shooter's face. She didn't need him in her life.

The impetus carried her to the top of the stairs, where the swell of emotion waned as rapidly as it had galvanised her, and she sank onto the top step. Sunny knew it would expose her to misery, but she determined to do it anyway. She was going to the Savoy tonight and she wouldn't return home until she'd confronted Nick Shooter.

* * *

Rose was meant to be compiling a portfolio of Nick Shooter photographs for a spread in the *Trumpet* that Sunday, but she kept drifting away, reflecting on Feargal's proposition. It would solve her financial dilemma if he did move in with her, but their relationship was still budding, it needed space to develop if it was to stand a chance of surviving. She shouldn't risk it by allowing the detritus from her Father Damien days to interfere. She cared for Feargal – she cared for him considerably more than she was willing to acknowledge – but it was too soon to live with him. Especially for a reason as spurious as convenience. Yet did she have the luxury of choice? How else was she to raise the money, short of selling her home?

Rose put on her rectangular rimless spectacles in the hopes of enlightenment. Just as she'd feared, they made no difference. Spinoza said life should be viewed from the perspective of eternity. That was both seductive and dangerous – how did saying either yes or no to Feargal measure up on the eternity scale?

"Why are you mumbling about eternity?" asked Gerry, the picture editor.

"It's a brand of perfume. I'm thinking about buying it for a friend's birthday," she extemporised.

"Not until after you sort through those Nick Shooter pictures – the Exalted One's clamouring for them."

An email from Feargal flashed on Rose's computer screen, as though he sensed she was dwelling on him. *Sorry, have to cancel tonight, taping segment for tomorrow's show from film premiere at the Savoy. Editor's must, we're linked in to a promotion with the film. Can we meet tomorrow evening instead?*

A breathing space: relief flared through Rose.

Linus Bell tossed open the door of his office, blustering about his wife's new job being meant to keep that woman off his back. Petulance emanated from him: he hated having to disappoint Imelda, who asked for nothing. Whereas that harpy he was married to made constant demands, quizzing him about when he'd be home, whining that he never brought her anywhere. "I have a newspaper to edit, woman," he'd explode, but his tantrums never fazed her. "Kitty, I need you to work tonight," snarled Linus. "I want you to write a colour piece from the Nick Shooter premiere and you'll have to arrange admission to the party afterwards. It's bound to be choked with celebs behaving indiscreetly."

"Won't all the places be allocated by now?" squawked Kitty. "This is the hottest ticket in town."

"Do it," he commanded and swept on.

Kitty reached for the phone and started begging, bullying and horse-trading with the publicists handling the event.

* * *

Sunny dressed with scrupulous care. She painted her face so that it was dominated by her bluebird eyes and the cherry-red of her mouth, sleeked her platinum blonde hair away from her cheekbones, and finally pulled on the gown she had bought by credit card two hours earlier and intended to return to the shop the next day. It was a crimson flapper dress, shoestring-strapped and fringed at the neckline and knee. She added a gilded snake bracelet just above the elbow, clipped a scarlet sequinned headband around her forehead and Sunny was ready. The effect was dramatic. She pirouetted once in front of the full-length cheval glass in her room: she looked outstanding and she knew it.

Her father was emerging from the basement as Sunny descended the stairs, towering over him in gold mules that pinched. She should have taken off her toe-ring, but it comforted her.

"Good Lord," he stammered.

"I take it that's a compliment." Sunny was arch.

"I pity the young man you're planning to work your wiles on tonight." He was dubious as he pushed back the brim of the baseball cap he'd been wearing in case of draughts.

"A girl likes to access her inner fabulousness from time to time, Denis." She blew him a kiss. "Don't wait up."

"Gave up doing that years ago," said her father. "Go and show yourself to your mother – she likes to see you all dressed up."

* * *

Sunny psyched herself in the taxi. There had been a wronged woman character in *Beat It*, the pilot police show which should have been her breakthrough role. Sunny had rehearsed the lines with the actor who'd played the victim, half-envious of her colleague's opportunity to slam doors, point accusatory fingers and generally flounce, whereas her own character was no-nonsense – although with an underlying hint of flirtatiousness. The cad had been a solicitor and the action had taken place in his office, as the distraught woman he'd abandoned had tackled him. Sunny was word perfect on the character's accusations. "I devoted myself to you for five years, your happiness was my happiness, and now you treat me like something you've just trodden in. I left a marriage for you, I turned aside from my children for you, yet suddenly I'm a pariah. Just tell me how it happened. How could I be loveable one day and not loveable the next?" Then she had pulled out a gun from her pocket and Sunny, who had been in the solicitor's office on police business, had wrestled it from her. All a bit far-fetched, of course, and maybe – Sunny frowned – scenes such as that explained why the network had declined to pick up the option on the series. But she could certainly empathise with that wronged woman. She closed her eyes, nurturing her sense of having been shamefully mistreated. Nick Shooter needn't imagine he could float through life taking whatever he wanted whenever he wanted. It was time someone pricked his bubble.

"Going anywhere special?" asked the taxi-driver, admiring the woman in his rear-view mirror. Girls in red dresses – they worked for him.

"No." Sunny was terse.

"You look like you're going somewhere special," persisted the driver.

"Looks can be deceptive." Now, where had she been? Oh yes, Nick Shooter had been walking on water for years, but he had a ducking due to him. Sunny folded her arms as Donnybrook Church flashed past; she owed it to other women to make a stand. This would be her swan song. Her final public appearance before switching to teacher-training college.

A knot of terminally excited photographers pointed their cameras at her as she stepped from the taxi in O'Connell Street, just in case she was somebody. A ragged cheer sprang from the throats of a couple of hundred fans trapped behind crush barriers, which rapidly died away when they realised Nick Shooter wasn't with her. Sunny drifted up the red carpet and flickered her eyes across the lobby – no sign of him yet. A burly man in a dinner jacket relieved her of the invitation her agent, Malachy Curran, had wangled, imagining she intended to go there and play the see-and-be-seen game.

"If you could take your seat, please." The usher guided Sunny towards the stairs. She moved on reluctantly, but there was no help for it but to go inside the auditorium, where a humming noise indicated it was already close to full. She sat beside a sandy-haired man with a discontented expression and a tanned woman with a sleek blue-black bob dressed in head-to-toe Gucci, who was maintaining a running commentary which her companion steadfastly ignored.

Sunny cast a desultory eye around the crowd. Same old faces. There were a few RTÉ presenters, a coven of models and a sprinkling of politicians. That former Miss Ireland with the bird's name, Penguin or something, was near the front, her hair so teased up the person behind had no chance of seeing the screen. Sunny nodded at the actor she'd appeared with in the bottled-water commercial and he blew her a kiss. Nick Shooter was twenty-five minutes late, during which time the sandy-haired man, whose temper appeared to be in free-fall, went outside twice for a cigarette.

In his absence the Gucci woman spoke to Sunny. "Wouldn't you just love to get your hands on that Nick Shooter fellow? He's gorrr-geous." She had an Australian accent and a chin sharp enough to pierce tin.

Sunny shrugged. "I've heard he doesn't believe in playing hard to get. Just sashay up to him and you might be in with a chance."

"You think I should?" The woman, who would have been stunning if it weren't for the discontented lines girdling her slanted eyes, seemed inclined to quiz Sunny further except her partner returned.

"Feckin' smoke-free cinemas," he complained. "It's time smokers took a stand. We're the most downtrodden group in this pathetic little country. If one more person mentions secondary inhalation to me I'll swing for them. Secondary inhalation's a myth."

Sunny gave him a sympathetic smile; she wouldn't mind a shot of nicotine herself right now.

"I've half a mind to light up right here," he added, to impress Sunny.

"That's all you have, half a mind," hissed the Gucci woman. "We'll be thrown out and I'll never forgive you, Linus. I'll make your life a misery, so help me."

A roar went up from the rows behind, so that everyone stopped talking and craned over their shoulders. Nick Shooter and his entourage had arrived. He walked to the front, hand upraised to accept the acclamation, his chiselled face managing simultaneously to convey surprise, humility and gratitude. Sunny's innards were churning, she wanted to turn tail and flee, but she kept her gaze fastened on him. His eyes, which she knew to be a startling shade of green, although he was too far away to see the colour, swept the audience, devouring their adulation.

Another man joined him, a tubby, balding specimen, and Nick slung his arm around the other's shoulder, allowing him to share the applause. The second man held up his hand for silence. "Ladies and gentleman, we're overwhelmed by your reception." Nick nodded, overwhelmed on cue. "My name is Tibault Brown, ladies and gentleman, and I'm the director of tonight's film. It could never have been made without one man, a man who fitted the lead role as though it was tailor-made for him. Ladies and gentlemen, I give you Nick Shooter, the finest damned actor I've had the pleasure to work with!"

The clapping, whistling and feet-stamping was tumultuous, but eventually Nick was able to speak. His voice was a modulated instrument, a stage actor's repository of timbres and nuances, and Sunny quivered to hear it again.

"It gives me enormous pleasure to be back in a city where I spent so many enchanted hours, a city which has given me so many precious memories." Nick Shooter's smile was an individual benediction to every member of the audience. "Some of you may remember that I played Antony here in *Antony and Cleopatra* at the Gate a couple of years ago" – his smile faded, replaced by an expression of rapt ardour – *'We have kissed away kingdoms and provinces!'*" The spectators applauded and he laughed. "That's when I acquired a taste for Guinness and honed my love for Yeats." More cheering.

Liar, thought Sunny, he could never tolerate Guinness – he's playing to the gallery.

A woman bolted from her seat and raced up to him. "Hone your love for me, Nick," she cried, touching his sleeve before security hustled her away. It was Ella Jackson.

"Leave your number with my people, sweet thing. Whoops, nobody heard me say that," he quipped. Some joke. Sunny's mouth set in a grim line. "Now then, where was I before I was so charmingly interrupted? Of course, my affinity with your fair city. You made me feel welcome during those three-and-a-half months I lived among you" – Nick allowed his eyes to mist over – "and you've made me feel welcome again tonight. People of Dublin, I salute you." He made an obeisance from the waist down.

Predictably the audience was beguiled and Nick received a standing ovation as he took his seat in the front row.

Bastard, thought Sunny. He's so convincing, he'll have us all thinking he wants to move in next-door. She was fermenting with indignation at Nick's reference to his precious memories of his months in Dublin – did they include his time with her, or had she been airbrushed out? She was relegated to subsidiary status as part of the local colour as far as he was concerned.

The lights dimmed and the credits were rolling. *A Tibault Brown film. Starring Nick Shooter. Too Late For Love, Too Soon For Death.*

The title was excessively long, thought Sunny, but she was soon engrossed. Nick was lambent on screen, simultaneously chilling and vulnerable as a gangster in Roaring Twenties' Chicago. The camera lingered on his defined jaw-line, his graceful carriage. When he traced the barrel of his pearl-handled gun along the blind heroine's throat, before crumpling and weeping against her breast, the audience sighed in unison.

"Feckin' egomaniac, he's in every shot," muttered the sandy-haired man in the seat beside Sunny. "I'm off for a smoke."

* * *

A fleet of cars was waiting to convey guests to the party afterwards at the Guinness Storehouse.

"Sunny, what are you doing here?" called Kitty, emerging from the cinema and forgetting, momentarily, that she wasn't speaking to her malicious, secrets-selling sister.

"I could ask you the same question." Sunny wasn't pleased to see Kitty – she didn't want any distraction from the task in hand. "Clarke not with you?" Sunny feigned insouciance.

"Of course not, I'm working. Anyway I understood he'd gone back to the States."

Typical, thought Sunny, Kitty was better informed about Clarke's movements than she was.

Kitty peered at Sunny's feet. "Those are my gold mules you're wearing – I thought they were lost."

"They're too tight anyway." Sunny appraised Kitty's fawn work suit. "You'll have to do something about this tendency towards pastels – it's the Noreen-dear factor emerging in you. I don't believe you have a single primary colour in your wardrobe. Could you not have rustled up a little black number?"

"No, you've colonised anything of mine that's halfway glamorous," retorted Kitty. "Look, I can't stand here blathering, I don't want to miss the party. I'm supposed to capture the social-climbing essence of this plastic-coated affair in twelve hundred words." Kitty jumped into a car. "Don't even think about getting in beside me, Sunny. I don't want to be in an enclosed space with someone as toxic as you."

Her sister pulled a gargoyle face and climbed into the Mercedes immediately behind.

They arrived at the same time and took the moving staircase up to the Gravity Bar, trying to pretend they didn't know one another. Kitty cracked first. She was on the thread above Sunny and they were on eye-level. "You're here because of Nick Shooter, aren't you?" Her tone was intended to be snide, but emerged as sympathetic. Sunny swallowed. Kitty's pity was unwelcome.

"Don't –" Kitty paused. "Don't do anything you might regret."

"Kitty-cat, I'm always doing things I regret, it's my second rule in life."

"I'm probably going to be sorry I asked, but what's your first?"

"Never turn down a free drink." With that, Sunny stepped off the staircase and lifted two crystal saucers from a tray held by a waiter dressed in the Roaring Twenties' theme, arm-bands on his shirt-sleeves, hair parted in the middle and greased to either side. Sunny tossed back first one champagne cocktail and then the other, blinded the waiter with a full circumference smile and lifted another two saucers, before stalking towards the party. "I'm coming to get you, Nick Shooter," she warned.

Chapter 33

"Great balls of fire!" Sunny surveyed the scene, one hand on her hip. The dimly lit room was crammed with people laughing, drinking and talking, and the sense of well-being wafting from it was almost palpable. "There's no end of men here. There might even be one for you to have an affair with, Kitty. When the one you're currently embroiled in ends badly, as it's bound to."

"When will you learn it's nothing as seedy as an affair I have in mind? I intend to be a mistress."

"Nothing seedy about that." Sunny was languid, setting her glass on a passing waiter's tray and lifting a brimming replacement. She winced, as the party's gangster theme struck her. "I've been upstaged. Half the women in this room are wearing flapper dresses – people will think I'm a waitress and palm off their empties on me."

Nearby, Feargal was engrossed in discussion with his producer. "Listen, Niall, you can't start laying into the free Guinness until we're in the clear for tomorrow's show. We need a couple of sentences on tape from Nick Shooter, then you can drink yourself into next week. Where is he, anyway?"

"He's giving an interview to TV3; we're next up."

"The television boys will take forever," Feargal groaned.

"Precisely, that's why I'm having a drink." Niall looked vindicated.

Feargal checked his watch. "I'm going walkabout to see if there's anyone else from the cast here. You find the publicists and remind them we're next in the queue for Nick Shooter. Someone said Bono was going to be here."

"They say that about every party in this town," muttered Niall, cradling his pint.

Feargal cruised the room, wishing Rose could be with him to share the spectacle. Picture windows framed the city lights twinkling below, but indoors a Chicago speakeasy had been recreated, with jazz music on the stereo system and staff in spats and fedoras or flapper dresses with kiss-curls stuck to one cheek. He spied Ella Jackson being comforted by a statuesque woman with dramatic silver streaks in her dark hair, who exuded serenity.

"I can't believe I did that, Flora," Ella wailed, pausing to take another sip of her strawberry daiquiri. "I can't believed I made a prize fool of myself in front of most of Dublin."

"It was only a thousand people at best, angel," the older woman consoled her, kneading between Ella's shoulder-blades with the heel of her hand.

Ella moaned. "A thousand people. I'm supposed to be a torch singer, a sophisticated woman of the world, not a star-struck groupie. I'm a laughing-stock, my career is in tatters. I doubt if I'll ever be able to step onstage again."

"Don't be silly, angel, nobody will remember any of this in the morning," consoled Flora. At the rate most of the revellers were drinking, they'd be lucky if they recalled their own names in an hour.

A couple of men walked past. "You lost the head in there, pet," smirked one. "Hone your love for me, Nick? I laughed till I wept."

Ella burst into tears.

"Cheer up, I'll mention you in my column on Sunday. We might even run a picture," offered a nondescript woman with artificially straightened hair. It was one of the diarists from the *Sunday Globe*.

Ella hiccupped. "I'll look ridiculous – that's not the kind of publicity I want. Besides, I'm still waiting for that double-page spread you promised me in exchange for the Joe French story."

The journalist shrugged. "I put your name forward, the big chief didn't bite. Better luck next time."

Ella was furious, her sobs arrested. "Better luck next time? There'll never be a next time at this rate. But I'm going to salvage something from the wreckage of this evening," she sniffed, dragging Flora to the Ladies' to help repair the damage to her face. "If anyone asks, you're to tell them the *Globe* paid me to pull that Nick Shooter stunt. But I'll give them a better reason to run my photograph in their papers before this night is over. Hand me my lipstick, Flora."

* * *

A man with copper hair stood alone with his elbows on the bar and his back to the throng. Kitty's slowing heart-beat recognised Joe French before her brain conveyed the information. She touched his elbow, incapable of staying away, despite her embarrassment over the Gresham episode. He looked startled to see her, casting a swift glance back to where his wife, sensational in a halter-necked lurex catsuit, was engrossed in conversation with Hubert de Paor.

"Kitty," he began, before grinding to a halt.

"I believe I owe you –" they spoke simultaneously.

"You first," she said.

"No, you," he insisted.

"It seems I . . ." she couldn't continue. It was so humiliating to admit she'd been drunk and passed out. She mustered her courage. "It seems I –"

"You don't have a drink, let me order one for you," Joe interrupted. "Champagne?"

Kitty shuddered. "Just some water, please."

There was a pause while a barman with a glued-on moustache that kept slipping conjured up another lager and a glass of Ballygowan.

Joe shuffled, then turned to face Kitty. "Nothing like that has ever happened to me before."

"Nor me." Kitty took a shallow breath and prepared to apologise. Perhaps he'd give her another chance if she explained she'd drunk too much between nerves and excitement.

"I can't believe I fell asleep in the hotel room," Joe launched in, before she had a chance to speak. "You must think me such a wally. The red-hot lover who couldn't keep his eyes open. I've been working really long hours with the company – you know we're on an expansion footing and I'm facing bombardment from all sides. Clodagh's been keeping me awake at night, too – it turns out she does have chickenpox, poor little mite. The nanny's with her tonight, but I have my mobile switched on in case she starts whimpering for us. I guess I'm not as handy at juggling balls as I thought I was." He rubbed the bridge of his nose, harassed. "But I'm determined not to lose you over something as ludicrous as nodding off in the middle of a romantic evening, Kitty. Please give me another chance. I hardly know where to begin telling you how much you mean to me. I know it sounds trite, but I think about you all the time and wonder how you are. You're permanently on my mind." He gulped. "I realise I don't have much to offer you. In fact, there's a good chance you think I'm a complete loser and a waste of time. I can't even promise that you'll come first with me, because that place belongs to Clodagh. But I can't manage without you – I seem to be addicted to you, Kitty Kennedy." He trailed to a halt, misery leaching from his eyes.

Kitty looked into them and saw flecks of yellow amid the golden-brown. A balmy wave washed over her, dissolving her tension. Joe wasn't angry with her, in fact he cared about her. He'd just told her he had feelings for her. That he was addicted to her.

"I know this probably sounds like a preposterous mish-mash to you," stuttered Joe.

"It doesn't sound preposterous, it sounds caring."

Joe's hesitancy began to recede. "I'm sure you're raging with me and you've every right to be –"

"I'm not raging, Joe, far from it. I have feelings for you too."

Joy exuded from Joe. Instinctively he started to wrap Kitty in a hug, but as his arms reached out he remembered his wife was in the room. His eyes darted towards Emma, who was still talking to that buffoon of an artist. Instead he embraced Kitty with his eyes. "Come away with me," he urged. "I know a place in West Cork where we can be together in perfect isolation. It's where my father used to send the family on holidays when I was a boy. We'd go for a month and he'd spend weekends with us – he could never get away from the post office for longer. You'd love it in Baltimore, Kitty. We can take long walks on the beach, eat fish chowder in a pub I know – maybe we'll be able to hire a boat, if the sea isn't too choppy, and visit the islands offshore. Say you'll come. I'll cancel everything at work and make up some excuse at home. When can we do it? This weekend?"

Kitty laughed, warming herself in his enthusiasm. "Yes, this weekend," she agreed. "On one condition."

"Name it."

"You bring your trumpet and play that Louis Armstrong tribute you've been dangling before me since we met."

"My horn. It's a deal. I'll be in touch, Kitty." Joe checked his back was to his wife, mouthed a kiss at Kitty and pushed his way through the bodies to join Emma French and Hubert de Paor.

"Kitty!" A voice that sounded suspiciously like the Exalted One's called her name and, turning in its direction, she collided with Nick Shooter.

"Well, hello," he drawled.

"You're not my editor," she gasped.

"I never said I was."

"Kitty!" came the voice again, more autocratic than before. It was unmistakably Linus Bell's.

"God of God oh God, it's bad enough having to talk to him in the office without this," she groaned.

"Ignore him," commanded Nick Shooter, who seemed to be wearing make-up, now that she was just inches away from him. Foundation, definitely, and had his eyelashes been smeared with Vaseline so they spiked outwards? He seized her by the arm, hustling her forward, and the company parted obediently.

"I can't go with you," squeaked Kitty. "You're the man who broke my sister's heart." Except she didn't say it, she only thought it.

Nick was smiling, accustomed to his charisma melting all opposition. He hadn't actually decided what he intended doing with this little blonde creature, but there was something rather winsome about her.

"Just a minute." An authoritative voice rang out. "I'm Feargal Whelan from CityBeat FM and we've been waiting for more than an hour for an interview with you, Mr Shooter. Please, it will only take a minute or two."

Nick was tempted to tell Feargal Whelan from CityBeat FM to take his microphone and shove it somewhere unhygienic. But his personal publicist was pulling faces at him, a curious knot of onlookers was gathering, and he had faithfully promised his manager he'd behave tonight. Scouts' honour. "Remember the family man image, Nicky-boy," he'd exhorted him earlier on the phone. Nick Shooter sighed, then unleashed a smile on Feargal. "There's a room set aside, if you'll follow me." He turned to Kitty and pressed his lips to her hand. "Wait for me, Wanda," he murmured, "wait as long as it takes. I need to know you're there for me." It was a line from *Too Late For Love, Too Soon For Death*.

That was a close escape. Kitty heaved a sigh of relief that Sunny hadn't seen her with the film star – if recriminations had been bitter about Clarke T Maloney, they'd be positively feral about Nick Shooter.

Sunny, meanwhile, was fast becoming best friends with Audrey Bell, her Gucci woman from the cinema.

"So you think a rich husband is the answer to all my problems, Audrey?" queried Sunny.

"Sure thing," confirmed Audrey. "My Linus has loads of wealthy friends from the private members' bar at Lillies Bordello. Captains of industry, senior executives, all sorts. You'd be right up their street, hon. You have to decide what you want in life: money or a guy with a cute butt. Money works for me."

"Is it really a compensation?" Sunny was curious.

Audrey nodded emphatically. "It's also a weapon. Take my husband. He nagged me to death until I got a job, although we don't need the cash. So you know what I did? I arranged to be paid in clothes instead of salary and I take taxis to and from the shop – it costs him every time I go to work." Her slanting eyes were alight with caustic humour. "Trust me, hon, you should find a man to marry. It doesn't matter what he looks like so long as he's attractive when he's standing on his wallet."

"It's just that men never seem keen to marry me." Sunny was slurring her words slightly, for she had been unstinting with the complimentary champagne cocktails. Since Audrey had been equally liberal, however, neither noticed her new best friend's intoxication.

"My sister Kitty, now, men are forever panting to drag her off and marry her. But me? Bonk her and boot her out."

"You probably sleep with them too quickly." Audrey was slicking on another layer of lipstick without bothering to use a make-up mirror. "You want to keep them dangling after you."

"But I like sex," complained Sunny. "Deliciously repetitive, gloriously life-enhancing, casual sex with a stranger."

"Go back to having that after you're married." Audrey was patient. "In the meantime, prioritise, hon. You need a wealthy husband, every girl should have one."

"Preferably her own," kidded Sunny.

348

"Speaking of fooling around, did you mean what you said in the Savoy about Nick Shooter being up for grabs? Have you heard something about it in the acting trade?"

Sunny felt the sudden onset of not entirely welcome sobriety. "Nick Shooter is always up for grabs." She climbed off her stool, swaying slightly. Where was that man? He was the reason she was here.

A lull in the conversation, as people paused to eavesdrop on him, indicated Nick's return to the room. A short man was beside him, chattering about CityBeat FM. It was now or never. Sunny filled her diaphragm with air and walked purposefully towards Nick Shooter, coming to a halt directly in front of him.

"Sunny." He looked mildly pleased to see her – not thrilled, but not discomforted either.

"Nick."

"You look terrific in that flapper dress, you'd have been perfect for *Too Late For Love* in it." He grazed her cheek with his lips.

The kiss galvanised Sunny. She rested the palm of her hand on his chest, flexed it and pushed – sending him toppling. A phalanx of security guards steamed over, but it was too late. He scrabbled for footing, but reeled backwards, crashing into a table and ending up flat on his back with the contents of a bowl of punch splashed over him. "Nick Shooter, you're at the bottom of the food chain. You pretend to love women, but you have nothing but contempt for them. The only time you feel love is when you look in the mirror. You use us shamelessly: mislead us, disrespect us, toss us aside. You imagine you're Casanova reincarnated, Nick Shooter, but I've got news for you. You're too self-absorbed to give any woman pleasure in bed." Sunny lifted her chin and pulled herself free from the restraining security guards, who let her go at a signal from Nick's chief publicist.

Nick leaned up on his elbows and lifted a piece of fruit from the punch off his chin. "Slice of lemon, anyone?" he inquired.

One of Sunny's long legs snaked out and coiled around an elbow, causing him to lose his balance and flop down again. "Improvising was never your strong suit, Nick." She wheeled around.

Chapter 34

A devastating silence settled on the Gravity Bar after Sunny left. Kitty, whose heart had relocated to the base of her stomach watching her sister's performance, assimilated the shocked faces. It seemed as though the room had suspended its breathing. A rush of sibling loyalty welled up in Kitty, obliterating the rivalry. Sunny was still her little sister. The one who used to crawl into her bed at night and link fingers for their wishbone embrace. All at once it was irrelevant what Sunny might or might not have told the *Sunday Globe* about her. Kitty straightened her shoulders, defiance shading her eyes to slate, stepped forward into the space vacated by Sunny and began to clap.

For a minute, hers were the only hands beating together. Then another pair joined her, skin thudding against skin, and Audrey Bell stood beside Kitty. Linus's pale blue eyes bulged in horror, but Audrey looked directly at him and applauded all the harder. Initially in ones, then in twos and threes, other women detached themselves from the crowd until the clapping grew to a crescendo. Nick, helped to his feet by two of the security staff, tried to pretend the applause was directed at him, bowing with exaggerated flourishes. But the clapping continued, inexorable, and unmistakably intended for Sunny. Nick's publicity staff ushered the actor away.

"Funny folk, the Irish," the actor tossed over his shoulder. "They turn on you for no reason."

As the tumult died down, Kitty stole away to the Ladies' and leaned her palms on the counter surrounding a washhand basin. Nick Shooter's face segued into Hubert de Paor's – which blurred and reformed as Joe French's. Each face was interchangeable. Pin-pricks of perspiration sprang along the hairline on her forehead. She raised her head to reach for a paper towel and caught sight of her reflection in the bank of looking-glasses. The woman who gazed back repulsed her. Kitty's eyes skittered away.

They alighted on a small laminated card left behind by someone. Perhaps by accident, although it looked as though it was propped deliberately behind a tap. She picked it up and read aloud the words of the *Desiderata*: "*Neither be cynical about love, for in the face of all aridity and disenchantment, it is as perennial as the grass.*" Kitty slipped the card into her pocket. She had started this year on a cynical footing, but it was time she unpicked her defences.

* * *

"You must have done something enormously wicked to Sunny Kennedy to make her behave that way," purred Ella. She'd managed to sidle through Nick Shooter's security cordon by borrowing a tray and a couple of glasses, and was now face to face with him.

"Unbelievably wicked," agreed Nick, accepting the cocktail she reached him. He was gratified to discover it was his favourite, a Vodka Martini.

"Are you always wicked towards women?" she continued, edging closer.

"Always," he confirmed. "Except when I'm spoiling them."

"It sounds as if we have something in common." Ella set down the tray and removed the cigarette from between his fingers, bringing it to her mouth. She moulded her mulberry lips around the filter, conscious of the effect she was having on Nick. Nick quirked an eyebrow, aware she was teasing him but prepared to go along with it. He shook his head at his chief publicist and that rugby scrum of security guards: *Loosen up, guys, it's time I had a little fun.* "What do we have in common, sweet thing?" he asked, indulgent.

"We both enjoy being wicked from time to time." Ella blew a smoke-ring and then licked her upper lip. Nick tracked the darting movement of her tongue, then drained his Vodka Martini. "I've had cramps in my lower back all evening. I've suffered from them on and off since I was thrown from a horse during filming in Tuscany last year. There's only one way to alleviate them."

Ella waited.

He took her hand, tickling the palm with his thumbnail. "A long, hot soak in the bath. I believe I'm ready to go back to my suite at the Four Seasons, sweet thing. Can I interest you in a bath? Wicked girls always need a good wash."

* * *

"You were home early last night," noted Noreen-dear.

Sunny mumbled something inaudible as she headed for the kettle.

"Didn't the evening turn out the way you'd hoped, lovie?" continued her mother.

A yawn ruffled through Sunny. "Actually, it turned out exactly the way I'd hoped." She brought her mug to the table. "Now that I've given up on acting, finally, conclusively and for all time, I'm going to spend the rest of the day ringing up teacher-training colleges. Today, Noreen-dear, is the first day of the rest of my life."

"Does that mean you aren't going to Hollywood any more?"

"It does."

They drank in companionable silence.

"A man with a lovely rich voice rang for you an hour ago," Noreen-dear remembered.

Sunny tensed. She'd exorcised Nick Shooter last night – surely she didn't have to do it all over again today?

"He said his name was Feargal something, he works for CityBeat FM. I wish someone would explain to me what FM stands for one of these days. Anyway, I made a note of his name and number on the pad by the telephone. Very polite young man, a credit to his parents." Noreen-dear rattled the teapot and eked out another half cup.

"What did he want?" Sunny was stumped. She didn't know anyone called Feargal from CityBeat.

"He said he heard your feast of the denunciation last night, whatever he meant by that – you didn't tell me you were working, lovie – and thought your voice was marvellous. He mentioned it to the station's editor and they want you to go in for a voice test as a newsreader and continuity announcer. Isn't that superb news?"

Sunny laughed, a joyous peal that propelled her father up from the basement. "Looks like I may be ready to let go of showbiz, but showbiz isn't ready to let go of me!" She wiped away tears of merriment.

Denis stole into the kitchen, enticed by Sunny's elation.

"I'm up and about so early, I may as well go straight into town and take their voice test today. You know," Sunny bent, adjusting her toe ring, "people who get up in the morning must be able to pack a huge amount into their days."

Her parents exchanged apprehensive glances, unsure whether their daughter had undergone a puzzling metamorphosis or was rehearsing another role.

* * *

Kitty had sat up all night after the premiere, making her plans – breaking the habit of a lifetime and taking her mother's advice. Imagine reaching the age of thirty-six before realising Noreen-dear occasionally talked sense. She was going to use Clarke's cheque to finance that world trip and write a travel book for single women. But she still felt a whiff of guilt that she couldn't share some of the cash with her friend. Rose has Feargal, she'll be fine, she consoled herself. Meanwhile, Kitty had to act quickly to set her plan in motion. She needed to remove herself from temptation in the shape of Joe French as swiftly as possible.

In work the next day, she intended asking Linus Bell for a sabbatical – and handing in her notice if he refused her. But for the first time in living memory the Exalted One took sick leave. Kitty was using the delay to draw up an itinerary.

She broke off to update Rose on the drama of the premiere party.

"Sunny didn't," breathed Rose.

"She did," confirmed Kitty.

"And Mrs Exalted One?"

"Oh yes."

"I wish I'd been there." Rose removed her glasses and scrubbed at a speck on them. "Did Sunny really. . .?"

"Really."

Rose sighed with pleasure. Then she roused herself. "I'm late, I'm supposed to be meeting Feargal."

* * *

Linus Bell had sent Audrey home in the chauffeur-driven Jaguar after her disgraceful hand-clapping episode, showing herself up and making him look like a man who couldn't keep his wife under control. Then he'd adjourned to Lillies Bordello after the Gravity Bar had closed, and when Lillies had indicated that patrons should clear off or have their membership rescinded, he'd taken a cab to Imelda's house. He'd been waiting for her as she'd finished night duty, perched on the garden wall with next door's carton of semi-skilled stolen from the step. Imelda had brought him in to sleep it off. He'd headed for Shrewsbury Road in the middle of the afternoon to change his clothes and stop by the office – only to discover that the feckin' Australian wagon had carried out the threat uttered so often he'd disregarded her. The locks on their house had been changed and she'd made an appointment with a divorce lawyer. That was all he needed – crippling maintenance payments and another woman clamouring to marry him. Linus Bell had scuffed his shoes kicking them against his own front door, before checking into the Merrion and ordering a bottle of Courvoisier and a clean shirt from room service.

As he was methodically emptying the bottle, droning about the lack of commitment to be found in life and racking up an unprecedented number of profanities, Rose was strolling home after work to Clonliffe Square hand in hand with Feargal.

"We won't talk about anything important until we're indoors," she insisted.

He told her about the party instead, astounded to discover that the striking blonde who had floored the film star was sister to Rose's friend Kitty. "Dublin is so small," he marvelled. "Everyone is connected to everyone else."

"You want to try living in Slane, then you'd know all about it," advised Rose.

"We've invited her along to the station to audition for a newsreader and continuity announcer's job – she has a terrific voice," said Feargal. "With looks like hers, she'll probably be snapped up for television before long. I can see her reading the evening news bulletin – ratings will sky-rocket."

Rose pinched him.

"I'm more of a radio man myself," he chuckled.

Indoors in her apartment, she rustled up a quick meal.

"I spoke to Ian Jackson about my lease on the flat in Liffey Street. He'll allow me to break it as soon as I like, provided I find him another tenant." Feargal buttered a slice of Hannah McBride's soda bread, carefully not looking at Rose in case his face betrayed his eagerness. He wanted her to lift her gaze to his and say, "Move in with me" – simple as that. He didn't feel it was too soon, or that they were rushing their relationship; he loved Rose and wanted to be with her. He was sorry she had money troubles, but they had paved the way for them to live together, and he was only suggesting something he'd have raised sooner or later.

Rose stiffened. "I rang Sherry FitzGerald today and spoke to the estate agent who valued my property for me. I've put the apartment on the market, Feargal."

His expression clouded and his stomach knotted itself in preparation for disappointment. He pushed back his chair, clattering its legs against the wooden floor. "So I presume this is a last supper?"

"No, Feargal, you're jumping to conclusions. Just because I don't want to live with you – yet – doesn't mean I don't want to see you. If and when we decide to move in together it should be because we want to share our lives, not because I owe my ex-fiancé money and your rent will help finance a bank loan." She walked over to where he was sitting and crouched by his side. "Look, it's a temptation to opt for your solution because I really don't want to move out of this flat. But I feel that it would jinx everything between us, and if we're going to give this a shot we shouldn't hobble it at the outset." Rose took Feargal's hands in both of hers. "I have to accept that I can't afford this apartment, sell it and buy somewhere cheaper. It's not critical, nobody's dying. In fact," she smiled, a little shyly, "life is fabulous right now because I've found someone I care about, who cares about me."

"Who loves you," Feargal corrected, pulling her onto his knee.

By and by, they discussed possible areas where she might look for another apartment – Rose pessimistic about their locations and Feargal resolutely upbeat.

"Blanchardstown?"

"Too far."

"Portobello?"

"Too dear."

357

"East Wall?"

"Mugged there once."

"You could commute from Slane."

"As a last resort." Rose chewed the inside of her cheek; she might be glad of that last resort before long.

"What is it you're actually looking for, apart from an identical flat to Clonliffe Square but cheaper?" asked Feargal.

"What is it I'm looking for?" Rose massaged her neck muscles and allowed her mind to drift. What did she want from life? When she spoke, it was in an undertone, but the words were imbued with an urgency that made Feargal pay close attention. "I want a man who'll love the residue of me. After I've lost my looks, my wit, my memory, that he'll love me – not for the woman I was, but for the ghost of the woman I am." Rose snapped out of her dream state. Embarrassed by her candour, she shook her black fringe into her eyes.

Feargal pushed it away from her face. "I'll go flat-hunting with you at the weekend. We'll find you somewhere you can feel at home, I promise."

Chapter 35

Linus Bell was suffering from a tumultuous hangover – and even more rampant apprehension about what that Valkyrie he'd been misguided enough to marry would do to him next. If she found out about Imelda he might have to kiss goodbye to their holiday home in Deauville, as well as the Shrewsbury Road six-bedroom house. He'd have to steer clear of Imelda for a time, a realisation which didn't improve his temper. "What is it?" he scowled, when Kitty knocked on his office door.

"I need a word with you." She opened the door and advanced.

"It'll have to wait," he barked.

"It can't wait." Kitty was determined to prise a sabbatical out of Linus and she wasn't going to let him fob her off. Ninety thousand dollars in the bank went a long way towards tempering her caution around him.

"Approach the bench then."

Kitty had rehearsed what to say and was succinct. "I've inherited some money and I'm going to use it to travel and write a guide book. I'd like a year's sabbatical, please."

"You can't have it," snorted Linus. "I'd be short a columnist if you left, *capisce?*" Just as he'd suspected, there was a commitment vacuum on this newspaper, even his senior staff were plotting to desert him. "Tell Valerie to bring me in a coffee on your way out." He scribbled something on a flat plan for the next week's newspaper. Looking up, he was surprised to see Kitty still standing there. "Well?"

"You leave me no choice but to hand in my notice. I'm owed two weeks' holidays so I'll be gone in a fortnight."

Linus sighed, ice-blue eyes resigned under their sandy lashes. Today was going to be a bleak one; he wouldn't be in the least surprised if Audrey delivered his suits, each minus a trouser leg, to the office. He'd no idea what had possessed the woman to change the locks, although she'd spent a suspiciously long time talking to that deranged blonde who'd floored Nick Shooter – who was probably some class of man-loathing lesbian. If he knew anything about women, your one in the red-fringed dress hadn't been near a man in years. Frigid, more than likely. He should assign a reporter to her case and track her down, though, to see if she had any dirt on Nick Shooter they could run in the paper. In the meantime, Kitty Kennedy was littering his office, a stubborn set to her face. Linus grimaced. "You can have six months," he bargained.

"I need a year."

"Bring a lap-top on your self-indulgent jaunt and file a column from whichever godforsaken hole you find yourself in. I'll pay you a third of your current salary."

Kitty hesitated, weighing the offer. "All right," she agreed.

She managed to keep her composure until she was outside Linus Bell's office. Then she executed a one-woman conga up the newsroom floor until she reached Rose's desk. "*Olé, olé, olé, I'm on my way, I'm on my way,*" she sang.

Rose was scouring the Internet for flats she could afford in areas where she wouldn't trip over syringes every morning. "That's fantastic news, Kitty. Easter Islands, here you come."

Kitty peeked over her shoulder at the screen. "Why are you

looking at places there? It's miles out of the city and there's no public transport."

"Desperation. I hear Sunny may be working with my Feargal – the station loved her voice test."

"Your Feargal, is it?" teased Kitty. "Someone's had a change of heart."

"It's a belated New Year's resolution," countered Rose. "I've decided to stop looking gift horses in the mouth."

"Thought you didn't hold with New Year's resolutions."

"I didn't hold with boyfriends thirteen years younger than me either." Rose's eyes shimmered. "But some certainties have a knack of dissolving."

"I do believe you're in love," crowed Kitty.

"I'm not sure if it's love, but it's definitely something worth having."

Just as Kitty was about to interrogate Rose, Irene from reception beckoned to her. "There's someone in the front hall for you."

"Tell me it's not my email stalker," begged Kitty. "He's been threatening to pay me a visit – he thinks we should go to Dublin Zoo and admire the flamingos."

Irene was impervious. "He didn't give his name, but he said he was a personal friend."

Kitty heaved a sigh. "I may as well see who it is. But if I'm not back by lunchtime, Rose, send a search party to the zoo."

She pressed the button for the lift, gave up waiting and took the stairs to the ground floor. To where Joe French was standing in the foyer.

* * *

A persistent knocking sounded on the door of Number 16, Hunter Crescent. When neither Sunny's mother nor her father answered it, she pounded downstairs. On the doorstep, a lugubrious face ducked under a black and white checked umbrella.

"There's something you should know before I fly home."

Clarke's eyebrows bristled with resolve. "Kitty was never in the least bit interested in me. I only latched on to her because I'm a chump who imagined I could turn back the clock and be seventeen again with the world at my feet. Instead of which I tripped over my options and wound up with a broken marriage and a kid I don't see enough of through my own fault."

Sunny closed the front door behind her. "So you're not holding a candle for my sister?"

"Not any more. She's a great gal, but she's not for me."

She stepped under his umbrella and took it from him, sheltering them both from the drizzle. "Does that make you susceptible to temptation?"

Clarke gulped. "It would, except I'm on my way to the airport. We took a detour."

His brown eyes, Sunny noticed, were the colour of maple syrup, and they reminded her of that feeling of contentment she experienced when she ate pancakes for breakfast. "I'd call it a hefty detour – the airport's in the opposite direction. So what are you doing here, Clarke T Maloney?"

"I guess I wanted to see you. To set the record straight. I'll be off, then. You have a great life, Sunny, you hear?"

Sunny watched Clarke walk towards the daffodil-yellow front gate, past the sundial – *I am a sundial, and I make a botch, Of what is done far better by a watch* – to where his driver was waiting in a limousine with darkened windows. She watched him jump into the car and the driver flash his indicator to pull away. The winking light roused Sunny. She dropped the umbrella, bolted down the front path, and tapped on the car window. Clarke's face appeared.

"When are you coming back?" She was breathless, spray sprinkling her hair.

"I'm not intending to come back."

"But what about the film? If new financing for it is arranged, won't you be back?"

"I never needed to come to Ireland to take charge of the casting, Sunny, I employ people who do that for me. Have a good one." He rolled the window back up.

Sunny rapped her knuckles on its surface again. "I have to say, I'm disappointed in you, Clarke."

"Why?"

"There's more than one sister in the Kennedy family, in case you hadn't noticed."

A slow smile wended its way along Clarke's heavy features, transforming them. "Actually, I had noticed. That's why I had my driver take this pretty lengthy detour."

"I'm glad to hear it. Now, here's the plan: I'm going to hitch a lift with you as far as the airport, during which time I'll explain about my lifetime's ambition to visit a place in California called Carmel. Oh, you know it? You live there? Good gracious, what a small world. Well, maybe we could meet up when I'm there."

Clarke wrestled open the door to his car, his face wreathed in a smile so blinding it no longer bore the least resemblance to Eeyore.

* * *

"Sorry to turn up unannounced, Kitty."

Joe didn't look sorry in the least. Closely shaven and discreetly scented, he looked every iota the successful businessman in a tailored navy suit. His trademark energy crackled as he took her hands between his, turning them over and pressing his lips first to one palm and then the other. "I know this is indiscreet of me, but I was driving past your office and I couldn't bear to miss an opportunity to see you. Could you slip out for half an hour? We could grab a coffee and talk over our plans for the weekend." His voice was a caress and Kitty felt cosseted within that sense of intimacy he fostered so readily. His hands retained hers, the skin reassuringly warm.

"Now's not a great time for me," she began.

"Come on," he entreated, a half-smile blurring his dimple, "live a little. Nobody will notice if you leave the office. Just take twenty minutes." He cupped a hand under her elbow and guided her outside the building. "There's so much I want to tell you about our special place in West Cork. I've been on the phone to the hotel already and booked it for two nights. It's a little family-run establishment; I know you're going to love it as much as I do."

"I'm not going away with you, Joe."

He didn't understand at first, engrossed in describing where he'd take her and how they'd spend their time. Then his smile started to falter. "Is this weekend difficult for you?"

She nodded.

"Well, let's make it next weekend. I want to be with you, Kitty, that's all that matters to me."

"But it's not, Joe."

"Sorry?" Puzzlement clouded those treacle-gold eyes with their faint yellow flecks.

"It's not all that matters to you. You have a wife and daughter who matter to you as well."

"I've told you about my wife." He was eager, the words colliding with one another as they toppled out. "I'm not in love with her, we hardly have anything in common apart from Clodagh. Emma goes her way and I go mine."

The temptation was almost irresistible, for Kitty wanted to let him persuade her. But she'd been offered a reprieve – and much as she regretted losing Joe French she'd regret even more surrendering to him, in years to come. She forced herself to adopt a harsh tone.

"I feel sorry for you, Joe – it's not the ideal way to live your life. But it's your choice. I have other plans for my life. I've taken a year's sabbatical and I intend to travel."

"Why?" The planes of his face sharpened, betraying his bewilderment.

To escape from you, Joe, thought Kitty. She shouldn't articulate it, he might dissuade her. Kitty shrugged. "Call it a bug. I've always wanted to check if there really are islands out there called Leeward and Windward, and if it's true that Banjul has the best patisseries outside France."

"I could come with you." He was eager, almost boyish. "Maybe not for the whole year, but I could meet you places if you gave me your schedule."

Kitty wavered.

"You could trek through the jungle, playing the lady adventurer, and when you emerged at the other side I'd be waiting in the best hotel in town with a gin and tonic and a hot bath drawn for you. I know you, Kitty Kennedy, I know you'd like that."

"I'm thinking about it," she confessed.

"Thinking about it is all wrong, try feeling it," Joe insisted. He opened his top button, loosened his tie and bent down. "I brought my horn to play for you. I always promised I'd serenade you."

She noticed a black case by his feet, from which he produced a gleaming gold instrument and brought it to his mouth. The music was as moving as it was unexpected, a melodic waterfall of pleading. Passers-by paused to listen, as captivated as Kitty by this sliding scale of notes. Joe's eyebrows were knitted with concentration while he blew, playing the ragtime tune with more heart than expertise, in truth, for it was a complicated piece. But a knot of office-workers broke into spontaneous applause when he drew away the trumpet from his lips, and several cars by the traffic lights tooted their own horns.

"What was that?" Kitty breathed.

"Cornet Chop Suey, one of Louis Armstrong's blistering solos. I didn't do it justice, I'm afraid." Out of breath, he produced a handkerchief and mopped at the base of his neck. A faint prickle of sweat was forming copper curls at his ears.

"It was wonderful." Kitty was regretful.

"It's a 'Wonderful World', after all. Or it can be, if we let it." Joe's smile was a beacon. "Louis believed that. He summed up his philosophy in that song: he insisted it could be magical if only we gave it a chance. Love – that's the secret, he said." She was mesmerised. Scenting victory, Joe slicked the salmon-pink tip of his tongue over his lips. "Let's create a universe in which we alone exist, Kitty."

The twitch in her gut warned her against it. "It's not possible, Joe. There's no way of blocking out the rest of the world. Not permanently." Kitty backed away from him – sluggish, reluctant steps – before she changed her mind.

Joe stretched out arms still holding his horn to draw her to him, persuasive, yet, in the dying seconds of their relationship. "Don't give up on us, Kitty."

Her eyes turned opaque. "There is no us."

Kitty spent the twenty minutes she could have been drinking coffee and making plans with Joe French in the Ladies'. Dry-eyed, but devastated. He was a man she could love for the rest of her life and she didn't want to share him. Except someone else had reached him first. Finally she rallied enough to go back outside, to the spot beyond the revolving door where she'd stood with Joe. Realising there was no Joe in her life any more. It was empty. But at least it belonged to her again. A somewhat flawed consolation, but Kitty had to take her solace where she could find it.

She listened intently, as if those wistful trumpet notes might be hanging in the air still, but there was only the snarl of traffic. The air was fresh, though, and as Kitty sniffed it she had the sense of a season on the brink of change – winter already preparing to yield to spring. "Now I need to behave like a human being," she said aloud.

* * *

Rose was sitting at her terminal, pretending to work, but in reality listening to Feargal's radio show on tiny headphones.

"Rose."

She didn't hear Kitty, immersed in admiring Feargal's masterful handling of an obstreperous listener.

"Rose." Kitty pulled out one of the ear-pieces.

"What is it?" Rose tugged out the other ear-piece, checking to see if the picture editor had noticed what she'd been doing.

"Remind me how much you owe Father Damien."

"Forty-five thousand euro."

Kitty scribbled rapidly and handed a cheque to the bemused Rose.

"What's that?"

"Forty-five thousand euro. You don't have to sell Clonliffe Square. Stay there and pay me back when you can." Kitty's blue-grey eyes were alight.

Rose gripped the cheque with the air of a woman who thought it might vanish at any second. "But what about your world trip and the guide book?"

"I still have half the money left. I can go on the trip – I'll just make a few economies along the way. Besides, I'll have some income on the road. The Exalted One has conned me into agreeing to do a weekly column. Mind you, how he thinks I'll be able to file copy from a rainforest is beyond me."

"I can't accept so much money from you," Rose prevaricated, although the idea of being able to stay in her apartment filled her with surreptitious joy.

Kitty placed her hands on her hips. "You'd be a fool to say no. What did you tell me only this morning about your New Year's resolution?"

"Never look a gift horse in the mouth," stumbled Rose, unable to tear her eyes off the cheque.

"Never look a gift horse in the mouth," repeated Kitty, her face curved in a smile.

Rose looked up, unshed tears glinting in her eyes. "I do believe, Kitty Kennedy, that you've converted me to New Year's resolutions."

Kitty hesitated. She wasn't sure how she felt about New Year's resolutions any more – except that maybe she'd had a narrow escape from one. Although it was possible she'd regret that escape as long as she lived.

"You were a long time in the foyer. I thought maybe you'd given into temptation and sailed off into the sunset with your email stalker after all," added Rose.

Kitty leaned over Rose's desk and brought her face close to her friend's. "I've learned something about temptation, Rose. The trick is knowing when to succumb – and when to resist."

The End